THE SHATTERED ALLIANCE

Undercover Series Book 2

SYDNEY KATT

RANDOM DISTRACTION BOOKS

The Shattered Alliance is a work of fiction. Any resemblance to actual persons, living or dead, events, or locales is entirely coincidental.

2013 Random Distraction Books Trade Paperback Edition

ISBN: 0615812961
ISBN-13: 978-0615812960

Cover art: Farah Evers
Editing: Tara M. Clapper

Printed in the United States of America

www.randomdistraction.com

987654321

For Beth, the biggest Skyce fan I know.
This book wouldn't have been possible without your
input and support. And yes, you can still be the president
of the Skyce Fan Club.

ALSO BY SYDNEY KATT

Agents of Deceit
Foresight is Flawless

Sarcastic sexy suspense titles being added all the time

Sign up for updates at www.authorsydneykatt.com for
information about new releases

PROLOGUE

Love is a fickle bitch. That's right. I said it. Someone had to.

It's not that I have anything against love, per se. I just...it's complicated. Suffice it to say, she and I have met and parted ways. A few times. Each time, she sucker punched me then kicked me while I was down.

In retrospect, all those little things I took for granted pop into crystal focus. All those tiny details I didn't care enough to see at the time reveal themselves to me as what they really were: pivotal moments. These are the insignificant pieces of life – picking up dry cleaning, smiling at a stranger in the coffee shop, answering the phone.

But here's the thing...life and death don't bow down to a simple trip to the cleaners. The fate of the world doesn't hang in the balance of a ringing phone.

Actually, that's a lie. Answering that one phone call a few weeks ago set a chain of events into motion that I could no more avoid than I could possibly hope to stop. Sending that call to voicemail would save my life.

The choice I made to answer it is what killed me. I know that now.

Answering that call killed the one I love most in the world, even if I didn't know it at the time.

Despite it all, I can't blame love for this. I'm the fool who ran blindly into this bank, thinking my eyes were open because I could see. Unfortunately, love chose this unique moment in time to restart our turbulent affair. Now things are...*difficult*, to say the least. Getting the love I've waited a lifetime for right now is cruel. How long did I get to revel in it? A few days?

Fickle bitch.

Does love realize that dying now is an unfathomable fate? Three weeks ago, I could be standing in this bank, staring down the barrel of his gun, and I wouldn't so much as blinked. The end of my life was little more than the bitter matching bookend to what started this whole mess those years ago. But now...

Now I have so much to lose. I have everything to lose.

Funny, I always thought my life would flash in front of my eyes during my last moments, not a contemplation on the nature of love. There's something ironic about that. Or is it something else? I never paid much attention to all those grammar lessons back in school.

Too late to figure it out now. He's done grandstanding. He's pulling the trigger.

Well, Love, I guess I'll meet you in hell...

ONE

No witnesses in the park today, as expected. March brought its chilly winds with it this year, but even if it hadn't, it was still much too early for children to be outside playing. No self-respecting adult would be out in this weather. And the unrespectable adults? They were sleeping in before a night of St. Patrick's Day debauchery at the bars.

Yes, this meeting had promise.

I pulled my auburn hair into a quick bun at the base of my neck and opened the door to my silver coupe, imagining what a passerby would think if they saw me. Not many twenty-four year old women would choose to wander alone in a near-dark park in this part of town. They'd probably think I was looking to score a fix for my addiction.

Close. My drug of choice was a little stronger than anything a drug dealer could offer. What the information dealer offered, well, it left me jonesin' for this meet worse than any withdrawal a heroine junkie would experience.

The wind cut through my trench coat the moment my heeled boot stepped out to touch the pliable dirt, but I knew turning back wasn't an option anymore. If I'd wanted to stay safely curled in my bed on the cold mornings, I should've figured it out years before now.

Without another thought for the frigid morning, I hurried to the benches on the far side of the pond.

My lips twitched at the thought of what might happen. It was the closest they'd come to a smile in years. If my instincts were correct about the cryptic call I received last night, I would succeed where the FBI failed. I would finally discover what happened to the man who murdered my father.

And I've wanted this for a very long time.

Just over two years, to be exact. That was when Raptor destroyed my life. That was when the FBI let the man who murdered my father during a bank heist get away like a wisp of smoke in the wind. One of the agents swore he'd do whatever was in his power to bring this man to the unfeeling judgment of Lady Justice. Apparently, he didn't have much power. His entire case evaporated when, one by one, Raptor's gang turned up dead.

I'm perfectly aware that normal people would grieve, not submerge themselves into Dallas's criminal underground. A normal woman might acknowledge her feelings of powerlessness over the loss instead of taking on the alias of Songbird. I'll get to that.

Once Raptor's dead.

But Raptor's been at this longer than me. I could put word on the street that I had a bank score planned and anyone willing to face some danger would get a big take, but I couldn't know if the man I sought would ever hear about it. My two-bit con connections probably didn't swim in the same lake as the man who walked away with millions from a single bank job.

Last night's call wasn't from just another low-level con though. The adrenaline marathon racing up my spine during the brief conversation told me as much. This guy could get me to Raptor. I knew it, even though Raptor's name never came up.

I was so caught up in the moment of the call that I never considered the isolated nature of the location a problem. Heeled boots had also been a poor choice. Sitting alone on the bench, I realized no one would hear me scream here. At five feet four inches, I was hardly physically intimidating. If things went bad...

No. Don't go there. Focus. Play the role. Sell the character.

I'd finally get to find out if the role of the ruthless bitch was as satisfying to play as I'd always imagined it to be.

Besides, it didn't matter if things went bad at this point anyway. With slight pressure from a trigger finger, I lost everything that

THE SHATTERED ALLIANCE | 5

mattered to me. That gave me a distinct advantage over every criminal in this city.

I didn't have anything left to lose.

"Well, this is a surprise. I never imagined Songbird would really be Skylar Montgomery. Interesting," a male voice said, startling me because I didn't hear so much as the rustle of a crunchy leaf under his shoe.

I turned around and looked into the piercing green eyes of a dead man.

His presence shocked her. Good.

Parker Ramsey wanted Skylar to understand how dangerous her little game was. Although she so ignorantly toyed with fire, he could still respect what she attempted to do. Few had the guts to go after Raptor. Including himself, he could count them all on one hand with a few fingers to spare.

Skylar rose to her feet, never wavering in her contemptuous stare. Was this supposed to intimidate him? The prom queen put on a trench coat and thought she could pretend to be a criminal mastermind. She would have to try a lot harder if she wanted to play games with him. She was out of her league and too clueless to realize it.

"You're dead. I watched them put you into the ground."

"You saw what you were supposed to see, Skylar. Nothing more." He curved his mouth into a smile that didn't reach his eyes. "But it's touching that you came to my funeral."

Skylar drew in a shuddering breath before sprinting towards the cover of the trees a few feet away. He caught her with ease and ducked when she tried to punch him. It was a good thing, too, because it looked like a solid punch. Considering the company she kept, knowing how to handle herself was smart. It wouldn't help her right now with him, but it was smart all the same.

Catching her shoulders, he pushed her back against a tree and restrained both of her hands in one of his, holding them firm against the bark over her head. With his free hand, Parker undid the top two buttons of the blue button-down shirt peeking out of her coat. He saw the defiance burning in her sapphire eyes when he put a finger into her bra and pulled out a small recording device. Why were people always so obvious about it when they wore a wire?

And why did women think their bra was a good place to hide anything when that was always the first place men looked?

"What the hell do you think you're doing? This isn't amateur hour," Parker demanded, releasing her. "Anyone with eyes and a brain could tell you were wired."

She buttoned her shirt and shot him an indignant look before answering. "I was expecting someone else."

"Really? Who?"

"Someone living, perhaps."

"I'm not exactly a zombie, so who were you expecting?"

Her eyes bored through him with laser precision and she remained silent.

He shook his head. "I know you're going after Raptor and believe me when I tell you he would have killed you over that little stunt. He is not the sort who appreciates having his conversations recorded." After a beat, "Neither am I, for that matter."

"Why is that any concern of yours?" Skylar asked as she rubbed her wrists. "You asked for this meeting so why don't you just get to the point already. I'm not in the mood for your little displays of dominance."

Little displays of dominance? She just kept on making this meeting more enjoyable.

"Look, Raptor double-crossed me and I'm out for revenge. You're probably the only person in this world whose distaste for him can rival my own. We're in a unique position to help one another and I think we should take full advantage of this opportunity."

"Why should I ever trust you? You're nothing but a thief."

"I never said you should trust me. In fact, you would be a fool to do that, but let's face reality for a moment. You may call yourself Songbird and have a few seedy connections, but you're no criminal. You're in over your head if you think you can take Raptor down on your own. You need me."

Skylar regarded him with skepticism and resumed her silent routine. It reminded him a bit of a petulant child stomping their feet in the grocery store when their mom refused to let them have candy. She would have to seriously work on this tough girl thing if she was going to be useful.

"Okay, I can tell you don't agree with what I just said, but hear me out. If I can't convince you, I'll walk away and you're welcome to go get yourself killed on your own." Parker paused and glanced around at their deserted surroundings. Although he'd released her, Skylar remained against the tree, almost as if she was creating distance for protection. "Why don't we go somewhere a little less secluded to talk? I can tell you think I'm going to kill you at any moment." When she didn't respond, he rolled his eyes and added, "I'm not, by the way."

Still no response.

He closed the gap between them, placing his arm on the tree to her left. Leaning his weight against it, he flashed one of his slyest smiles. "Of course, if you'd prefer to be alone out here with me, I can see potential in that scenario as well."

Skylar conceded, unflinching. "Fine. Meet me at the café on Frankford and the tollway in five minutes. You get the time it takes to finish a cup of coffee to convince me. Those are my terms."

"Then I'll see you in five," Parker replied before turning and disappearing into the trees.

It would be a miracle if he made it through her cup of coffee without bursting into laughter at her tough girl act.

Just as I expected, the café was quiet and I was able to get a booth in the back corner. Parker joined me as I was placing my order with the waitress. After he ordered his coffee and the waitress retreated into the kitchen, I said, "Your time starts now."

He nodded, all business. I liked that, even if I didn't like him.

"I understand your hesitation to work with me. In your shoes, I imagine I would feel much the same way, but you will get yourself killed without my help. Raptor is a very dangerous man."

"You don't think I'm aware of that?"

"Clearly you're not," Parker paused as the waitress deposited our cups on the table and left. "I've worked with him and I know how he thinks. What you have to understand is that Raptor is a pro at what he does. He could be talking to you and you would have no idea you were talking to a murderer unless he wanted you to know it."

I considered his statement as I took the first sip of my coffee, grateful to have something to do with my hands besides fidget. I didn't want him to have the satisfaction of seeing how uncomfortable I really was. With all of this. "That seems like an odd thing for someone who knows his face to say."

Parker shrugged. "I don't know his face. Criminals of Raptor's caliber are extremely cautious. He wore a mask every time we met in person. The only thing I ever got a good look at was his eyes, but I'd wager all of the gold in Fort Knox that he was wearing contacts to change their color. His voice was very distinctive, very cultured and European, but there's no guarantee that wasn't just for my benefit."

I frowned. "So, what you're really telling me is that you're useless to me."

An inviting smile played at the corner of Parker's mouth. "Raptor killed everyone who worked with us on that job and he tried to kill me, too. I had to fake my own death and go into hiding to get away from him. Do you honestly think I would choose now to surface if I had nothing to offer?"

"Go on."

"I have confirmation from my sources that Raptor is in Dallas and ready to pull another job. He thinks I'm in the ground, so seeing my face again should be just enough to draw him out. The man is incapable of pulling a job when there are loose ends. I happen to be the biggest loose end he has. We just have to find out who he is by day before I surface."

"I'm sure you understand that *we* implies I'll be helping you."

Parker shook his head, smiling slightly. No response. I posed my next question.

"You seem very confident that Raptor won't just kill you."

"He won't," he replied with an air of authority. "He'll know I'm up to something big if I'm willing to show my face to him. He won't be able to resist finding out what it is first." Parker eyed the empty cup I set on the table. "You've finished your coffee. Have I just been wasting valuable planning time or are you in?"

It wasn't hard to see why Parker was such a good con artist. With his easy smile and lean build I would have willingly believed any lie he wanted to tell me, that is, if I didn't know who and what he really was. Everything he made appear so casual – his tousled dirty blonde hair, his expressions, even the tone of his voice – were no doubt very carefully practiced and polished.

Working with Parker made absolutely no sense to me. Despite my quest for revenge, I considered myself a rational woman. Mainly. Still, there just might be something to what he said about drawing Raptor out. Unless someone else could corroborate Songbird's credentials as a thief, Raptor would probably never waste his time on her.

"Tick tock."

"I'm in."

Parker stood and nodded. "Good. I'll be in touch."

I turned around in the booth and called after him, "How will I contact you?"

"You won't," he called back as he left the café.

*****

Special Agent Jackson Caldwell sat down in the conference room at FBI headquarters in downtown Dallas to await a case and partner assignment. Again. Apparently, financial crimes were at an all-time low in the area.

Or his new Special Agent in Charge was just a dick who liked tormenting his new agents.

Considering that he'd been buried under mountains of point-less paperwork since his transfer to the Dallas Financial Crimes Unit at the end of last year, he imagined his impression of Hargrove was fairly accurate. Any other SAC would have been salivating at the prospect of getting a new agent with six years' experience with the Bureau. Even with his unusual recruitment and lack of Quantico training, his case closure rate really should've spoken for itself.

Instead, it was all sexual harassment seminars and training videos.

Under ordinary circumstances, Jackson might have welcomed the light workload. His last case ended almost six months ago and it was the most difficult he'd ever faced. Innocent people lost their lives – his partner included – before he'd been able to take down the would-be terrorist. If he had put together the pieces a little sooner or if he'd gotten to the scene a little faster or if he'd been honest with the woman he loved even once...But decisions were easy to second-guess in retro-spect.

Jackson frowned at his watch. Again. He'd already been there for over an hour, waiting for a juicy case. God knows, he needed a dis-traction from the current pathetic state of his life. It was sad that he spent most nights alone. It didn't bother him in D.C., but being here again...

He felt every lonely night.

Jackson was fully aware of the fact he was handsome. With his black hair, crystal blue eyes, and body kept in peak condition by a rig-orous workout schedule, he could have his pick of women. In his younger days, he would have filled his time with just that. Then again, having a failed marriage on his romantic resume by the time he was thirty-two had taken its toll on his ego. Now, there just seemed to be something unseemly about prowling around in clubs, looking for one-nighters.

Besides, there was only one woman he wanted in his bed and she was currently not returning his calls. Again.

The opening conference room door interrupted Jackson's thoughts. A man who he judged to be in his early forties stepped inside and closed the door behind him. Must be the new partner. He had the efficient movements of a paperwork-pushing agent who'd spent his career working white collar crimes.

He was about six foot in height, salt-and-pepper brown hair, soft green eyes, and a body that was fit enough, save the soft midsection that was apparently party to one too many donuts. Evaluating the man in front of him, Jackson guessed he probably did ok with the ladies. At the very least, he probably didn't spend his Saturday nights waiting for a woman to return his calls.

"Agent Caldwell, I'm Agent Brandon Dinsley. It appears we'll be working together."

Jackson stood and accepted the agent's extended hand.

"It's good to meet you. Do you know what case we've been assigned to work?" He knew his voice had an edge to it. He was aching to get back into the field.

Agent Dinsley nodded and set a small stack of file folders on the table.

"Our bank robber is known as Raptor. He committed dozens of bank robberies in the area, but during his last heist an innocent man was killed. That was two years ago."

"Two years ago? Why the hell are we working a case that's two years old?"

"Because it was never solved and you're the new guy."

"Figures. What did you do to get stuck with it?" Jackson asked.

"I asked for it."

"A cold case. Why?"

"I have my reasons, Caldwell. Why don't I get you acquainted with this case?"

Dinsley didn't wait for Jackson to respond before continuing.

"On December twelfth, five masked men entered First Alliance Bank and Trust. They were well organized and took over the bank lobby. Within minutes, they had all of the staff on the ground and called the bank president out of his office to open the vault. It wasn't until they had almost eight million dollars loaded into black gym bags and were on their way out of the building that Raptor realized there was an unnoticed customer in the president's office. The man was on his cell phone with the police and Raptor fatally shot him.

"Once the shot was fired, a customer by the name of Parker Ramsey stood up and started yelling at Raptor as they all fled the building. That man, along with the rest of Raptor's crew, showed up dead within the next six months. We have no proof that it was Raptor, but we can assume it was not mere coincidence."

"Do we have any leads?"

"Our last real lead dried up over a year ago, but I have a source who's told me Raptor may be about to make a move," Dinsley replied.

"Do you have any details?"

"Not really, but I know how Raptor operates. He always has an inside man. In his last heist, Ramsey opened an account and established a relationship with the bank employees. After the robbery, they all said they liked Ramsey and they were surprised by his involvement."

"Shocker."

Dinsley ignored him. "Apparently, he was able to get close enough to several of the employees to find out when would be the best time of day to strike, as well as when the largest amount of cash would be on the premises. He spent over two months staking the place out for Raptor."

Jackson mulled over what his new partner had said for a moment. He was annoyed to get a case full of dead ends, but was determined to crack this case and prove himself to his new superiors.

"Is your source reliable?"

"Probably not, but I am certain Raptor will need someone to be on the inside just as Ramsey was," Dinsley answered. After a brief pause he added, "He may already have someone."

I tossed my keys on the entry table as I closed the door behind me. After Parker's abrupt exit from the café a few hours ago, it took an emergency appointment with the best therapist in town to get me back to a semi-calm state of being. I say semi-calm because even an hour under the skilled hands of my massage therapist still wasn't enough to rid me of all my tense muscles.

For some reason, having coffee with a dead man was unsettling.

Had it really only been a year since I attended his funeral? At the time, it was therapeutic to witness the burial of all the men who were a part of my father's murder. Now that I knew it was a ruse I wasn't so sure how I felt.

I could understand Parker wanting vengeance; I was more than familiar with that concept. That he wanted to team up with me was what didn't quite ring true. Why would he want to work with Songbird when he supposedly didn't know she was me until we met in the park. I had to be missing something and I knew I would have to make sense of all of it before I got in any deeper.

There was still time for me to walk away from this. All of it.

I couldn't deny wanting to bring down Raptor. In fact, I wanted it so badly I could taste it, and it tasted fabulous, but wanting and doing were different animals. Parker Ramsey worked with Raptor once before – once that I knew of – and it was possible they were working together again. Maybe they were trying to pull me in so they could set me up to take the fall on their next big heist. Maybe Raptor wanted to take me out before I could become a problem.

Maybe I was paranoid.

After a long, hot shower I decided to call my contact and see what he knew about this. Chill was one of the few people I'd met who I felt I could trust since submerging myself in the underworld. I wasn't sure why I felt that way, considering he was a criminal, but my instincts were usually correct. Now was not the time to stop trusting them.

After several rings, Chill answered his cell phone.

"Songbird, it is good to hear from you again. To what do I owe the pleasure?"

"I've heard through the grapevine that Raptor is back in town and ready to take down another bank. If anyone knows anything about that, I figured it would be you, Chill," I replied, crisp and down to business, hoping he would also get straight to it.

"You figured right, sweet. I can confirm that he is both back and ready to boogie."

"Do you know the alias he's using?"

Chill laughed. "Very cute, Songbird. No one knows who Raptor is by day and I can guarantee that anyone who learned is dead and buried by now. All I know about this cat is that he does the social scene in a big way."

"How do you mean?"

"This guy is cultured and he probably comes from money. He does this for the challenge, not the take. From what all of my sources have told me, he has a good life in this town."

I thought that over for a moment before I asked, "Can your sources be trusted, Chill?"

"Can anyone I know really be trusted, Songbird?"

"Good point. Do you have any reason to believe they would feed you bad information on purpose?"

"No. My sources want to live to see tomorrow."

Charming thought.

"Okay, Chill. If you find out anything else, you have my number. You'll get your next payment by the end of the week."

"You know, Songbird, there are other services I can provide for which you would not be charged," Chill said seductively.

"Keep it in your pants. You know I don't mix business with pleasure."

"Oh, Songbird, apparently you still have not looked in a mirror. You can hardly blame a guy for trying, can you?"

"I suppose not." I was about to disconnect the call when a thought occurred to me. "What do you know about a man named Parker Ramsey?"

Chill was silent for a moment. "I know that Parker Ramsey helped Raptor pull off his last big heist and he was rewarded with a bullet. Ramsey is dead and buried, has been for quite some time. Why do you ask?"

"Because Parker Ramsey approached me in the park this morning about working with him."

"Well, I know you do not ever ask for my advice, but I think you should take it this time. Watch your back, Songbird. If Parker Ramsey is magically back from the great beyond, there is definitely trouble brewing. Besides, there simply are not enough fine-looking women in this town for one of you to go out and get yourself killed," Chill replied before hanging up.

I thought about what he said as I ran a brush through my damp hair. No, he definitely did not have to tell me Parker was trouble. The fact he was charming, blonde and knew how to fake his death told me that much. I couldn't help wondering if Chill was being straight with me this time. Every other piece of information he'd sold me was spot on, so I didn't have a reason to doubt him now.

Still, he'd hesitated just a second too long when I asked about Parker Ramsey.

Parker let his cell phone ring only once before he answered it. He could count on one hand the number of people who had this number and he didn't want to talk to any of them right now. Unfortunately, not answering a call from any one of them would be a fatal error at this stage of the game.

"I'm taking a risk in calling you now, Ramsey, so I hope you have something good to tell me," a gruff voice demanded.

"I've made contact with a little lark and I think things should run smoothly and according to plan." Parker put more confidence into his voice than he felt. Skylar being in and Skylar being useful weren't exactly the same thing.

"Can you be certain? I would not have expected she would be pleased to see you."

"She won't be a problem for us. I'm a good con man and she won't have any idea what we're up to until she's already in too deep."

"See that she doesn't, Ramsey. I'm taking a big risk on you and she'd better not cause me any problems."

Parker cleared his throat before speaking. "Look, it was my call to pull her into this. You don't have to worry about a thing."

"For your sake, you had better be right about that, Ramsey. You had better be right."

Perfect. Thinly veiled threats. The cornerstone of any successful partnership.

"Either you trust my judgment or you don't. I know what I'm doing. If you want this score to go down in your favor, we need her to play her part."

"Don't get cocky, Ramsey. I think we both know I don't trust your judgment. Make one wrong move and you'll find I can make things very uncomfortable for you."

"Considering my circumstances, that would be a feat."

"You have no idea what tools I have at my disposal to make that happen. Just get the plan on schedule and contact me once you have something positive. As I've said before, you don't have much time to save your skin. Clock's ticking."

TWO

Since the death of my father, I was reclusive to a fault. I was self-aware enough to realize that. My self-imposed solitude never bothered me before, but it was a liability now that I had what I hoped would be a solid lead on Raptor. Did I know who was part of the elite local social scene? Even if I did, would I have any clue how to get cozy with them?

It's a damn good thing I remembered to check the mail today because my bank statement – and a stroke of genius – was waiting for me.

Michael Traymoore, the president of First Alliance Bank and Trust, was just the person to see. In life, my father trusted him completely; in death, he became a close friend of mine. He handled many of the more profitable account relationships personally and he was always invited to any event of importance in this town. I also had the vague recollection of him telling me about heading up the planning committee for an important charity gala this year to benefit children with cancer.

If Raptor was in town, Michael would unwittingly be my key into his life.

After waiting in the bank lobby for over half an hour, Michael finally walked out of his office and greeted me. "I'm sorry to keep you waiting for so long, Skylar. I had a conference call that ran late," he said as I followed him into his office.

"Don't worry about it, Michael. I knew I was taking a chance in dropping by without an appointment."

Michael shook his head as he closed the door behind us. I fought to suppress the smile his action caused. Every time I saw him, his light brown hair was so carefully gelled into place that even those wicked Texas winds couldn't move it. Today was clearly no exception.

"Don't be silly. You know you don't ever need an appointment to come by and see me." He sat down across the desk from me. "So, what brings you by today?"

"I just thought I would come by and see how you were. I know I've been a stranger, but I've been a little depressed lately, I guess."

"Frankly, Skylar," he began. The concern in his soft brown eyes was evident when he spoke. "I've been a little bit concerned about you. I've been meaning to call you, but this silly fundraiser has been eating up every free moment of my day."

Well, hello there, perfect opening. I think I'll pounce on you.

"How's that going anyway, Michael?"

He shrugged. "Oh, I just don't know anymore. It seems like the closer the gala gets, the more problems we encounter. I never imagined when I volunteered to take the lead this year that it would involve quite so much planning."

"Well, you know," I began, tentative, "I have quite a bit of free time on my hands if you need anything. I don't really know much about planning a charity gala, but I would be glad to lend a hand."

A smile broke across Michael's face and I could tell exactly what he was thinking. I was certain he thought this would be a good opportunity to get me out of my townhouse and back into the swing of things. If that also meant getting me face to face with Raptor, we were on the same page. "I might just have to take you up on that, Skylar."

I shrugged. "If you do, you do. I can find a way to fill up my time if not, but it might be nice to do something that benefits someone else for a change."

"If you mean that, the next meeting is tomorrow evening. It might not be a bad idea for us to meet first so I can fill you in before I throw you in with the sharks."

I suppressed a laugh. If he had any idea what I was really up to, he would not be referring to a bunch of bored housewives and soccer moms as sharks. "Why don't I meet you at Yvette's for lunch then, Michael?"

"I'll see you at eleven-thirty."

I didn't feel quite like myself after I left Michael's office this afternoon, so I drove around until the sun started to fade behind the fluffy grey clouds scattered across the sky. Like that was a surprise. I hadn't felt like myself in two years, but lying to Michael...it just felt wrong on so many levels. At the very least, my involvement should still take some of the details off his plate. The white lie about my true motives didn't have to matter.

Did it?

While parking my coupe, I wondered what I was getting myself into with Parker Ramsey. I knew what he was after, but how was he planning to get it? Was there more to his agenda than I knew? Probably. At this point, I didn't even know how I'd let him know about the fundraising gala.

As soon as I got home, I went straight into my closet to change into my college sweatshirt and a pair of faded jeans - an outfit which always comforted me. It wasn't until I was pulling my hair back into a ponytail at the base of my neck that I realized I was not alone in my bedroom. A shadowy figure sat on the window seat, reading the book I'd left on my nightstand last night.

"I was wondering if you were ever coming home." Parker didn't bother to look up from the book.

"What the hell are you doing in my bedroom?" I snapped. "How do you even know where I live?"

"I was waiting for you to come home," he replied, still without looking up. "And I have my ways."

"How did you get in here?"

"I let myself in."

"My security system was armed."

Parker glanced up at me. My anger must have been evident because he put the book aside before speaking. "That thing is a joke. You might as well put out a welcome mat for burglars."

I placed my hands on my hips, fuming. "I'll have you know, that system is top of the line."

"You forget who you're talking to, Skylar." He stood up to meet my glare and advanced on me until he was so close I could smell his cologne. He had to be at least half a foot taller than me. "I'm the best at what I do."

"Fine. What do you want?" I wanted to step away from him, but I wouldn't give him the satisfaction of knowing how off kilter it threw me to be standing this close to him in my bedroom.

"I told you I'd be in touch."

"I assumed you meant by phone."

A smile played at his lips. "Assumptions are dangerous things, Skylar. Besides, I don't like to talk about these sorts of things over the phone or in public. I hardly figured you would be comfortable coming to my hotel, so here I am."

Though I was not pleased to have Parker in my bedroom, at least this solved my problem of letting him know about the fundraiser.

"Did you have anything specific to tell me or are you just here to annoy me in general?" I asked, finally letting myself step away from him and retreat to my kitchen.

"Annoy you in general and, yes, I'd love a drink."

Was he really accepting a drink I hadn't offered and making himself at home on my sectional?

"I have bottled water and soda. Take your pick," I called to him, still trying to figure out how the hell he got in.

"Water."

I handed him a bottle before I sat down on the far side of my sectional sofa from him. "Should I be expecting you to just let yourself in here whenever you like?"

Parker took a sip and shrugged. "If you expect it, then you will most certainly be disappointed, but it is a definite possibility as long as you have that particular alarm system."

I set my can of diet soda on the edge of the coffee table and rubbed my temples with my hands. Parker had the annoying habit of answering a question with a lot of words that told me nothing at all. "Well, as annoying as you are to me, it's a good thing you're here. I've been busy today and I think I have a way in."

I filled him in on my conversations with Chill and Michael. Parker appeared thoughtful as I spoke, but remained quiet. I suppose I expected him to have some sort of reaction to what I was telling him, so I finally asked, "Well?"

After a moment he nodded and said, "I think it just might work. From what I gathered during our conversations, I always figured him as the high-society type. This just might work." He paused and the gleam in his eyes brightened. "I'll surface at the gala."

"Is that really such a good idea, Parker? Michael knows who you are. You would be taking a huge risk to expose yourself to a man who would like to see you behind bars."

He dismissed my concern with a wave of his hand. "I never spent much time with Michael and he probably hasn't given Parker Ramsey a thought since I turned up dead."

"Even still...you can't just walk into a fundraiser, uninvited, and introduce yourself to everyone as Parker..."

"You have this all wrong, sweetheart. First off, you're going to invite me as your guest. Second, you'll introduce me as Jonathan Price, antiques dealer."

"And why, pray tell, would I invite an antiques dealer to be my guest?"

"Because I'm your new boyfriend," he said as though it was an obvious fact.

"You have got to be kidding me."

"Think about it for a minute before you completely dismiss it. What if Raptor tips his hand at the gala and we need to formulate a new plan? No one would think twice about your boyfriend pulling you off into a deserted corner and talking to you in hushed tones."

"You sound pretty confident."

"I sound that way because I am confident. I always am."

I relented. "Fine, but I do not mix business with pleasure, so don't get any ideas. I'll play along, but if you lay a hand on me the wrong way, I assure you I'll break it off."

"Promises, promises..." Parker replied as he stood up.

I also rose to my feet. "I'm not joking."

"I'm sure you're not, but you don't have to worry about anything from me. Don't misunderstand, you're a beautiful woman and I know I'm easy on the eyes, but I don't need that particular *distraction* as long as we're dealing with Raptor. After this is all over, well, we'll just have to see what happens."

His arrogance infuriated me, but I did not give him the satisfaction of a response. I watched in silence as he left through my front door without another word to me. It was unnerving to me that my mind failed to provide me with a snappy comeback whenever I was around him. I was normally so quick with those.

I shook my head as I locked the door behind him and rearmed the perimeter. My life was quickly becoming complicated and I knew what was coming next would just further aggravate the situation. Too bad that it was unavoidable at this point.

There was something about him – and I couldn't say what it was – that was so familiar to me. Did he remind me of an old boyfriend? An actor? The star of an X-rated dream I'd once had?

Whoever it was...this familiarity was powerful.

It had to be my mind conjuring old feelings for someone else onto him because it wasn't even possible for me to have the hots for a man I hated. When all this was over, I needed to see a shrink.

The day was a long one for Jackson. After Dinsley gave him the quick overview on the Raptor case, he proceeded to produce every case file there was for Jackson to read. By six o'clock he'd read almost all of the material and decided that he had learned enough for one day. If Raptor hadn't struck in over two years, one more night was definitely not going to make much difference.

Besides, he was still pissed off that his first assignment was a cold case.

Traffic was light and Jackson made it to the Collin County Prosecutor's office in less than an hour, which was excellent time for Dallas traffic. He knew Jenna was keeping unusually late hours over the last few weeks and figured she would still be there. At least, he hoped she would since she hadn't returned any of his calls over the last week.

Jenna Monroe, the woman Jackson loved and the woman who still did not trust him, was sitting at her desk, engrossed in a file she was reading when he arrived. It struck him as odd that, though she changed very little in appearance since he first met her the previous September, things had changed between them so markedly. Her eyes were a deep brown, taking in everything she looked at. Her hair was the color of a chocolate bar and Jackson remembered it always smelled as sweet. As he watched her from the doorway, he couldn't help but hope she would soon be able to forgive him for everything that had happened between them.

She glanced up to meet his gaze and tucked a loose strand of hair behind her ear. "How long were you going to stand there before you said something, Jackson? So far, I have you clocked at five minutes."

"You looked intent on what you were reading and I didn't want to bother you," he replied as he entered the room.

"Don't worry. I could really use a distraction right now. Trista left over an hour ago and I've actually gotten to work since then. I think I'm probably about to cut out anyway."

"Do you want to grab a bite to eat?" Jackson asked, hopeful.

"I'm not hungry."

"Oh."

The look in Jenna's eyes softened at his obvious disappointment. "What brought you by, anyway?"

"Business," he lied. "I've been assigned to a case that's two years old and was never closed. Do you remember hearing anything about a robbery at First Alliance Bank and Trust?"

Jenna bit her lip in thought. "The location in Frisco?"

"Yes."

"I think that happened about the time I was moving back from Boston. I remember hearing something about it, but I was hardly in the frame of mind to retain facts. All I remember is that a customer was killed."

Jackson nodded. "That's the one. Oh, well. I guess I'll let you get back to what you're doing so you can get out of here."

"If you want, I can look in our archives tomorrow and see if we have anything on it. Your agency would be the one with jurisdiction, but I'm sure we have some record since most of Frisco is in our county."

"That would be nice. Thanks, Jenna," he said, before turning to leave.

"You realize this means you'll owe me dinner if I find anything out for you."

"I think I can manage that," Jackson said as he fled her small office.

He just hoped she hadn't seen the huge smile her comment triggered. Was it wishful thinking or was there something sly in her tone? Either way, this might be the signal from her he'd been waiting months to get.

Thursday, March 18

I hadn't slept well the previous night, probably because I was now paranoid about my security system. I gave up on sleep early that morning and headed to the gym around seven. After two and a half hours of cardio, yoga and weight training, my lack of sleep finally caught up with me, but it was too late for a nap. I was the kind who could never just sleep for an hour when I was this exhausted.

And I couldn't miss my lunch with Michael if I was going to be ready for society *sharks.*

As I applied the last of my makeup, I didn't get the apparent attraction Chill and Parker seemed to have to me. Maybe they were in to bitchy chicks with body image issues. My last boyfriend certainly hadn't been. He'd always loved my kindness and my easy confidence. But those weren't the things that helped you catch a murderer.

Okay, well...maybe confidence, but I didn't have any genuine confidence in being able to catch him so bitchiness would have to fill the bill. Eric wouldn't recognize the woman I'd become if he were to see me today. Did I recognize myself anymore?

It didn't matter. I was scrutinizing criminals right now, not dwelling on the last five pounds I'd never be able to lose.

Maybe I looked good to them because a life of crime didn't leave a lot of time for dating and they were both hard up for some action. Doubtful. I couldn't say for sure about Chill, but something told me Parker wasn't one to sleep alone unless he actually wanted sleep.

God knows, I wouldn't let that man sleep.

Where the hell did that come from?

I pushed that thought out of my head as I drove to Yvette's. There was plenty for me to be concerned about without starting to fantasize about my new partner. Michael had known me for several years and I would have to keep up my guard around him if I didn't want him to discover that my motivations were anything other than pure.

I got to Yvette's early to get a table. They were one of the most popular Italian restaurants in Plano and I didn't want to burn a lot of time standing around. As usual, Michael arrived promptly at eleven-thirty. In all of the years I knew him, Michael was never late or early to anything: he was always precisely on time.

After we had ordered our meals, Michael got straight to the point.

"The gala is in less than two weeks. All of the RSVPs are in, but it seems like new details keep popping up that we should have handled months ago."

"How many people are on the committee?"

"Besides you and I, there are five people involved. They're a good group of people and I think you'll enjoy working with them," Michael said as the waitress arrived with our salads. It never failed to amaze me how swift the service here was.

"Good. I'm looking forward to getting back into the swing of things. Why don't you tell me a little bit about the people I'll be working with?"

Michael nodded. "Reyna Vinson takes care of most of the details. She comes from old money and has been involved with this particular event since she was a child and her mother was overseeing things. Even though I'm the event chair, there's no doubt in anyone's mind that she's in charge of the gala."

"What's she like?"

"She's very nice. You would never guess her net worth by talking to her. She has a level head on her shoulders and she does a considerable amount of charity work. Suzanne Wyndham is completely the opposite." Michael paused as the waitress set our plates on the table beside the salads we'd only just started eating. "Her husband, Drake, is the CEO of the bank. Don't get me wrong; Suzanne is a lovely woman, but she has the tendency to talk down to everyone else. I don't think she means any harm by it though."

"I'll keep that in mind."

"Trevor Brightman is a real estate developer, so there's scarcely a meeting that goes by without his cell phone interrupting. It seems like he's always in the middle of a big deal requiring his attention. He's nice enough in small doses, but his girlfriend is one of the most annoying people I've ever met. I think her name is Chelsea, but I might be wrong about that."

Michael was the most tolerant person I knew. For him to dislike someone made it worth noting to me. I wished I could tell him what I was up to so I could gain his insight on the situation, but I knew he would never go along with what I was doing. I decided to keep that little drama to myself.

Especially since I didn't have a clue what I was doing.

"What's wrong with her?"

"It's just a feeling I get about her. I suppose it doesn't really matter, though. She'll be at the gala with Trevor, but she isn't on the committee so you shouldn't have to deal with her until then."

"That's good." Having someone annoying at the gala might distract Michael enough that he didn't realize my date to the event was a bank-robbing con man.

"Elaine Whitman is the best fundraiser I have had the pleasure to work with. She is relentless on the phones, but she has a heart of gold. Her parents died shortly after she was married and she took in her younger sister until she went away to college."

Another orphan. Like me.

Michael fell silent. I had always been good at reading people and I could tell there was something he didn't want to tell me. Whatever it was, I was ready for it. None of the first four *sharks* sounded so bad.

"Who's the fifth person, Michael?"

"Eric Sauters," he replied, voice soft, fatherly.

Maybe I was less prepared than I'd thought.

Parker was glad his connections within the county were still intact; otherwise, he might have ended up spending hours standing in lines and flirting with lonely looking clerks to no avail. He set down the blueprints on the desk and retrieved a pad of paper from the drawer. From his first glance at the diagram, he knew this would not be an easy task.

His cell phone rang as he was detailing the security systems.

"Yeah," he barked into the phone.

"You are a difficult man to track down, Ramsey," Chill said.

"Dead men normally are. What do you need?"

"Skylar is asking questions about you. How do you want me to handle it?" If he caught the irritation in Parker's tone, he wasn't showing it. Cool as usual. There were many reasons why they called him Chill and that was among them.

Parker thought about that before answering. "What have you told her so far?"

"Just to watch her back and that you were dangerous."

"Good. Tell her as little as possible."

"I can try, but she pays me well and is...*persistent*, to say the least. I may have to throw her a bone here and there."

"All right. We go way back, Chill. I trust your judgment. You know what's going on here, so tell her whatever you feel like you can without showing our hand. I can't have this compromised this early in the game."

"Done. Just make sure you give me a little notice before you need me for the other thing."

"You don't have to worry about that. I'm probably at least two weeks out, but it'll go down this side of a month."

"I will stay available. Keep me posted." Chill disconnected.

Parker frowned at the blueprints. Bank security turned more complex over the last two years than he thought possible. Despite the skeleton of his plan coming together in his mind, he was grateful he had some time to pull off this job. Designing the perfect crime was always the easy part for him and this time would be no different.

The hard part would be convincing Skylar Montgomery to go along with the real score.

Jackson waited for his partner to get off the phone. He'd spent the better part of the morning going over the details of the case until he felt like he had a good handle on the facts, but something about it was still bothering him. The file had to be incomplete.

"Why were no suspects listed in any of the case files?" Jackson asked as soon as Dinsley hung up the phone.

"We could never substantiate anything and the higher ups didn't want to risk potential lawsuits."

Jackson raised an eyebrow. "Lawsuits?"

"We had a few suspects, but all of them had alibis that checked out. They were all prominent men in the community, so I had to drop my investigation of them."

"What kind of evidence did you have on them?"

"Nothing substantial, but it could have been the kicker if we had anything else to corroborate it. All of the men had large amounts of money deposited into their bank accounts shortly after the robbery."

"How large are we talking about?" Jackson asked.

"About five million."

"And I suppose they all had an explanation."

"Yep. Drake Wyndham was just made the CEO of First Alliance and had to liquidate his ownership in a limited partnership as one of the conditions. Trevor Brightman claimed he just collected the rest of his money on a real estate deal. Eric Sauters put the money into his business account for a customer who wasn't sure where to put it yet. They all had the paperwork to back up their claims, but I've always thought there was something fishy about the whole situation."

"Do we know what happened to each of them since the investigation died down?"

"They all still live in the area. Of course, since we never had anything solid on any of them, there would be no reason for Raptor to relocate. If he is one of those three, of course."

"There was one other person I wanted to ask you about. Skylar Montgomery's name was mentioned throughout the file. Who is she?"

Dinsley frowned. "She's the daughter of the man who was killed during the robbery. She was upset when our investigation turned up nothing but dead ends and she made that known to anyone who would listen to her."

"Will she be a problem during this investigation?"

"She shouldn't be, but I might make a trip out to talk to her in person if I were you."

Dinsley wasn't telling him the whole story, but he decided not to act on it. A confrontation at this point would be premature. He would need to dig up some more details to substantiate his hunch before he said anything.

Raptor paced around his office restlessly. Two years was a long time to walk the straight and narrow. The First Alliance heist had been his largest take by far, but it still gnawed at him that it didn't go exactly according to the plan. His plan. Down to the last detail, everything was perfect.

If only Ramsey hadn't lost his cool at the end of things and blown his cover. Eliminating the crew was never part of the plan. At least, they would've lived until they helped him launder the money.

Fucking Ramsey and his mouth. Shoot one little customer to tie a final loose end and he came unglued. If Ramsey hadn't let his name slip, Raptor would've pulled a dozen more jobs by now.

Instead, he was bored.

"At least you got what you deserved, Ramsey. Even if it wasn't at my hands," Raptor said to himself as he sat down at his desk.

It was time to find a new score that would put Raptor back in the papers. Unfortunately, bank security was tighter since the last heist and he would need someone on the inside if he was going to make it work. Despite his intense hatred for Ramsey, he wished he were still alive.

No one was better at disarming people's skepticism than he was. He'd had the sort of face people would trust in an instant and forget as soon as he was gone. Wheelmen and muscle were a dime a dozen, but an inside man with such versatility was a rare find. The only person Raptor had ever known who could match Ramsey's skill was himself, but he could hardly play that role.

His face was far too recognizable in this town.

THREE

I left Yvette's just after one o'clock that afternoon. I was grateful the committee meeting wasn't until six-thirty. My mind was racing and I knew I would need every millisecond of the time to pull myself back together. It figured that the first time I chose to try and get my social life back that Eric would be somehow involved.

Pulling one over on Michael was hard enough, but no one on the planet knew me the way Eric did.

Eric Sauters. Two years ago, I thought he was the man I was going to marry. I met him at the end of my sophomore year in college while trying to study at a coffee shop. I didn't realize how crowded it was until Eric asked if he could sit down. We spent so long arguing about politics that I was almost late for my class. He got my phone number under the pretense of continuing our argument at a later time.

Of course, I didn't find out until our second date that he only picked the fight with me so he would have an excuse to get my number, not that he needed one. With his golden blonde hair and brown eyes, I would have asked for his number if he hadn't asked first. I wasn't exactly the sort to sit back and wait for the guy to get around to making the first move.

I was also never one of those girls who thought she was in *love* with every boyfriend, so when I realized I was in love with Eric, I fell especially hard. If people really only got one great love in their life, he was mine. A few weeks before my college graduation, I found the ring in his sock drawer and faked puzzlement at what his big surprise for me was.

That was the way my life was supposed to turn out: Parents still alive and me living in married bliss to the man I still thought about each night before sleep claimed me.

Fate had other plans for me, I guess. One phone call destroyed my life. It changed everything. It changed me.

I didn't even find out about the robbery until after I walked across the stage. I can still remember scanning the crowd for my parents and never seeing them there. On that horrible day, the emotion that crystallizes in my memory for me is anger. My father was dying and I was angry they weren't watching me graduate.

Eric was an angel through everything, but I couldn't stand to have him around me, loving me. I didn't deserve him and I sure didn't deserve his love, so I pushed him away. It was for the best, I always told myself. What happened in the month after my father's death left me an empty shell with nothing left in my heart except bitterness and vengeance. That wasn't something I wanted to dish out to the man I loved.

No, the blackness in my heart was all for Raptor.

Eric was shattered when I told him I didn't want to see him anymore. I always hoped he would move on and find someone who could offer him more than the murderous thoughts that consumed my mind. It was too painful for me to try to be his friend so I severed all ties to him. The last I heard he was making a name for himself in the investment business.

I really shouldn't reminisce when I was behind the wheel. I had no memory of driving home from the restaurant.

As soon as I closed my front door, I knew I was not alone. Why did it seem like Parker was always around when I least wanted him to be? I was not in the mood to play his games right now.

"Come out, Parker. I know you're here," I snapped into my living room.

Parker needed a break from his planning so he went to Skylar's just before one o'clock that afternoon. When he realized she wasn't home, he let himself in to wait. It annoyed him that she was never home, even though she had no way to know when he was coming over.

He needed to tell her the truth, but every minute that ticked by while he waited took away a piece of his nerve.

Parker summoned his thoughts back once he heard Skylar's voice and walked out into the living room where she waited. "That was no way to greet a guest," he chided.

She rolled her eyes. "*You* are not a guest."

"True," Parker responded, nodding. "I'm your boyfriend."

"I am not in the mood for this right now. What do you want?" Skylar asked as she slumped down onto the sectional.

"I needed to talk to you about something." Parker paused. "What's your deal?"

"Nothing. I'm just sick of coming home every day to find a burglar waiting for me."

"Well, maybe I wouldn't be waiting if you weren't always out when I came over." He shook his head. That didn't matter. "Besides, I'm a con artist, not a burglar. There's a difference. One takes finesse."

Skylar touched her hand to her face and let out a loud sigh. "Why can't you just use the phone like a normal person?"

Parker smiled. "I'm not a normal person. And I already told you I didn't like to discuss this sort of thing over the phone."

"Fine, you win. What did you come here to tell me?"

Why did she look like she was about to cry? No power on this earth could make him tell her the truth if this was a PMS thing. "Are you sure you're okay? You don't look so good."

"Wow. You really are a smooth talker, aren't you?"

"I didn't mean..."

"I don't care." She dropped her gaze to the carpet. "I'd like for you to stop spending so much time in my bedroom when I'm not here." Her eyes shot back to his with sapphire flames burning inside. "I don't know you. It's creepy."

Clearly, she wasn't about to cry anymore. "It's not like I'm rifling through your panty drawer, sweetheart."

"I don't care if you're in there washing the windows, it's still my private space, even if you can apparently walk in here whenever the hell you feel like it."

"Look, I can't wait out in the open for you to get home and I can't be sitting on the couch in case you have someone with you when you get here. I can either wait in your bedroom or the bathroom." The corner of his lips twitched, but he didn't let the full smile form. "But I think it would be creepier for me to be waiting behind the shower curtain for you." The smile won the battle. "Unless you'd like me to surprise you while you're in the nude, that is."

Skylar regarded him for a moment, then shook her head. "Oh, I bet you'd enjoy that." She tapped her index finger against her lips a few times. "Is the real reason I always come home to find you here that you're trying to get a peek at the goods?" She shrugged and lifted her arms out to either side. "You can get your fill of looking, but it's still hands off."

Parker was about to answer her when a knock at the door interrupted them. Whoever it was had damn good timing. When she'd moved her arms, it changed something about the angle with her shirt and a lacy edge to her bra was beckoning to him from the low neckline of her blouse. It would help him sell his answer if his eyes weren't glued to her breasts.

She rose and brushed by him on the way to the door. Against his will, his eyes strayed to her ass. Fitted black slacks were a definite improvement over the baggy jeans she seemed to favor. He tore his eyes up to meet hers as she looked back to him from the viewer.

Her eyes were wide with an annoyance that didn't seem to be because she caught him ogling her.

"Who is it?"

"I don't know, but it looks like he has a badge in his hand," she whispered, urgent. "You shouldn't be here when I open the door."

Parker nodded. "I'll wait in the bedroom."

"Are you kidding me?" Even though she was too short to be intimidating, she advanced on him and caught his arm before he made it to her room. "Didn't we just talk about this?"

His eyes swept over the room. "I'm pretty sure a cop will notice me hiding under the coffee table, so where did you want me to go, sweetheart?" He inched nearer to her. "Or did you want me to wait in the shower for you? You balked at that suggestion before, but never gave me an answer of substance."

Was now really the time to test the limits of the sexual tension between them? A cop was standing on the other side of the door and he was considering breaking his number one rule when on a con. Like the seething woman in front of him, he didn't mix business and pleasure unless it was a necessary part of the plan.

And he didn't need to seduce her to get to Raptor.

Yet Parker still found himself considering it. For Skylar Montgomery, he would toss out all his carefully constructed rules of the game. If this were about anything other than Raptor, he would take her to bed without a second thought for the score he was blowing. Based solely on the sexual chemistry smoldering in the few inches of space separating their bodies, the trade would be worth it.

Well worth it.

But this was about Raptor. For that reason - and that reason alone - sex with Skylar was off the table until after the last play was made. It didn't matter that she still hadn't released his arm, or that one of her fingers was stroking it.

It figured that she wasn't going to make this easy on him.

She stared at him, barely breathing until they heard another knock at the door. Skylar finally shook herself out of it and shoved him into the bedroom. "Just be quiet and leave my underwear alone."

"I wouldn't think of touching a thing until I get an invitation."

"Keep dreaming. Not gonna happen."

"We'll see." He grinned and stepped out of sight from the front door. "You were thinking about the shower. We both know it."

Unfortunately, so was he.

When the door opened, a pair of untrusting blue eyes greeted Jackson.

"Can I help you?"

"Are you Skylar Montgomery?"

"I am. What can I do for you?"

He flashed his badge. "I'm Special Agent Caldwell. Can I come in for a moment? There's something I'd like to discuss with you."

"Of course," she replied, opening the door wider for him to enter.

Jackson scanned the living room while she closed the door behind them. He could have sworn he heard a male voice, but there was no evidence in the room to support that. He waited for an invitation to sit, but received only a hostile glare from where she stood beside the door.

Yeah, this was going to be a fun one.

"Miss Montgomery, I've been assigned to the First Alliance robbery," he began.

"I figured. Why else would the FBI be at my door?"

Her tone matched the hostility in her eyes, so he tried to make his own sound soothing when he spoke. "I understand you must be frustrated by the amount of time that's gone by and I want to assure you I will do anything in my power to find Raptor and bring him to justice."

Skylar laughed a mirthless laugh.

"You understand? I am so glad I finally have someone assigned to the case who understands what it's like to have your family ripped apart by a criminal. Tell me, Agent Caldwell, what was the name of the man who murdered your father in cold blood?"

Jackson remained quiet. He knew better than to interrupt her tirade. He'd grown up with two sisters and this was nothing new to him. Of course in this particular instance he couldn't wait for her to become bored with the argument and stomp off to her room.

"Oh, I can tell from your silence that when you say you *understand*, you really mean you feel sorry for me. You can save your pity for someone else because I don't need it. Why don't you tell me why you're really here?"

"Miss Montgomery, I'm here to tell you in person that I'm on this case and to find out if there is anything you feel I should know that may be useful to me in the investigation."

"So, I take it you rushed over here to talk to me before bothering to read the files?"

This had to be Dinsley's idea of a joke. A little advanced warning might have been nice. "No, I'm here because I've been doing this long enough to know not everything is always included in the case files. I'm here to make sure nothing you feel is important was left out of the official report."

"Oh. Well in that case..." The brunette regarded him for moment in silence before circling around him, her fingertips lightly grazing across his back as she moved. Jackson watched as the anger from before gave way to a more playful look. Skylar came to a stop in front of him and toyed with his tie, fingers tickling his neck in the process.

"What are you doing, Miss Montgomery?" Jackson asked, though he had a pretty good idea.

She moved in closer and rose to her tiptoes to bring her lips nearer to his ear, pressing her body against his in the process.

"You asked if there was anything I thought you should know. I just wanted to see if you and I would be able to play nice and get along," she whispered before she began to kiss his neck softly. "I can think of all sorts of ways to make your investigation more enjoyable for you. Just say the word."

Her previous hostility would've been preferable to this. Jackson was annoyed to be there on official business while she was apparently trying to seduce him. Even if he wasn't involved with Jenna, well sort of involved, he still wouldn't have invited her advances. If nothing else, the bomb that struck his relationship with Jenna after she learned the truth about him had taught him not to mix his personal life with his cases.

It was just too bad it was a valuable lesson he'd been forced to learn more than once over the course of his career.

Jackson pushed her back gently and gathered her hands in his. "I'm sorry, but I really don't think this is a good idea."

Skylar nodded and moved around the sofa to sit. She gestured for him to have a seat at the far end. "Good. You and I will get along just fine then, Agent Caldwell."

"Excuse me?" He sat down, trying to figure out if this was another game or sincerity.

"Let's just say the last agent on this case spent more time trying to figure out how to get into my pants than he spent trying to figure out where Raptor was. I just wanted to make sure I wouldn't have the same problem with you."

As if he'd really need to spend any time trying to figure that one out. Getting clothes off women was an art he'd perfected a long time ago.

"Unless you've got an address for Raptor or a map to the money sewn to the inside of your pants, I don't see the relevance in taking them off."

"Of course." She looked anything but convinced. "And you're here because...why? To chat with me about the worst days of my life? A phone call might have been more appropriate. Besides, I have no idea what's included in the file and what was left out."

"And nothing strikes you about that day as more important than the rest?"

An odd mixture of emotions swam through her eyes. She closed them and took a breath before answering.

"I'm told the 9-1-1 emergency response was a little sluggish that day, which is probably why my father bled out before anyone could get to him." With obvious effort, she opened her eyes, revealing anger and hatred within. "I think it's important that the shot wasn't an instant kill shot, meaning he suffered before he died."

"I didn't mean to bring up..."

"Your very existence in my living room is a reminder that my father's dead and the man who murdered him is still out there because your office couldn't catch him. I don't need a reminder, Agent Caldwell.

I wake up every morning, and sometimes in the middle of the night, feeling the loss as though it just happened."

"I'm sorry."

"Good. That's the first productive thing you've said since flashing your badge. Maybe you're actually sorry enough to do something about it. All of the agents and police officers were just around to follow their little investigation checklist, but none of them were sorry." She turned her attention to her folded hands in her lap. "Now, I have a very full evening planned and I have quite a bit to do before then. Be a dear and let yourself out."

Jackson stood. "I'll be in touch, Miss Montgomery."

She didn't look up. "I expect so."

He left without another word. The thought entered his head that this was just the sort of thing his last partner, Collin, would love to hear about. Too bad he was dead.

Another regret.

Once the initial slap in the face of thinking about Collin's death wore off, something else occurred to him. Dinsley alluded to the fact he'd previously worked this case. Was it even possible the conservative man who was his new partner was the same man Skylar just referred to?

If Dinsley was more interested in Skylar than solving the case, Jackson knew he would have to keep a close eye on his partner. It was the least logical answer, but it was the only one he had that made any sense. Besides, Dinsley certainly wasn't offering up any information.

Why else would he request this cold case?

As though on cue, Parker returned to the living room. He shot me a look, but I pretended not to notice. I wasn't in the mood to talk about the past anymore. I'd just vocalized the most painful detail of my father's murder and I would have to relive another painful portion of the past in a few hours.

How many memories of pain could one person endure before they crumpled? I was just about there.

"What was that all about, Skylar?" he finally asked.

"What was what?"

"Okay, I admit I didn't have the best viewing angle, but it looked like you just threw yourself at that agent."

"Jealous?"

He gave me a noncommittal shrug. "I thought it might be nice to know whether you were planning to work with the other side of the law on this one."

I smiled, or I got as close to a smile as was possible right now. "I had to be sure he was on the up and up. Either he is or he's gay. Regardless, I'm not worried about him."

Parker gave me another strange look. "What happened to the agent you were talking about?"

"I don't know. I always suspected there was something off with him, but then he stopped coming around one day. I didn't question it since it was a good thing for me."

"Maybe this new agent will be just what the case needs?"

"I lost my faith in the FBI a long time ago. I think you and I will find Raptor long before they realize he's in town." I paused, remembering he was still here for some unknown purpose. "What did you want to talk to me about, anyway?"

Parker shrugged. "It wasn't that important and I can tell you're tired. You should try to get some sleep before your meeting tonight. You need to be at your best for that."

He didn't give me the opportunity to process what he said, much less respond before he left. Given the innuendos he made before the FBI came to play, I didn't expect him to leave without more of the same. I don't think Parker even bothered to look me up and down during our brief exchange.

Odd.

Then again, I didn't know him well enough to read him yet. Maybe he was one of those guys who hit on everything that moved without realizing it. Or maybe he just enjoyed trying to get under my skin by pushing my buttons. If he was as good at what he did as he kept saying, he should already have figured out that the hot-cold routine wasn't the way to get me into bed.

But he was right about one thing; I was exhausted. If I crawled into bed now, I could get in a decent nap before I had to face the socialites. And my ex.

I couldn't say which terrified me more.

I opened my eyes just before five that evening. Good thing, too, because I didn't set my alarm. Part of me wished I had overslept, but I knew there was no turning back for me now. I knew that from the first moment I locked eyes with Parker Ramsey. Raptor would never expect me to come after him. I couldn't let my feelings for Eric get in the way of that.

What were my feelings for him? With so much time between us, it was hard to say.

It would undoubtedly be a difficult night; however, I couldn't remember a night since the murder that wasn't full of pain. The thing I had to keep in mind, that had to keep me going, was that this wasn't about me at all. This was about payback. I was doing all of this to settle a score that had long gone unresolved. My father deserved so much more than to be just another name in a file passed from agent to agent as the years went on.

As I let the hot water cascade over me in the shower, my thoughts invariably turned back to Eric. They usually did when I wasn't consumed by anger. And, really...how angry could I be when I was in the shower?

I hadn't spoken to Eric in the last year. Before that, I didn't know how much time elapsed since I last saw him. I didn't even know if he was seeing someone. Come to think of it, he could be married by now...

That thought hit me hard as I dried my hair. I needed to rethink my whole tough girl, mask of stone routine when I was around Michael. If I hadn't spent so much energy trying to pretend the prospect of seeing Eric Sauters tonight didn't completely unhinge me, I might've thought to ask about that.

Or did it even matter? After all this time, I wasn't still in love with him. No way. I'm not sure of much, but I'm sure of that.

Probably.

Ugh.

How was I going to pull off lying to Raptor when I wasn't even capable of lying to myself? I didn't ask Michael because I didn't want to get an answer. For another few hours, I'd wanted to imagine he was still single and we'd get a second chance as soon as this mess with Raptor was finally over. It wasn't a question of whether I still loved him; it was a question of whether I could keep my poker face intact during those first moments when I saw him. Especially if there was a ring on his finger...

I couldn't even bring myself to imagine that.

It was selfish to hope he spent the last year of his life alone and pining for me, but I...I didn't know how I was supposed to be okay with his moving on. The only thing I was sure of was that I was not ready to see Eric again. If he was with someone, I knew I would feel hurt, but I would feel worse if he wasn't.

"Stop it, Skylar," I ordered my reflection in the mirror. "None of that matters. Raptor is close and you are going to bring him down."

I dressed quickly and managed to get to First Alliance by a quarter after six. When Michael greeted me at the door, he let me know I was the first to arrive. I supposed all of the society types would be fashionably late. The airs these sorts of people put on drove me nuts. It was going to take all of my patience not to lose it on any of them, or so I imagined.

After I settled into the boardroom of the bank, Michael left me alone so he could keep watch for the others to let them in as they arrived. I was only alone for a few minutes when an energetic raven-haired woman entered the room. She could've passed for a high school student. The woman plopped down next to me. Her sea blue eyes were shining when she spoke.

"You must be Skylar. I am so excited to finally have another woman on this committee who isn't like a hundred years old. Oh, I'm Reyna Vinson, by the way."

I instantly understood what Michael meant at lunch. Reyna did not act like someone who was worth tens of millions of dollars. In fact, she looked like she should be at the mall hanging out with her friends and gossiping about boys.

I accepted her outstretched hand. "It's good to meet you, Miss Vinson."

"Please, Sky, it's Reyna. Do you mind if I call you Sky?" She didn't wait for my response before continuing. " Of course you don't. I'm not one of those stuffy housewives who are hung up on formalities. Anyway, I am so glad I have someone to help me with all of this planning."

"What about the others?"

Reyna made a dismissive gesture with her hand before she spoke. "Please. Most of these people are at the meetings just so they can get their name out in front of people. 'Laine is a whiz at fundraising, but she isn't much for the details. Michael tries, but that man is just too busy with the bank. I mean, you know how he is. Everyone else could vanish and I would probably still get the same amount of work done," she replied.

I wasn't sure why, but I liked Reyna in that instant. It wasn't every day you met someone who told it exactly as it was. She shot from the hip and that was refreshing. Even though she was acting completely informally, I could tell she was also capable of presenting herself in the dignified manner I was sure her family would expect.

I noticed a figure out of the corner of my eye, but Reyna jumped up before I could make sense of who it was. She grabbed his arm and led him into the room towards me.

"Sky, this is another one of the slackers I was telling you about. He only comes enough to keep me happy. Sweetie, this is Sky. She's going to help me out with all of my million errands."

"We've met," Eric replied in soft voice. "It's good to see you again."

As the meeting began to wind down, Michael chided himself for not warning Skylar about Reyna and Eric. While she seemed to be dealing with the surprise well enough, he knew she was a mess inside. Monty had always described his daughter as having a level head when it came to everything except for *that* boy.

If nothing else, at least Reyna appeared blissfully ignorant of the occasional sidelong glances Eric and Skylar were sneaking at each other whenever she leaned forward. Monty would've been kicked back in a chair, arms crossed over his chest and shaking his head over the whole thing.

Michael felt his throat start to close at the thought of his old friend. Monty was the kind of man who always had something kind to say no matter what was going on in his life. Skylar used to take after her father, but recently she turned into a sullen young woman who rarely smiled. When he told her about the one piece of good news after her father's death, she just looked through him as though he wasn't even there.

Maybe the old Skylar would come back one of these days, Michael mused as he stood up to rescue her from the others. Especially Trevor. It was hard to say whether the man was hitting on her or trying to sell her something.

"We'll have to do lunch, Sky," Trevor insisted.

"You're ridiculous, Trevor. No one *does* lunch anymore," Suzanne snapped.

Reyna locked her arm through Skylar's. "Back off, you lot of vultures. No one is stealing Sky away from me until this gala is over," she interrupted, cheerful, as usual.

"Thanks," Skylar whispered.

Michael clapped his hands to get everyone's attention. "Okay everyone. I think we all know what to do and I need to get everyone out of here so I can arm the alarms."

"That's Michael's way of telling us his wife made something good for dinner and he wants to get home before it's too cold to eat," Reyna told Skylar.

Michael took pleasure in the smile Reyna's comment caused to appear on Skylar's face. He noticed when she hung back once everyone exited the building. After he made certain the alarm was armed and the doors were locked, he joined her in the parking lot.

"You should have told me, Michael."

"I know, but I was afraid you wouldn't come if I did."

"You still should have told me."

"I know."

"Then why didn't you? We both know you don't care whether I help with this or not."

"Would you have given Reyna a chance if I told you she was seeing Eric?"

"No, probably not." Emotion broke across her face. "It's not like I have any reason to be upset about them, but...It's just harder than I thought it would be to see him again." She shook her head. "I want to hate her."

"Reyna's a good person. She was the one who finally got Eric to cheer up and get back out into the world."

Skylar smiled. "I said I want to hate her, Michael, not that I do. I spent all evening trying to hate her, but I can't. She's just too damn nice. It's almost like what I used to imagine a little sister would be like."

"She reminds me a little of your cousin Alexa."

"I haven't seen her in so long, I don't even remember."

"Maybe you should plan a trip to California to see her."

"I don't know. Maybe one of these days."

He was pushing too hard. Michael knew that, but he didn't know when he'd have another opening to talk to her about visiting the last few members of her family who were still alive. "You know your aunt and uncle moved back to the area last year."

"I know. We were never...close." She let out a sigh. "That's a lie. I just can't stand how pretentious my aunt is. I don't know how Alexa puts up with her."

"Well...maybe you could start with your cousin then. You could head out there after the gala and get away from this unpredictable weather."

Something flashed through her eyes, but it was too dark for him to tell what it was. She cleared her throat. "Um...yeah. If nothing's going on."

FOUR

What was that God awful sound? Why wouldn't it stop when I smacked my alarm clock? Oh. I didn't set my alarm. Wow. It's already after one o'clock? How did that happen? Sure, I had to take something to help me sleep last night after seeing Eric again, but...still. I should've been up hours ago.

I rubbed my eyes and opened the door, not bothering to see who it was first.

Or change out of the tank top and yoga pants I slept in.

"Oh my gosh, were you still asleep? I am so sorry," Reyna said, as usual, talking at the speed of a jet.

I shook my head. "I just overslept, that's all. Do you want to come in?"

"Yes." She hesitated, then nodded and stepped inside.

"Would you like some coffee or..."

"I'll get it," Reyna interrupted. "I woke you up, so I bet you probably need a minute to get used to being awake. I know I would. I am so not a morning person."

I watched Reyna disappear into my kitchen. Did she have to be so much like me? Well, except for looking like she just stepped off the cover of a magazine. And she was perky.

It was as though she was trying to make this difficult on me. I took advantage of the opportunity she gave me to brush my teeth and change into a comfortable pair of jeans and a soft grey sweater.

Reyna handed me a cup of coffee as soon as I emerged from my bedroom. "Here you go, sunshine. Wow. That is an awful color for you." She looked embarrassed. "Sorry."

I shook my head. "Thank you for the coffee. You're entirely too peppy."

"I know. I do that when I'm nervous." The hesitation was back.

I led her into the living room to sit down before I responded. "Nervous?"

"I wanted to apologize to you for last night. I had no idea about you and Eric. I probably made an awkward situation even worse and I'm sorry about that." She paused and looked suddenly embarrassed. "Well, I mean, of course I knew about you and Eric. I just didn't know that you were...*you* before last night when he told me that you were."

"First of all, there is no me and Eric anymore and there hasn't been for quite some time. If anything, you made the situation less awkward because you didn't know. You have nothing to be sorry for."

"Are you sure?"

"Yeah. Don't worry about it, Reyna."

"Okay. So you aren't quitting then?"

"No. Why would I?"

"Oh, thank God. You're like the only normal person on that committee. Couldn't you just have died when Suzanne and Trevor started fighting about the right way to serve salmon mousse? Don't they realize they're talking about whipped up fish?" She wrinkled her nose.

I couldn't suppress my laugh. "That was a waste of time."

"I know, Sky. It's like this every week. Last time it was some-thing about whether the centerpieces should be pink or bubble gum, even though they both look *exactly* the same. I honestly don't know how my mother managed to do this year after year. These people are absolutely, certifiably insane."

"What can I do to help you?"

"I was hoping you would say that," Reyna replied, producing a piece of paper from her purse. "I know Suzanne wanted to pick out the floral arrangements, but I need someone to go who won't spend two hours trying to decide between the closed buds and the slightly closed buds."

I accepted the paper from her. It was the address to the florist we were apparently using for the gala. The color scheme was also listed for me. Clearly, Reyna was a bit of a control freak, though I completely understood why after having met Suzanne.

"I'll take care of it. How many arrangements do I need to get?"

Reyna stood up as though she were trying to visualize the room in her head. "Let's see...We'll need about a hundred table centerpieces. There will be seven buffet tables that need a little color. It may be too cold, but I want something out on the terrace as well, just in case. I guess sixty feet of greenery ought to do the trick. Eh, whatever else you think we might need." Reyna scrutinized the room. "I can tell you have good taste. I won't have to worry about anything strange from you. I hate to give assignments and dash, but I have to get to the caterer's and make certain that we are not having whipped fish at my gala. You have my cell if you need anything," Reyna said breezily as she left.

"She seems nice," Parker commented as he entered the room.

"I wish you would stop doing that."

I guess I could at least rule out him picking the lock on my front door since Reyna and I would have seen him come in.

"You know you're starting to like me, Skylar. I can tell; you only raised your voice a little that time."

"I don't have time for this. What do you want, Parker?" I snapped. And how do you keep getting in without my knowledge, a voice inside my head was screaming.

Seriously...was the man magicianing himself through my bedroom wall or what?

"I thought I would come see how you were doing today. That's supposed to be a good boyfriend behavior, right?"

I shot him a dirty look. He probably wouldn't know a good boyfriend if I hired one to keep him out of my living room.

"Okay, okay. I get the hint. I actually thought it might be a good idea if we got to know each other a little better."

"Pass."

"Excuse me?"

"Business and pleasure rule."

He rolled his eyes. "I think we both know that wasn't what I meant." Before I could protest that I knew no such thing, he added, "We should get to know each other better because you're going to have to pretend to be smitten with me soon."

"Smitten? You are out of your mind. I've never been smitten before in my life."

"You get my point," he said.

"Yeah...but I don't see why you expect me to fawn all over you like you're something special." It really pissed me off that a smile was playing over his lips. "Besides, *smitten* isn't my style and there will be people at this thing who know that about me."

"Fine. I'll pretend to be smitten. Either way, we still need to have a little more knowledge about each other than we do right now. We'll only get so far working with me being a dead con artist pretending to be your boyfriend and the obvious contempt for me you don't bother to hide."

"I suppose that would be a good idea, but I get to go pick out flowers," I said, holding up the address for him to see. "You're welcome to come with me, if you like."

Parker shrugged. "I've been dead for over a year. I have no plans."

"I was kidding. Don't you think it will be dangerous for us to be out in public together before the gala?"

He grinned. "I doubt Raptor will be casing a flower shop. It's ever so slightly beneath him, I imagine."

"Whatever," I sighed. "Let's just go."

"Aren't you going to change first?"

I did a double-take. "Why?"

"The kid was right. You should burn that sweater."

Why did everyone hate my clothes today? "But comfortable is my favorite color."

"That's fine, but if you show up for the gala wearing that, we'll need to rethink the whole smitten thing." He shook his head. "I'm the best out there, but no one's *that* good."

The time at the florist was unbelievably boring for Parker. After an hour and a half of waiting on a stool in between displays of roses and carnations, he was beginning to think he should meet up with her once she was done here. This was about flowers for a gala that didn't matter to her, not the cure for cancer. At least she didn't have him babysitting her purse as women liked to do while shopping.

He cracked his first smile since parking next to her car in the flower shop's parking lot. Skylar probably thought he'd snatch her wallet if she let go of her death grip on it.

Things weren't all smooth sailing after she selected the final arrangement either. Although she accepted his offer of an early dinner, it took more negotiating than a nuclear disarmament summit to choose a restaurant. For someone who said whatever was fine with her, she sure did shoot down plenty of his suggestions. By this point, Parker imagined it would be faster to cook a gourmet meal from scratch than to continue this devil's game of twenty questions.

Mercifully, she told him to meet her at a Mexican cantina adjacent to the coffee shop. This was Parker's first time to this restaurant chain and he was surprised at the quiet atmosphere and the dim lights. Intimate was the word that came to mind. Intimate was hardly the kind of atmosphere you chose when you didn't want to blur the fine line between professional and passionate.

"I thought I wasn't supposed to get any ideas," Parker said, casual, after the server took their orders.

She glanced around as though seeing the scenery for the first time before saying, "You still aren't. I thought it might be dangerous to go somewhere you could be seen."

"Good call." After a beat, "Who was that this morning?"

"That was Reyna Vinson. She pretty much heads up the gala committee."

"What was she talking about?"

"My super-exciting floral errand we were just on."

"Don't be coy."

"What do you mean, Parker?"

He cocked his head and gave her a sharp look. "It sounded like the two of you were talking about a man."

"And that makes it your business...how?" Skylar snapped. "Hmm, that's right. It doesn't."

"True enough, but I think you should tell me anyway."

"And why is that?"

"From your little outburst, people on the other side of the room know it's a touchy subject for you. If you're going to make this big of an issue out of something, it's exactly the kind of thing I'll need to know about you. As your boyfriend."

"I'm really getting sick of hearing you say that."

"I'm sure you are, but you need to get used to the idea of it before we come face to face with Raptor." Parker paused long enough for the plates to be set down in front of them. "You're going to have to look at ease with me if this is going to work. Right now, I'd say you don't look comfortable with the concept of food, much less having it with me."

Skylar sighed and averted her eyes. "I just found out that I'm on the committee with my ex."

"Ah, and I take it Reyna's the new girlfriend."

"Yes, but I couldn't tell you how new she is or isn't." She snatched a chip out of the basket and tore off tiny pieces of it while she considered her next words, letting the crumbs pile on the tablecloth. "If it's all the same to you, I'd really prefer not to talk about it."

"Okay, but before we can drop it, I need to know if this is going to pose a problem for us."

"It shouldn't. It was a long time ago and I just don't want to re-hash the past."

"You have to realize how ironic that sounds coming from you."

"What's that supposed to mean?" Skylar snapped.

"Nothing. Let's just drop it."

"No. I want to know what you meant by that." The demanding tone matched the intensity of the scornful look she tossed at him. "I'm sick of you answering my questions with more questions, if you bother to answer them at all."

Parker considered his words before he spoke. "I just thought it was an odd thing for you to say considering what you're up to with me. Revenge scenarios aren't usually indicative of leaving the past lie."

Skylar set her fork down and glared at him. "My involvement with you is about catching a killer. Some things need to be left in the past; other things cannot be."

"If you say so. I'm only trying to understand you a little better, not pick a fight with you."

"Fine. What do you want to know, Parker?" Between her prick-ly body language and the edge to her question, it was clear she didn't care what he wanted.

"For starters, I would love to know how a woman without a job finances this kind of a crusade," Parker replied, deciding he didn't care whether she wanted to answer him or not. Sometimes, cutting to the chase was more effective than beating around the bush and finessing a mark.

Skylar took a sip of her tea. "How did I know you were going to ask me that?"

"Because it's important for me to know." When several seconds ticked by without a response, he added, "I have ways to find out any-thing about you I'd like to know. I'm asking you now, rather than digging into your life, out of professional courtesy. Either way, I will get an answer."

Her eyes registered momentary shock and then regained the usual icy composure. "I must say, I love the way you make yourself out to be this noble guy doing me a favor while being a complete prick."

"Trust me when I tell you that you'll know when I'm being a prick. That isn't it."

"Oh, well, gee. Aren't you a nice guy then? I don't feel bullied and insulted anymore." She pulverized another chip while she spoke. "In fact, how about we get out of here so I can give you a blow job and then thank you for letting me when I'm done?"

She really must say whatever popped into her head at any given moment. Parker didn't know what to do with that. What he did know was that she wasn't actually offering. Rather than trying to analyze what would even make her think to say that, he directed the conversation back on point. "You're evading."

"Am I?"

He leaned forward to cut the distance between them by half and spoke in a low, firm voice. "Unless you're serious about getting out of here and proving it to me, I suggest you quit playing games with me." He held her eyes captive with his steady gaze. "And I can assure you of one thing, Skylar. Once we start down that path, I don't quit until you can't remember how to count to ten, much less whether you thanked me." Unnoticed, he slid his hand across the table and she jumped slightly when he stroked the top of hers. "Start talking...unless you want me to get the check and give you several reasons to thank me tonight."

She continued to stare at him for a long moment, not bothering to recoil from his caress. Whether she did so because she enjoyed his touch or because she wouldn't give him the satisfaction of the response was anyone's guess.

"You really are a legend in your own mind, aren't you?"

A sly smile spread across his lips. "I'm a legend in many people's minds, sweetheart."

"Ugh." She rolled her eyes and withdrew her hand from his touch, using it to pick up her tea glass. "I'd rather tell you than continue listening to this unoriginal display of the male ego."

She sipped her drink before continuing.

"My father let Michael invest his life savings in risky tech stocks. Michael pulled the money out right before the dot com market crashed again and then he made several more wise investments for him. Apparently, my father was going to tell my mother and me about it after my graduation. His early retirement date was set and he was going to take my mother on the trip around the world they always planned to take one day.

"After his murder, we discovered he was heavily insured, probably from back when he owed the full balance on the house and cars. I don't know why else he'd keep such a high policy on himself."

"Men with families will over insure themselves to make sure their families are provided for."

"And you're supposed to be the shining champion of family men everywhere?" She pushed her food around on her plate with a fork, not having taken a single bite. "Anyway. As you say, my mother would have been very well provided for, but she couldn't handle it. She always blamed herself for what happened to him. She kept saying that if she hadn't forgotten to pick up his suit from the dry cleaner's, he wouldn't have stopped in at the bank while he waited for her that day."

Skylar reached for her glass again, gulping it down as though iced tea had the same power to steel her resolve as hard liquor. "She fell into a bad depression after the funeral. I guess she couldn't live with herself, thinking she was somehow to blame, that she killed her husband." Dropping the pretense of eating, she leaned back in her chair and folded her arms over her chest. "I came home one day and found her on the bathroom floor with a half-empty bottle of pills next to her and whatever vodka from the bottle she hadn't drank soaking into the carpet. I got there too late to do anything."

Parker's expression softened as he listened. "I'm sorry to hear that."

"Yeah, well, anyway...she was also well insured, apparently. I couldn't stomach the thought of staying in that house, so I sold it. I kept just enough money to buy my townhouse and I gave the rest to Michael to invest for me. Six months after that, I got a call from him telling me I wouldn't have to worry about money again." Void of any emotion, her eyes burned through him. "And that's all there is to tell. At least, that's all there is to tell unless you'd like to review my financial statement to confirm everything."

"I hardly think that's necessary."

"Well, if you change your mind, I can have my people put something together for your people to save them the time of hacking into my life." She averted her eyes. "Dinner was a bad idea. I'm not even hungry." Skylar pushed away from the table and rose to her feet. "I'm leaving. If you don't mind, I'd prefer not to have any intruders this evening."

Parker watched as she walked out of the restaurant. He signaled for the check and considered things. He didn't like the realization that her trust would not come easy. With most women, he could play to their emotions, but that wouldn't work with someone like Skylar. If she had emotions hiding under her stony façade, she'd long since lost touch with them.

To compound the issue, he knew there wasn't much time to waste. He'd never conned someone as detached from their emotions as Skylar Montgomery clearly was. If he was going to get past her defenses and get her trust, he'd need to take a different approach.

And trying to do any of this without her trust would mean conning her while he conned Raptor. Bad plan. No, Parker would find a way to earn her trust so he could let her in on the real play.

"Caldwell," Jackson said into his cell phone.

"I don't think I'll ever get used to the way you Bureau guys answer your phones," Jenna replied. Without waiting for a response, she continued, "I think I have something you might be interested in, Jackson."

He could think of many things Jenna had that he wanted, but he didn't figure she would appreciate his saying so. Better keep it neutral since she was probably talking about the case. "Really? What have you got?"

"Un-uh. I found out something that could be valuable to you and you owe me dinner now."

"Gee, Jenna...Sounds like you don't think you can trust me to make good on dinner when I've been offering it for months."

Jackson heard the faint sound of laughing on the other end of the phone. Either he was reading too much into it or she was flirting. "No. I'm just saying that it's almost six and I'm starving. I say we save time and make it a working dinner."

"A working dinner?" After starting out as fiery lovers, they were barely back to being friends. Now she wanted to move even further away to the realm of colleagues? No way, he thought to himself. It was going to be difficult to win Jenna back if he couldn't get her to go on a real dinner date with him.

"Hey, you want the info and I want food." The hint of something sly entered her tone. "Or you're welcome to come by my office on Monday morning and we can try to pencil in dinner for another time."

No, getting penciled in was even worse than a working dinner. A pencil made it far too easy for her to erase him from her schedule. And life. "No need to pull out the calendars. I'm free tonight. Do you have anywhere special in mind?"

"Yeah," she answered, casual. "My place."

That didn't make sense. "I thought I owed you dinner."

"You do, but I'm not in the mood for a noisy restaurant tonight. I thought it might be nice if you picked up something on your way. I'm leaving the office now. Can you be over in about an hour, Jackson?"

"Sure. I'll be there."

"Good. I'll see you soon then."

Not soon enough, he mused, slipping his cell into the pocket of his black suit jacket.

Dinsley didn't seem to be in his office, so Jackson picked up his keys and left the building without bothering to look for him. After his stunt of sending him to see Skylar Montgomery without so much as a heads up about her attitude, he reasoned his new partner didn't care much where he was. For that matter, Agent Brandon Dinsley may not care about catching Raptor either.

But Jackson sure did.

As the lingering doubts about his partner's loyalty to the Bureau faded from his mind, Jackson crossed the parking lot to his car. He wasn't sure what Jenna had discovered – since he cared more about seeing her than finding out – but he was intrigued by her invitation all the same. Whether her playful demeanor on the phone signaled good news for the case or for their relationship was anyone's guess.

If her good mood held up once he got to her condo, maybe tonight was the time to make it clear to Jenna that she was more to him than just a professional contact.

Remembering the way it felt when she told him she didn't love him at the airport on Christmas Eve, his grin faded from his lips. Was he ready to hear that, not only didn't she love him, but she wasn't even interested in dating him? Could he handle that?

It didn't matter. Jackson Caldwell was a man of action. Sitting on his hands and waiting for the right time to confess his feelings to Jenna was killing him in ways he'd never imagined possible.

If the axe was going to drop, severing the last thread supporting their second chance, it would drop tonight.

*****

Rushing out of the restaurant the way I did was a mistake; one I didn't realize until I was already home. Saying I wasn't hungry was a total lie, but I couldn't handle being out in public. As it was, I barely made it into my car before the hot tears burned through my eyes and slid down my face.

Now I was just pissed off.

One, I don't cry, but more importantly, my rumbling stomach was an annoying reminder that I didn't keep much food in the house. I was really in no mood to go back out to pick up something.

I don't know why the rush of emotions at talking about my mother's suicide caught me off guard. Other than Michael, I hadn't uttered a word about it to anyone after answering all the necessary police and insurance questions. Not even Eric. Obviously, he knew what happened; I just never talked about my feelings. I couldn't. Talking about feelings would be the first step towards feeling something on the matter.

Numb was so much better.

At least I didn't cry in front of Parker. Nothing about our arrangement was comfortable; adding a fresh layer of humiliation into the mix was unthinkable.

Angrily, I wiped the last traces of moisture from my eyes and I flopped down onto my couch. I frowned at the clock and picked up my cell phone. It was still too early to contact Chill on a Friday, but I dialed anyway. I didn't have anything else to distract myself.

"You do not really get the whole man of the night thing, do you Songbird?" Chill snapped without saying hello.

"Not really. No. I just wanted to find out if you had found out anything I should know about yet."

"You sound upset, Songbird."

"No. I'm just...tired, that's all."

"Oh. Do you want me to come over and tuck you in?"

"Chill," I warned, even though I was sure he'd provide ample distraction for the evening if I gave him the slightest indication of interest.

"Okay, okay, but we are going to have to work on that business and pleasure rule you have going. You should not torture yourself that way."

I cracked a smile. "I'll take it under advisement. Now, do you have anything for me or not?"

"Chill has lots for you, baby, but nothing on the information front. The streets are abnormally quiet, which means something is most definitely brewing. I just do not know what it is yet, but I will long before anything goes down."

Wonderful, more dead ends.

"What about Ramsey?"

"What about him?"

"Have you heard anything about him?" I pressed.

"Not really anything new. I have it confirmed he has been after Raptor since he faked his death, but the details are sketchy. He is good at covering his tracks, Songbird."

The doorbell distracted me from my train of thought. "Well, Chill, keep your ear to the ground for me. I've got to go."

I set my cell phone down and went to the door. I knew my face had to register my surprise once I opened the door, but I didn't care. Parker was on the other side.

I honestly wasn't sure the man knew I *had* a front door.

"This is a surprise," I said as he walked in past me.

"You said you didn't want any intruders, so I figured that included me, even though I'm hardly a common prowler. I thought you'd be hungry later, so I brought you your dinner," he replied, vanishing into the kitchen.

I heard the rustling of a plastic bag and my refrigerator door open and shut before he reappeared.

"Thank you." I was still in awe he'd used the door.

Parker shrugged. "No problem. Okay, I'm out of here."

"You're leaving?"

He walked over to the door and put his hand on the knob before speaking. "Yeah. You don't seem into playing twenty questions tonight and somehow I don't see you wanting to kick back to watch a movie with me."

Huh? "Are you saying you'd like to stay to watch a movie with me?"

The faintest of grins touched his lips. "No. My mind's usually too active for an activity so...*passive*." He opened the door. "The weekend is yours. I'll see you on Monday."

The way he said 'passive' made me wonder if he wanted to say 'platonic' instead. Given the current state of my emotions, I could be okay with that. In fact, if he could really make me forget how to count to ten, he could certainly take my mind off these painful memories. No question I was okay with that.

But I really didn't like to mix business with pleasure, not that I knew why. I'd never been in business like this before. Maybe uncomplicated sex with my partner wouldn't be a big deal. He was attractive, fit, seemingly interested in more by his sexual banter and standing in my living room. Hopping in the sack might even help alleviate some of the tension between us, which would make working with him easier.

Breaking my rules appeared to have plenty of benefits, but Parker was gone before I could suggest a more active way to use the couch than watching a movie.

After I locked the door, I went into the kitchen to reheat my enchiladas. I always hid my emotions from people, especially those I didn't trust, but it was like he read my thoughts anyway. It was just as well he left before I made any sort of move on him. His ability to read me was unnerving and I could use a few days in solitude to fortify my mental defenses against him.

Still, I had to admit I didn't know what I was going to do with myself over the next two days. Though little time elapsed since our first meeting, I was accustomed to Parker appearing at random moments. As I sat down to eat, I let myself wonder about how he'd be spending the weekend.

In a strictly professional way, of course.

"Did they ever prove if the agent was on the take?"

Jenna shook her head and started gathering the dinner plates from the coffee table. "They turned over the information to your office, but you know how you guys handle everything internally. No one on my side ever heard what happened one way or the other."

This new information cast more suspicion on his partner. Dinsley's behavior was already suspect before this, but if he were on the take...Hopefully Jenna could turn up something more. Once he had something solid, he could confront Dinsley about his true interest in the case.

"Did they think he was working with Raptor?"

She considered that. "Some do, some don't, but I'll see if I can find a connection."

"I appreciate that, Jenna," he said, gazing up into her deep brown eyes.

"It's no trouble," she replied. She held his gaze for a moment and then hurried out of the room.

Jackson followed her into the small kitchen. Once she set the plates in the sink, he placed his hands on her shoulders and turned her to face him. "What are we doing?"

"Clearing the dinner dishes."

"No. You and me. What are we doing?"

"I...don't know anymore."

"Babe, I don't know either." He searched her face for a long time, unsure what to say. Was there even anything left to say? "Jenna...sometimes it's like you aren't even here when we're talking."

She offered an apologetic smile. "Sorry. I was just thinking about something."

"Care to share?"

"The time Blaine walked in and caught us fooling around in here."

He remembered that day well. It was a good day. It was when they went from strictly friends to being on the verge of something more. "You were so embarrassed you could barely look anyone in the eye for the rest of the night."

"And you were so turned on you could barely keep your hands off me back then."

"Even now, it's still all I can do to keep my hands off you."

Standing here now, it was as if they were different people than they were in the fall. The old Jenna wouldn't have been wearing a slinky black skirt and deep blue silk blouse on a Friday night. And she sure wouldn't be in shiny black heels. Looking at the woman he desired more than anything else in existence, it was almost as though what they shared those long months ago was a mirage.

Jackson couldn't accept that.

He wouldn't.

On some level, he realized this was it. There was a difference between taking things slow out of respect for the other person's wishes and taking things slow because you didn't want anything more. Jenna needed to know exactly where he stood, on the very off chance she didn't already.

"You know how I feel about you and you know what I want. The only thing that's changed for me from before is that I don't have to hide my job anymore. Well that, and the fact that I never imagined missing you before the way I've missed you since I lost you." He tried to read her face to see if he was getting through, but she was doing her lawyer face. No emotion. No real reaction. "Jenna...I have never stopped loving you. I haven't stopped wanting you. Not for a single day. If you'd let me, I'd touch you and never take my hands off you again."

She opened her mouth to say something, but no sound came out. Instead, her eyes locked on his, holding him captive. When she looked at him like that, Jackson forgot why it was he had to try so hard to keep his hands off her. With the tension between them turning into a thick curtain, he couldn't remember why months had passed since their last kiss.

He lowered his lips to hers in a tentative kiss. He didn't hurry, didn't press for more. Instead, the kiss unfolded on its own accord. In his mind, no more talking belonged in the night, just this. Even though he wanted more from her, wanted her in every way, he was content in this moment.

Her fingertips grazed the back of his neck and contentment yielded to desire. She may believe their entire relationship was a lie, but to Jackson, nothing in his life was more real than when he was with her. Waiting for her to realize what he already knew approached the limits of what he could stand. The honey almond scent of her hair mingling with her lightly perfumed skin was intoxicating.

What he felt went beyond wanting her; it was need.

Her lips grew urgent against his and whimpering cries fluttered from her throat. He wasn't imagining anything. She needed him, too.

She moved her hands to clutch at the front of his crisp white dress shirt. "Jackson...ohhh..."

That was it.

He couldn't handle slow for another instant, not unless he stopped right now. With effort, he tore himself away from her and stepped back, fighting for self-control. No matter how much he wanted to make a move, to make her his tonight, he couldn't do it if it meant risking everything he wanted from her. A single night wasn't close to good enough.

Jenna's eyes flew open, confused. They regarded one another for several seconds before she closed the distance between them, wrapping her arms around his neck to pull him back to finish their kiss. Unthinking, Jackson pressed her against the wall, desperate to feel her body against his. Any moment, she'd push him away and accuse him of rushing her, but until she did, he wanted to enjoy the perfect way her curves melded into him.

She didn't push him away.

Her tongue sparred against his, taking what she wanted, demanding satisfaction. More demanding was the leg that crept up around his waist, tightening and pulling him even closer. All his reason told him to stop, while every inch of his body begged him to ignore reason just this once.

He had to stop himself, yet he couldn't. If it were any random woman, he could control his instincts and urges. With any other woman, reason would win the day.

This wasn't any other woman though. It was Jenna. His senses didn't respond to reason concerning her.

"We should stop this," he said, even as his fingers made short work of her blouse's buttons.

Her hips writhed against him. "I know."

It was becoming less and less possible to tear his lips from hers or to keep up with his line of thought. "Stopping is the responsible thing to do." A hand stole into her shirt, molding around the thin satin of her bra.

Her breath came out in a shivering sigh at his touch. She tugged at his tie until she was able to loosen it. "I don't want to be responsible. Not tonight."

"You're killin' me." His free hand slid up her thigh, moving under the skirt already bunching at her hips.

She arched her back and ground her hips against him in need. "Getting noble on me now? Unless you're not as interested in me as you say, don't you dare leave me unsatisfied tonight."

"I want you bad right now, but..."

She grazed her lips against his throat. "I have protection, if that's your hold up." Her eyes met his as she pushed him back, wrestling with his belt until it was on the floor. "Bedroom, Caldwell. Now."

Though it was nearly six months since they last made love, Jackson still remembered the exact number of steps to get there. What he didn't remember was how much her fluffy grey cat loved to walk in the way. Jackson stumbled at the threshold to the bedroom and Jenna tripped over his feet.

They hit the carpet with a soft thud and didn't miss a beat. Jenna pushed him onto his back and straddled him. In the near darkness of the room, he could see the look of determination on her face as she fought with his shirt buttons. Seeing how much she wanted him fueled a fresh wave of lust. So much blood was flowing to his erection that he'd be lightheaded if he were still on his feet.

The hips grinding over him while she worked the buttons didn't help either...Or, more likely, they helped too much.

He rolled her onto her back and covered her body with his, lips moving along her jaw line. "God, I want you so much right now." He slipped a hand under her skirt to toy with the elastic of her panties. "I can barely stand it."

In some ways, being with her like this, feeling the supple skin trembling under his fingers didn't feel real, almost as though she'd vanish in a puff of smoke if he let her out from under him.

She grabbed his face with both hands, kissing him hard before she spoke. "Then cut the foreplay already and get inside me." Shoving his hand out of the way, she shimmied off the panties.

No, this was definitely real. Not even in his most elaborate fantasies had she ever been this desperate to have him. Come to think of it, Jackson couldn't remember her ever wanting him with so much urgency in the past. Whatever caused the abrupt change in her behavior towards him, he wasn't going to blow it. He wasted no time moving off her and heading for the nightstand drawer.

But he didn't find what he needed inside. Not even close. "If your idea of protection is completely turning me off, crime scene photos are probably the way to do it."

Jenna let out a throaty laugh. "I study cases before bed, so I needed to clear out the condoms. The last thing I need is one falling out of a case file while I'm in court."

"Then where..." His words trailed off when he turned back to her. Instead of where he'd left her on the carpet, Jenna was leaning a hip against her dresser, arms folded, foil packet flipping between her fingers, beckoning with the faint glimmer as the foil caught the light.

"I guess we can call it a night if you're too turned off now."

"Oh, to hell with that."

Jenna made short work of his zipper and sheathed him with the condom the moment he closed the gap between them. "Good call."

"Jenna..."

"Shut up." She hopped up onto the dresser and pulled him close. "You always did talk too much."

Probably. He slid into her in one thrust, savoring the way her body felt around him. At the same time, she felt just the way he remembered, yet it was like nothing he felt before.

His rhythm was slow and even, his kiss soft and thorough. After the long months without her, it tested the very limits of his willpower to avoid a frenzy that would be over much too quickly. In truth, he didn't want it to ever be over, which went against everything his body was screaming at his mind. The only compromise he could imagine was later taking his time to do it right, keeping Jenna awake long into the night.

How many sleepless nights had they both wasted during all the time spent apart?

She tore her mouth away from his. "Harder," she demanded. Her hands gripped the edge of the dresser at either side of her hips. "I'm not going to break, Caldwell."

"Someone's demanding." But he gave her exactly what she wanted, driving into her over and over with enough force to make the mirror bang against the wall.

"I'm not apologizing for knowing what I want." She wrapped her legs around him, the point of her heel digging into the back of his thigh. "Ohhhhh...just like that."

But Jackson was barely paying attention anymore now that animal instinct took control. His hands were sliding under her skirt again, this time to grip her hips to hold her in place. Somewhere, his brain registered her screams of ecstasy, but the muscles contracting around him as her orgasm ripped through her were what captured his attention. He luxuriated in the way it felt to drive the woman he loved wild with pleasure for a single instant before his own release nearly knocked him from his feet.

For an eternity, Jackson stayed inside her, wedging her against the smooth wood finish of the dresser. The ragged gasps as they caught their breath were the only sounds in the dark stillness of the room. Gradually, his vise grip on her hips lessened and he'd regained enough control of his breathing to brush a soft kiss against her smiling lips. He always knew they'd get past their problems, or he'd hoped they could. He just never imagined it would be quite so explosive.

Or on her dresser when the bed was a few feet away.

"You have no idea how much I needed that tonight."

The lazy quality to her words made him grin. "If you thought that was good, give me about ten minutes to recover and we'll do it right."

Jenna pulled back when he tried to kiss her again. "I didn't think there was anything wrong with that."

"Well...no. But I think you know I can make it a hell of a lot better for you between the sheets."

"Ummm...It's just getting sort of late."

He pulled out and discarded the condom in the wastebasket. "We don't have to do anything you're too tired to do." His fingers brushed the chocolate brown strands of hair from her eyes, getting momentarily lost in the way the small amount of light in the room sparkled in them. "I'm fine with just holding you tonight."

She hopped off the dresser and started buttoning her shirt. "Actually, I wasn't thinking you'd stay."

"You want me to go?"

"Yes. I think that's probably best."

What the hell? "If you didn't want that, I wish you'd said something to me. You know I would've stopped."

"Jackson...I did want that." A note of exasperation crept into her voice. "Now I want you to go home." She moved to the bedroom door and flipped on the light. "I really don't see what's so difficult about this."

Jackson let out an aggravated sigh while he zipped his fly. "Then help me understand. If you don't want me then why did you start it?"

"Excuse me?" Jenna poked a finger into his chest. "You kissed me, Caldwell."

"And you kissed me back. It's the same thing."

"No it isn't."

"Well...I stopped and you started it again."

"You aren't going to win this on a technicality."

He shook his head. What the hell was there for him to win when she was intent on sending him home? "We aren't in the courtroom, Counselor, but if you'd like to get technical then you started all of this. I was in D.C., trying to get on with my life when you showed up at my door to tell me you missed me. Either you want me or you don't."

"So it's black and white now?"

"Yeah."

"I can't believe you! You used to be a lot a better at the whole seduction thing," she began, folding her arms across her chest, "or was that just part of your cover, too?"

Jackson threw up his hands in disgust. "I might have guessed you'd throw that in my face sooner or later."

"And? You lied to me and you used me for your case. If you didn't want to be reminded of what you did to me then you shouldn't have done it in the first place."

"So...what is this? You needed to get laid and I just happened to owe you dinner? Did it even matter to you that it was me inside you? Or would any guy around have done the trick for you tonight?"

"Are you kidding me with this?" Anger bit into her tone. "You're actually getting pissy with me because I had sex with you? Sex you made it clear to me you were interested in having before you kissed me?"

"No, I'm fucking pissed off because you apparently just used me for sex as some sort of sick way to get revenge on me for doing my job last year."

Jenna shook her head and moved into the kitchen, Jackson hot on her heels. "Oh, you're really one to talk. You could've made your case against Chad without screwing me and we both know it. You're damn lucky I didn't file a complaint on you over it." Her eyes tore through him. "I still could."

"Yeah, good luck with that. My boss practically ordered me into bed with you that night to find out what you knew."

"She what!?" Jenna picked up his belt from the floor and threw it at him. "So, not only did you use me, but you didn't even want to sleep with me in the first place?"

"No, I ignored eighty percent of the orders I got when I was out here before. I took you to bed because I'm a man and there was only so long I could control myself around your constant cock tease."

"You really are some piece of work."

"Yeah, well so are you. You came all the way out to D.C. to tell me you thought we should start over and then blew me off the minute I got out here." He left the room to snatch his suit jacket off the office chair. "Either you're one cruel bitch or you're fucking insane."

Jenna's eyes narrowed. "You know what? I was wrong about that. Starting over with you after everything you put me through was never a good idea."

Her words hit him with an unexpected force. Jackson thought nothing could hurt him the way it did when she'd told him she didn't love him, but he was wrong. Hearing Jenna say their second chance was a mistake caused a peculiar reaction. Rather than hurt, he felt un-contained rage bubble to the surface.

"No, Jenna. The mistake was mine. I'll never know how I honestly thought I was in love with you this whole time." He stormed over to the door. "And for the record, there are plenty of women in this town who wouldn't be so annoyed at the thought of having me in their beds all night long."

"Then maybe you should go find one of those women and leave me the hell alone."

"You know what? That's the first intelligent thing you've said to me in a long time about this sick joke of a relationship we have." He shook his head in disgust. "If you end up hearing anything about Raptor, fine. If not, lose my number. You're more trouble than you're worth." He stepped out into the hallway, slamming the condo door behind him.

Jackson took exactly two steps, basking in his rightness before the enormity of what just happened hit him. Why did he say that? What was he thinking?

As he turned to go back inside, the deadbolt snapped into place with an air of finality.

If it hadn't been over months before, it sure as shit was now.

FIVE

"Wow." I tossed the paperback book near my feet on the couch. "How do people come up with that stuff?"

I rubbed my eyes and glanced at the clock. Nearly ten-thirty. True to his word, the weekend had indeed been mine. It struck me as odd that I didn't know what to do with the spare time. Not long ago I worked completely alone and never minded the endless hours stretched out before me, but now that I had a real plan, and someone who had a connection to Raptor, it annoyed me to spend a single minute on anything else.

More than that, I think catching up on my reading annoyed me. My choice of fiction did little to take my mind off things. In fact, everything I read reminded me either of my father's murder or the criminal I was out to get.

But, if nothing else, the weekend was enough alone time to get my impulses back under control. Hopping into bed with Parker would be a mistake, regardless of how hot he was or how many times the idea crossed my mind. I barely knew him. What I did know of him, I wasn't sure I liked.

I stood up to stretch, but was interrupted by the ringing of my phone.

"Hello?"

"Sky, did I wake you?"

"No, Reyna, I was just reading. What can I do for you?"

"I just wanted to let you know I went by the florist today and the arrangements you picked out look great."

I frowned at the phone. "Are you in the habit of checking up on what you assign everyone else to do?"

Reyna laughed. "Actually, yes."

"Doesn't that just make more work for you?"

"It does, but when you've seen some of the things the others have picked out, you tend to be more cautious. Don't worry. I now trust your judgment one hundred percent," she replied breezily.

"Well, I suppose that's good to know." Was I really supposed to care? My purpose in life wasn't to be committee member of the year.

"Anyway, I called to make sure you knew the next meeting was tomorrow night. Same time and same place."

"I'll be there, Reyna."

"Oh, I also wanted to let you know that I have a dinner at my house every year for the committee members. You know, to thank everyone for their help. It's next Sunday night at six. I hope you'll be able to make it. Of course, you can feel free to bring a guest."

I sighed. I wasn't really looking forward to spending more time with her and Eric than necessary, but it could give me more of an opportunity to observe everyone if Raptor didn't show himself at Saturday's gala.

"I'll try to make it."

"Good," she began cheerfully. "I'll see you next Sunday, then. Oh, and I'll also see you tomorrow night."

Something seemed different when I hung up the phone and I glanced around the room in expectation. I could sense Parker's presence. A smile crept across my lips, but I suppressed it. I had to remind myself I wasn't happy to see him.

Mostly.

"I thought the weekend was mine, Ramsey," I said into the empty room.

Parker walked out of my bedroom and leaned against the doorframe. "Weekend's over, sweetheart. Where is it you'll try to make it to?"

"Reyna is having a dinner next Sunday at her house for all of the committee members. I get to bring a guest."

Parker smiled. "Good. We'll be there."

"Very presumptuous of you to think I'll be inviting you," I said as I plopped back down on the couch.

"I didn't realize you had another fake boyfriend to escort you places."

"Never said it was a fake boyfriend. I do okay with the guys, you know."

"Of course. That explains why you're always alone when I come over." He continued before I could say something smart in reply. "I guess I'll have to start working on acting fake boyfriend jealous."

Since I didn't even have another fake boyfriend in the wings, much less a real one, I let that part of the conversation die. "I presume we have something to do since my weekend is over?"

"Very presumptuous, but yes Skylar, we do. Get dressed. We need to get going."

I could tell he was mocking me with his tone and word choice, but I chose to ignore it. I had to pick my battles with this guy. Pointing out I didn't like the way he was always so amused by me didn't rate high on my list of things to bicker about tonight. Besides, he always touched me when our arguments turned heated.

And the combination of heated argument adrenaline and his touch always made me think about doing him on the carpet right in the middle of the room.

I didn't give myself long to dwell on that mental image in my head since we had to go somewhere, even if that didn't make much sense. Where could we possibly need to go this time of night on a Sunday? Wherever it was, I knew I would end up with more questions than answers.

I looked down at myself. "I'm not wearing the sweater everyone hates. What's wrong with what I'm wearing?"

Parker eyed me cautiously. "The color of your sweatshirt is better, but the frump girl thing would draw too much attention where we're going."

"Where are we going?"

"You'll see when we get there." He must have caught the question in my eyes because he added, "Just show a little skin."

"Is that to fit in where we're going or because you want to see me in less?" Why did I ask that? I didn't need to know the answer when I was trying to avoid conversations that would lead to me wanting him.

His grin widened. He was amused again. "The attire would be place appropriate, but we can call it a bonus for me, if you like."

"That wasn't an answer, Ramsey." Seriously, shut the hell up, Skylar.

"It wasn't meant to be." He placed his hands on the back of the couch and leaned close enough for me to feel his breath on my ear. "Now I suggest you go change so we can leave. Unless you need help getting out of these clothes, that is."

I jumped up, putting immediate space between us. "Nope. I'm good. Just be a minute."

I hated the faint sound of chuckling as I retreated to the privacy of my bedroom. Though it was nearly over as it was, this was going to be a long night.

I looked out the window of Parker's car as he pulled into the parking lot. "Blaine's Rain? I thought this was important. I'm really not a fan of clubs."

"We have someone to meet." He cut the engine and grinned over at me...again. Seriously, what was his deal? He'd done that at least a dozen times since I'd walked out of my bedroom in a short black skirt and electric green halter-top that didn't quite hit my waist.

He could grin all he wanted, but I was cold. Apparently, my trench coat would've made me look too much like a prostitute, so I was huddled in his black leather jacket that did exactly zero for my frozen legs. At least he had heated seats.

Actually, if I knew anything about cars, I'm sure I'd be impressed because the word 'car' didn't do justice to this sleek yellow machine. At all.

Before I could let myself dwell on whether I was sitting in a stolen car with an idiot who couldn't stop grinning, I got back on point. "Who?"

Parker's grin widened. "Come on."

With reluctance, I followed Parker into the crowded nightclub. Since he wasn't set to surface for almost a week, I could only assume I was meeting one of his underground connections. I hoped he knew what he was doing.

Because I sure didn't.

"Here. Sit down, Skylar. Do you want something to drink?"

I shot him a look and shrugged out of his jacket, hanging it on the back of the chair before sitting. "Are we really meeting someone or is this a ruse to get me drunk?"

He knelt beside my chair until he was only inches from my face and dropped the volume of his voice to little more than a whisper no one else would be able to hear over the hum of people and music. "Sorry to shatter that high opinion you have of me, but if I was really into taking advantage of women while they're not thinking clearly, I could've done so on Friday." His eyes locked on mine. "And I believe we're both aware of that."

Yeah, I knew it, but I didn't realize he did as well.

He held me prisoner with that intense gaze for the most excruciating moments of my life before rising and giving me an expectant look. When I didn't respond, he said, "To be clear, we really are meeting someone here. The drink offer is just a drink offer."

"No. I'm good. Thanks."

"Suit yourself. I'll be back in a second," he replied, leaving in the general direction of the bar. It wasn't lost on me how many interested looks he drew from women as he moved effortlessly through the throng of people in his way.

Would I attract the same amount of attention from men if I were dressed as simply as he was? I doubted it. I didn't own a pair of jeans that fit me the way those dark blue jeans fit him: not tight, but well-fitting; perfectly tailored to him. And Parker could pull off the long-sleeve black button down, untucked and also perfectly tailored to his torso, but I'd just blend into the crowd wearing it.

I glanced around the club while I waited for Parker to return, toying with one of the auburn strands that was in my peripheral vision. He'd made me take my hair out of the usual ponytail, not that I knew why. I didn't have hair that cascaded around my face in alluring waves. It just hung there like curtains, shiny and straight. When was the last time I'd even worn it loose like this?

Probably not since ending things with Eric. He'd loved me enough to think everything about me was beautiful, even my hair...

To derail that painful train of thought, I let myself really see the club around me. This was just the sort of place I would love to hang out in when I was in college, but now it was annoying to me how loud the techno music was. Back then, I would think the purple haze cast by the black lights gave the club pizzazz; now I thought there was something sinister about the shadows. I had to be the oldest twenty-four-year-old on the planet.

Then again, how many other people my age knew monsters really existed in the world?

I felt a hand slide onto my shoulder, slipping under the strap of my top near my neck before squeezing slightly.

"I thought I told you not to get any ideas," I snapped as I turned around, freezing when I met a pair of gleaming red eyes.

"I know you keep saying that, Songbird, but I also know you are bound to come to your senses sooner or later."

He sat down across the table from me and flashed a wicked smile my way. Parker walked up and set down three drinks on the table. I watched in silence as the two men shook hands and embraced before Parker took the remaining chair to my right.

Even pissed off, the brush of his jean-clad leg against my bare calf was a momentary blip on my attention radar.

"It's good to see you again, old friend," Parker said to the man. "How long has it been this time?"

"At least three years, but you were dead for two, so who can truly count?"

"That is the rumor." To me, he said, "I know you said you didn't want anything to drink, but I figured you'd change your mind." Parker gestured to the drinks. "You can pick your poison, but I know you'll go for the rum and diet coke."

"Don't play games with me, Ramsey," I snapped at him. "I want to know what in God's name is going on here and I want to know right now."

"Oh, you will know everything, babe, but trust me when I tell you God has nothing to do with this little gathering," Chill replied in his usual icy demeanor.

I looked at the men in shock. Not only was Chill not surprised to see Parker, but they went way back. That was information I should have gotten long before this moment. I didn't fully understand what was going on yet, so I remained quiet and sized up Chill.

No matter how many times I saw Chill, his appearance was always startling to me. His hair was spiked and dyed the same shade of blood red as his contact lenses. His lanky figure was always shrouded in black clothing and I could tell he kept his complexion ghostly white on purpose.

"So, the two of you are friends," I said finally.

"Do not be cross, Songbird," Chill answered.

"Cross, Chill? No, I am beyond that. I knew you were hiding something from me when I asked you about him."

"Ramsey wanted for you to draw your own conclusions about him without any outside information from me."

I narrowed my eyes. "Really? How nice. Should I also assume that all of the information you've sold me is bogus as well?"

Chill took a swig of his beer. "I am not in the business to betray my customers."

"You could have fooled me. The only question I still have is why I'm even here right now."

"Keep your voice down." Parker leaned forward in his chair and said, "I'm telling you this because you need to know Chill is in this with us."

"Oh?" I said, picking up my drink from the table. Too late, I realized it was the drink I said I didn't want.

"If Raptor wants to set up a deal in this town, he will contact me," Chill answered, smug.

"That's right," Parker agreed, "Raptor will need someone to hook him up with a crew and all of the specs needed to pull off a job. It's just a matter of time now."

I looked Chill squarely in the eyes. "Were you just toying with me when you warned me about him?"

Chill shook his head with purpose. "No. I still think this cat is one dangerous dude. We may go way back, but I would sleep with one eye opened around this one."

"You always sleep with one eye opened, Chill, regardless of who it is," Parker joked.

Chill stood up. "That is true, Ramsey. Sorry, but like I told you on the phone earlier, I have got some business to attend to in a few. Got to jam." He turned his gaze on me. "Always a pleasure, Songbird."

I sat in silence long after Chill left us, sipping on my drink. Parker eyed me, but seemed to know enough to keep his mouth shut until I was ready. Finally, I said, "Is there anything else I should know, Ramsey?"

Parker shrugged. "It was Chill who first gave me your number to contact you about the job, but I'm sure you've already figured that out by now. Of course, he doesn't have a clue who you really are yet."

"Well, at least I'm not the last one to know everything."

"There's no reason for dramatics, Skylar."

Oh, did he want to see dramatics? "It isn't being dramatic if I'm right. I don't like being lied to."

"I haven't lied to you." His leg brushed against mine when he leaned close. "So, yes, you are overreacting right now."

"I am not...and you did."

"You never asked me if I knew Chill." He reached out to straighten the silver rose dangling from my choker – or, I assume that's what he did. His hand lingered for a moment, fingertips grazing my neck. "So, why don't we fast forward through the part where you acknowledge I'm right and get on with the conversation?"

With the exception of Raptor, I don't think I've ever hated someone as much as I hated Parker Ramsey right now.

Even more annoying was the distraction of his leg brushing against my bare legs. I couldn't stay sufficiently mad when his close proximity was wreaking havoc with my hormones. This had to be the result of the alcohol.

All five sips of it.

"Why is Chill in this with us?"

"We already answered that for you."

"No," I replied, shaking my head, "I want to know the real reason."

Parker sighed. "His brother worked with us on that last heist. He met the same fate as everyone else." His hand slid across the table to cover mine. "Chill wants revenge and he's every bit as motivated as you are."

We'd just have to see about that.

Monday, March 22

Jackson glanced at the clock on his desk and realized it was finally late enough to call the Collin County prosecutor's office. He grabbed his cell phone and went into one of the conference rooms, pulling the door closed behind him. Even though there was a phone on his desk, it was out in the open and he didn't want Dinsley to walk by and find out that he was going outside the Bureau to find out about him and the case.

"Good morning, Jenna Monroe's office," Trista said once she answered the phone.

"Good morning, Trista. How was your weekend?" Jackson asked, making small talk despite his hatred of it.

"Better than yours, Jackson." Trista's tone meant she clearly already knew about Friday night. "Do you want to talk to Jenna? She's here already."

"No, thanks. I was hoping to just leave a message for her. I don't think she wants to talk to me right now."

"You're reading her all wrong, you know, but I'll take the message."

Besides being Jenna's assistant, Trista was also her best friend. If anyone knew what was on her mind, Trista would be the one. Jackson was tempted to ask for her advice, but he thought better of it. He had never been the sort to put his love life out on display and he didn't intend to start now, no matter how much he might need the help.

Of course, he had serious doubts that he still had a love life where Jenna was concerned.

"I wanted to let Jenna know who our suspects were before to see if she was able find out anything about any of them." That sounded flimsy to his own ears, even though there was truth to it. He was looking for any shred of anything to give her reason not to lose his number.

"I still think you should tell her yourself, but go ahead," Trista chided.

"Trevor Brightman, Eric Sauters and Drake Wyndham."

She whistled. "Wow, you sure know how to pick 'em."

"I guess so."

"Is there anything else you want me to tell Jenna for you?"

Jackson considered that for a moment, but didn't think it would be a good idea to relay apologies through her. "No, thank you Trista."

"Suit yourself, Jackson, but take my advice. Jenna is going to come around. She loves you and we all know it. It's just going to take her a little time – especially since you turned into Captain Dickwad on Friday. What were you thinking, anyway?"

"I wasn't," he admitted.

"Clearly. Calling a woman you just slept with a sadistic psychopath isn't the most endearing pillow talk I can think of."

"I didn't say that."

"Whatever. Close enough. It really sounds like your bedroom skills have gone rusty since last fall."

"Excuse me?"

"Well, maybe I should say your bedroom conversation skills. She actually said there were no complaints in the physical department."

Did he really want to hear the dissection of his sexual prowess from Jenna's best friend? It was bad enough she clearly already gave Trista the play-by-play. Rather than encourage the current conversation, he remained quiet.

Her sigh came through the phone loud and clear. "Are you sure you don't want to talk to her? She told me to put your call through."

"She knew I'd call?"

"Well, she's not stupid. It wasn't like you were serious when you told her to lose your number."

"I was when I said it."

"Yet here you are calling her bright and early on a Monday morning, using the pretense of business to cover."

Jackson remained silent.

"Look, I'm sure you've noticed by now that she tends to hold onto things for a long time before letting them go. Hang in there. You know she's worth it, even if you're too stupid to admit it."

Hours later, Trista's words were still fresh on his mind. At least it was somewhat reassuring that he wasn't still on the bad side of Jenna's closest friend. Trista made her anger very clear to him when she found out he'd lied to all of them about who he was.

Jackson only hoped she was right this time. He wasn't ready to turn the page on the chapter of his life with Jenna in it.

I opened my eyes and squinted at the sunlight streaming into my bedroom. I started to roll over and go back to sleep, but I remembered that I had pulled my curtains closed before I'd gone to bed last night. Rubbing my eyes, I sat up and frowned.

"Dammit, Parker!"

I watched as he walked into my room with a skillet in his hands. "Good morning to you too, or I guess I should say good afternoon."

"Huh?" I asked as I pushed the covers aside and got out of bed.

"It's well after noon, but I thought you might still want breakfast food."

I followed him into the kitchen still blinking at the brightness of being awake. "Let me get this straight. Now you're breaking into my house to cook me breakfast? This isn't going to make me less angry about being lied to. What are you trying to pull here?"

"I'm not trying to pull anything. I thought it was time to continue our conversation from Friday. I was just trying to do something nice."

I resigned myself to the conversation that was about to take place and went to brush my teeth and hair. After only a few more minutes, we were seated at my dining room table.

"This actually isn't half bad," I admitted to Parker.

"I did what I could with the lack of ingredients you keep in your kitchen. Luckily, you had enough for an omelet. Do you ever go to the store?"

I shrugged. "Rarely. I'm not much of a cook, so I don't see the point of buying stuff to spoil in my fridge."

"What do you do about meals, then?"

"Fast food, if I eat."

Parker eyed me up and down. "Well, that would explain it."

"Explain what? And don't look at me like that," I snapped at him.

"You're thin as a rail. I didn't mean anything by it. I guess I just didn't figure you for one of those dieting types."

I shook my head, wincing at the way my neck cramped. "I never diet; I'm just not really ever hungry. I do work out quite a bit, though."

"Yoga, right?"

"Among other things. Why do you ask?"

"No reason," he answered with a shrug. "I just like trying to figure you out."

I set my fork on the plate and tried to rub the kink out of my neck. "Really? So I suppose you think you have me all figured out then."

He nodded. "Very nearly." His expression changed. "What's wrong with your neck?"

"It doesn't matter. Fill me in on this vast knowledge you have about me," I said with a smirk.

Parker stood and circled around behind my chair. "Well, if you insist."

"What are you doing?" I tried to turn to look at him, but the sharp pain in my neck stopped me.

"Giving you a neck massage." Strong fingers went to work on my neck. "It's not as fun to be right when you're wincing in pain and trying to hide it."

"Your confidence is a bit premature."

"Nothing about me is premature, Skylar." I could hear the smile in his voice. He continued without missing a beat. "I'd say that you used to be a blast to hang out with, but until Raptor's caught or dead you have this brooding thing going. You work out, not because you need to, since you don't eat, but as an outlet for all of the anger that you've never bothered to deal with. I'd wager that you haven't opened a single bank statement since your father died because you don't want to be reminded of where the money came from. How am I doing so far?"

He was doing pretty damn well, but I wasn't going to tell him that so I remained quiet. Just like I wasn't going to tell him the kink was gone. I also wasn't going to tell him how good his touch felt now that he'd soothed my knotted neck muscles.

There was a lot Parker Ramsey didn't need to know at that moment, I suppose.

"It's okay; you don't have to admit it. I already know. I'm also going to go out on a limb and say that you're into all of this."

"Excuse me?" I'm sure there was a better response to that, but I couldn't think of what it was with his massage now spreading to my bare shoulders.

"Come on, bad things happen to good people all of the time and they never alter their lives as drastically as you have. I think it excites you to walk on the wild side like this." Parker knelt behind me until I could feel his breath on the back of my ear. "For that matter, I think I excite you."

"You don't know what you're talking about."

The smile was back in his voice. "If you say so." His fingers slid under the thin straps of my camisole.

Was he still massaging or was this a caress. I didn't care. The faintest of whimpers escaped my throat and Parker's breath turned hot on my neck.

"The only thing I haven't been able to figure out is why you go by Songbird."

I sighed, but didn't say anything. Had I just felt his lips graze my skin?

"Waiting for an answer here," he prodded, tension in his voice.

Did he actually care or was he just trying to keep the conversation on track as a way to distract himself from touching me? I let my head droop forward and whimpered again, louder this time. I wasn't sure I wanted him distracted.

But I wasn't sure I wanted anything else, either.

"Skylar?"

Ugh. He cared. "Skylar is derived from the word skylark. Skylarks are known for their singing. My dad always used to call me his little songbird when I was a kid."

"I'm sorry to bring it up. I should go now." But he didn't move.

"So you just came by to cook me breakfast and bother me this time?"

"No. I came by to make sure that you were still in."

"But you never asked."

"I didn't have to ask to know." His lips brushed against my ear, lingering after he spoke. "Plus, I got to find out that you're into me." He rose and crossed to the door, grinning. "Not bad for a morning's work."

The sonofabitch had just played me. But...still. It wouldn't kill him to be wrong once in a while.

SIX

Later that night I was beginning to wonder if all of this was really worth it. I didn't even know what Eric and Trevor were going at each other for this time and I really didn't care anymore. Even Reyna had lost interest in the conversation and was flipping through a magazine.

I had to hand it to Trevor, though. He was amazingly poised for someone being attacked from both sides by Eric and Suzanne. Come to think of it, he always seemed very calm and in control of himself. I couldn't help but wonder if that was a quality Raptor...

The front door to the bank slamming shut and a set of keys banging against them interrupted my thoughts. I knew the bank was closed and all of the committee members were already present so I shot a worried glance in Michael's direction. He rolled his eyes and shook his head. I realized why as Drake Wyndham entered the conference room.

I met Drake only a few times before my father's murder, but I never liked him. At the time I first met him, he was the vice president of the bank and it was obvious to me that he was nothing more than a corporate mouthpiece. My father hadn't thought much of him either.

And my father was an excellent judge of character.

I never fully understood what happened, how Drake managed to maneuver himself into the CEO's chair that should have gone to Michael. Michael told me once that it was all just corporate politics and Drake was better at the game than Michael ever cared to be. I respected Michael for that. Even though there was no love lost between the two men, they were always quite cordial with one another.

Though he carried himself with all of the poise of a politician, his eyes always gave away what was going on behind his careful façade. Or, that too, was a part of the façade. His inky black hair had the casual appearance that must take quite a while in front of the mirror to achieve. His face might be etched from stone for as much as his expressions ever revealed. Still, I would think he was up to no good even if I didn't know of him from my father and Michael's perspectives.

Never in my life had I seen such a fire in anyone else's grey eyes before.

"Excuse me everyone," Drake began as though he were addressing the board of directors. "I'm terribly sorry to interrupt, but I need to borrow Mr. Brightman for a few moments."

Without a sound, Trevor rose from his chair and followed Drake into the hallway. Though the door was shut, I could still see them through one of the panes of glass in the wall. I couldn't hear what they were saying, but it was obvious this was not a pleasant discussion among pals. I strained my ears to hear, but the chatter in the room overshadowed it.

Elaine leaned closer to me and whispered, "It's always something with those two. You would never know that they used to be close."

I looked at her in surprise. "What happened?"

Elaine shrugged. "I'm not sure. I guess they were doing a business deal together a while back. I don't know all of the details, but I've heard things went sour – with the deal and the friendship."

"How long ago was that?"

Elaine pursed her lips and looked up. "I guess it was just about two years ago."

When Trevor walked back into the room, Michael clapped his hands to get everyone's attention. We decided that we would have to meet again the following evening and then we adjourned the meeting. I said good-bye to the others and headed to my car. I needed a drive to clear my head and sort things out.

I'd witnessed a total change in Trevor's demeanor when he was outside with Drake. I didn't have any idea what they were talking about, but I knew whatever it was had been enough to transform a mild-mannered real estate developer into something potentially dangerous.

Granted, Drake always had that appearance to me, so Trevor's reaction might not amount to much. Still, I had to wonder what they were discussing and what might cause such a rift between friends. Was it even possible one of them was Raptor?

If so, was the other covering it up?

Parker frowned at the caller ID on his cell phone before he answered it.

"What?"

"Don't take that tone with me, Ramsey."

"Sorry. Hello, how are you this evening? What?"

"I just wanted to check in. Have there been any developments since we last spoke?" the man asked, his voice filled with irritation.

"Not really," Parker answered.

"And why the hell not?"

Parker ran his hands through his dirty blond hair. "Most of my contacts have dried up since I've been off the scene. Besides, everyone I've spoken with has informed me of how quiet things have been lately."

"Quiet?" he questioned.

"It happens. You know as well as I do that people stop talking right before something goes down."

"Okay, Ramsey, I get it, but you had better not be letting yourself get distracted by your new little playmate. I don't have to remind you what will happen if I don't get what I want."

Parker continued frowning long after the end of the call. No, he didn't need a reminder of the consequences. Even if this wasn't personal for him, failure wasn't an option this time.

Too much hung in the balance.

Raptor looked at the woman next to him in his bed to make sure she was asleep. Hearing some inane question of whether he was asleep when he obviously was not would be enough to drive him to murder again that night. He slipped out of the room and went to the kitchen before he could contemplate choking the life out of his slumbering bedmate.

Although the woman sharing his bed was annoying enough that no jury alive would convict him, he couldn't allow his thoughts to linger on how perfect the skin of her neck would feel straining for air under his death's caress. Killing her was a reckless fantasy. He couldn't indulge. Not yet.

God, how long had it been since he'd last watched the life drain from someone's eyes at close range, knowing he alone held the power to decide who lived and who died? Too long. The last set of kills were all by bullet.

Killing his team in such a plain manner was necessity. The real tragedy all those years ago was not choking the life from Andrew Montgomery that day in the bank.

Montgomery. That was a new problem.

He poured himself a glass of water and quickly downed it. "What the hell are you up to, Skylar Montgomery?" he said to his glass.

He knew Skylar just enough to know she could be a threat to him. Perhaps it was simple coincidence she chose now to leave her solitude. But Raptor was never a man who bothered with idle things like coincidence, fate or luck. If foolish fate had plans in store for him, it was too bad.

Raptor made his own luck. He decided fate...for himself and everyone around him.

Still, he couldn't know for sure if Skylar's sudden appearance meant anything. His guard would stay up at all times around her, just in case. It was impossible for her to know he was the reason she mourned her father.

No, he would go on just as he planned before Montgomery turned up at the committee meetings. He was the best at taking down banks. It would take more than some grieving bimbo to mess with his plans. This time would be no different for him.

This new score would go off without a hitch. He'd waited in the wings of respectable society too long to set things aside now. Skylar Montgomery would not pose a problem for him.

And if the bitch did, he would put a bullet in her just like he had her father...even if guns lacked his usual finesse.

Tuesday, March 23

It was still relatively early when I pulled out my journal to write what I knew so far. It's funny...Michael gave me this journal just after my mother's suicide to help sort out my feelings and begin to heal. After two years, this was the first time I opened it.

Something told me destroying Raptor wasn't exactly what Michael had in mind, but it was all I had.

I frowned down at the page. My hope was to gain more insight about the situation if I wrote everything I knew and reread it. Unfortunately, it didn't work. My subconscious didn't seem to know any more than I did.

So far, I only knew that everyone seemed suspect to me, but I didn't have enough to narrow things down. It was also possible that none of the people I was spending time with were Raptor or knew anything about him. All my hopes rested on what may be little more than a fool's errand.

Awesome.

As much as he annoyed me, I wished Parker was here so I would have someone to bounce ideas with. Then again, I was just as grateful he wasn't here. He was always filling my head with more unanswered questions than I already had. Did he distract me or did all those new questions help me focus? Who could tell anymore?

Wow, I'm stupid. When did I turn into the chick who sat on the couch asking herself questions she had the answers to instead of things that mattered? Ugh. Having Parker Ramsey as a partner must've made me regress a good decade in maturity.

Giving up on the journal idea, I unrolled my yoga mat and attempted some basic poses. No matter what I did, I couldn't find my center. I couldn't blame this one on Raptor, either. Now Ramsey was ruining my workouts.

Parker was a distraction to me because I was attracted to him and that was all there was to it. He was right in yesterday's observations. He was right about all of it. The danger excited me, but even more, he did. Having any sort of feelings for him beyond contempt would be foolish and I knew that. I did.

It was too late to tell myself to place the safe bet. Even when I couldn't tell if he was toying with me or coming onto me, I wanted to be around him. He could piss me off all he wanted and I couldn't make myself wish him gone. Not anymore.

Would I even have the will to rebuff his advances, should he make one he meant? I couldn't answer that question any more than I could pinpoint Raptor's alias. If Parker were in this room with me right now, even I couldn't guess how I might behave.

Just like that, I wasn't alone.

*****

Jackson looked at Dinsley in anticipation. Dinsley seemed disinterested in the tip he got from a source about their three suspects. The more he dug into this case, the more it appeared his partner didn't want to close it.

"You're ahead of yourself, Caldwell. It doesn't matter that these three men will be at the same place on Saturday night. That fundraising gala is an invitation-only sort of thing. If we had any sort of hard evidence, it would be no problem to crash the party. Until then, we have to step lightly."

Jackson left Dinsley's office and went to the records area. He didn't know why Dinsley was so standoffish with him, but Jackson was ready to get to the bottom of it.

Getting the file clerk out of the room was easy enough. Lower level agent files weren't exactly under state-of-the-art security once you had building clearance and were alone in the room. A quick glance at Dinsley's personnel file revealed all the standard information he'd expected. All details so standard, Jackson was about to give up.

Then he found it. It wasn't a safe deposit box key to Raptor's millions, but it was what he needed to confirm his suspicions just might be warranted after all.

He slipped the file back into the cabinet and returned to his desk. Jackson considered calling Jenna to let her know what he had found out, but dismissed the idea. She was busy enough with her own work without having to show him how to put two and two together to make four. Besides, she would probably slam the phone down in his ear as soon as she heard his voice, regardless of what Trista said yesterday.

If Jenna really wanted to talk to him, she would've called him. Phones worked both ways.

But he didn't need Jenna's call to figure out what was in front of him. Two years ago, Raptor robbed First Alliance Bank and Trust. Two years ago, Skylar dealt with an agent who didn't seem overly interested in capturing Raptor. Two years ago, an FBI agent was under suspicion of being on the take.

And two years ago, Special Agent Brandon Dinsley was placed on administrative leave.

*****

"What do you want, Ramsey?" Skylar asked, her voice ripe with irritation.

Parker tilted his head to the side to regard her. "Well, at the moment I would love to know what position that is. Yoga might not seem like a waste of time and energy if there's more of that."

She glared up at him from between her legs. "You are such an ass."

And she had a great ass...especially in those clingy pants and from that angle. "Look, I came over here to talk to you. You're the one *presenting,* as they'd say in the animal kingdom."

"In yoga it's called the downward facing dog." She shot him a lingering dirty look before killing his view by standing up. Skylar stretched her arms over her head, still with her back to him, to stretch. "So, I'll repeat my previous question. What do you want, Ramsey?"

"You really need to start calling me by my alias if you're going to be used to it by Saturday. It wouldn't be a wise move to slip in front of Raptor and call me Parker."

"Fine. What do you want, Price?"

"Better...not exactly affectionate, but better." In a strange cop-show kind of way. This whole thing would be so much easier if she'd just let her guard down, he mused. "I wanted to go over our story with you so you can get it into your head before Saturday."

"Okay," she replied with a nod, still stretching her arms, effectively ignoring him. "I was beginning to wonder if I needed to come up with that on my own."

Parker tried not to let his horror at the thought of letting someone else come up with the back-story show on his face. "You had an antique statue in your possession that you wanted appraised. You asked around and got my number. I appraised it for you, helped you to find a buyer for it and asked you to dinner once our business transaction was complete. We hit it off and that's that."

"That isn't much to tell," Skylar commented.

"That's the point. It's never a good idea to get elaborate about these sorts of things. Excess details can be misconstrued. Stories get confused. If we aren't careful, we end up telling two different versions and I guarantee Raptor would pick up on that."

At first, she seemed to accept that. Then she spun around, fresh annoyance marring her face. "Why are you so certain I'm the one who'd mess it up? How do you know you won't be the one who slips? What if Raptor knows about antiques?"

He shrugged. "I know more. One of my degrees is in art history."

"*One* of your degrees. How many do you have?"

"Enough that *I* don't need to worry about blowing our cover."

Skylar rolled her eyes. "Well, I don't think we have to worry about me mixing up *that* story."

"Good." Parker tried to read her face, but it was expressionless. Why couldn't he ever tell what she was thinking?

Her hands went to her hips. "Was there something else, or were you just planning to stare at my ass while I stretch?"

"Tempting, but there actually is something else."

"And that is...?"

"Come here." Before she could process his words, he reached for her, pulling her to him by the hips. Her lips were on the verge of forming a question when he silenced them with his mouth.

The kiss lasted perhaps three seconds before Skylar pulled away. "What the hell, Ramsey?" Her deep blue eyes registered her confusion for another two seconds after that.

Then anger came to play.

Parker heard the crack of her slap before he felt its stinging effects on his cheek. "I've made myself very clear. You've had your little fun, now you can get the hell out of my house."

He caught her wrist before she could unlock the door. "I had to test something, Skylar."

"Other than my patience?"

"I wanted to see what your reaction would be to that."

"You might need to head back to school if you really didn't know."

He closed his eyes and let out a frustrated sigh before continuing. "I know you're an intelligent woman, so I'm sure you can appreciate how much of a mistake it would be to have that particular reaction to me around Raptor. Especially if you use the wrong name when you do it."

Skylar opened her mouth to protest, considered his words then let out her own sigh. "I see your point. I guess I just wasn't expecting it." She hopped around on the balls of her feet while rolling her neck and shoulders like a prizefighter revving up for battle. "Try it again. I'm ready this time."

"I didn't realize you'd have to psych yourself up quite that much."

"Just shut up and kiss me. I can do this. I'm a great actress."

"Are you now?" Parker circled his arms around her slender waist and pulled her close to him. He held her gaze, taking note of her steely determination. That would do for now, but she'd have to do a hell of a lot better than this if she planned to fool anyone.

Especially Raptor.

"Were you planning to kiss me anytime this week? I've got plans later, you know."

"So impatient." He brushed a loose lock of hair from her face and she shivered in response. Without a second thought, he released her and shook his head. "This will never work."

"What's that supposed to mean?"

Did she sound annoyed because of his comment or because he hadn't kissed her again? "I think it's pretty obvious you can't hold this together. No one's going to buy us as a couple." He scrubbed his hands over his face. "I'm pulling the plug on this operation."

"Like hell you are. Get a grip on whatever your deal is, Ram...Jonathan, and just kiss me."

"My deal? No." He advanced on her until her back was pressed against the door. "You're the problem."

"Me? How?"

"Oh...come off it, Skylar. I can't even touch you without you doing this weird shivery thing." He accented his point by dragging a slow finger from her cheek to her neck to her bare shoulder, eliciting the same shiver in response. "What the hell is wrong with you?"

"Nothing."

"Dammit, Skylar! Stop playing around and answer the fucking question. Unless you plan to wear a Victorian dress to this gala so that you don't have any exposed skin for me to touch, no one's going to buy us as a couple if you can't even stand still when my hand brushes across your skin."

She rolled her eyes. "You're an idiot, Price."

"Excuse me?"

"It's because we haven't had sex yet."

That might be the last thing he thought she'd say. Ever. Sure, they both probably thought about it multiple times each day, but he never thought she'd admit it.

Oh, to hell with it. Sex with Skylar might be all he thought about. Plan or not.

"Are you trying to say you want to have sex with me?"

Skylar met his eyes. "Well...yeah. Don't you?"

SEVEN

I watched his reaction closely, but Parker's poker face was too damn good. For all his expression gave away, I might have just complimented his haircut, not put sex on the table for discussion.

While I studied his expression – and tried to ignore the fact he still had me sandwiched against the door – I realized the folly of my words.

"Parker, you understand I was in character when I said that. Don't you?"

He wasn't buying it. "Character?"

I nodded. "Look, why would I – or any woman – not want to sleep with her boyfriend?"

"You tell me, Skylar."

I sighed. "I'm not even going to stand here and pretend you aren't attractive because you'd know I was lying." I paused. This was stupid. I wasn't having this conversation two inches from his face. "Will you back up?"

He lifted his hands in truce and took a step back, just enough to give me breathing room, but not enough to give me actual space. "You were saying how you wanted to sleep with me."

"Anyway. What I was actually saying is that the character I'm pretending to be wants to sleep with her boyfriend, but they haven't yet."

"Why not?"

"How should I know?"

"This is your story. Don't you think you should?"

Why was he being so difficult about this? "Fine. Things keep coming up to interrupt their plans."

"What things?"

"Parker, what the hell is wrong with you?"

"You're the one who's improvising with the story. I'm just trying to get on the same page so we don't tell different versions. Maybe I think *things* means unexpected business trips and you think *things* means the gala committee errands. If you want to make up some elaborate fiction about why you react the way you do when I touch you, at least finish developing the lie."

"Fine. You had to go out of town and now I have the gala stuff and those are the *things* that got in the way. Does that work for you?"

"I suppose. It does seem like a lot of extra story just to cover the fact that you want me and can't hide it."

"Dammit, Parker, I was in character. I told you I was a good actress."

He nodded. "Sure you are."

"What's that supposed to..."

Gentle, yet demanding lips silenced me before I could finish my question. Was this a test? Or was he kissing me because he's a man who wants me? The answer didn't matter to my response. Whether I was in character or out of character, I wanted him.

Parker's hands started on my shoulder blades, but didn't stay there long. One hand moved to the small of my back, pressing me against him, while the other hand crept past my neck to pull the elastic band out of my hair. What was his obsession with me having my hair down?

Or was he just trying to distract me?

Instead of losing myself to the kiss that may well be a test, I decided to up the ante. I pressed back against his shoulders just enough to make him take a few slow steps back without breaking the kiss. Since I knew the layout of my living room better than he did, I knew exactly when to push him hard enough to make the back of his knees hit the side of the couch and fall over backwards. The moment his back hit the cushions, I was on him, straddling his waist and leaning over him until my hair was tickling his face.

"Do you believe it now?" I grazed my lips over his. "Do you believe I'm a good enough actress to pull this off?"

"Yes and no." Before I could protest, he grabbed my face with both hands and pulled my mouth back to his. Against my lips, he whispered, "I believe you can pull it off – if you ever start using the right name, that is – but you weren't acting, Skylar."

"Okay, *Price*, I'm sorry your ego can't take it, but I was acting."

His lips grazed my jaw in the most delicious manner. "I can tell when women are acting. That's not what it's like. At all."

"Gee, don't all men think they can tell when a woman's faking?"

"We could test that." His meaning was unmistakable.

"We probably could." I glanced over at the wall clock. "I don't have anywhere to be until this evening, but..." I couldn't come up with a way to end that sentence.

Parker's hands toyed with the lower hem of my shirt before gripping my hips. His smoldering gaze captured my eyes. "But?"

Someone knocked on the door and I nearly jumped out of my skin. At least I didn't have to come up with an answer now. I pushed away Parker's hands and climbed off him to go to the door. He shot me a look and pointed to himself then the bedroom after I checked who it was.

"Only if you need a minute to cool down," I mouthed.

He glared at me and gestured for me to open the door. I retrieved the elastic band from where he left it on the floor to pull my hair into a quick ponytail before letting Reyna in.

She walked into the room and glanced at Parker. "Am I interrupting anything?"

I shook my head. "No. This is Jonathan Price. Jonathan, this is Reyna Vinson."

I watched as he walked around the couch, cooler than a frozen cucumber, to shake Reyna's hand. He must've learned that icy sense of control the same place Chill did.

"It's a pleasure to meet you," she said to him before turning back to me. "I just wanted to pop by and see if you already had a dress for Saturday."

I shook my head. I'd been too focused on the aloof man standing next to me and a vicious killer to do anything practical like that. "I tend to do things at the last minute."

"Perfect." Reyna smiled. "I'm the exact same way because I hate shopping for those silly things. Do you want to go with me to see what we can find before the meeting tonight?"

No. I wanted to shove her out the door and attack Parker...no matter how bad an idea it was.

"It sounds like that's my cue to leave if I don't want to get stuck outside the fitting room all afternoon holding purses." He grinned, but the last of the heat from just moments before still burnt in his eyes. "I've got to be going anyway, sweetheart." He walked over to me and dropped a light kiss on my lips. "I'll see you tonight."

Did I imagine the very clear implication to his statement? He turned to Reyna. "Help her find something sexy."

"Oh...I will," she replied as he left.

The moment the door snapped shut, Reyna blew out a breath and turned to me. "He might be the most intense man I've ever met. Who is this guy?"

I smiled at her. If only I knew. "I've been seeing him for a while, but I don't know if it's anything serious yet. Just let me change and I'm ready to go."

Reyna followed me to the bedroom. "Based on the way he looks at you, I'd say it's serious."

"You know, I usually like to get dressed alone."

She laughed at me and disappeared into my closet. I heard the rustling of hangers for a moment before she reappeared with a brightly colored sweater and solid black leggings. "I thought I'd save us a little time by picking out an outfit for you that actually looks good." She hooked the hangers over my wrist and retreated from the bedroom. "I mean, we are going out in public."

When Jackson saw the number on his cell phone's caller ID, he ducked into the nearest conference room before answering.

"I'm glad you called."

"So, you actually bothered to see who was calling this time." If there was any trace of hostility left from Friday night, Jenna wasn't showing it in her voice.

"I wanted to tell you how sorry..."

She cut him off. "I know, but don't. It happens and it isn't worth discussing."

Did that kind of thing really just happen to anyone? Even if it did happen to people, this was Jenna. "But..."

"No. It isn't an issue. I don't have time to talk about it anyway. I'm calling about your case."

"Oh." Did he expect she'd call him out of the blue about anything else? "What have you got?"

"Quite a bit. Or nothing. It's hard to tell. Can you meet me at the café on Frankford and the tollway?"

Jackson considered that. He didn't want to explain to Dinsley what he was doing, especially since he now had a strong suspicion his partner was on the wrong side of the case and in it up to his eyeballs. But, if his time doing busy work these last months had taught him nothing else, he at least knew how to get in and out of the building without anyone noticing him.

Dinsley didn't need to know he was going anywhere.

"Sure. What time?"

A lengthy pause stretched across the phone connection before Jenna spoke. "I can send Trista with the information, if you'd prefer."

"Why would I prefer that?" When Jenna didn't say anything, he added, "Unless we've hit the point where Trista officially hates me less than you do, I would always prefer to see you instead of her."

"I don't hate you, Jackson." A measure of sadness crept into her tone. "I never did." Another moment of uncomfortable silence passed between them before she said, "I have a few phone calls to make before I can leave. Two hours?"

"I'll be there. See you then. Jenna...I will see *you* then, right?"

"I've got another call. Two hours, Caldwell."

Caldwell. Great. First they went from lovers to friends. Now, they were down to colleagues.

This might be a good time to stop pretending he didn't notice the outrageous flirting of the woman who rang up his wheatgrass juice protein drink at the gym each morning.

Parker watched the two women get into a sleek BMW and drive off. Skylar was going to play right into his hands without him having to put too much effort into it. A smile crept over his face as he put the car in gear and pulled into the traffic.

Absently, Parker reached for his cell phone and realized it wasn't in his pocket. A quick glance revealed it wasn't on the passenger seat either. Damn. Must've fallen out of his pocket when they were on the couch.

He flipped a U-turn and headed back the way he came. Skylar getting her hands on the numbers in his cell phone was the last thing he needed to happen. What she found would be a deal breaker for her at this point.

The two women should be away for hours, so he didn't bother parking away from the townhouse or going around to Skylar's bedroom window. Instead, he walked straight to the front door, pressed the extra button on his car alarm remote to disable her home security system and unlocked the door with the key he made a week before their first meeting.

If people knew how easy it really was to program auxiliary remotes, they wouldn't bother paying for alarms.

As he thought, the cell phone was buried between two couch cushions. He started to leave, but thought better of his hasty exit when he noticed a journal on the coffee table. A quick glance might give him some insight into the unreadable mind of Skylar Montgomery.

No such luck. It was blank. Every page.

Just like her face during the kiss.

When he told her she wasn't acting, it was a bluff. Unless he caught her by complete surprise, she wore a mask of stone that not even the world's best archeologists would be able to decode. Even then, the surprise normally wore off within a few seconds.

Based on her racing heartbeat, she was into the kiss...or the game she was playing on him during the kiss. Whether she genuinely wanted him or not was another question entirely. If only the girl hadn't interrupted him, he might have gotten his answer.

Parker struggled to remind himself that taking things any further with her was a complicated indulgence he didn't need, but he had trouble mustering the will to care. Acting or not, she was one hell of a kisser. Based on that alone, he knew she'd be a hellcat in bed.

Either way, ruse or real desire, she could still give him exactly what he needed from her. One way would just be more fun than the other.

He hit the redial button on his phone. It rang several times before he heard the familiar and gruff voice on the other end. A little time spent under Skylar that morning made the interaction less unpleasant than usual.

"I'm set," Parker said evenly before he disconnected the call.

*****

Raptor hung up the phone from the morning's most recent call and drummed impatient fingers on the expansive desk. Time enough for one more call before he got on with the façade of his day. He knew it was still too early in the day for Chill to be up, but time was a luxury he didn't have right now.

The prospect of a good heist always hyped up his system.

When he answered, Raptor said, "How do you maintain any sort of clientele if it takes you that long to get the phone?"

Chill couldn't hide the surprise or the grogginess in his voice when he spoke. "Most of my clientele keep the same hours as do I." After a beat, "It has been a long time, Raptor."

"That it has, that it has."

"Does this mean the rumors are true and your hasty retirement is at its end?"

"As usual, you're well informed. I'll need a crew, standard size."

"That will not be a problem. It has been slow around here of late and you should have your pick of the crop."

Exactly the way he liked it. "What do you know about a con named Songbird?"

"I know Songbird is a woman and an excellent planner. Plenty of connections."

"Good," Raptor said. "I have to go out of town for a few days, but see if you can get something set up with her when I get back."

"I will see what I can do, but she is not big on face to face meets."

Prima donna cons were a dime a dozen in Raptor's world. He could break her down to agreeable compliance, of that he was certain.

He heard a soft knock at his office door. "See what you can do. I'll be in touch."

Raptor hung up the phone as his assistant entered his office. "The car is here to take you to the airport, sir."

"Excellent. Keep my schedule light for next week. I'm anticipating some last minute appointments to hit the books."

I was amazed at how much fun I was having dress shopping with Reyna. I expected her to drag me off to one of the ritzy dress shops on Preston Road in Dallas, but instead she took me to the mall.

In the second department store, Reyna held up a gaudy pink sequined dress and said, "This dress scares me. The sad thing is that someone will come in here and think *this* is a good idea and wear it on Saturday."

I shook my head and laughed. "I love it."

A look of horror came over her face. "Tell me that you are kidding, Skylar Montgomery, or I will die of a heart attack right here, right now."

"It's hideous," I agreed.

Reyna hung the dress back on the rack and walked over to the rack in front of me. She flipped through a few dresses before she asked, "So, what's the story with this Jonathan guy?"

I smiled. "He's an antiques dealer. He helped me sell a piece I had a few months ago. He asked me to dinner once our business was complete."

"It always happens that way," Reyna said. "Right when you stop caring if you ever find someone, they pop up out of the woodwork."

I cocked my head to the side and looked at her. "Is that how it happened with you and Eric?"

Reyna looked uncomfortable. "You don't want to hear about that."

"Why not? I'm glad he found someone nice like you."

She shrugged. "Okay. You know how all the brokerage firms harass you when you have money, right?"

"Probably not to the degree you do, but yes. I've had to change my phone number three times to get rid of the calls."

"Well, Eric was one of them. He was the first one who called and actually seemed to acknowledge that I was a person and not a dollar sign. I agreed to meet with him face to face. He didn't have anything for me to invest in that I wasn't already in. Most brokers would have tried to force me into the package they were offering anyway, but he admitted I was in good hands. I liked his honesty and I asked him to have a drink with me. He turned me down a few times, but I'm persistent."

I had to admit to myself that Reyna reminded me very much of myself. Before my world had crashed down around me, I wouldn't take no for an answer either. If there was something I saw that I wanted, I would go after it with everything I had until it was mine.

Now, the only thing I devoted any attention to was finding Raptor.

"I'm glad you were persistent, Reyna."

She smiled again. "Me too." She glanced at her watch and frowned. "This store doesn't have anything, so we should get out of here. I can't afford to be late to the meeting tonight."

"How come?"

"Conveniently, about half of our committee had to leave town on business, so we'll get to pick up their slack. I imagine you and I will be very busy over the next few days."

I followed Reyna out into the parking lot and got into her car. Something kept telling me Parker would also come up with numerous things for us to do. It was a good thing Reyna didn't know exactly how busy I'd really be.

Brandon walked back into his office and sat down. It was only two o'clock and his partner was nowhere to be found. Caldwell was trying his patience and the email he had waiting for him further exacerbated the situation.

He had to deal with this situation, sooner rather than later.

Caldwell was asking questions about him and the file clerk admitted that he may have left him alone in the room for ten minutes. It didn't take much imagination to figure out his partner pulled his file. What he might be after in the file, Brandon didn't know. He did know that his new partner was quickly becoming a problem.

Every other agent Brandon worked with over the last few years was content to do the bare minimum. This guy was different. Brandon could only imagine that Agent Caldwell was out right now trying to solve the case. In any other situation, that would be a good thing. Bringing bad guys to justice was what they did. It was the reason Brandon became an FBI agent in the first place.

But this case was different.

He couldn't afford for Caldwell to uncover certain details about the case. Not yet. Not until he was ready.

If his new partner did too much more digging, he'd uncover the very thing he couldn't know. That couldn't happen. It was time to take steps to ensure his fellow agent didn't get too close to the truth. But what steps?

How far could he go to safeguard himself against exposure?

Brandon leaned back in his chair and rubbed his temples. "What am I going to do about you, Agent Caldwell? What am I going to do?"

*****

Jenna was in a booth at the far side of the café when Jackson arrived. He sat across from her and she treated him to a warm smile.

"Thanks for meeting me on such short notice, Jackson."

By her tone, it was almost as though Friday night never happened. Jackson didn't know if it was a good idea to play pretend, especially since the reason there were so many problems between them was because he tried to pretend his job shouldn't matter to her. Still, he wasn't going to be the one to bring it up again.

"You're the one doing me the favor, Jenna. What did you find out?"

"I wasn't able to find out anything else about the agent I told you about, but I've got Trista working on it for me. However," she said, retrieving a file folder from her briefcase, "I was able to dig up some dirt on your suspects."

Jackson thumbed through the file. "You have been busy."

"Your case is more interesting than mine is right now." She made a dismissive gesture with her hand. "Anyway, it seems that Trevor Brightman and Drake Wyndham were involved in a partnership together a few years back. Drake had to sell off his share when he became CEO of First Alliance, but I can't find a record of who he sold it to."

"Do you think that could be something?"

Jenna bit her lip, thoughtful. "I don't know. Maybe. It's possible."

He nodded. "I'll see what I can find on that."

"Okay. Trevor has been under suspicion of insurance fraud twice in the last five years, but he was never charged."

"That isn't much to go on."

"Well, I could have dug up more on him if he existed prior to seven or eight years ago. No record of Trevor Brightman before then."

"An alias maybe?" Jackson asked.

"Could be. I don't really know what to make of this guy. And the other guy, um...what was his name?"

"Eric Sauters."

"He's a straight arrow. I couldn't find anything on him, but I'll keep digging. I went ahead and requested his Articles of Organization from the County Clerk's office, just to see if there was anything damning there. From what I can see, he either keeps his nose clean or he's very good at covering his tracks."

Jackson closed the file and looked her in the eyes. "I really do appreciate all of the effort you've put into this for me," he said, voice soft. He wished there was something more to say, a magic bullet of words to repair all the damage, but there wasn't. "I don't know how I can ever thank you enough for this."

Jenna stood up and tossed a mischievous grin in his direction. "Well, you could go with me to this fundraising party thing Elaine is making me go to on Saturday night."

The gala Dinsley wouldn't let him crash? "You love to make me go places with you where I have to get dressed up, don't you?"

"But you look so good when you do, Jackson," she joked, as her eyes took in his casual wardrobe of blue jeans and a button down. "Besides, a girl does need an excuse to get you out of those casual clothes every now and then." She paused as though she realized how her words sounded and shook her head. "You know what I mean. So, will you go? I hate going to these things solo."

"Of course." Even if he didn't love her, he wouldn't pass up the chance to observe his suspects.

"Good. Pick me up at seven."

Jackson sat in the booth for a few minutes after she left, reading the file she put together for him. Finally, he smiled and walked out to his car. He didn't want to dwell too much on her invitation for Saturday or he'd make more of it than it was. Jenna just needed an escort to keep drunk society types from pawing at her all night.

It wasn't a date.

Knowing that wouldn't change his feelings for her, though. He had too many memories of the last time they got all dressed up to go somewhere. It was the night she almost died. It was the last night he was the man she loved instead of the agent who lied to her.

At least now he had an excuse to go and observe his suspects. That was still something to look forward to, even if getting out of the colleague zone with Jenna wasn't. She may think he was doing her a favor, but Jenna had no idea how much she was helping him.

Parker sat quietly at his table and pretended to read the newspaper. After a respectable period of time passed, he left the café and got into his car. It appeared the FBI was investigating Raptor more actively than he thought.

Never before could Parker match a real name to Raptor, so he was glad he decided to stop in at the café for a cup of coffee after completing a few tedious errands. He knew each of the men in question, which was to say he saw their pictures in the paper. Well, with the one notable exception he knew for quite some time. Unfortunately, there was no way to know if the man he knew was Raptor. All of the men were of a similar build so it would not be possible to narrow it down from that alone.

But, the build they all shared was the same one Raptor possessed.

Parker picked up his cell phone and dialed Chill's number. It was far too early to bother a man of the night, but he couldn't avoid it. He needed to know if there was any word on the street about any of the men. Chill would forgive the early call once he stopped complaining long enough to realize they were a step closer to catching his brother's murderer.

"Dammit, Ramsey! I was just getting back to sleep. This had better be worth it," Chill said, just as irritable as Parker imagined he would be.

"I think I could have his real name."

"I am all ears, brother."

That was faster than Parker expected.

"The FBI is checking out Drake Wyndham, Eric Sauters, and Trevor Brightman. Do you know anything about any of them?"

Chill was silent for a moment. "Sure, I know lots about them. Pick up the paper and turn to the front page of the society section after a big photo op shindig." He snorted. "Men of stature cannot risk being associated with me. But you already know that. You only call me from beyond the grave."

Parker ignored the dig. "Thus the Raptor persona."

"You got it, but I will see what I can find."

"Okay. Be discreet. We don't want to tip him off until we're ready," Parker warned.

"You forget; you are talking to the Chill Man." He yawned. "Oh, Raptor called, by the way."

"And you're just now telling me?"

"Do not bust my balls on this. You woke me up. Anyway, he wants a crew. He also wants to meet our little songbird."

"What did you tell him?"

Chill let out a second, more exaggerated yawn before answering. "I told him she does not do meetings in the flesh – no matter how much I would like her to. He asked me to see what I could do. He wants to meet with her when he gets back into town. Do you think she would do it?"

Parker sighed. "I know she will, but I don't know if she's ready to without burning our cover. When did he say he'd be back?"

"A few days. This conversation bores me. Is Songbird in all the way yet, or are you still tossing breadcrumbs?"

"Breadcrumbs."

Parker could hear Chill laughing on the other end of the phone. "You do love to toy with the ladies, do you not Ramsey? Take a lesson; I have known Songbird longer than you have. If she figures out the play before you fill her in, game over. You lose."

Parker grinned. "I'll keep that in mind. I'll let you know what to tell Raptor about Songbird."

"Done. Should I assemble a crew yet?"

Parker thought about that before he spoke. "No, hold off on that for a bit. Raptor will want to feel like he's in control of this. Besides, I want to make certain Songbird's in, really in, before we add her to the roster. I don't like having to replace people at the last second."

"Hmm. Too messy. Keep me in the loop, but do not call me again until a more respectable time of the night." Chill paused before adding, "The FBI's investigation seems to be hitting a little close to home for you. Should this concern me?"

Parker considered his words carefully. "That would be premature since we can't be sure it really is him. If he is Raptor...that complicates things. Regardless, the plan remains unchanged."

"Your call, Ramsey," Chill replied before disconnecting.

Parker started his car and debated what to do with this newfound information. All of the men in question were in some way involved with the gala Skylar was working on. He instinctively drove his car to her townhouse and let himself in to wait.

"Now I just have to wait for you to come home and tell me who wasn't at the meeting tonight. I just hope it isn't who I'm beginning to think it might be."

And if it was, could he do all that was necessary to bring down a man he had so much history with?

Reyna dropped me off at just after nine o'clock that night. The meeting was as exhausting as she warned me and I was completely void of energy. It was a chore just to carry my dress inside.

If Parker felt the need to try something on me tonight, I hoped he was in the mood to do all the work.

It amused me that Parker greeted me at the door before I could even remove my key from the lock. Someone was clearly impatient. He took the dress and bags out of my hands and vanished into my bedroom. I decided to sit down on the couch while I waited to find out what he was up to. My feet ached from all of the walking.

That was when I remembered a dress and shoes weren't my only purchases for the day. Reyna talked me into purchasing an epic supply of sexy underwear. She had a rule that a new relationship deserved new panties...or something to that effect. Since I had a rule about not wearing underwear until I washed it, Parker would not get the pleasure of seeing me in any but the old stuff.

Assuming I was willing to let things get that far with him tonight...

"How was the meeting?" he asked as he sat next to me on the sofa.

"Hellacious." I shot him a sidelong glance, trying to figure out why we were making small talk. "It was just Reyna, Elaine, and me."

"What happened to everyone else?"

"Suzanne went with Drake to some meeting in New York so she could get her new spring wardrobe. Eric went to a seminar. Michael went to help his wife at the elementary school she works at. His assistant was vague, but I guess it was an open house for the spring semester. I don't know what happened to Trevor. Reyna said he left her a message, but his cell phone was cutting out so she didn't understand anything he said."

"Convenient that everyone skips town just a few days before the party," Parker commented.

I nodded my agreement. "You know, I really like Reyna as a person, but she isn't very organized. I think we could have been out of there in an hour flat if Michael was leading things."

"Do you have much to attend to?"

I rolled my eyes and let out a sigh. "You don't know the half of it."

"Okay. I'll let you focus on it. Go ahead and take the next few days to get everything done. I'll meet you there on Saturday."

His statement surprised me. "Don't we have quite a bit to accomplish ourselves?"

He shrugged. "Raptor left town. I don't think he'll be back until the gala anyway." His eyes took in my weary appearance. "Besides, I want you fresh on Saturday."

Parker didn't give me a chance to respond before he left. I was grateful – if not a little disappointed – for the extra time to myself. He was right, I couldn't risk being off my game around Raptor.

Still, I wondered what he would be up to. I didn't know where he was staying and he never gave me his cell number, so I would just have to wait until Saturday to find out.

It wasn't until I was changing for bed that his behavior struck me as odd...well, odder than usual. I was beginning to understand him a little better, but I couldn't figure out what he was hiding. Parker kept acting like he had something on his mind or something he wanted to tell me, but something kept him from it.

Was it important or just commentary on my ass?

As I waited for my sleeping pills to kick in, I tried to focus my mind on what he told me about Raptor. It couldn't be a mere coincidence that several of my committee members were out of town at the same time as Raptor.

I tried to get my mind around that idea and remember if any of the men had done or said anything that might make them stand out to me, but I couldn't focus long enough. My mind kept wandering back to Parker and what might've happened on the couch without Reyna's interruption. Despite knowing how much he loved toying with me, I knew the kiss on the couch wasn't the same thing. The look in his eyes was too real.

But then again, he was a con artist.

EIGHT

For the second time today, I was in the swanky ballroom of the Wellington Hotel in north Dallas. Reyna booked the largest ballroom, which was enormous even considering the hotel we were using for the gala. Despite the army of event coordinators on staff, she insisted we be here in the afternoon to oversee the decorating.

Seeing everything during the day didn't do our work justice. Now that I could see it in the moonlight, I could truly appreciate how stunning everything looked. The ballroom was on the fifth floor and the terrace had a spectacular view of the courtyard and swimming pools. When the wind wasn't gusting, it felt wonderful outside. I only hoped it would stay this way long enough for the guests to enjoy it.

Wait, what was I thinking? It didn't matter if the guests enjoyed anything and I didn't care if things were perfect. I didn't join the committee to help them raise money for kids with cancer and I didn't do it to make sure a bunch of dressed up stiffs could walk around and feel important.

I was here for Raptor.

I hadn't seen or heard from Parker, no, Jonathan, since Tuesday night. I had no idea what he was up to during that time and Chill hadn't answered my calls the few times I'd tried to contact him. My curiosity was piqued, that much was a given, but I accepted the truth last night. I was anxious to see my ally again and it had nothing to do with Raptor.

When the guests arrived, Reyna disappeared and I decided to start looking for him. After looking with no success, it was evident he wasn't here yet. I saw Michael mingling with a group of newcomers and I went over to him just as they were leaving him to find a table.

"Everything looks perfect, Skylar. You and Reyna did a wonderful job."

I smiled. "She did most of the work, but I'll take the credit anyway."

The string quartet began to play and Michael extended his hand to me. "May I have this dance?"

I let Michael lead me out onto the dance floor despite my better judgment. How long was it since my last formal dance? Several years, unless I missed my guess. I wasn't sure if I would even remember how to move without tripping all over him. We – but mainly his feet – were in luck because Michael was a wonderful dancer and it was easy to follow his lead.

I felt a tap on my arm as someone said, "May I cut in?"

Michael looked at me for my agreement before he replied, "Of course."

"You look beautiful tonight, Sky," Eric said as he took me into his arms.

"Thank you." That was all I could manage.

I was over Eric, in theory. Seeing him at the meetings with Reyna made it easy to tell myself all the old feelings were long gone, but now...it was far more difficult to pretend when I could feel his hand on the bare skin of my back. It made me wish I hadn't let Reyna talk me into this dress. With its nonexistent back and plunging neckline in the front I felt exposed as we danced.

It was all too familiar; being wrapped in Eric's arms, his hands on my bare skin...I couldn't do this. I shouldn't be here. Trying to dance with the man who should be my husband as though we were just old friends while he probably spent every night with his new girlfriend – who I considered a friend – was sick. What the hell was I doing?

Not even I knew the answer anymore.

I thought I was doing a good job of keeping my emotions in check until I felt his arm tighten and I found myself drawn closer to him. I wanted to resist him, to stiffen and hold my ground, but I couldn't. Being so close to him again felt natural.

It was *Eric.*

"Where's Reyna?" I asked instead, praying my voice was as neutral as I hoped.

"Overseeing the caterers, of course."

His face was inches away from mine now. Oh, God, please don't let him kiss me. I respected Reyna too much to do this to her, but I didn't know if I had the willpower to stop it before it started.

"Sweetheart," a voice said from behind me, "I've been looking for you everywhere."

I felt myself jump away from Eric and he released me. Parker kissed me lightly on the lips and turned to Eric. "I'm Jonathan Price."

I watched as Eric accepted his outstretched hand. "Eric Sauters." His face said it all. Parker's appearance was the only thing that stopped him from kissing me right there on the dance floor. "It's good to meet you, but, if you'll excuse me, I should attempt dragging Reyna away from work."

After Eric left, Parker turned to me and said, "I take it that was the famous ex."

I sighed and nodded. "That was him."

"He seems like an okay guy. What happened?"

"Raptor happened." Please, don't ask me more. Not now. Just...read my mind and know to shut the hell up about whatever you just saw.

"Ah. Of course." Parker took my hand and spun me into his arms.

"What are you doing?"

"I'm dancing with the most beautiful woman in this room."

"Don't be cute," I snapped, remembering to leave the smile on my face for appearances.

"I'm not. I love the dress." His hand slid to the small of my back as though it belonged there. "Burgundy is a good color for you. Very sexy." A sensual fire burned deep within his green eyes, just as it had before Reyna interrupted us earlier in the week. "Your friend clearly has excellent taste."

I decided not to respond to his remark and I let him dance me around the sizable floor. Parker's touch was electrifying on my bare skin. When I let my eyes lock on his, I realized this might be the most natural thing in the world for me.

Instead of thinking of ways to put up my defenses or dwelling on the lingering feelings for Eric that kept bubbling to the surface, I gave myself to the dance. As long as the band played the song, I could simply dance. As long as his possessive touch claimed each part of my skin it touched, I could focus my thoughts only on the man in front of me. As long as Parker played his role and kept looking at me the way he was, I could be the woman falling in love with her antiques dealer.

I just wished I could figure out why the bleached-out blonde in the trashy red dress by the bar kept staring at us.

Jackson and Jenna arrived just before eight o'clock. She was oddly quiet during the ride over, but Jackson didn't press her for the reason. At some point he knew he would have to face the truth and accept it. He was in love with a woman who didn't love him back. Their relationship was too damaged by the way they met to recover.

Jenna kept enough distance between them as they walked from the car to remind him that any chance of romance was out of the question. They were friends and it was killing him. Every time he saw her, Jackson's arms ached to hold her. Last Friday night's incident crystallized something for him. Jenna wasn't the only one who couldn't let go of the past. She was holding onto the bad while he was holding onto the good and he knew he wouldn't soon forget about how good they'd been together.

He finally understood why people didn't often remain friends after a break-up. It was too painful. In fact, it was so painful that he decided to apply for a transfer back to D.C. as soon as his case was closed. Running into her wasn't an option for him any longer.

Almost as soon as they checked their coats and entered the ballroom they ran into Dinsley. Jackson assumed he wouldn't be there based on what he said about it being an invitation-only event. He was certain his surprise was evident on his face, but Dinsley was mirroring his reaction so Jackson didn't think much of it.

"It's so good to see you again, Brandon," Jenna said as she gave Dinsley a hug.

Jackson narrowed his eyes. "I wasn't expecting to see you here."

He also wasn't expecting a rush of bitter jealousy towards his partner to flow through his veins. Was Jenna dating? Had she been dating the entire time they were apart?

If she'd slept with his partner, he'd take a dive off the balcony...

"Nor was I," Dinsley replied.

Jenna shot him a quizzical look after Dinsley left. "How do you know Brandon?"

"He's my new partner."

"How nice. You two are going to get along great. He's a really nice guy."

Jackson cocked his head to the side. "How do you know him?" He tried to keep the seething jealousy out of his tone.

He failed.

By the look on her face, Jenna caught the edge to his voice. "Elaine used to date his younger brother when she was in school. The guy was a jackass, but Brandon's been a real friend to her over the years."

"Is there any chance that he's the agent you found out about?"

"Brandon?" The look of horror on her face would be comical if his blood weren't still boiling over the mental images his mind conjured to torment him. "No. He's as strait-laced as they come, by the book all the way." Jenna paused and a smile played at the corner of her lips. "You aren't jealous, are you Agent Caldwell?"

"No."

"Uh-huh. Were you ever planning to ask me to dance?"

"I was thinking about it."

"Well," she said with a glint of mischief in her eyes, "I see Elaine and Daniel over there. I'm going to go say hello. You come find me when you're done thinking about it."

Jackson watched Jenna cross the dance floor to find her sister. He wanted nothing more than to follow her and find out what was causing her sudden playful mood, but he needed to deal with Dinsley first. If Jenna said he was all right, he probably was. Still, Jackson needed to find out for himself, which would prove much more difficult than he first thought.

Dinsley was gone.

Raptor knew the moment the man walked into the room that it was Parker Ramsey, back from the dead. He didn't know what he was doing here or why he was dancing with Skylar Montgomery, but he knew he didn't like it. Why had Ramsey chosen now to reveal himself?

Until tonight, his concern about Skylar's reappearance in the world was only mild. Now...well, he may have to deal with her before the next heist, just to be on the safe side.

He maneuvered through the crowd to get a closer look at Ramsey as the couple danced. It was him. There was no doubt about it. The question wasn't if this man was Ramsey, but if Ramsey knew who he was.

Raptor went to the bar to get a drink, a stiff drink. One glance at Chelsea was all he needed to be certain it was Ramsey. She looked shaken.

As he leaned on the bar to accept his drink he whispered, "You look like you've just seen a ghost." His hand brushed against her bare shoulder. "Why ever could that be?"

She glared at him, hatred burning in her eyes. "You're an ass," she whispered back before walking away, the material of her red dress hugging her ass as she moved.

Raptor smiled and turned his attention back out to the dance floor. Chelsea's response to him never failed to amuse, much the way a new toy amused a small child. Soon enough, her appeal would wear off as well.

God help her when that moment came.

But he couldn't dwell on the things he could do to that firm ass just now. If Ramsey was back from the dead, something was going to happen tonight. He would just have to find a way to isolate him from the rest of the crowd before it did.

Raptor had never liked witnesses.

Parker led Skylar off the dance floor. "As much fun as I'm having, I think you should start introducing me to the others."

Parker caught the look of annoyance Skylar tossed his way, but ignored it. He was certain she thought he was being sarcastic. He wasn't. If he didn't have a very strong suspicion Raptor was here tonight, keeping this beautiful woman in his arms for the whole of the night would be his first, last and only priority.

The way she looked at him during the dance...If she were acting, she was a lot better than he gave her credit for being. Holding her in his arms, he had the strong urge to lead her into any of the dozens of dark corners he could find in a hotel like this. Or get a room.

No. No room. Not yet, anyway.

Raptor first.

He let Skylar lead him to a small group of people. One of the men looked at him strangely before he spoke.

"Hey, Sky. Have you met my girlfriend Chelsea Varner?" he asked.

Skylar smiled, but Parker could tell it was forced. "No, I haven't, Trevor." She turned to the blonde next to him. "You must be her."

"It's a pleasure to meet you."

"Oh, this is my good friend, Jonathan Price," Skylar said.

Parker studied the couple as they made the usual small talk. Chelsea Varner. He knew her from somewhere, but he couldn't quite place her. There was a terrified look clouding her hazel eyes as she looked at Parker, almost as though she knew who he was.

And then he knew.

Raptor must know, too. Her new look wasn't much of a disguise and her tight red dress was made to draw male attention. Not smart on her part. Not smart at all.

When Parker knew her, she kept her hair a short bob at her chin in the natural brown it really was. Now, her hair was past the middle of her back and bleached white-blonde. She must wear contacts as well because she used to wear glasses at all times.

"Trevor, I'm going to get a drink."

Parker realized she knew she'd just been made. After she left, Skylar turned to him as if to ask what that was all about, but he shrugged it off. He couldn't keep the thought away that Trevor couldn't be Raptor. There was no way Chelsea would hang on his arm if he were.

Would she?

They mingled for another half hour before someone else caught Parker's eye and he began to look for a way to sneak away from Skylar's side. There was a man present he needed to talk to, but couldn't risk doing so with Skylar around. It was too soon.

Slipping away proved more difficult than he hoped. They got caught in a rather long and pointless conversation with Suzanne Wyndham once she learned he was an antiques dealer. Her husband wasn't a treat either. He glanced at Parker once as if to size him up before dismissing him and walking away from the conversation.

Just like Raptor did during their first meeting...

It was unnerving to Parker to be out in the open and still not have an idea of who the man he was looking for was. He had his suspicions about the man he knew, of course, but it could just as easily be either of the other two men. His old *friend* had the ultimate poker face; he hid his reaction to Parker well.

Parker got his opportunity to slip away during the next set of introductions.

"This should be fun," Skylar muttered under her breath as another couple approached. "Agent Caldwell, when you said you would be in touch, I had no idea it meant in a social setting."

The agent didn't seem any happier about running into Skylar than she was to see him. "I'm not here in an official capacity tonight."

"Then I hope you're an invited guest." Skylar's tone was pure ice. "Oh, where are my manners? This is my good friend Jonathan Price."

Parker accepted the agent's hand and sized him up. Caldwell was studying him as well, but he knew he wouldn't have to worry about this guy. They never met and Parker was more than positive the only picture the feds had of him was an unflattering bank surveillance photo.

Before he could learn the name of the agent's curvy companion, Skylar continued her verbal assault on the agent, so Parker took that as his cue to slip away.

"So, are you crashing then? Because I didn't see your name on the guest list."

I could tell the agent was fighting to remain calm, just like I could tell he didn't like me very much. He should have tried to hide his reaction better though, because knowing that just made taunting him more fun. The petite brunette at his side didn't seem to enjoy it as much I did.

"Actually," she said, "He's here with me and I can assure you that I'm on the list." Her eyes narrowed. "I'm always on the list before there's even a list."

Though I was certain we'd never met before, I felt as though I'd seen her somewhere. High school? Doubtful. She looked older than me. College. Nope. Same logic.

Then I knew.

"Wait. You're that author right? Monroe, something Monroe."

"Jenna."

From her tone, she didn't like me more than her boyfriend did. Go figure...A woman who didn't like me. Like that was anything new. At least now I knew why Caldwell turned me down cold.

"I just finished reading your book. Not bad."

Jenna's voice was dripping with irritation when she spoke. "Thank you."

"There was some pretty racy stuff in there, but I guess I know where you got your inspiration." I turned my attention back to Caldwell. "Maybe I was wrong about you." I fiddled with the lapels of his jacket. "Perhaps I should have come on a little stronger. Might have made for a fun afternoon."

He scowled at me, but remained silent. From the look on Jenna's face I could tell he hadn't filled her in on his visit with me. That was just the opening I'd need to *really* have a little fun with the two of them, but I thought better of it. He did, after all, pass my test. There was the scant possibility he was a good man.

Not that I thought that meant he'd catch Raptor before we did...

"Don't worry," I said, flashing a smile in her direction. "You have nothing to worry about. I was just testing him and he passed. Your boyfriend here turned me down cold. You should feel lucky because most men don't." I smoothed his lapels. "But if you were blonde, I might not care that you have a girlfriend standing right here."

I didn't give either of them the opportunity to reply before I turned and left them where they stood. Ramsey wasn't with me and I had no idea when he walked away from the conversation. It surprised me that I was anxious to find him, but I suppose it shouldn't have. Against my better judgment, I was smitten.

But I'd slit my wrist with one of the pins holding back my loose curls before I'd admit that to him...

When a search of the ballroom didn't turn up my *boyfriend*, I decided he might be on the terrace getting some fresh air. I was about to open the richly sculptured French doors when I saw Reyna, looking frazzled. Since I was still pretending to give a damn about the committee stuff through the end of the gala, I figured I should help her first.

"Is everything all right, Reyna?"

She sighed and shook her head, her black ringlets bouncing as she spoke. "No."

Uh-oh. Did she see me dancing with Eric? Was it obvious to her that I could barely control myself around him, much less in his arms? Stay calm. "What's up?"

"I'm just annoyed. I don't like these things as it is and we're already out of cream puffs. I never should have agreed to use Suzanne's caterer. They've been nothing but a headache for me this entire evening."

Cream puffs? She really needed better priorities. "So what? There's nothing you can do about it now besides giving yourself an ulcer. This is a party. You should be out there on the dance floor having fun."

Reyna sighed again. "I suppose."

"Where's Eric? It's his job to make sure that you're having a good time."

She shrugged. "I don't ever know what he's up to, but uh, while we're on the subject...where's Jonathan? He did come tonight, didn't he?"

"He's here. Somewhere."

Reyna started to laugh. "We are pathetic, aren't we? Here we are; two sexy women and we can't even keep track of our men."

"I'm sure they're around."

Reyna's blue eyes grew serious and her tone was confidential when she spoke. "Watch out for Chelsea."

"What?"

"Look, your man is hot and she's not someone you can trust."

"How do mean?"

"I don't believe in spreading gossip, but...in this case I know it's true. She goes after men who are married, mainly, but she was trying to cozy up to Eric a while back, too."

"Married men. How do you know?"

"Let's just say she used to be Drake's assistant until Suzanne made him fire her."

"Oh. I think I'm on the same page."

Reyna's eyes grew wide. "If I were you, I'd get back to looking. We can chat more tomorrow. I promise I'll be better company then."

After I assured her I would come to the dinner at her house the following night, I headed back towards the terrace. Even though he wasn't really my boyfriend, I felt strangely jealous of Chelsea. It wasn't as though I had delusions of a relationship with him or anything; I just didn't want to see some other woman weasel her way into bed with the guy I'd been having verbal foreplay with for the last few weeks.

It was my turn to get what I wanted. I couldn't have Eric because Reyna was in the picture, but Ramsey was mine. The trashy blonde could just wait her turn.

I was not prepared for what I found on the terrace.

After Skylar walked away, Jackson couldn't shake the feeling that he knew her date from somewhere.

"What is it, Jackson?"

"That guy looks familiar to me, that's all."

"I didn't realize you'd be working tonight," Jenna said, something familiar yet unfamiliar in her voice.

Not good. "I wasn't planning to actively work, just observe." He eyed her with caution. "It's not like this was a real date or anything, right? You just needed an escort."

"Something like that." She frowned and stifled a yawn. "I can't do this anymore. I'm going home."

Panic flashed through Jackson's mind. Even though they hadn't been on a date, this was not the way he wanted their night to end. Who did he really think he'd been kidding, anyway? He was hoping he could make her change her mind.

"Okay. I'll take you home."

Jenna shook her head. "No, you can stay. I'll get a ride with Elaine."

"Look, uh...I'm sorry I didn't tell you about what happened with Skylar, but..."

Jenna made a dismissive gesture with her hand and stopped him mid-sentence. "I don't care about that. I know you would tell me if there was anything to tell. I trust you."

Her statement caught Jackson off guard. She hadn't trusted him in almost six months. Why now?

"Is everything all right?"

"Things are better than all right." Jenna left the ballroom, stopping short of the coat check long enough to retrieve something from her purse. "I'm not stupid. I get it."

"O...*kay?*"

"I do understand you need to concentrate on your case before all of the people you're observing head out." She pressed an object into the palm of Jackson's hand. "So observe them."

"What's this for?" Jackson asked, looking at the key in his hand.

"I know you have to work now, but I want you to come over after. I won't wait up, but I'd like you to wake me when you get there."

"I...don't understand."

"I know." Jenna sighed. "I know I said some things on Friday – things I meant – but..."

"But what?"

In lieu of a response, she grabbed him by the collar of his shirt, pulling him to her as she stepped into the shadows of a nearby corridor. Her lips met his in a hungry kiss that he couldn't help returning with equal passion. For a non-date, this sure as shit felt like the way a date should end.

Granted, a kiss like this really deserved total privacy, not the low hum of music and conversation a few yards away.

With her palms splayed across his chest, she broke away from the kiss and stared up at him in heavy-lidded anticipation. "Say you'll use the key tonight." She paused to take in a shaky breath. "I don't care how late it ends up being. Come over."

He gathered her hands in his. "Jenna...what's going on with you?"

She averted her eyes. "I can continue to shut you out of my heart and my bed to punish you, but I end up punishing myself as well." Her eyes returned to his. "Besides, I never did thank you for saving my life. Not properly. I know Chad would have killed me if you hadn't found us in time."

"I was doing my job."

"It was more than you just doing your job. It was always more than your job between us. We both know that."

Did they both know that? How many months did he spend trying to convince her of that same fact? "You don't owe me anything for saving your life that night. And you don't have to invite me to bed to thank me."

"But you have to admit it's the most pleasurable way to thank you." Raising up on her toes, she pressed her lips to his again, lingering. Against his lips, she whispered, "You know I'm right."

Jackson framed her face with his hands, tilting her chin up so he could delve his tongue fully into her mouth, leaving her knees quivering by the time he was done. Feeling his own resolve waver, he pulled away from her, putting several inches of space between them. "You may be right about the pleasure, but I don't want you to sleep with me just because you feel like you owe me."

"That's not what I'm doing."

She seemed sincere enough about that. "Are you sure this is really what you want? I understand if it isn't." He would die a little inside, but he'd understand.

Jenna brushed a softer kiss across his lips. "I'm positive. I know you have a lot left to do tonight and I'll understand if you don't make it over. I just really hope you do."

With a fleeting glance, she turned and left. Jackson stared after her until she vanished from sight to collect her coat. She was right; he did have a lot of work left to do tonight. He had to prove himself to his new superiors by cracking this case.

Not that he had a clue how to accomplish that while his partner looked guilty as sin.

He pocketed the key and smiled to himself as he went in search of Dinsley. Hell would freeze over before anything kept him from Jenna's bed tonight.

NINE

Parker met him in the most secluded corner of the terrace. The air was crisp, but the wind subsided so it was semi-pleasant. Actually, he found it surprising they were the only two people outside.

"I think your partner recognized me."

Dinsley frowned. "We may have to bring him in then. I know you didn't want to, but I'm sure we can trust him. From what I can tell, he's on the up and up." The usual gruff expression cracked into a smile. "The little bastard's even been checking up on me behind my back."

"Fine. Tell him if you absolutely have to, but I'd rather not have more people in on this than is necessary. Skylar doesn't even know the truth yet and I don't want her to find out from him. I get the sense that she doesn't like him very much."

"What truth is that, Price?" Skylar angrily demanded from behind him. "Dinsley, I suppose it's good to see you again."

"I'll just leave you two alone," Dinsley replied, retreating to the safety of the party.

"What the hell is going on here?"

Parker pulled her into the shadows far enough from the party that her raised voice wouldn't carry through the door. "I always had every intention of telling you..."

"Stop dancing around the point and get to it. Be straight with me or I walk right now."

Parker ran his fingers through his light hair and let out a sigh. "I've been working with the FBI for the last six months."

"Okay," Skylar said. "And I'm the Tooth Fairy." She pointed to her bare back. "My wings are invisible, but trust me, they're there."

He ignored her sarcasm. "I tracked Raptor for as long as I could, but my leads dried up and I needed the resources of the FBI behind me. I met up with Dinsley and we worked out a deal. If I can help them catch Raptor, Parker Ramsey stays dead and Jonathan Price can enjoy his life without looking over his shoulder – for them or for Raptor."

"Why didn't you tell me?"

"I didn't think you would be willing to work with me on those terms. I was going to tell you about it the other night, but you reacted so strongly to Caldwell that I didn't think the timing was right."

"What else have you been keeping from me, Price?" she demanded.

Parker thought he heard a noise and he pulled her close to him. He pressed his lips against her neck and whispered, "I think someone is coming and I'm going to kiss you to cover. For the love of God, don't hit me."

Parker felt the tension in Skylar's body subside as his lips met hers and her arms slipped up around his neck. As her fingers played through his hair, he thought she was getting good at this charade. If he didn't know she was still seething from his deceit and faking her feelings, he would believe she was enjoying the kiss.

Parker pulled back enough to speak. "I think it's just us again."

"Good," Skylar responded as she pulled him back in for another kiss.

Still seething or not, she wasn't acting. If it was even possible, she was more into kissing him than she'd been on the couch when she was moments away from giving him the 'go' signal.

"What are you doing?" Parker asked once he was able to free himself from her grasp.

"I was getting into character." Sly blue eyes slanted up at his. "I thought you liked it when I got into character?"

"I do, but..." He didn't mean to admit that. "I thought you were pissed off at me?"

Skylar shrugged and a slight shiver raced over her when the wind picked up. "You could be working with Raptor and playing me right now. In the scheme of things, what I just walked in on wasn't the worst thing I could find out."

On instinct, Parker reached for her, pulling his jacket around her to block some of the wind. It was a move meant to shelter her from the cold, but she took the opportunity to nuzzle her face into his neck. Standing on her toes, her lips and hot breath grazed behind his ear.

"You're playing with fire, Skylar."

She made a small, nonchalant sound in her throat. "Good. I like fire." She pulled away to look up at him from beneath heavy eyelids. "Just kiss me." Her lips quirked into a grin. "And none of this acting bullshit, Price. Kiss. Me."

He didn't intend to let things get this far until after Raptor was under control, but a man had his limits. Pressed against him, looking into his eyes the way she was...this was what Parker Ramsey's limit looked like. It didn't matter that the wind was picking up, or that the woman in front of him wasn't over her ex. It didn't even matter that the fire she so casually played with would consume them both without hesitation.

He wanted her. That was it. Thinking about all the reasons he shouldn't was futile.

"No acting, huh?" He reached up to toy with a dark strand of hair softly dancing in the wind by her cheek. "Thank you for wearing your hair down. I like it."

"I figured you might. What else do you like?"

"I like when you do this." His fingers trailed down her neck, eliciting the now familiar shiver of excitement. "You were never faking that, were you?"

"What do you think?"

He walked her backwards until his hands hit the brick wall, careful not to scratch even an inch of her smooth skin against it. "I think you wanted me the first day we met in the park."

"You think?"

Parker's hands moved to tilt her face up to his, straying to the strands of hair around it. God, he loved her hair. She should burn every one of those damn rubber bands she used to tie it back.

"I think you weren't acting on the couch either, Skylar." His eyes locked on hers. "I think the only reason we didn't spend the whole day in your bed was because of that damn knock at the door."

Skylar held his gaze with a sensual sapphire fire burning in her eyes. "I think you're still not kissing me." Her hands made a bold move to squeeze his ass, pulling him closer still. "Has it been so long since you kissed a woman without acting that you've forgotten how to do it or what?"

"If I didn't know better, I'd say you were taunting me to try making me lose control."

She lifted an eyebrow and slipped her arms around his waist, tapping the buckle of his belt without saying a word.

His lips grazed across her jaw, drawing a low moan from her. What the hell was he doing? This was *not* the way to get to Raptor.

Fuck it. "Let's get a room." He kissed her hard, tugging lightly on her lower lip with his teeth. "Now."

She opened her eyes at his request, dazed by both his kiss and his words.

"As sexy as you are in this dress tonight, I can't think about anything but getting you out of it."

He didn't wait for her to respond, instead pressing fleeting kisses all over her neck. "Come to bed with me, Skylar. No acting."

Her hands clutched at his dress shirt and she looked at him, unsteady. "Price..."

"Eh-hm. Skylar, can I talk to you for a minute?" Michael interrupted.

Raptor waited until Skylar left with Michael before he approached Ramsey.

"What the hell do you think you're doing here with Skylar, Ramsey? Oh, I'm sorry, Price," Raptor demanded.

"You know how it is, old friend. Meet a pretty girl; get invited to a party..." If he was surprised to see Raptor, he hid it well.

Raptor took a menacing step towards him. "Don't be flip with me. What's the play?"

He shrugged. "She's loaded and lonely. I wanted to see what I could get out of it."

"A love con, Ramsey? Isn't that a little beneath your skills?"

"It is, but I need an off the books bankroll for anything truly worthy. I didn't get to walk away with millions from our last heist like you did." A smug smile tugged at his mouth. "Besides, this con isn't exactly a hardship, if you catch my meaning. I'd consider bedding this one even if there weren't a payoff at the end."

"Touché," Raptor replied.

"Anyway, I was hoping to draw you out."

"In a hurry to die for real, Ramsey?"

"No. I knew you wouldn't kill me."

"The night isn't over yet."

"You were always smarter than that. You must know what lengths I went to in order to vanish. The reason I've chosen now to re-surface must be important to risk your wrath again." He made a dis-missive gesture with his hand. "Or I'd rather get a bullet than a BJ from my current mark. I'll let you figure it out."

"Keep talking."

Raptor didn't know what Ramsey was up to, but he knew it would be good. A con of his caliber would never risk death unless it was for something important. Whatever it was, Raptor knew he want-ed a piece of it.

"I heard you were looking to take out another bank and I have a tip on one. I can use Skylar as the insider without her even knowing it. We all know you're the best at taking down banks and I figure you owe me. Help me pull this job and I'll forget you double-crossed me and tried to kill me. This is a win-win situation for the both of us. The only real question left is: are you in or are you out?"

"I'm in," Raptor said without missing a beat.

"That's what I thought." Another of his condescending smiles tugged at his mouth. "Now, if you don't mind, I have a mark to continue seducing."

I followed Michael into the room the caterers were using for their equipment. Mentally, I tried to prepare myself for what he was about to say, but I found that to be a difficult task. The situation with Parker was at a level I couldn't anticipate prior to tonight and it was now beyond the distraction phase; it was dangerous.

I should be keeping a close eye on my potential Raptors, yet all I wanted to do was find my partner and get a room as he suggested.

"What's going on, Skylar?"

"What do you mean?"

"Who's this guy you're with?"

"Oh. His name is Jonathan Price," I said, knowing he wanted more than a name and hoping he didn't know anything about him be-yond it.

Michael couldn't conceal the worry in his eyes when he spoke. "What do you really know about this man?"

"He's an antiques dealer, Michael. Why are you suddenly so concerned about my love life?"

"You know I worry about you in general, but this guy...I feel like I should know him from somewhere, Skylar."

"And his familiarity is a bad thing? Besides, aren't you always the one trying to push me into getting on with my life, meeting new people, and so on?"

He sighed and shook his head. "I just don't want you to end up getting hurt."

Making my tone light, I answered, "That's two of us then."

"I'm being serious and I wish you would take this seriously as well. You don't seem to know much about this man you're obviously close with..." His voice trailed off. "You should understand that not all men make their intentions clear."

Was Michael actually taking the protective father posture with me or was I just too off my game to read him right now?

"I'd say he was making his intentions pretty damn clear a few minutes ago."

"For the night...maybe. Have you considered he's after your money?"

Was he serious with this? "He doesn't seem to care about money all that much. It's not like we talk about my bank balance or anything."

"Look, I know you're a big girl, Skylar. I know you can take care of yourself, but we both know Monty would be asking these questions if he were here right now." He paused to clear the sudden emotion from his voice. "And I know I'm not your father and could never, ever take his place. I wouldn't try, but you're the closest thing to a daughter Margo and I have. We love you and we worry."

Wow.

"I don't know what to say to that."

"Promise you'll be careful...with everything."

"Michael, I promise. Jonathan Price...he's one of the good guys. You don't have to worry so much about me." After a few moments of awkward silence, I added, "I saw Margo chatting with Suzanne when we were on our way in here. You should probably be more concerned about her right now."

Michael finally cracked a smile. "If that's the case, I'd better go rescue her." He turned to leave, but paused to say, "Just...be on your guard. With any guy."

I allowed myself to breathe in a sigh of relief after Michael exited the room. Lying to him was the worst part of this situation, but things would've gone bad if he realized how he knew Price. Luckily, Michael believed him to be someone after my money. Or my virtue.

Such as it was.

Long minutes ticked by on the wall clock while I regained my composure. For so long I isolated myself, yet I still had people who thought of me as family. And he was right about what my father would've said in this situation.

Michael's words of caution reminded me of my father's famous 'Guard Your Heart' speech. Though it annoyed me as a teenager, they were the words that helped me to avoid heartache for most of my life. In fact, the only time my guard ever slipped was when I met Eric.

And now with Price...

I walked back to the party and tried to find my partner. I half expected him to already have a room and to be making pointless small talk while waiting for my return, but a quick search told me that wasn't the case. To cover my bases, I decided to head back to that quiet corner of the terrace, just in case he was still there.

Trevor cornered me before I could feel the icy blast of air from the doors. "Sky, have you seen Chelsea anywhere?"

Why did this guy think he could use a nickname that almost no one got away with using? I only tolerated it from people I considered friends, not that I had many. Trevor sure wasn't one of them.

"No, I haven't. I was actually just looking for Jonathan," I replied quickly, hoping he might take the hint and realize I wasn't in the mood for pleasantries.

He did not.

"So, we really did quite a job on this one, didn't we?" he asked, oblivious.

I resigned myself to the conversation. After all, this was the whole reason I was here, socializing with people I'd never talk to, wearing a dress I'd never wear. I needed to take my hormones out of the driver's seat for a while.

Maybe he'd say something to help me determine whether or not he was Raptor if I kept him talking. "I suppose so, though I'm probably not the best judge of this sort of thing."

Trevor smiled. "Then you can take my word for it. This shindig went off without a hitch. I've been to a million of these things and this is the first one that I haven't seen some drunken CEOs make fools of themselves on the dance floor."

I considered what he said before I spoke. "How often do you assist with these?"

"Every chance I get, but I'm out of town quite a bit these days. I only end up helping to plan about three a year, but I attend dozens."

That sounded like an exaggeration, but I didn't comment.

Raptor supposedly left town after the bank heist. I made a mental note to see what I could turn up on the travel habits of Trevor Brightman. That was when I realized how fidgety he was this evening.

At all of the previous meetings, he was the picture of poise and confidence. But now...He kept glancing around the room and shifting his weight from foot to foot. I wondered if Parker was right in his theory that surfacing at the gala would throw Raptor for a loop.

I also wondered if this was what it would look like.

"For the last time, are you in this?"

"You're hurting my arm, Parker," Chelsea whined.

Parker had crossed paths with Chelsea on her way out of the ladies room. Something was in her eyes every time they saw each other that went way beyond knowing who the other really was. She had to be working with Raptor; she was just too nervous.

Since no one was around, Parker decided now was the time to find out. He'd grabbed her by the arm and shoved her out onto the terrace. Michael looked worried when he interrupted them, so Skylar would be occupied long enough to find out where Chelsea's alliances really were.

Parker released Chelsea's arm and leaned against the railing. "I know you're hiding something, Cherry. You know as well as I do that I'll find out anyway. Save me the trouble and start talking. I've already been approached by Raptor tonight, so you can stop trying to pretend you don't know.

Chelsea's eyes grew wide. "But you're still alive! Parker...How did you pull that one off?"

"My little secret. Start talking or I'll tell him you ratted him out to me," he threatened. After a beat, he added, "You don't want to test me on this one. We both know I'll do it."

Defeated, Chelsea slumped against the railing next to Parker. It was obvious Raptor still terrified her. What wasn't so clear was why she would stay so close to the man who murdered her fiancé two years ago.

"After the last of you guys turned up dead, I figured Raptor would be long gone and I came out of hiding. I tried to go legit and get a job walking the straight and narrow, but they don't really pay well."

She shook her head. "And I sucked at being a secretary anyway, no matter what the pay was. I ended up waiting tables at a bar. I didn't know Raptor lived here until I put a drink down in front of him one day. I'd never actually seen him without his mask, but I'd know those eyes anywhere," Chelsea said, voice soft.

"Did he realize you'd made him?"

"Yes. I think the man has a sixth sense about that sort of thing. He threw down some cash and left the bar in a hurry, but he was waiting for me at my car when my shift was over. I thought he was going to kill me."

"Why didn't he?"

"I've never fully understood. He made a pass at me. I didn't know what to do and I wasn't ready to die. I guess I thought if I rebuffed him he'd kill me, so…" Chelsea's voice trailed off.

"You're lovers, then?"

Chelsea looked at the ground and shuddered. "If you can even call it that. I don't know how to get away from him. I tried, once, but he was at the bus station waiting for me when I got there." Her eyes clouded. "He *really* didn't like that. Made it clear death wouldn't come quick if I tried it again without saying a single word." She shuddered again and hugged her arms over herself in a protective manner.

"I'm sorry, Cherry. It never occurred to me that I was leaving you here unprotected when I faked my death."

"How could you? Besides, I was the first one to go underground after he…*died.*"

Apparently, Cherry's pain was still every bit as fresh as Skylar's was. She couldn't even say her fiancé's name or that he was murdered after two years.

"You have a plan, don't you Parker? That's the whole reason you're here, isn't it? I'm telling you right now that whatever you have in mind to destroy Raptor; I'm in. I don't care what it takes. I don't care how dangerous it is. Say the word and I'm in, Parker."

Just when the boredom from talking to Trevor was reaching epic proportions, Parker and Chelsea joined us. Even though Trevor was cordial enough, I noticed something in his eyes when he spoke to Parker. For some reason, there was a strange tension simmering between the four of us. I didn't understand it at all.

The only people who reacted strangely to *Jonathan Price* besides Michael were Eric, Trevor, Drake, and Caldwell. Caldwell was probably in the clear since he was a fed and taller than the others. But the other three men? They all needed to stay on my list, at least until I could figure out the meaning behind their peculiar reactions to my date.

My date...that was another problem.

I needed to deal with him before the night was over. Hell, I needed to deal with myself. Instead of focusing on who was Raptor, I kept practically going into heat just because Parker looked in my direction. That wasn't productive.

But the man was so damn frustrating that it wasn't all my fault. Just before Michael appeared on the terrace, Parker was ready to toss our night's mission over the balcony and take me up to a hotel room to spend a sweaty night between the sheets. Then he vanished and was nowhere to be found.

Until he reappeared with Chelsea...

Unfortunately, I didn't get a chance to talk to him about his alternating spurts of interest and disinterest in me. Instead, we made pointless polite conversation with people. Michael and Margo, Suzanne and Drake, Trevor and Chelsea. It was like everyone I knew was making the "Goodbye, we're leaving" tour around the room and I was their first stop.

Even Eric and Reyna stopped us at the coat check to say goodnight. Reyna was a tired version of her usual self. Eric was quiet, keeping his eyes glued to mine through most of the pleasantries. In fact, he only broke his gaze when Parker retrieved my coat and helped me slip it on.

The whole thing felt wrong. I was leaving with Parker and he was leaving with Reyna. It wasn't the way things should be.

It just...*wasn't.*

For one thing, I didn't have a real boyfriend. I had a con man who couldn't decide if he wanted to take me to bed or get away from me. If there was something real between the two of us...I don't know. Maybe it wouldn't hurt so much to see Reyna snuggled against Eric as they waited for the valet.

Why didn't I use the valet? It would beat walking to my car in the cold wind with a silent man. I didn't even know why he was so silent.

Once he made certain I was safely in my car and it started, he walked off, still without a word. Was he dreading a conversation about his FBI affiliation or was there more going on? I knew I should be grateful he was working with the FBI to catch Raptor, but...

It didn't provide much comfort.

I rolled down my window to call to him, but with the howling wind, I didn't think he'd hear me. I didn't know what to say anyway. If he would hide something like working with the FBI from me, I knew I could expect him to do the same if there was something sinister going on. What else was Parker Ramsey hiding from me?

It was time to find out. Tonight.

Sunday, March 28

After standing outside her door, key in hand, for fifteen minutes, Jackson heard a clock strike midnight. He'd made a half-assed attempt to find Dinsley before hurrying out of the gala and making the obligatory stop at the convenience store. Even if Jenna had a drawer full of condoms, it was still his responsibility.

Then he sat in his SUV for a half hour in the store's parking lot before letting himself put the key in the ignition and drive to her condo.

Jenna asked him to come over and wake her up if she was already asleep. Coupled with her statement about wanting to thank him, he took it to mean sex. From her behavior just before leaving, there was no question in his mind about whether he was right.

The question was whether he was okay with a quickie or a night or however she planned to thank him. More than that, it was about whether he was okay with getting tossed out of her life again by sunrise.

Was emotionless, no strings attached sex with Jenna better than no Jenna at all?

"Fuck it," he muttered under his breath as he unlocked the door.

She wasn't asleep, he realized as soon as he closed the door behind him. Her bedroom light was on and the bathroom was still steamy from a recent shower. He closed his eyes and groaned. Did he have to remember how much fun they once had in that shower?

Jackson saw her before she realized he was there. Her hair – still damp and wavy from the shower – clung to the back of her blue silk robe as she struck a match to light a candle on her nightstand. He let out a breath as he watched her. The robe, the candles, the wet hair, the overwhelming scream of desire ripping through his body...it was all too familiar.

He had to get out of there. Now.

"You're earlier than I expected," Jenna said without turning around.

"I wasn't having much luck at the gala after you left." He hoped his voice wouldn't give away his thoughts. "I still have a few more hours of work ahead of me this weekend, I imagine. I can come back later, if you'd like."

Jenna shook out the match and turned to face him, an amused look on her face. "Do you really want to go, Jackson?"

"No, I don't want to go." She moved close while he spoke and, unbidden, his fingers moved to the robe's sash. "But I probably should."

She tilted her head to the side. "Why's that?"

"Because I'm not in the mood to get kicked out after a quickie again." He hadn't meant to say that aloud

"And?"

"And nothing." Without his permission, his fingers tugged at the sash until it gave way, but he didn't break the connection between their eyes.

"We seem to be on the same page then." Jenna shrugged out of her robe and let it slide to the floor. "I'm not in the mood for a quickie tonight either."

The earlier confusion left his mind when he looked at her, replaced with the burning image of red lingerie. It was the sleekest silk and lace mingled together to show off her perfect breasts and thighs while still making him itch to take it off her. Two fragile strands of material on either shoulder were all that held the slip on.

"I'll take your silence as a sign of approval." She placed a hand on his chest, pausing there before loosening his tie. "I've been waiting to wear this for you since I bought it last October."

"You have?"

His eyes stayed glued to her, but he didn't touch her. He must be having a psychotic break from reality. The woman he loved was throwing herself at him and he couldn't reach out to touch her.

She met his gaze. "I bought it right before my reunion so I could wear it that night." She began unbuttoning his shirt. "If I get you out of these stuffy clothes you dislike, will you loosen up and touch me?"

That was it. Jackson pulled her to him and kissed her with all the passion he fought to bury over the past months; the passion he believed dead after last Friday. Jenna kissed him back while impatiently tugging at his shirt. When it was off, she pulled away to look at him, grinning. "You've been working out."

Jackson kicked off his shoes. "I haven't had much else to do since I got here," he replied, moving to the bed.

"Oh, please," she snorted, pushing him back onto the mattress and straddling him. "I can't imagine you really had all that much alone time since you got to town."

"Huh?" Jackson muttered, only half-paying attention. With one hand moving under the silken hem at her thigh and the other molding over her breast, the last thing he cared about was why he had time to work out. "Oh, yeah, I guess I did have to meet a bunch of people when I transferred offices." He slid his hand to one of the thin straps and slid it off her shoulder, ready to remove the lacy barrier. "That only takes up so much time, I guess."

"So," Jenna began, leaning over him to graze her lips over his, "Have you met many women then?"

Wait. What the fuck was this? It was like she was...*jealous.* "Quite a few, but I'm not sleeping with anyone else, if that's what you're asking."

Placing a hand at either side of his head, she pushed herself up so she could glare into his eyes, clearly not believing him. "How come?"

Jackson maneuvered until he was able to slide out from under her and sit up. "This is clearly a mistake. I should go before..." He shook his head and rose to his feet. "Look, I thought I could do this, but I can't."

Fixing her straps to keep the lingerie from tangling down around her, Jenna also rose to her feet. "Do what? Why exactly are you leaving?"

"I thought I could come over here and sleep with you like it didn't matter or mean anything." He retrieved his shirt from the ground and stepped back into his shoes. "I really thought I could do it your way and...God, I can't believe I'm saying this, but I am not interested in being your fuck buddy or colleague with benefits or whatever the hell this is supposed to be."

"Okay, I don't really know what's wrong with you right now, but I was just asking you a question. It seems like you could at least give me a straight answer without flying off into hysterics."

He nodded. "Oh...so it was just a question? That's interesting because it felt more like you were flinging some kind of an accusation at me."

"Well, I just want to know if there's anyone else. Okay? It doesn't change anything tonight, but I still want an honest answer."

"Fuck this."

Jenna reached out to stop him when he started to leave the room, but he pulled away from her touch. "You want to know why I haven't been with anyone else, Jenna? Do you really?" He spun around, grabbing her by the shoulders, glaring. "I haven't been with another woman because I've been waiting for you to come around since I got back to town. I've been waiting for you to realize that I'm in love with you."

She opened her mouth to speak, but he cut her off. "I know it shouldn't piss me off that you only want sex from me. I should be a guy and just do it. I should be able to use you the way you want to use me. But sex isn't all I want from you." He paused, grasping at the point he was desperate to make. "If I can't have all of you, I don't want any of you. I don't care how pathetic that is."

Jackson pulled his shirt on as he hurried to the front door. Jenna was fast at his heels, but he pretended that she wasn't as he reached for the doorknob. "You should know that I'm requesting a transfer back to D.C. as soon as I close this case."

"No!"

The pain in her voice surprised him, but he couldn't turn back to look at her. "Whatever the hell this is that we keep doing...I'm not interested." He paused to collect his thoughts. "I'm going to go and you're not going to try to stop me or call me. This is how it ends."

"Wait, Jackson. You need to know something before you go."

"What's that?" he asked, keeping his back to her. He still couldn't look at her. His resolve was already wavering.

"You're wrong about something. I do feel the same way about you." Jenna put her hand over his on the doorknob and waited for him to look at her. "What you think I want...It's not. I want more, too."

"But you said that it was a mistake?"

Jenna took a steadying breath. "Trying to start over was a mistake. I thought if I put distance between us that my feelings for you would go away and I'd be able to get over you...I couldn't. You can't start over with someone you were already in love with. That's the point I should've made."

Were, he thought to himself. His love was current; hers was past tense.

"Anyway, I'm not blameless for our fight. I, uh, I did use you."

"Okay."

She let out a sigh. "It's just that I tried so hard to convince myself while we were apart that the only thing ever really between us was the sex. I thought I wouldn't feel anything for you if I slept with you. I thought that might be enough to finally let you go and move on. I wasn't trying to use sex to get back at you, I was using it to get over you."

"That's not really any better. I have to go."

"Jackson. Don't."

"Why? Now you're telling me that you used sex to move on with your life, yet you apparently don't want me to date anyone else even though you don't want me. Give me one decent reason why I should stay."

"Because I'm heart and soul in love with you, stupid. My plan backfired on me. I was only trying to kick you out because I needed space to think. I was still so in love with you that my heart ached from it. I was a goner once you were back in my bed and I knew it. I wasn't ready to stop lying to myself yet. And then you pissed me off with the things you said. Fighting with you was just...easier."

"And now what's easier?"

She rose to her tiptoes to press a fleeting kiss to his lips. "Doing the right thing...admitting the truth. I don't know."

"If you don't know, I don't know either."

"Look, the only thing I really know anymore is I threw the deadbolt after you left to keep from running out after you. I dialed your number on my cell phone and kept my finger on the call button while I stared at it for hours that night, not sure if you'd even answer if I called you."

"I would've answered."

Her eyes glistened with unshed tears. "And if you did answer, I was afraid you wouldn't be alone."

"I would've been alone, Jenna. And drunk."

"But you said..."

"Just because I probably could've found someone to sleep with doesn't mean I wanted to." Squeezing his eyes shut, he added, "You were all I wanted. You always have been."

"Stay the night with me. The whole night, not just an hour or two."

"What about tomorrow?"

"Can we figure that out in the morning?" Jenna asked. She led him down the hallway to the bedroom, pausing briefly to flip off the light so only the soft flicker of the candle's flame lit the room. "I'm not going to get you out of my system in one night, Jackson. Probably not in a thousand." She stopped beside the bed and kissed him softly. "More realistically, I'm never getting enough of you."

He wanted to take her at her word, but he didn't know how to get his hopes up only to have her destroy them again. "Are you really sure about that?"

"It's been so long since I've felt your touch, *really* felt your touch...I don't want to waste another second without it, without you."

"Jenna, that's not an answer."

Her eyes locked on his. "I've never been so certain about anything else." She swallowed hard. "Without you, my heart is...empty. We can talk things through at length tomorrow if that's really what you want. But tonight...right now...I can't talk anymore. I need you. Just you. You're everything I want."

Jackson laid her down on the bed and said, "And we'll talk tomorrow."

"Yeah." She touched his face with both hands, tears finally spilling down her face. "I love you so much I don't know how I survived without you in my life...or whatever it was since I've only been going through the motions since you left."

He knew exactly what she meant. Without her, Jackson's life was little more than day after day of a hollowed-out shell performing the tasks of living. In that instant, with her arms around his neck so tight he could hardly breathe, he knew she felt exactly the way he did about her.

Her eyes filled with horror. "You can't go back to D.C.! You...*can't.* Please...don't leave me."

His heart burst from the desperation in her voice. He cupped her face with gentle hands. "Jenna Monroe, I will never leave you."

"Promise?" Her voice broke with emotion. "I'll hold you to that, you know."

"I swear it."

TEN

As Parker took his hotel's exit from the highway, he realized the same car was following him since he left the gala. It was too dark to see who the driver was, but he suspected it might be another of Raptor's games. Raptor wasn't the most trusting person to work with and it would be just like him to track him to where he was staying.

"I'm not in the mood for games tonight, Raptor," Parker said to himself, pulling into the hotel's underground parking garage.

With purpose, he passed dozens of spots on the first few levels and drove to the lowest level. Parker knew it was the least popular level with the other hotel guests and could safely assume no one would be around to witness anything if a confrontation ensued. He slipped into the dimly-lit stairwell next to the elevators and made certain the door closed with a loud thud.

Then he waited.

After only a few minutes, the door hesitantly opened and his tail entered the stairwell. Parker grabbed the person by the wrist and slammed them up against the wall. It was odd. Raptor was never that easy to trick in the past.

"Ouch, Parker, it's me," Skylar whimpered.

Parker released her and stepped away. "What the hell are you doing here?"

Skylar rubbed the back of her neck where it had hit the wall. "I needed to talk to you."

"Then you should have said something at your car. Why were you following me?"

She shrugged. "I didn't realize I needed to talk to you until you were already gone. Trust me, it's not like I would've followed you if I knew you were going to attack me."

He sighed. "I thought you were Raptor."

A smile played at her lips. "I get that a lot."

Approaching footfalls on the stairs above them stopped Parker before he could reply. Without thinking, he pulled Skylar to him, putting enough passion into the kiss that no one would suspect they were anything other than impatient lovers, least of all that they were conspirators. She didn't hesitate in the slightest and melted against him.

After the person exited the stairwell, Parker pulled back just enough to look at Skylar. The look in her blue eyes mirrored the look he was sure was in his. His earlier meetings with Raptor and Cherry were enough to distract him at the gala, but now...

There were no more distractions.

In wordless agreement, Skylar followed him from the stairwell to the elevator. It stopped at the next level and an employee joined them. In an unconscious and possessive gesture, Parker took her hand in his, reveling in its softness.

The tension grew between them until it was a thick curtain of desire as they waited for the elevator to make its next stop. The elevator stopped at the lobby and the employee exited with a nod to them, leaving them alone. They stared straight ahead at the closing doors, fingers entwining and tightening. Parker brought her hand to his lips, brushing a soft kiss against her knuckles.

Skylar turned to him and Parker lost control the moment their eyes met.

He felt the wall at the back of his hands and realized he'd pressed her against it while kissing her, making certain he could feel every inch of her against him. Parker opened her trench coat and moved a hand to cup her breast through the thin material of her dress. No bra, he realized right away. God.

Nice touch.

Skylar made a small sound in her throat and he moved his other hand under the hem of her dress. Grasping her hip, he coaxed her leg up so he could get even closer to her. By the time she arched her back and tightened her leg around his waist, his need for her was urgent. If he wasn't certain a bored security guard was watching them at that very minute, he would take her right then against the elevator wall.

In another thirty seconds, he wasn't going to care about even that...

Though the elevator didn't stop at any other floors on the way up to his, it moved far too slow. When he couldn't stand the barrier between his fingers and her body, Parker slipped his hand under the dress to feel the soft skin of her breast. Skylar gasped when she felt his caress and clutched at the collar of his starched shirt. He moved his hips against her and she bit her lip to keep from screaming.

Longest. Elevator. Ride. Ever.

When the doors finally opened, they stumbled out into the hallway, tripping over each other's feet. There were only two suites on the floor and Parker was grateful his was the closest door to the elevator. In a perfect world, they'd be in his suite and stripping off their clothes in under a minute flat, but the reality was that neither was willing to break the kiss or stop their exploring hands long enough to make it to the door.

He made several attempts to operate the card key lock and open the door with his one free hand until he dropped the card on the plush carpet. With an impatient growl, Parker knelt to retrieve it. With her skirt twisted, he was able to see a thin line of bare skin over the top of her stockings, distracting him from the card in his hand. Instead of standing up right away, he pressed his lips against her leg, pushing the dress's fabric out of his way as his lips worked their way up her thigh in a slow, methodical manner. When she couldn't stand his sweet torture a moment longer, Skylar ripped the card from his hands and unlocked the door.

Parker was barely able to close the door to his room before passion again sparked. Skylar shrugged out of her trench coat and let it fall to a heap on the floor. Moving backwards in the general direction of the suite's bedroom, she unfastened her dress and stepped out of it. His breath caught in his chest at the first sight of her nearly-nude body. She was even more breathtaking than he imagined – and he'd imagined it quite a bit since Tuesday's romp on the couch.

The possibility of pursuing something with Skylar was ever present on his mind since their first meeting in the park. She was so utterly annoyed with him when he found the wire concealed on her that Parker could only squelch the rush of desire at the first touch of her skin when she slanted that look of defiance at him. Even that was barely enough.

Parker realized this was crazy, that everything he worked so hard to build would come crashing down around him if he took this thing with Skylar any further, but none of that mattered to him at this moment. As soon as he felt the deadbolt click shut in his hand, he approached her, drawing her into his arms. Their lips met and the intensity of her kiss was a surprise to him.

Was it possible she'd spent as much time fantasizing about this as he had?

They left a trail of clothes on the floor as they made their way to the bed. Parker laid her down gently, but a twinge of guilt kept him from ravishing her. Fuck it all. He had to tell her.

"There's something you need to know."

"Shh...I know all I need to know. Just kiss me," Skylar said, breathless.

Parker looked down at her and hesitated. "This is important."

"Unless you have two dicks, it isn't going to make a lot of difference to me right now." She regarded him for a moment. "Do you? That might be sort of fun."

He blinked. Twice. "I'm being serious."

"Okay, fine. Look. Unless you have Raptor bound and gagged in the closet then it can wait." Her voice was thick with desire. "And right now, even that evil bastard can wait."

Parker didn't respond. Somehow, he doubted she would still feel that way after he told her the truth. The real truth. As much as he wanted to believe she'd never be the wiser, she had a knack for finding out things before he was ready to tell her. Their partnership would come to a screeching halt if that happened.

But he had to have her.

Skylar looked up at him intently before putting her arms around his neck and pulling his lips down onto hers. Without warning, Parker felt his knees knocked out from under him and realized he was flat on his back. The smell of her auburn hair all around his face was intoxicating as she kissed him and he knew the time for using caution with her was gone.

"Nice move," he commented once her eyes met his.

Skylar nibbled on his lower lip and said, "I knew my self-defense classes would come in handy for something."

"I didn't realize I was attacking you."

A smile crept across her lips. "You weren't. That was the problem. Sorry I had to get rough with you."

Effortlessly, Parker knocked her over and pinned her on her back. He placed his lips close to her ear and whispered, "Don't worry about it, sweetheart. I don't mind the rough stuff as long as I know what rules we're playing by."

Her breath quickened as he kissed down her neck to her breasts. Between her sounds of enjoyment and the ethereal feeling of her smooth skin against his lips, it was almost impossible not to take what he wanted without a thought for her pleasure. Over the years, he shared his bed with many women, but he couldn't remember the last time he felt the desire burning in him he felt now.

He was driving Skylar crazy with the kisses he planted all over her body; that much was obvious from the way she whimpered and twitched under him. He could feel the tension coiled tight inside of her as he moved lower to taste her, but he resisted the urge several times to give her the release she so desperately sought. Her shuddering body told him he could give her what she craved by moving only a fraction of an inch to the right.

Tempting...

Despite wanting her more than he wanted any of the women who came before her, he wanted her wild with want first. And she was almost there.

Parker felt Skylar's fingers tangling themselves in his hair before he felt her lightly tugging his head back to hers. Her kiss was liquid fire when he closed his mouth over hers and he could feel her hands on his back, firmly pressing his body against hers. She pulled away slightly and lightly brushed her lips against his ear before she spoke.

"I want you," she said hoarsely.

Parker kissed her neck. "I know you do."

"I'm serious."

"Well, let's hope. Otherwise this is just damn mean if you're not."

"Dammit, don't tease me anymore," Skylar breathed, airy. "Just make love to me."

When Parker felt her hands slipping down to his hips, he realized he couldn't deny himself any longer. Their lips met again and he knew he would have hell to pay for this, but he didn't care anymore. He let everything he knew slip from his mind as he entered her. Their eyes met for a split second before her lids fluttered closed and her body arched against his.

But just as suddenly, her eyes flew open. "Wait. Stop."

Mother. Fucker. He knew she was going to figure out that she didn't like fire as much as she said she did. Couldn't she have figured it out fourteen seconds sooner?

"What's wrong?" His voice was soft, tone comforting even though he wanted to strangle something over this.

"I can't do this. I need…"

"Yeah, I figured as much." He started to slide out, but her legs tightened around him. "What?"

"You don't understand." A smile broke across her kiss-swollen lips. "You've got about ten names going on here. I just need to know which one I'm supposed to be screaming when I come. Assuming you're up to the task, that is."

For the first time, he let his shock over something she said register on his face. Would that mouth of hers ever stop surprising him?

One of her bare heels nudged him in the ass. "Been pretending to be other people for so long that you can't answer the question? Just pick anything at this point and let's get to it. Or I can just pretend you're Ethan Hawke. Either way."

"Price," he said, automatic. "Just call me Price."

To hell with the consequences.

God. How long had it been since my body last felt this relaxed? Years, probably. Too damn long, at any rate.

I shut off the faucet and dried my hands, annoyed by the trembling tension in my upper thighs. This was ridiculous. I really needed to get laid on a more regular basis. Sex with Price was good, but not so good that I'd be incapable of walking afterwards.

Without a care for my nudity, I tossed a leg onto the smooth marble counter and leaned in for a deep stretch. Repeating the process on the other leg, I tried to remember when my last yoga class was. Pretending to care about the gala was really getting in the way. At least that was over now.

Of course, I didn't have a clue what might be about to take its place.

What I did know was that this was the most obscenely large bathroom I'd ever seen in a hotel. Either the FBI was being good to their new partner or being a con man paid extremely well. Considering

I was naked in his hotel room and had no immediate plans to change that, I pushed both of those unpleasant thoughts from my mind.

Flipping off the light, I returned to the suite's bedroom. The lights were off now and the moon's pale glow filtered into the room through the cover of hazy clouds. "Nice view."

Even in the near-darkness, I could feel his eyes flicker over my body. "It really is."

"I meant the view you have of the downtown Dallas skyline."

"It pales in comparison to what I was looking at," he said, handing me a champagne flute once I was next to him in bed.

Where did this come from? I looked around and noticed a tray of strawberries, cream and chocolate sauce on the bed. "How long was I in the bathroom?"

"Not as long as you think. I called room service while you were asleep."

"I was asleep?"

Price sipped his champagne. "Briefly." He dipped an oversized berry into the whipped cream and hovered it in front of my lips until I took a bite.

The almost ripe tartness of the berry was perfect mixed with the delicate cream. I took a sip of my champagne, then burst out laughing. He really knew what he was doing. He was good. I'd give him that much.

"Something funny?"

"Well, isn't it a little late for your whole seduction scene?"

"It's never too late to enjoy a good bottle of champagne with a beautiful woman." He grabbed the bottle and refilled our flutes. "Besides, I wasn't aware I needed a seduction scene." He raised an eyebrow. "Or that one would work on you. I might've tried it sooner if I thought there was any chance of success."

"No, you would've been shot down cold." Probably. Maybe. Whatever. I might have blown him in the park if it hadn't been so cold when we first met and he hadn't given me the opportunity to get out from between him and that tree...

"I figured as much." The humor left his eyes. "We really should decide on breakfast. I'll forget to set out the little card if we don't do it now."

Was he kidding me with this? "You're really talking to me about breakfast right now?" I dipped my finger into the chocolate and licked it off. Slowly. "You can't think of a better use of time?" I made a production of sucking the chocolate off that clung to the base of my nail.

"Several, but I thought I'd be a gentleman first."

My finger was back in the chocolate, smearing it over his bottom lip before I responded. "And what ever gave you the impression I wanted a gentleman in bed?" I licked clean the chocolate from his lips and darted several kisses over his mouth, never giving him the chance to answer my question. I didn't really want an answer anyway; I wanted him.

Again.

Now.

I have no clue when he put the whipped cream on my breasts or pushed me onto my back sideways across the bed, but I do remember him dragging the strawberry through it on its path down my abdomen, his mouth following in hot pursuit. Holy. Hell. The things that man could do with his tongue...and a rough strawberry.

Wait. Why was champagne pooling on my stomach? Pleasuring me with a strawberry was one thing, but champagne in the belly button was my line in the sand. Well, sand would also be my line in the sand because...it's sand. Do I really have to explain that?

"Hey? Ethan Hawke? Question."

His eyes cut up to mine from between my legs. "Did you seriously already forget what name you were screaming out a half hour ago? I'm pretty sure guests five floors down could remind you."

"Well, I got your attention, Price, didn't I? Otherwise you might just think I really liked what you were doing."

His lips twitched. "And you didn't?" He slid two fingers inside me.

My eyes fluttered and my breath hitched in my chest. "I...I...didn't...say that." If he could just still the fingers for a few seconds, I'd be able to talk again. "Champagne. Belly button. Why?" I bit my lip. No more words for me. I didn't care about the answer anymore. If I'd just shut up then I might get the pleasure trifecta of fingers, tongue and strawberry.

No such luck. "It probably dripped off my hair."

I peeked open a single eye. "Why do you have champagne in your hair?"

"You spilled it all over me when I was trying to take it from you."

He pulled his fingers out and tried to shake out the remaining champagne from it. The bastard actually took the fingers away. No good. I arched back until my head was hanging off the side of the bed and scooted away from him until the mattress's edge hit me at mid-shoulder blades.

"What are you doing now, Skylar?"

I couldn't really see, so I felt around on the carpet over my head. "I'm looking for something I can use to clean up the champagne. Can't have sex with it pooling in my belly button like this."

"But you're unconcerned about the whipped cream all over your breasts?"

"Well…" I pulled myself up enough to meet his amused gaze. "Yeah. It's different."

He rolled his eyes at me and pulled me back to him by my hips. Before I could protest, he'd slurped the champagne away and polished off the strawberry. "Better?"

"Actually…yeah."

"Then let's see what I can do about that whipped cream."

I smacked his shoulder to get his attention when I felt his erection pressing its way up between my thighs. Enough was enough. I was never a big fan of foreplay anyway. "I'm on top."

Amusement twinkled in his eyes. "Point of fact, babe, I'm on top right now."

"And now it's my turn." When he just stared at me, I added, "Look, I really prefer to run things."

"As do I."

"Then like I said, it's my turn." I shoved him off me. "Sit back."

He shrugged and complied, eyes never leaving mine.

Finally, something he wasn't going to give me a hard time about. I positioned myself over him and took in those first two delicious inches of him. Grasping the headboard at either side of his head, I steadied myself to ensure I could keep my balance while moving up and down only those first inches, adding the third, then the fourth, and so on and so on as I decided I wanted more.

It had not felt like this the first time with Price. Good, yeah, but he hadn't filled me in quite the same way. Just another reason why I should always be on top.

Always.

My hands slipped from the headboard to his chest as I slid down the length of him again. Letting my head fall back, my eyes closed and I bore down on him, making sure I had every piece of him. "Ooh…"

Rough fingers were in my hopelessly tangled hair. I didn't realize why until I felt his tongue glide past my teeth, eliciting a tiny moan of surprise that was lost somewhere in my throat. One hand cupped the back of my neck, while the other trailed down my body to coax my hips to keep moving. Focusing on two things at once was never my strong suit in bed.

Apparently, he'd noticed.

Damn. It was dangerous for any one man to feel this good. I pulled back from the kiss and let myself lean away from him to get a deeper angle. I could only wonder if those green eyes piercing through mine in burning intensity could read my thoughts. I hoped not.

No time for complications in my life. Even though this was approaching the best sex I'd ever had territory, I didn't want a boyfriend. Just this.

But as good as it felt, there was this sense that it would be better if I could just get a different angle. I leaned back and to the right, chasing the sensation until my left foot was on his shoulder. Better, but not quite. I continued contorting my body until my other foot was on his shoulder as well and I was practically in a tricep dip for support.

"I have never seen a woman do that before," he murmured, lust ripe in his voice.

If this had ever been one of Cosmo's featured positions, I sure didn't remember it.

And if it wasn't, it needed to be.

The angle limited my range of motion, allowing me only a small measure of movement to grind against him, but the feeling of it...God. Unimaginable. Nothing like it because the spot he was hitting had never even existed until this instant.

My arms shook, burning. "Pr...Pri...Ohhhh!"

Strong hands were at my back, moving me – or did he move? – until his tongue was licking away the last of the sticky sweet cream between my breasts. "I've got you."

But I still fell...straight through the fabric of reality and into darkest oblivion.

When the darkness lifted, I was on my back with my head at the foot of the bed, Price moving in a slow rhythm inside me. Were we still having sex or was this again? Didn't matter. The man had stamina. Some part of me probably loved him for that, but I was beyond thought or reason. I was spent.

His lips grazed my ears. "This feels so good, I could actually do this to you all night if you let me. Come for me again so I'll know when to stop."

"Can't." My voice was hoarse. "Nothing left. I'm done."

"Oh, you're not even close to being done." His teeth nipped at my neck. "You're going to have to come for me one more time or you're not getting out from under me."

"I might die if I do."

"That's asinine."

Something about his tone pissed me off enough to rally my energy. "After you."

He pulled back to meet my eyes, grinning at the challenge to my words. "I don't think so. It's my turn to run it."

"I don't have to be on top to run it." To make my case, I focused on squeezing every internal muscle I had around him, eliciting a surprised yelp of pleasure from him. "In fact, I know I'm winning this one."

"Not a chance, babe." His rhythm quickened, his hips slamming into me harder. I could feel my fingernails slicing into his back, momentarily giving me a distraction to focus on while I tried not to come unglued. Then he took that away from me, slamming my hands down at either side of my face, fingers interlocked with mine, without missing a single exquisite thrust.

"I'm not giving in," I growled at him, tightening around him like a vise.

"We'll see." Perspiration beaded on his forehead, but his eyes never left mine, locked on me in failing determination.

"I always win." Even to my own ears, my voice sounded like a woman who was on the verge of losing everything.

On their own accord, every muscle in my body contracted to the point of pain. The look I found in his eyes was some sort of shocked bliss. As violently as my muscles contracted, everything released in a dazzling display of bright colored sparks behind my eyes. Price collapsed on top of me, the grip on my fingers lingering yet light.

When I found my voice – or some small shadow of it – I asked, "Who won?"

He made no attempt to move from where his face was buried in my tangled hair. "Does it fucking matter? That wasn't even sex. It was like having an epiphany of perfection." His breath was ragged and hot on my neck. "I'll never win anything after that."

That sounded about right to me.

*****

Jackson opened his eyes and glanced at the clock next to the bed. It was just after three in the morning. Despite wanting nothing more than to stay in bed with Jenna, he knew it was time to get up. He had only intended to stay until she fell asleep, not the entire night...despite her earlier request.

He wouldn't be able to concentrate on whatever it was between them while he still had so many lingering doubts about his partner tickling the back of his mind.

As quietly as possible, Jackson got out of bed and got dressed. He paused at the bed only long enough to kiss her forehead before leaving. It had been bothering him since he left the gala that he hadn't been able to find Dinsley after Jenna left. He had a feeling in his gut about the situation he knew he couldn't ignore any longer and he had a pretty good idea of what it was.

When Jackson got to FBI headquarters he was surprised to find his partner was hard at work in his office. "Burning the midnight oil, Dinsley?"

Dinsley looked up from the stack of papers on his desk, obviously startled. "I had to finish something. What are you doing here, Caldwell?"

Jackson sat on the edge of his desk and glanced at the files. "Apparently, I'm doing the same thing here that you are. I think that Jonathan Price is really..."

"Parker Ramsey," Dinsley interrupted. "I know."

"You know?"

He sighed. "Yes and I have for quite some time now."

"And he's not in custody...why?"

"He's working on our side, Caldwell."

"Excuse me?"

"I said that he's working on our..."

"I heard you," Jackson snapped, cutting him off. "What I want to know is why I'm just now finding out about this."

"Okay. Shut the door and I'll tell you."

Jackson raised an eyebrow. "Why? We're the only people here."

Dinsley stood and crossed the room to the door. Once it was shut he replied, "I have to make sure I take every precaution. No one in this office knows about the deal I made."

"Really? I always had you pegged as a straight arrow," Jackson replied as he sat in one of the chairs.

Dinsley crossed the room back to his desk and took his seat before he said, "That assumption is mainly right, except I know you've had me pegged as anything but. I only made the deal to help capture Raptor. Once he's in my custody, I planned to fill in everyone else about the deal I'd made. It's a lot more difficult to reprimand someone who just caught a notorious bank robber."

Jackson looked at his partner incredulously, but didn't respond.

He closed the file he was reading and then continued. "I know you pulled my file and I'd like to know why."

Jackson shrugged. "You weren't giving me a lot to work with and, frankly, you were looking damn suspicious. I think I have a right to know whether my partner is on the right side of the law or not."

"I suppose you're referring to the administrative leave I was placed on."

Jackson nodded.

"My partner was killed during a bust that went bad. I didn't handle it well and they put me on leave."

"I'm sorry to hear that. I know what it feels like." While death was nothing new in his profession, the death of his last partner cut him to his core.

"Oh, yeah, I forgot you were partnered with Agent McShae when he died. He was a good man, but you don't have any idea what I'm talking about." Dinsley's voice was sterner than made sense.

"All right then, paint me the picture."

"Strictly off the record, Sophia and I were in love. You know the Bureau's policy on that as well as I do, so I don't need to explain why my superiors couldn't understand my inability to get past her death."

Jackson knew what policy he was referring to. The FBI had zero tolerance for interoffice romance. It caused complications that could potentially get in the way of good police work.

And good judgment.

"Okay. So why are you so attached to this case?" Jackson asked.

"After the First Alliance robbery, I was called back from leave and partnered with this cocky Quantico punk. I think I got close to finding Raptor at least a dozen times, but he always seemed to be one step ahead of me. We found out a while back that my partner had been on the take. We weren't able to prove if he was working for Raptor because he skipped town before we could arrest him, but I've always thought he was. I know I would have nailed Raptor if I had just realized my partner was dirty sooner." He shook his head. "I'm a better agent than that." Squeezing his eyes shut, he added, "Sophia would've been ashamed of me for missing the obvious like that."

"And that's why you asked to stay assigned to this case," Jackson concluded for him, sidestepping the apparent emotional time bomb ticking away in front of him.

Dinsley grinned. "You aren't as dumb as you look."

Jackson folded his arms over his chest. "No, I'm not, but I think we're going to have our work cut out for us if we keep running separate investigations. You fill me in on what you've got and I'll do the same. Deal?"

"Deal," Dinsley agreed. "We'd better get started. There's a lot you don't know."

Jackson narrowed his eyes. "Ditto."

"Well that was certainly unexpected," Parker said, still trying to catch his breath.

I couldn't fault him for that. How long did it take before we finally wore ourselves out in what he described as perfection? My muscles would probably ache from the exertion in the morning, but it was worth it – completely and totally worth it. In fact, I still didn't know how he got the pillows down to the foot of the bed and covers over us. Good thing he did though. There was no way I would've had the energy to crawl back up to the top of the bed after that.

I propped myself up on my elbow and smiled down at him. "Oh, come now. You had to expect that we were bound to do that sooner or later. I know I did."

He looked up at me and returned my smile. "It never occurred to me." Before I could call him on an obvious lie, he added, "I thought about getting you in my bed, of course, but it was never like that even in my wildest fantasies." His smile faded. "You never seemed...*approachable*. Not before tonight, anyway. I figured you hated me."

Resting my head against his chest, I thought about what he said. At the beginning, I really did hate him, or at least, the thief in him. However, he was not the man who put a bullet in my father's chest. Except for the fact he was a criminal, he wasn't a bad guy.

"I didn't realize you would have to think so hard about that one...especially now," Parker said. "Guess that's my answer."

"Sorry, I was thinking...I don't hate you. I don't know that I ever really did."

Parker kissed my forehead and changed the subject. "Didn't you say you needed to talk to me about something?"

"I think I might have said something like that, but why are you in such a hurry to get back down to business?" A smile tugged at my lips. "I'm still completely nude and you want to talk shop."

He moved his hand down the length of my back, softly tracing a finger down my spine. When the familiar shiver chased his finger, I could almost hear the smile in his voice. "I'm not, trust me, but I thought it might be nice to get that part out of the way so there aren't any distractions later."

"So...pending business can distract you from me, but I can't distract you from business? That is wrong on so many levels."

"No, you definitely know how to distract me...from everything." He sighed. "Besides, I need a minute here."

So did I. I still wasn't convinced I wouldn't die after that.

"Okay, then. I wanted to find out if you noticed anything strange at the gala. I think I have it narrowed down to three suspects, but I was hoping you could help me narrow it down further."

Parker appeared thoughtful when he spoke. "Who are the three?"

"Eric Sauters, Drake Wyndham, and Trevor Brightman. They all seemed to have a strange reaction to your presence at the gala."

"You're right," Parker said quietly. "It is one of them."

I tried to hide the shock I felt, but knew I failed. "What?"

"I've suspected Raptor's true identity from the moment I met him this evening. He confirmed it for me when you were talking to Michael."

It suddenly occurred to me that I was naked and a feeling of self-consciousness – my first of the night – washed over me. I sat up and clutched the sheet against my chest. Parker placed a hand on my shoulder, but I shook it off.

"Why didn't you tell me?" I demanded as I scanned the room for my clothes.

"I did tell you," he countered.

"Don't you think you could have told me before I took my clothes off?"

"You didn't give me much of an opportunity. Besides, I tried to tell you and you told me it could wait until later. What's wrong with you all of the sudden?"

I jumped out of the bed, pulling the sheet with me. "I don't know where my clothes are. That's what's wrong with me," I snapped.

Parker leaned over the side of the bed and said, "They're over here and over there and by the door."

"Didn't give you a chance. You could've told me when you walked me to my car...or in the stairwell...or the elevator." I hurried to retrieve the articles of clothing from the floor, but I didn't have the patience for stockings. I knew I needed to get out of here and now. I picked up my trench coat and wrapped it around me.

I could hear Parker pulling on his pants behind me, not bothering to defend himself against my unreasonable rant. He couldn't have told me in the stairwell or the elevator. That would've required him to not be kissing every last shred of logic from my head.

Once I fastened the coat, I turned around and asked, "Who is it?"

Parker didn't respond right away. I was so angry. He knew that the purpose of the evening for me was to find out Raptor's true identity. It infuriated me that he didn't tell me the second we were alone. He could have waited the extra five minutes to lick whipped cream off of me.

"I can't tell you."

His voice was so soft when he spoke, it took a moment for his words to register in my exhausted brain. "Why the hell not?"

Parker walked up to me and tried to put his arms around me in an attempt to calm me. The temptation to let him was strong, but I resisted. Parker was not going to get out of this without an explanation.

And it had better be damn good.

"Well?" I demanded sharply.

"If I tell you who it is, I'll just put you in danger."

"I think it's a little late for that now. Just tell me."

"I can't. If I tell you, I know you won't be able to pretend you don't know."

"So what? The whole point of this was to find out who Raptor is. I can't believe you're double-crossing me like this."

I watched as anger flashed through his eyes. Fear is probably what I should feel, but I was too angry to feel anything else. Everything I had spent so much time searching for was within my grasp and he was trying to take it away from me.

"I can't believe you would say that to me, Skylar. I know what it feels like to be betrayed at the end of the game and I would never do that to someone I was working with," Parker said in earnest. "Especially not you."

Yeah, like I was supposed to believe that I meant so much to him after a few hours between the sheets. "If you'll steal, you'll lie. Now quit playing games with me and tell me who Raptor is."

"I can't do that. I don't think you've given this any thought."

"You're kidding. Right?" I snapped. "I haven't thought about anything else since the day he murdered my father."

"What are you going to do once I tell you who he is?"

I didn't have an answer for him. Parker was right that I hadn't thought that part through. I always assumed once I knew who it was that I would figure out what to do next.

Parker continued without waiting for me to respond. "Raptor is a prominent citizen in this town. I'm the only proof you have that he's Raptor, but as you say, I'm expected to lie. If I tell you and you kill him; you'll only create a headache for yourself. The police aren't going to let his murder go unsolved. I think you know that."

Did he always have to be right?

"I suppose you have a plan."

"I've had a plan the entire time," he answered.

"And you didn't think you should let me in on it." I knew I was right before he responded.

"I couldn't be sure I could trust you with it."

Was this a joke? "That is one hell of a thing for you to say to me."

"Look. Once you've been burnt you tend to be more careful." Then he quickly added, "It wasn't personal."

"Fine. I'm going home now and you can go meet up with your good buddy Raptor."

"I don't appreciate your implication."

"I don't care," I said as I snatched up the last of my belongings and stormed out of his room. "You can both go to hell."

Parker followed me out of the hotel room just as the elevator was opening. "Skylar...just come back inside so we can talk. You're making this into a bigger deal than it needs to be."

"No, I'm finally seeing things the way they really are." I shook my head as I turned to face him from inside the elevator. As the doors started to close, I added, "You are *exactly* the man I thought you were."

ELEVEN

For once, fortune was smiling down on me during my drive home. No cops. I whipped in and out of the sparse traffic I encountered, narrowly avoiding several collisions. My mind was still reeling from Parker's betrayal.

A car was on the street in front of my townhouse when I arrived and...Wait. It wasn't just any car; it was *his* car. How did he beat me here? Pissed off, I cut the engine and jumped out. He grabbed my arm on my way to the door, but I shook him off.

"Skylar, we need to talk about this."

"No, you need to get the hell off of my property before I call the cops and report a prowler," I snapped back.

I slammed the front door in his face and went into my room to change...well, put something on, I should say. Parker was waiting for me when I came back into the living room. I could feel the blood pounding in my ears when I saw him and I knew he could tell how enraged I still was.

The look on his face said it all.

"I thought I told you to get out of here." I fought to keep my voice measured, dispassionate. Really, it was a fight not to reach for something close at hand to throw at him.

"This is stupid."

"No, this is Texas and we shoot to kill intruders here."

He rolled his eyes. "You and I both know you don't have a gun."

"Fine, but I have a big ass knife in the kitchen." Somewhere.

"Am I really supposed to believe you're going to stab me? Or that you really believe you could stab me if you wanted to?" He shot me the same look one might give a petulant child. "Whenever you're done playing games..."

"Oh, I'm not playing games, but I am done with you. I told you to get out. I meant it. Goodbye."

"You did, but I'm not going anywhere until we talk this through."

I placed my hands on my hips. "Unless you are planning to tell me who Raptor really is, you have nothing to say that I care to hear."

"Dammit, Skylar! We both know this isn't about that, but that it's about what went on between us." He advanced on me, but seemed to think better of touching me and stopped short, running his fingers through his hair in an awkward gesture. "Things got real between us and you can't handle that I'm not at arm's length anymore."

Yeah, that was part of it. No matter how much I wanted to deny it, it was still true. The way he'd put back on his shirt but left it untucked and unbuttoned, giving me a glimpse of the hard body underneath was almost enough to distract me. Almost.

"Don't flatter yourself." I shook my head. "It was just sex. You were tension relief after a busy few weeks. You're nothing more than the first available guy I ran into when I needed to get laid."

"You're trying to con a con. Don't you understand that we don't have time for games right now?"

Why was it that he got to lie to me and then act like I was an unreasonable child for being pissed off about it?

"You're right," I yelled, gesturing my hand back and forth between us. "*We* don't have any time because there is no more *we*. It's over. Get out."

"No. Raptor is within our grasp. Quitting is not an option. Not anymore, Skylar."

"Since when?"

"You were committed the moment you pretended to be my date at the gala tonight. Now, you'll just blow my cover with Raptor."

"Not my problem."

"Yes, Skylar, it is. If my cover's blown, so is yours. That means he turns into a wraith in the wind and we both lose our shot at taking him down." The muscle in his jaw tensed when he paused. "The only thing you're accomplishing right now is signing our death warrants."

I let out a deep breath in an attempt to control my temper. Sure, I was mad as hell, but I couldn't say I wanted to see him dead. "What do you want from me, Price?"

He looked at my slyly. "Actually, I want a lot of things from you, Skylar, but mostly I just want you. Naked. In my bed. Preferably with a side of strawberries." His shoulders shrugged a little. "Or your bed. It's closer. I'm not picky."

A sensual fire burned in his eyes as he stared at me, holding my gaze in such a way that I couldn't avert my eyes or turn away. With our eyes locked across the few feet of sizzling, intense space between us, I knew his mind was replaying how we'd spent the last few hours for him in vivid detail. There was no way he didn't know I was thinking about the same thing.

When I didn't respond, he added, "But I can see everything I want will be out of the question until I can regain your trust."

"You never had my trust."

"Have it your way. I need Songbird if this is going to work."

I glared at him. "Fine. You can have Songbird, but you'd better keep your damn hands, strawberries and anything else you can think of off me."

"Done."

Damn. That was faster agreement than I expected. "But, I have one condition."

"I'm still not telling you who Raptor is."

I shot him a dirty look. We wouldn't be standing here fighting if I thought I'd get him to cave that easily. "I'm not playing your little games anymore, Price. If I'm in, you're going to tell me exactly what the plan is. I want every last detail of how you plan to bring Raptor down." I paused for deliberate effect. "You want me to trust you? Give me a reason."

Parker looked me directly in the eyes and told me everything.

Except for Raptor's identity.

Parker let out a sigh of relief as he got into his car and drove back to the hotel. Giving into temptation almost cost him everything, but at least he was able to semi-smooth things over with Skylar. The situation could've gone bad very quickly if he hadn't.

As it was, he wasn't excited about the keeping his hands off her part of the deal. Not now. Not when he knew just how good they were together.

He swore under his breath and changed lanes before picking up his cell phone. Chill answered after only one ring. "S'up?"

"Songbird is in all the way," Parker said swiftly.

"Hmm...I can only imagine what you had to do to make that happen, Ramsey," Chill replied.

"Not now, Chill. I'm not in the mood. We could have a situation on our hands."

"Oh? Besides your need to bed every attractive woman you meet?"

He ignored that, unwilling to let his friend goad him into a re-action. "Cherry Sims is with Raptor now." Parker waited for the back-lash from his statement.

"That filthy little tramp! What kind of damned whore would fuck the guy who killed her fiancé? I ought to find her and..."

"Don't finish that sentence," Parker warned. "She's on our side and she's in."

"Oh. Well, in that case, things are just peppermint candy fresh, aren't they then?" Chill's voice was back to its usual cool demeanor.

"Here's the deal. Raptor knows about me now. Tomorrow is business as usual, but we take it underground on Monday. Things are going to go down fast now that the players are in place."

"I told you I would stay available. We get dirty on Monday," Chill replied before disconnecting the call.

Parker smiled slightly as he dialed another number. He let it ring once and hung up. Within two minutes, his phone rang.

"Skylar's. Monday."

The stage was set.

I went to bed as soon as Parker left, but I did not sleep. The de-tails of the plan stayed on my mind for a long time. It was something I never would have thought up. Then again, I wasn't a criminal.

There was definite merit to Parker's plan. I knew it would cap-ture Raptor's interest and the end game would keep him hooked until the very end, but there were so many intricacies that would have to go off without a hitch for it to work.

My involvement as Songbird was one of them.

I wanted Raptor so badly I could taste it. There would be nothing more satisfying than seeing him behind bars for the rest of his life, but I didn't know if I was really capable of what I would have to do to bring him to his knees. With the exception of my reckless driving, I was a law-abiding citizen and this plan was borderline illegal.

Who did I think I was kidding? The plan was illegal as hell.

Parker was another variable I couldn't gauge. Despite marching myself right up to his room and jumping into bed with him, I most certainly did not trust him. Honestly, I had no idea what I was thinking in the first place. I suppose I wasn't thinking at all.

The one silver lining I had on this storm cloud was Parker's assurance things would be over quickly now. Once we set the trap, it would only be a matter of days before Raptor was at our mercy. Within a week, Parker would be out of my life.

As I drifted off to sleep, I tried to decide if that was a good thing.

I normally liked to attend a power yoga class on Sunday mornings, but I was still in bed after three that afternoon. Fighting - among other things - with Parker had taken a lot out of me and I was exhausted. Besides, I reasoned I'd already gotten in my workout for the day.

Maybe for a few days...

Or a lifetime. Damn. I'd never had sex like that before. Doubtful I ever would again.

Parker picked me up at five-thirty and I gave him the silent treatment during the ride to Reyna's house. He tried to make light conversation a few times, but he finally gave up and turned on the radio to a talk program featuring a host with what may well be the most monotone voice on the airwaves. Might've been talking about the previous week on Wall Street, but I couldn't pay attention long enough to focus on it.

If Parker honestly believed I'd wake up magically not still pissed off at him...

He pulled over to the side of the road just short of Reyna's massive circular drive. "Pull it together."

"Excuse me?"

"Look, you can hate me all you want in private, but you need to get a grip before we go in there. You know as well as I do that Raptor's in there."

"I didn't realize Raptor was so concerned about your love life."

He shot me a scathing look before rolling his eyes. "Not a person alive, least of all Raptor, is going to buy us as a couple. Much less the couple we were last night."

"I don't see the problem."

"You don't see..." His exasperation with me was plain on his face. "You were into me last night at the gala. Now, you can't even look at me without scowling."

"Oh...so you want all the tension and anticipation?"

"I'd like you to fake it, yes."

"We had sex. Tension and anticipation are gone."

"Skylar..."

I shook my head at him. "Stop talking to me like I'm five. "Nobody's going to buy that we didn't hit the sheets after the way we were carrying on last night. If we go in there acting like we did last night, they're bound to think something's wrong with us."

"Fine." He bit out the word like it tasted of rancid vinegar. "That explains the lack of sexual tension between us." His eyes locked on mine. "That doesn't explain why you're acting so hostile."

"Maybe you were bad in bed."

Parker started to respond, but instead put the car in gear and pulled into the driveway. "Whatever you need to tell yourself." Once he parked, he added, "But it would be easier for you to plaster a smile on your face and pretend to like me. It'll save you from having to explain to everyone that I was bad in bed...with a straight face."

"Do you have to be so cocky?"

"From how vocal you were last night, I was under the impression you enjoyed that."

"This conversation is over. Reminisce about last night on your own time, not mine."

Reyna greeted us warmly once we reached the door, but she had to attend to something in the kitchen and instructed us to get comfy. I decided to do just that and started wandering. My father once told me you could tell everything about a person from their home. I imagined the thought would stroll through my mind unbidden every time I visited someone's home for the first time.

Thinking of Dad was good, especially right now. It would help me keep my anger in check with Parker in front of the others. If he could help me destroy the monster who killed my father, I could give him sappy looks at the dinner table.

I guess I wandered off farther than I intended because I found myself in what was the study, judging from the numerous bookcases filled with expensive looking leather-bound books, books that probably hadn't been read. A painting on the wall to my left caught my attention. I was scrutinizing a painting of the Trojan War when the door closed with the faintest of clicks.

I felt a pair of strong arms encircle my waist and I let out an exaggerated sigh. "I'm not in the mood for this, Price."

"Then I guess it's a good thing I'm not him," Eric whispered in my ear.

I freed myself from his embrace and spun around to face him. "What are you doing?"

"You know we belong together, Skylar."

"I'm with someone."

His eyes were hypnotic when he spoke. "And? You aren't serious about him. You can't be. It's not us."

"There is no us, Eric. Not for years now."

"If I had a say back then, there would be." He sighed and cleared the building emotion from his throat. "What are you even doing with this guy?"

"I enjoy his company. Besides, you're with Reyna."

"I don't have to be." The back of his hand brushed across my cheek. "She isn't you. Skylar…it was always you for me. Only you."

Eric tried to pull me into his arms again, but I pushed him back with one hand and stepped away. The deadening of my emotions was the one good thing to come from Parker's betrayal. I was now void of my former foolish romantic notions.

"Eric, I don't give a damn whether you're with Reyna or not, but I'm not going to give you a reason. I have a lot of respect for her and, what's more…I like her." Belatedly, I added, "I like my boyfriend, too."

"I don't believe you."

Yeah, I probably could've mustered a little more feeling for that one.

"It doesn't matter what you believe. We both moved on and it was hard for me to rise up from the rock bottom crap I lived through. I don't want to go backwards." I took a breath, grasping for the words I'd need to let him go. To get him to let me go. "You're in my past. He's in my present. That's just how it is."

"And I could be in your future." He gathered the hand I'd used to push him away into his hands and took a step forward, nearly closing the chasm between us. "Skylar…"

"I can't."

"Stop thinking about everyone else's happiness before your own." He pressed my hand against his heart. "This has always been yours."

"Eric, I...*can't.*"

"You can."

The tension had been ratcheting up since he came in and I had to stop it. While I wasn't really feeling my emotions right now, I knew they were still there, simmering below the surface.

"If you're really over me, if you're really sure you'd rather have this other guy instead of everything we had together, what we could still have together...stop me from kissing you."

Out of the corner of my eye, I saw the door to the study open. This had to look bad to anyone walking in on it, but I hoped it wasn't Reyna. I was sure Eric would realize the mistake he was making right now once he came back to his senses.

Fortunately, it was just Parker.

He shot me a worried look, but I smiled at him, waving him over to us while Eric casually released my hand. "I'm so glad you found me, sweetie. You have to take a look at this painting. It's like the one you were telling me about last month, right?"

Might as well make it sound like we'd been together longer than the few weeks I'd known him.

Parker walked over to us and slid an arm across my shoulders, electrifying my skin while positioning himself between Eric and I. Turning his attention to the painting. "You're right. It's from the same collection. Good eye...and memory, sweetheart." It could be my imagination, but his little term of endearment sounded very much like a man staking his claim in front of the competition. "Everyone has arrived and I think Reyna wants us all in one place."

"I'm sure you're right. Excuse me," Eric said, slipping out of the room with haste.

Once he was gone, Parker let his arm drop from my shoulder and asked, "What did I just walk in on, Skylar?"

"An old boyfriend who probably had too much wine before we got here, that's all."

"It damn well better be. I'm the only man you have time for until we see this through to the end."

"See what through? The plan or your desire to keep talking about last night's mistake?"

He shook his head at me, eyes gleaming with, I don't know, non-specific male pissed-offness at being questioned, I guess. "Don't be stupid. You're too smart to pull that one off."

"O-*kay?*"

Rather than answering my question, he continued as though I'd never said anything at all. "And next time an ex has too much wine, be a little more convincing about who you're with instead of wavering the way you were when I walked in."

I shot him a sidelong glance. "Jealous?"

When Parker didn't respond, I moved past him to the door. "Does this situation ever get less fucked up?" I paused with my hand on the knob. "I'm so ready not to have to think about this crap anymore."

Before I could turn the knob, Parker's hands were at either side of my head, one palm glued to the wall, the other holding the door shut. I turned to meet the intensity in his eyes. "I thought I told you to keep your hands off me."

An arrogant smile spread across his features. "You'll notice neither hand is on you."

"Technicality. Move."

"Nope." He shook his head, still grinning. "If you don't want to think, you know I can help you with it...mistake or not. Come back to the hotel with me after dinner and I'll make sure you don't have to think about anything until the sun comes up."

"Get over yourself."

"Why? You're not."

I opened my mouth to protest, but snapped it shut when he moved closer. He wasn't touching me, but if there were an inch of open air between any part of our bodies, I'd be shocked.

His lips hovered just a hair's breadth away from mine and I released the doorknob, unsure whether I should push him away or pull him close.

After too many seconds ticked by, he lowered his hand to the knob. "It's your call. I can take you home or you can come with me." He opened the door and turned back to me with a look of deadly seriousness. "Take that whichever way you like."

People began to scatter once dinner was over. For a while, Parker stayed at my side as we mingled, but after his offer in the study, the sexual tension level between us was back to almost unmanageable levels. Combined with the way he insisted on keeping his arm around my shoulders, fingers grazing the bare skin of my arm, it was more than I could handle when I was trying to keep my resolve firm on having him take me straight home.

I wandered from conversation to conversation until I realized Drake was nowhere to be found. Neither was Chelsea. After the morsel of gossip Reyna told me about the two of them last night, I couldn't let it go when I saw Suzanne standing by herself. I decided to see what I could find out from her.

"How are you, Suzanne?"

"Bored, Skylar. What do you want?"

"Nothing. I just saw you standing by yourself and thought I'd come say hi." I pretended to look around. "Where's Drake?"

"I don't know, but I'm sure I don't care."

A comment like that was normally one said with scorn or irritation. It puzzled me that hers was monotone, bored. "Is everything all right?"

"I'm just tired of that little bitch."

I knew exactly who she was talking about, but I didn't want to let on that I knew more than I should about her marriage. "Excuse me?"

Suzanne narrowed her eyes at me. "Don't play innocent, Skylar, it doesn't become you. I'm sure the gossip mongers on the committee already filled you in on my husband's *recreational* activities."

She apparently didn't like to beat around the bush. "If you know, why are you still with him?"

She flashed a condescending smile my way. "Oh...you must still be idealistic enough to believe in love. I used to be that way, but then I turned eleven and got over it."

"Grim way to see the world."

"Look, I don't ask Drake about what he does in his spare time and he doesn't ask me what I do in mine." Suzanne paused to feign a smile at Elaine as she passed by us. When she was out of earshot, she continued, "Frankly, I don't care who he's with as long as it keeps him off me."

Wow.

"So, why did you even bother to marry him?"

She sipped her drink and gave me a condescending look. "Drake and I are what you might call a power couple. He had the drive and the degree. I had the brains and the breeding. It was a natural partnership. Besides, you don't get very far in this world with a last name like Zuckermann."

I shrugged. "Well, at least you know what you want...I guess."

"Very true. I give as good as I get and I have no intention of ending up like Reyna's mother. Lovely woman, by the way."

"What do you mean?"

"Her mother had no idea what she was getting herself into when she married into money. She tried to fit in, but she could never accept her husband's *behavior*. He would gallivant around town, throwing his affairs in her face." She shook her head in disgust. "I think that man made a point to show up with his new mistress at whichever restaurant his wife went for dinner." After a beat, "On the same night."

Poor Reyna. My parents had their share of arguments, but they never lasted more than a week, were never in front of me and never involved an affair. I couldn't imagine what it would be like to grow up in that atmosphere.

"It's such a pity Reyna is going to end up just like her," Suzanne said absently, gaze resting on Drake as he reentered the room.

Now that I thought about it, Reyna never mentioned her parents – at least, not in the present tense. "What happened to them?"

"Her father is in Europe with his new toy girlfriend and her mother is in a psychiatric hospital. She had a breakdown and never recovered."

That sucked. "Why would Reyna end up that way?"

"Look at those three, thick as thieves. It's so obvious he doesn't love her. I don't think that man loves anything."

I followed her gaze to where Drake, Trevor and Eric were talking on the far side of the room. "What makes you think that?"

"It's in his eyes, dear. Take a real look at them sometime. Now, if you'll excuse me, I must speak with Elaine before she leaves."

After Suzanne walked away, I did just as she told me, finding a corner of the room where I would be able to study Eric without him being able to see me. Parker caught my eye across the room, followed my line of sight, then shook his head at me while Daniel was looking away. I could already hear him chastising me for trying to figure it out on the ride home.

And home it would be. I wasn't going back to the hotel with him. I wasn't.

Probably...

Turning my attention away from Parker, I looked into Eric's eyes. I tried to focus on what was within, not just on surface details like color and shape. No, watching him while he didn't know he was being observed – and wasn't trying to win me back – I thought I might understand what Suzanne meant.

Although Eric was on my list of suspects, I never honestly believed he would be capable of something so terrible. I mean, my almost fiancé robbing a bank and murdering my father? That was an absurd notion, especially since I was basing my suspect list on reactions to Parker's appearance at the gala.

And how else would I really expect Eric to react to me showing back up in his life with a boyfriend? I'm sure it didn't help the reactions stay normal when Parker always managed to walk up on us when Eric was in the middle of making a move on me. Considering Eric had a girlfriend of his own to worry about finding out, how could I expect him not to get away from the two of us as fast as possible?

So, it was really nothing more than a formality for me to keep him on my list. However, I needed to look into his eyes as an impartial observer rather than a woman who was still in love with him if I was going to see what Suzanne saw. At first glance, there was nothing out of place, but something changed in his expression and I knew the truth.

Eric Sauters was a man capable of committing murder. Now, I just had to figure out if he already had.

TWELVE

For the first time in months, Jackson felt like his life was finally back on track. Jenna was annoyed he'd been gone when she awoke Sunday morning and he had to spend part of the day working, but she understood once he explained why. Knowing his partner was on the right side of the law lifted a huge weight off his shoulders.

To make it up to her, he made a quiet dinner for them at his apartment. The intent was to give them time to have the conversation they needed to have, to give them a fresh start at trying to make a real go of it this time around. The reality was barely getting to finish his explanation of why he had to leave in the middle of the night before they ended up in bed.

Watching her get dressed shortly after midnight to head home nearly killed him...

When Jackson arrived at Headquarters on Monday morning, one look at the expression on Dinsley's face told him his high spirits over being able to see Jenna again that night wouldn't last for very long.

"We have a problem," Dinsley said sharply as he led Jackson into his office and closed the door. "Ramsey is gone."

"What do you mean he's gone?"

"One of our informants called me this morning to let me know Raptor and Ramsey are working together again. I tried his cell phone, but the number was disconnected. I just got confirmation he's checked out of the hotel."

"How did he slip past the tail we had on him?"

"Probably easily since there wasn't anyone watching him."

Jackson lifted an eyebrow. "Excuse me?"

Dinsley sighed. "He approached me. We all thought he was dead, so I assumed he wouldn't burn his cover and risk prison if he wasn't being straight with me."

"Have you called Skylar yet? I would almost guarantee this involves her," Jackson said. From the glimpse he caught of the two of them on the balcony at the gala, he was willing to bet this was anything but just business between them.

Dinsley nodded. "I got her voicemail. If I don't get a call back soon, I'll drive over in person and wake her up."

"You said you thought Ramsey was trying to pull her into his scheme to catch Raptor. Do you think he might cut ties with her as well?"

He shrugged. "After the surveillance tapes I had pulled from hotel security, I'd say she probably knows something more than we do." His face creased into a thoughtful scowl. "And whatever it was, she didn't like it."

Jackson couldn't ask for details because of a soft knock on the door.

"Yeah," Dinsley responded, voice gruff as ever.

An intern poked his head into the room and said, "Miss Montgomery is holding on line two for you. She said she was returning your call."

After the intern left the room, Dinsley pulled a headset from his desk and plugged it into the phone. Once Jackson put it on, Dinsley picked up the receiver and said, "Dinsley."

"What the hell is going on?"

"I was hoping you could fill me in on that," Dinsley replied, the picture of Zen, despite the nightmare they were in with Ramsey gone and working with Raptor.

"I just called Ramsey's hotel and they told me he checked out. I need to get in touch with him." There was an edge to her voice, one Jackson only heard when his younger sister was about to come completely unhinged with rage. "Where did you move him to?"

Jackson caught Dinsley's attention and mouthed, "She doesn't know."

Dinsley nodded and said, "I'm afraid that information is classified."

"Classified? Are you kidding me with this..." She let her voice trail off and paused in an obvious attempt to calm herself. "Fine. Then maybe you wouldn't mind giving him a message for me. You can tell him I did my part. I got him an invitation to the gala, but that's as far as I'm willing to take this. God knows I want Raptor behind bars more than anyone else, but this is all getting too close for me. I truly hope that you guys catch him, I really do, but I'm not ready to end up dead too. Tell Ramsey I'm out of this from now on."

"When did you decide that?" Dinsley pressed.

"What difference does that make?"

"I was just curious if you had your change of heart before or after you followed him up to his room."

Skylar was quiet for a long moment. "How the...surveillance tapes. Did you get an eyeful, Dins?" She regained her composure. "Look, everyone is entitled to a momentary lapse of judgment."

"Or a three-hour lapse, in your case," Dinsley offered.

Jackson was grateful they weren't having this conversation in person. His partner was entering a realm he didn't want to be in, not with a woman who undoubtedly wouldn't think twice before trying to beat a federal agent senseless.

"I was drunk. Extremely so, if you must know. Besides, I hardly see what my sex life has to do with your investigation."

Dinsley grinned, but managed to keep his tone serious. "I'm not fishing for details, Miss Montgomery, but I am interested in why you left in so much of a hurry you felt it necessary to carry your clothes."

"I have got to see these tapes," Jackson mouthed to his partner.

"We had a disagreement."

"About?"

"Let's just say I thought he understood how I felt about the man who murdered my father, but I don't think we see eye to eye on that."

"I see. When was the last time you saw him?"

"Last night when he brought me home from a party at Reyna's house. I told him I was out, but I want you to make sure he understands I meant it. I don't want him to come near me again."

"Do you have some reason to believe he didn't understand you?"

For the first time, she hesitated. "Yeah...I do." After a lengthy pause, "Let's just say he was pushing me for a repeat of what happened after the gala. I refused. He was pissed. Things got a little handsy in the car and I had to walk the last few blocks home. So, yeah...I have no idea if he was listening to anything I had to say because he sure didn't seem concerned about what I wanted." Another pause. "Or didn't want."

"Miss Montgomery..."

"No. No more questions. I'm out of this. You can't keep using me as a pawn in your investigation into a man I'm not convinced you'll ever be able to catch. Just keep Ramsey the hell away from me from now on," Skylar ordered before hanging up.

Jackson looked at his partner with concern. "How did she even get involved in all this?" If Ramsey had gone too far with her and she reported his behavior to anyone in the Bureau, things would get bad for Dinsley. He didn't have to say it to know his partner was already thinking it.

He shook his head. "I don't know the whole story. Ramsey said he needed someone to get him inside Raptor's world. I never thought it was a good idea to involve Skylar, but he said he was able to convince her he wanted to take out Raptor. She's had a rough time of it since her parents died. I guess she wanted some closure on the situation and figured this guy might be able to give it to her."

"Do you believe her story? That she doesn't know where he is?" Jackson asked.

"I don't know, Caldwell."

"What are we going to do about this? If we show up at her door in person and she's telling the truth then we blow it. If we let it go and she's lying, we blow it."

"Tell me something I don't know." He shook his head. "I can't order surveillance on her house without revealing that I made an off the books deal with a wanted criminal."

"So unless you and I take turns staking her out..."

"Yeah, that's about the long and the short of it."

"Shit." Jackson paced the room until he could think of something more productive to say than the string of profanity running through his head. "Do you want me to see if Jenna can get someone to watch Skylar's place for us?"

"Yes...No...Fuck, I don't know anymore. I'd like to believe she sobered up, came to her senses and realized what she was doing, but...I don't know."

*****

"So, how was that?"

"You could have been more convincing, but I think they'll still buy it." Price shrugged and kept an even tone, but he looked annoyed. "I can't believe you turned me into some kind of sex-starved would-be rapist."

"Whatever," I replied. "You did make the offer. I just jazzed it up a little."

"Yes...an offer. That's not the same as trying to force you. My hands were never on you."

That man didn't have to use his hands when his body language was persuasive enough. Almost too persuasive. "Well...you think Dinsley would've bought my insistence that they keep you away from me if I'd mentioned you never touched me?"

His eyes narrowed, but he didn't respond right away. "The drunk comment was uncalled for. I don't take advantage of drunk women. And you and I both know you didn't have enough to drink to impair *anything*."

I ignored the barb and looked at his suitcases in the middle of the living room, growing even more annoyed. It felt like they'd been sitting there for hours already. "Are you ever going to put those up?"

"You never told me where I was staying, so I don't know where I'm supposed to unpack."

I sighed as I considered what to do about that problem. Even though I had a spare bedroom, I never bothered to furnish it. Of course, I couldn't if I wanted to. The townhouse's second story was meant to be a master suite, but I used it as storage and slept in the downstairs bedroom. All the things from my parents' house...I wasn't ready to part with them and I couldn't stomach the thought of letting them rot in a dingy public storage unit.

Besides, I was never a fan of stairs.

"I still don't see why you have to stay here, Price." I kept my eyes fixed on his luggage for an excuse to not meet his eyes. "This is Dallas. You can't tell me there isn't another place you could stay."

"We went through this last night."

"I know, but I'm not convinced yet." I lifted my eyes to his. "We also went through you trying to get me back in bed last night. You'll have to forgive me for being wary."

"Skylar, if it was really just about me trying to get laid, I wouldn't bother hiding out here under false pretense." He shook his head. "Too much work for my taste."

"I'm suddenly too much work?"

"Any woman who makes it clear she's not interested is too much work. My bed only stays empty when I choose for it to. I don't have to waste time trying to convince women why they should share my bed for the night."

Well...nice for him. Nice, but irrelevant. "Whenever your ego's done talking, I'd love an answer to my original question."

Price glared at me for a long moment. I couldn't tell if he was pissed off at me because I'd questioned his motives or because my clothes weren't magically falling off because we were in the same room. "Look, I think we can both agree the FBI will just screw up the plan if we involve them. As long as Dinsley knew where I was, there was always the chance he would pop up at the wrong time and get in the way."

"Couldn't you just stay with Chill? Seems like you know each other pretty well."

"Would you want to live with Chill if you didn't have to?" I shrugged my answer and he continued. "It doesn't matter. I don't have to prep Chill, but I do have to make sure you're ready for all this. Besides, Raptor thinks we're sleeping together. He would eventually think it was odd for me to be living in a hotel."

I cocked my head to the side. "Why would Raptor assume we're sleeping together?"

"Because everyone else does." He shrugged. "And probably because I told him we were."

When I remained silent, he added, "It's not like I'm asking you to *be* my girlfriend. I'm not even asking you to pay attention to me while I'm here. Unless we need to go over something, you're welcome to pretend I'm not even here."

"Fine. You can keep your stuff in my room, but you're sleeping on the couch," I snapped.

Price rose to his feet and glared at me. "I don't like your tone. I told you last night you didn't have anything to worry about from me while I was here and I meant it. I may be a con artist, but I do have my ethics. Rape and sexual coercion are not tools in my arsenal."

Rather than brushing by as I thought he'd do, he stopped close to me. "I wish you would quit treating me like I'm going to attack you at any minute. There were two of us in that hotel room Saturday night and you started just as much as I did. Until the moment you freaked out and ran out of the room, you were having as much fun as I was. Don't waste my time by pretending otherwise."

I watched him pick up his suitcases and storm into my room. I honestly didn't know why I was going out of my way to be so hateful to him. He was right...about all of it. It wasn't as though he raped me; I was a willing participant and probably even the instigator of the encounter.

And it was fun. A lot of fun.

Damn.

When Price came back into the living room, it appeared he was completely over his anger. I waited for him to tell me why he had his laptop out, but he turned it on in silence. After a minute he glanced up from it and said, "I know you don't eat anything except fast food, but I do. If you'll pick up a few things from the store, I'll take care of all of the cooking over the next week."

I looked at him skeptically. "So you're shooing me out of my own house to go to the store for you?"

"Well, yes. It isn't like I can go in the light of day."

I hated the grocery store, but it was still early enough to go without being caught in the crowds. I sighed and said, "All right. Make me a list and I'll go."

Price nodded and handed me a piece of paper. "I'm one step ahead of you."

That was nothing new. I took the list from him and waited for him to look my direction. He didn't. I sighed, loudly. Still not so much as a glance.

"How long can I expect you to be pissed off at me because I don't want to have sex with you?"

"I'm not pissed off." Eyes still focused on his computer screen.

"Well...whatever the hell you are then. How long?"

He cut his eyes to me. Shaking his head, he gave me his full attention. "Let's be clear about something, Skylar. Not wanting to have sex with someone isn't the same as telling yourself you don't want to have sex with them. I'll respect them both equally, of course, but I'm not going to help you lie to yourself about it." He turned his attention back to the computer. "But no, I'm not pissed off that you're trying to convince yourself that you don't want me. I'm just busy and would prefer you get the store out of the way while I don't have anything for you to do."

I opened my mouth to speak, but he cut me off before I could. "And until you're done trying to con yourself over there, you've made it very clear where we stand. We're business associates, not lovers, not even friends." He frowned at the screen and quickly hit a few keys.

"Don't set the boundaries if you're not okay with where you're putting them, sweetheart."

I left without another word.

Something occurred to me as I was getting into my car. I wasn't sure when I stopped thinking of him as Parker. It was odd to finally be used to what I was supposed to call him now that it didn't matter anymore. Of course, it was his real name.

Had to be. Right? Jonathan Price sounded real enough.

I guess.

Raptor drummed his fingers impatiently on his desk while he waited for Chill to answer. What it would be to have that man's life. No responsibilities in the light of day. No need to function by society's timetable.

But that was half the fun, wasn't it? To be part of society while working at the level above it all. Above everyone else.

Operating in plain sight of those who hunted him and those he hurt; talking to him without so much as an inkling of suspicion in the back of their minds.

"Speak."

"It's about time, Chill. I've been calling you all morning," Raptor snapped.

"Do not pop a blood vessel. I've been working a deal for you."

"Does that mean Songbird will meet with me?"

"It was tough to get her to do a face to face, but I finally got her to agree on one condition."

"And what might that be?" Raptor demanded.

"She wants me there."

"Done." Either she required a safety net or Chill thought too highly of his own importance. A bullet would knock him down a peg or two when the time came for tying loose ends. "Where and when?"

"Eleven-thirty tomorrow night. Frisco. The underground parking garage of the office building on the tollway and Gaylord."

"Un-uh. That's too early for a meet. Push it back two hours and you have a deal," Raptor countered.

"I will run it by the bird, but we will most likely see you then. Oh, she has a daisy of a plan worked out for you."

"Really?"

"You will be pleased," Chill answered.

He'd better be. Raptor was about to ask for details when his assistant knocked softly on the door before opening it. "I'm sorry sir, but Michael Traymoore is here to see you."

"Send him in," he replied. To Chill, "Must go. I'll see you tomorrow."

Parker was so intent on what he studied that he jumped slightly in surprise at the doorbell. He crept to the door, silent, and peeked through the viewer. When he saw who it was he breathed in a sigh of relief and opened the door.

Skylar could talk a good game, but not so good he was certain the FBI wouldn't be an ongoing issue.

"You were supposed to be here an hour ago," he snapped after he closed the door behind them.

"I know," Cherry responded, unusually upbeat for someone sleeping with the enemy, "but it couldn't be helped. Trevor is suspicious every time I go somewhere."

"Shouldn't he be?"

Cherry laughed. "Probably. Where should I set up?"

Parker thought about that for a moment as he looked around the room. "Dining room, I guess. Do you need an internet connection to encrypt?"

She shook her head. "Nope, I have better equipment than I used to. The wireless encryption I'm using is second only to the stuff the government uses." She patted her laptop. "And the connection is as close to untraceable as you can get. We'll be invisible to anyone looking before they know to look."

"Not bad, Cher," Parker said, nodding.

After setting up, Cherry asked, "So, I never would have figured Skylar as a part of the criminal element. You must've pulled one hell of a con on her."

"Why do you say that?"

"Oh...come on, Parker. There's something about people like us you can see in the eyes. A spark."

He considered that. "And you don't think Skylar has it?"

"No. Absolutely not." She shook her head for emphasis. "She looks so dull and refined. She doesn't strike me as someone who'd be interested in or able to pull off what we're doing."

"Then you should take a closer look, Chelsea. Price, take these bags before they cut my hands in half," Skylar said as she entered the room on her way to the kitchen.

Cherry shot him a questioning look, but he gave his head an almost imperceptible shake. Skylar, still struggling with groceries and annoyance, didn't seem to notice either. On the outside he didn't let his relief over that show. But on the inside?

It was a fucking party of relief.

Parker took the bags and fled into the kitchen with Skylar close at his heels. Skylar hadn't cared much for Cherry when they met at the gala. That much was obvious, but he hoped she'd be professional enough to overlook it. He meant to tell her she was coming over earlier in the morning, but let her behavior distract him from the task at hand.

Distraction. It was an all too familiar experience when it came to her.

"What's going on here, Price?" she demanded while they put away the groceries.

Parker sighed. "Her name is really Cherry Sims. She's with us on this."

"You think I care what her name is?" Skylar glared at him. "I thought I knew the whole plan."

"You do. I told you we needed to hack the system. Cherry is our hacker," Parker said defensively.

"She's a hacker," Skylar said, skeptical. "Isn't she a bit *blonde* for that?"

"I wasn't always a blonde, Sky," Cherry snapped as she leaned against the doorway to the kitchen. She lifted a strand of the bleached hair in front of her face to scrutinize before dropping it in disgust. "I only look this way to get better tips. Men prefer blondes."

"That's debatable," Parker said, casting a quick glance in Skylar's direction.

"Right." A small smile crept over her lips. "Men who aren't Parker prefer blondes." Her smile faded. "Don't let my appearance fool you. I happened to learn from the best."

Skylar folded her arms across her chest. "And who might that be?"

"My brother," Chill said, walking up behind Cherry.

I recognized the voice to be Chill's, but I definitely did not recognize the man standing in front of me. His usual red hair and red eyes were a stark contrast to the jet black hair and soft grey eyes. I had to admit he didn't look half bad as a normal person.

He noticed my confused stare and turned to me to say, "Aw, we've not met. I'm Crandall Covington and before you say anything I do not know what my parents were thinking with that."

"You look so…"

Chill flashed his usual smile and cut me off. "It would hardly have gone unnoticed for me to show up at your door in club attire." He turned his attention to Cherry. "Should you not be hacking or something since you don't have anyone to fuck?"

His statement rolled off her. "It's been a long time, Chill. How've you been?" I detected the cautiousness of her tone.

"Don't be coy, Cherry. I'm trying very hard to stop myself from ringing your neck, you damned whore."

"Oh really?" The insult seemed not to affect her.

"Have you no decency, Cher? How can you sleep with the man who killed my brother? I thought you loved him."

"Trevor?" I said in surprise.

Cherry looked over at me and rolled her eyes. She turned her attention back to Chill before responding, "I didn't get much of a choice. I could either turn him down and end up at the bottom of a lake, or I could defile myself and live another day. I chose the latter and now I get to take him down, you pompous prick. And yes, I do have a system to hack…and I loved him more than you'd ever understand."

With that, Cherry pushed passed him and went back to the dining room. I was utterly lost now. Even though she was with Trevor, I also knew she slept with Drake. It was possible she'd also slept with Eric. For all I knew, she'd been sleeping with Price this whole time. I was no closer to narrowing Raptor's identity down any further.

And, apparently, everyone knew who Raptor really was but me.

Awesome.

"So, you are Andrew Montgomery's kid? I imagine all of this is as personal for you as it is for the rest of us," Chill said softly.

I shot him an irritated look. "More."

I heard Price shut the refrigerator behind me. "That's the last of it. Are you thirsty, Chill?"

"I'm good, bro."

Price led us to the dining room where Cherry was working and we sat down. I still couldn't get over Chill's appearance. His skin actually had color to it.

And this was probably an insane thought to be having with three criminals sitting at my table, but it sounded like Chill's whole way of speaking was different. Less formal somehow.

Weird. I had a blonde hacker who didn't want to be a blonde, a guy who spoke in formal, cryptic tones when doing business as a red-eyed crazy man and...Price. And here I didn't remember falling down the rabbit hole into whatever messed-up world I now inhabited.

Awesome.

I heard Price clear his throat and I focused my attention back on him. "Where are we, Chill?" he asked.

"The meet is set for late, late tomorrow night."

"What meet?" I asked.

Chill glared at Price. "You haven't told her yet?"

"Haven't told me what?"

Cherry glanced up. "Oh. This is Songbird? Wow." She shook her head and went back to work. "At least you being with her at the gala and last night makes sense now, Parker."

Before I could ask what the hell that meant, Price replied, "Raptor wants to meet with Songbird before he commits to the deal. Chill has been spreading the word that you were a master planner."

"How good of you to tell me. I thought he didn't know I was involved," I snapped. "If he gets to know who I am, I think I damn well get to know who he is."

Chill put up a hand to quiet me. "You'll be well disguised and I'll be there with you as the broker of the deal. There's nothing to worry about."

"Well we still have one problem, Chill. I'm not a planner of any sort, much less a master planner."

"Correction," Cherry interjected. "We have two problems. I can't hack this system."

Price and Chill exchanged looks. "We have to get someone else, then," Chill said finally.

Cherry shook her head. "Save your money, boys. This system is unhackable."

"Every system can be hacked, Cherry. There's no shame in admitting you can't do it," Price said.

I could tell how frustrated Cherry was by the look on her face. "Listen, I'm telling you this system cannot be hacked. It's a Footprint system."

"What's that supposed to mean?" Price asked.

I sighed. "It means we're screwed."

"Thank you," Cherry said with a nod. "Finally someone who gets it."

"Well don't leave us in the dark. Flip the switch," Chill demanded.

I didn't know how to fully explain it so I remained quiet, letting Cherry take the lead.

"A Footprint system is bad news for hackers. It records every move you make in the system, like a trail of footprints. It has multiple functions. The first keeps a log of what information has been compromised so it can be changed."

Price appeared thoughtful. "So, you're saying any information will be no good to us when it's time to pull the job."

"Basically, but that isn't the real problem," Cherry answered, grim. "The second function runs a trace on you and reports it to the security center of the company."

"How long does that take?" Chill asked.

"It depends on how good the hacker is, I suppose, but if I go any further into the system, we'll have the cops at our door this side of a half hour."

"Can't you cover your tracks?" Chill asked. "Marcus always could."

"Low, Chill. Even for you." She shook her head. "I'm already routed through about fifty different servers across the globe and four different satellites. It won't make enough of a difference to add more layers; we'll still get caught."

"I don't accept that, Cherry," Chill said. "There's always a flaw and someone who knows how to find it."

Something occurred to me. "Did you ever hear about the kid who hacked the White House?"

"Who didn't," Price replied.

"What about the one who hacked into a CIA spy satellite program in order to keep tabs on his girlfriend?" I asked.

"I'm not familiar with that," he said slowly.

Chill smacked his shoulder. "That one was priceless. The kid thought his girlfriend was sleeping with his best friend. When the CIA showed up at his door, he was finding out the girlfriend was sleeping with his best friend's dad. Classic."

"Anyway. They co-developed the technology. They know every trick and no one can bypass their system," I finished.

Chill eyed me skeptically. "How do *you* know all this?"

I shrugged. "I was an E-Business major. They had a special ethics class for us. It's a good school; we had lots of high-powered guest speakers." I gave Chill a long look. "And it was the best friend's mother, not his father."

Chill looked at me in silence for a moment, then slammed his fist down on the table. "This is a pickle, Ramsey. Songbird would have known about something like this a long time ago. What are we going to tell Raptor tomorrow?" he demanded.

Price ran his hands through his dirty blonde hair. "This is just a minor set-back, but we can deal by tomorrow night." He turned his gaze in my direction. "I'm afraid I'm going to have to ask you to do something you won't like."

I raised an eyebrow. "So? What else is new?"

"I know this will put you in an awkward position, but I'm going to need you to steal something from a friend," Price replied.

THIRTEEN

"What brings you by this afternoon?" Michael asked, rising from his desk.

I lingered at the door and leaned against the frame. "I was hoping I could talk to you for a few minutes."

"I just need to fax this off," he replied as he picked up a small stack of paperwork I estimated to be about fifty sheets. "I should just be a minute. Make yourself at home."

The smile faded from my lips the instant he left the room. Michael was the most detail-oriented person I knew and I was certain he wouldn't return until he received confirmation his fax was received. I reasoned I should have ample time to get what I came for.

The Rolodex was on the far side of his desk. I walked over to it and flipped immediately to 'S.' Just as I had predicted I was able to find the phone numbers for all of the security monitoring companies we needed. The handheld scanner Price gave me worked slowly, but my luck held out long enough to get all of the information into my purse.

I glanced at the door and once I convinced myself Michael wasn't about to return, I sized up the rest of his office. I knew him well enough to know he would have a list of all of his employees' security access codes. The question was where. My time was running out, but all our careful planning would be for nothing if I couldn't find them.

The door to the copy room shut with a loud thud and I glanced at the door to Michael's office. In desperation, I picked up the keyboard to his computer. Taped to the bottom was the list I wanted. I quickly committed the one I would need to memory and replaced the keyboard to its tray. As the sound of approaching footsteps grew louder, I fixed my gaze on his monitor.

"What are you doing, Skylar?" Michael asked, closing the door behind him as he entered the room.

I walked to the other side of his desk and sat down before I answered. "I was trying to get a better look at your screensaver. I've always found lightning strangely soothing."

"So have I, but it doesn't seem to be helping me much today," he replied.

I was puzzled by his statement. "I thought you would be less stressed out now that the gala is behind us."

"What can I say? My boss is an ass," Michael said with a sigh.

"What did Drake do now?"

"He took away the daily cash pick-ups. I've been cut back to armored car service on Mondays and that's it." He shook his head. "Sometimes I wish I could go back in time and fire him when he still worked for me."

"How often were you having pick-ups?" I asked, trying not to sound too eager for the answer.

Michael shrugged. "Every day. I could have twice daily pick-ups this week and it wouldn't be overkill. All of the major charities bank with me and they're all going to make their heaviest cash deposits this week. Drake knows how much I hate keeping that kind of cash on hand."

His tone told me he was more than a little upset. "Why would he do that, Michael?"

"The man has tunnel vision. All he can see is the money he'll save by cutting me back. He never considers the consequences of any of his actions," he said.

I tried to make my smile sympathetic. "I'm sure everything will be all right after this week."

"Oh, I know it will, but Drake is going to have to go if this bank is ever going to run the way it's meant to." Michael smiled back at me and cocked his head to the side. "I know you didn't come up here just to hear me rant. What did you want to talk to me about?"

"I wanted to apologize to you."

Michael arched an eyebrow. "For what, Skylar?"

"I was rude when you were asking me about my date and I'm sorry for that," I said.

"I've been meaning to talk to you about that," he said. "I overstepped my bounds and I'm the one who should be apologizing. I just..." Michael's voice trailed off and he looked away. There was a hint of pain in his eyes.

"What?"

"I never told you this, but I made a promise to your father before he died," he began uncertainly, his voice faltering. "I promised him I would take care of you and your mother. I should have realized she wasn't handling things, but...I don't want to fail Monty a second time."

I always considered Michael a friend, but it never occurred to me that he was trying to watch over me for my father. It explained so much. He seemed just a little bit too concerned about me, especially after my mother's suicide. The look in his glistening eyes made my heart break at the thought of what I still had to do.

"You couldn't have known, Michael," I said quietly. "None of us could have known what was in her mind."

After a moment he replied, "I know there was nothing I could have done, but it hurts all the same."

Knowing he felt the loss as deeply as I had set loose an unexpected rush of emotions and I went over to him. I knelt beside his chair and looked him squarely in the eyes. "You know I love you, right?"

Michael nodded. "And you know," he said, "but this is depressing talk and I think the last thing you need is me dragging you back down." He glanced at the clock and frowned.

"You have an appointment coming in, don't you?" I asked, even though I could read him like a book.

"I do."

We stood up and his fatherly embrace caught me off guard.

"You don't have to worry about me so much, Michael," I whispered.

He pulled away and gave me a stern look. "Yes I do, Skylar."

"What?"

"I can tell that you're up to something, but I'm not sure what it is yet."

I feigned innocence. "I really don't know what you're talking about."

He nodded and opened his office door for me. "Okay, you don't have to tell me. I just hope you know what you're doing."

As I left the bank, I wondered if I did.

*****

My house was empty when I got home from the bank. I didn't know where the others went, but I was grateful for the peace and quiet. The encounter with Michael was more unsettling to me than I expected. Knowing what he was trying to do all this time made it even more difficult to steal from him – especially now that he knew I was up to something.

Hopefully, Michael would never have to find out what it was.

I tossed the information in my purse onto the couch and walked into the bathroom. My muscles were overwrought with tension and it was annoying to me how slowly the deep garden tub filled with water. While I waited, I went into my bedroom to retrieve one of the books I purchased two weeks ago. After adding twice the recommended amount of bubble bath I went into the kitchen to get something to drink.

The hot, sudsy water did a lot for my aching muscles, but the citrus aroma of the bubbles didn't have the invigorating effect on my spirits they usually did. Where was Price? I thought it would be a welcome change to get rid of him; however, I found he invaded my thoughts even when he wasn't around. For all I knew, he was off with a woman who was less effort...like Cherry.

With a sigh, I picked up my book and flipped it open to the page I left off on.

Several chapters later, and now completely relaxed, I reached an absent hand over the edge of the tub for my bottle of water. Instead, I felt the top of a sneaker. I looked over and was startled to realize I was no longer alone. The book slipped from my hands and made a soft splash as it fell through the mountain of bubbles into the water.

"Dammit, Price," I said as I attempted to shake the water off of the soaked paperback. "Can a woman not get a moment's peace with you around?"

"Not usually. And never when she's naked." He knelt next to the bathtub, a smile playing at his lips. His eyes were full of mischief when he looked at me and said, "I didn't mean to interrupt you in the middle of your romance novel."

"Cute, but I don't read that fluff," I snapped back at him. "I was just about to find out if they make it out of the country alive."

"Hmm, seems fitting. Did you get everything?"

I gave up on the book since the pages were hopelessly stuck together and tossed it onto the floor. "It's on the couch."

"I saw that already. Did you get the codes?" he asked.

"Yeah."

"I didn't see them with the rest of the stuff. Where are they?"

I tapped my temple lightly with my index finger. "Right here. I didn't have time to write them down." I tried not to be annoyed by the look on his face. "It's an easy code and I have an excellent memory."

"Can you imitate the voice?"

I nodded. "Of course, sugar," I said, letting the hint of a southern drawl enter my voice. "Now, what have you been up to today?"

Price leaned in until his face was only a few inches from mine. "Wouldn't you like to know," he replied as he dipped a finger into the water, "but your water is starting to cool."

I caught my breath, but didn't respond. His nearness was both unnerving and exciting. When my eyes met his, I cursed myself silently because I knew he could read exactly what I was thinking. His hand was dangerously near my thigh and I could feel his fingertips graze my skin.

"What are you doing?" My voice was barely a whisper when I spoke.

He kept his piercing emerald eyes locked on mine. "I'm keeping you from pruning up," he replied as he opened the drain to let the water out.

As the water level dropped, the bubbles clung provocatively to my skin. Despite the fact Price was trying to play it cool, I could sense the quickening of his pulse. I knew he could vividly remember what went on not forty-eight hours prior, just as I did. I could still feel my body pressed up against his, under his, around his and I realized something with more force and clarity than I had ever before known.

I wanted him.

Still.

I understood the insanity associated with that thought just as I understood the heightened desire I felt for him. Price was a skilled lover and I knew how enjoyable it would be to let him take me to the brink and beyond during the time he spent here with me. Of course, I also knew that, in all probability, he would be gone within a week once we dealt with Raptor. And then there was the issue of the trust that did not exist between us.

Minor details.

I traced his jaw line with a finger and said, "Be a dear and hand me my towel, won't you."

Price stood and removed the towel from the rack on the wall. I noticed the hint of mischief in his eyes again as he extended the towel to me. As much fun as it would be to have him in my bed, I knew it would be a dangerous path on which to walk and now was not the time for any extra danger.

But I could still have some fun. Scratch that. A lot of fun.

I twirled my sudsy finger in a circle. "Turn around, dear," I said with a smile.

He shot me a look and turned around. I rose to my feet, letting the last of the water droplets spill off of me. Plucking the towel from his hands and wrapping it around me I said, "You can turn around now, Price, and you never answered my question."

When he turned around, I could see the tension in his face, but his tone remained light, casual. "I know. I thought we could talk over dinner."

"Trying to buy some time?" I asked as I cocked my head to the side.

He shook his head. "No. It'll be ready in about fifteen minutes."

"Oh," I replied, looking up at him from beneath lowered lashes. "I'll just get dressed then. Unless…"

"Unless what?"

I shrugged. "Unless strawberries are part of the meal."

As he set the plates on the table, Parker hoped his irritation hadn't shown. Skylar was playing with him and not by accident, a fact of which he was well aware. Women didn't usually have the ability to get under his skin, but Skylar seemed to push his buttons like no woman before her.

The problem seemed to boil down to his inability to read her. Parker was an excellent con artist and could normally anticipate the reactions of his mark, men and women alike, just as if they were a rerun on television, but there didn't seem to be any rhyme or reason to the way Skylar reacted to things. One moment she would be snapping at him and the next she would be tossing him the most alluring smile. He didn't ever know with certainty if he should be stepping away from her or pulling her to him.

And Parker was a man who hated uncertainty.

A typical con for Parker was a quick, surgical procedure rarely involving outside help. Having a woman around was a complicated indulgence he wouldn't allow himself until the con was over and his plane tickets were purchased. Their feelings were definitely never an issue that caused any sleepless nights – for him, anyway.

Unfortunately, Parker found himself taking Skylar's reaction to things into account more and more during his planning. Despite her outward toughness, he knew there was something softer in her that she fought to keep hidden. As much as he tried to deny it to himself, Parker wanted to see that side for himself one of these days, after their business together was long since complete.

As Skylar emerged from her bedroom dressed in the usual blue jeans and college sweatshirt, Parker reminded himself that he was on her turf now. He would have to play by her rules, even if that meant squelching the almost overwhelming desire to feel her soft skin against his again. There would be plenty of time for that once he convinced her he wasn't quite the scoundrel she made him out to be.

Glancing at her he asked, "Don't you ever wash that?"

"Very funny. It's comfortable and I have more than one, for your information," she replied, her tone scathing, as she joined him at the table.

"Wow," Parker replied, "you're in a fun mood all of the sudden."

Skylar shrugged. "I'm just not in the mood for games right now."

"You could have fooled me."

She shot him a look and continued as though he hadn't said anything. "Did I miss much while I was at the bank?"

Relieved by the change of subject, Parker answered, "Not really, unless you were enjoying Cherry and Chill taking shots at one another."

"Not especially," Skylar replied before taking a sip of her water. "There's certainly no love lost between those two, is there?"

"You'd be surprised."

"I doubt it, Price, but tell me anyway."

"They dated, briefly, before she met his brother. It was a long time ago, long before he ever became the Chill we all know and tolerate today."

Skylar arched an eyebrow. "Exactly how far do y'all go back?"

Parker took a long drink of his water as he considered the answer to that question. The truth was an elusive thing and it would be unreasonable to assume she would discover the truth just from the answer to that question. Still, Skylar Montgomery was far more perceptive than Raptor gave her credit for being.

"Boarding school," Parker finally said. "It was there we discovered we had the knack for, um, finessing certain situations."

"You make it all seem so poetic."

He shook his head. "I don't mean to, nor do I intend to try to justify my occupation to you."

Skylar grinned. "Your occupation," she said, her tone mocking. "Now you're making it sound like you actually earn a paycheck."

"Not in the traditional sense," Parker replied. He leaned back in his chair and folded his arms over his chest in an attempt to rid himself of the thought that there was something exhilarating about fighting with Skylar. "I may not have a paystub, but I do my fair share of work."

"Oh, really."

"Smirk all you want, but the perfect crime doesn't often magically appear in your mind. There is quite a bit of research and planning involved in what I do."

Skylar's blue eyes were wide. "You don't have to get defensive about it. I wasn't trying to call you lazy or anything. I just…"

Parker shook his head. "Don't worry about it. You'll have to bring your A game to offend me."

"Noted," Skylar replied evenly. "Am I still set to meet with Raptor tomorrow night?"

"Only if you think you're ready. It isn't too late to back out if you have any doubts about this."

A look of panic flashed through her eyes, but as quickly as Parker noticed it, it was gone. She set her jaw in determination and narrowed her eyes at him slightly. "I can handle it. I'm ready."

"No, you aren't," Parker said, "but you will be by the time I'm finished with you."

Skylar tilted her head to the side and said, "I can hardly wait to find out what you have in mind, Price."

Chill walked into the club and surveyed the crowd. After greeting a few of the regulars he had come to know over the years, he headed to his usual table to await the man he was meeting. Despite the business at hand, he found his mind was clouded and not in the usual, liquor induced kind of way he enjoyed.

"Damn you, Cherry," Chill murmured into his vodka tonic.

"I didn't realize you knew I was here," Cherry purred, walking up from behind him.

He cursed lightly under his breath before saying, "I didn't. Did Raptor let you off your leash?"

A look of pain passed through the blonde's eyes as she sat across from him. "Even a slut like me gets a night off now and again, Chill."

"Cherry, you know I didn't mean…"

"Yes, you did," she interrupted softly. "Of course, I would probably feel the same way in your shoes."

"You have no idea how I feel," he snapped.

"I'm sure you're right," Cherry replied. After lighting a cigarette and puffing a few times she added, "I have no better an idea how you feel than you have of why I've made the choices I have."

Through the numbing wave of pain Chill felt every time he was around her, he heard the logic in her words and relented. "Fine. Why don't you explain it to me, sweet?"

"Look, none of us are exactly angels here. We all have to play the hand we were dealt, but I didn't get the same wild cards you and Ramsey got. I don't have a trust fund, or connections, or the ability to pull off cons without a hitch. The only thing I have going for me is that Raptor pulled me into his bed. Granted, it is the last place I would ever want to be, but you know what they say about keeping your enemies closer than friends."

Chill looked at her incredulously. "You had alternatives. You could have come to me for help."

"No, I couldn't have. You made it abundantly clear to me at Marcus's funeral that you didn't want anything more to do with me."

"I had just buried my kid brother," Chill countered.

"Yeah, so you, of all people, should have understood how I was feeling." She took a few more drags on her cigarette to calm herself. "Besides, I couldn't have come to you for help regardless of your behavior. I've never forgiven myself for the way things ended between us."

He sighed. "Water under the bridge, sweet."

"Anyway, I've put myself in an excellent position to betray Raptor and Ramsey's plan is the way I'm going to do it."

"Do you really believe that Raptor trusts you?"

Cherry shrugged absently. "No. I'm quite sure he does not trust me, but he'll still ask me to be part of this. When he does," Cherry's tone became excited, "I will enjoy pounding the last nail into his coffin."

He laughed. "Such vivid imagery. I'd almost believe you had been planning this."

"There isn't a night that goes by without me thinking of some new way to kill him. I woke up in the middle of the night once with the thought to smother him in his sleep. He grabbed my wrist before I could ever reach for the pillow." Cherry looked at her watch and frowned. "I have to go."

"Lose your taste for the night life?"

"Trevor was supposed to have drinks with a builder he's been working with. It would annoy him if I wasn't home when he got there."

"Maybe he'll loosen your leash one of these days if you're a good little girl," Chill bantered.

"Or I'll cut it myself."

Chill considered everything she said for a long while after she left his table. Cherry was playing a dangerous game, but she couldn't possibly understand that. Raptor was far more calculating than she seemed to give him credit for and he would be able to see through any change in her behavior, no matter how slight, which is why she'd have to stay in his bed for another week.

Fuck.

As a frail-looking man approached, Chill decided he would have to put Cherry out of his mind. There was business to attend to at the moment. His chemist had finally arrived.

I watched from the counter as Price washed the dishes after our meal. My feet swung restlessly over the edge, occasionally banging into the cabinets as I waited for him to finish. He dropped the subject of my meeting with Raptor after telling me he was going to prep me for it and I was grateful for that. Outwardly, I could talk a good game, but I knew the truth on the inside. Raptor was a hardcore killer and I was way out of my league. Despite what I said, I wasn't ready.

Not even close.

I didn't realize the sound of water had stopped until I felt a warm hand covering mine on the counter. My face must have given away my inner turmoil because Price's eyes were clouded when he looked at me. Softly, he asked, "Are you all right?"

My first reaction was, oddly enough, to tell him how I felt, but confiding my feelings to people was never really my style. I tossed a pointed look at his hand and then met his gaze. "I was."

Price sighed and removed his hand. "I wasn't trying anything, Skylar. You can drop the attitude."

"Whatever," I said, rolling my eyes.

"No," Price replied. He placed his hands firmly on the counter on either side of me and looked me square in the eyes. "We need to get whatever the problem is out in the open and we need to do it right now."

I pursed my lips. "I'm sure I don't know what you mean."

"Yes, Skylar, you do. Look, as arousing as it is to fight with you, I don't think this argument has anything to do with me."

I shook my head absently. "It probably doesn't, but I'm not in the mood to talk right now."

"Then what are you in the mood for, besides taking potshots at me every chance you get?"

He asked the question seriously, but I decided to have a little fun with it anyway. Deliberately, I slid off the counter onto my feet. My movement caught him off guard, so he didn't have the opportunity to step back or to move his hands. My body was pressed between the counter and his when I looked into his eyes.

After holding his gaze for a moment I replied, "What do you think?" I curved my lips into an alluring smile. "You are supposed to be able to read people and all, right? You tell me what I'm in the mood for tonight."

"I don't have the slightest idea."

"I think you do."

He gave his head a slight shake, but made no move to back away from me. "I can't read you, Skylar. I never could."

"Really? Does that happen to you often?"

His eyes were locked with laser intensity to mine. "Never. Not even once."

"That must be...frustrating."

"You have no idea."

"No, I don't. I can read you, Price. I know exactly what you're in the mood for tonight." I flicked my tongue over my lips.

Then I waited.

As expected, his eyes dipped down to my lips before returning to mine. "You think so?"

No question in my mind now. "I know so." I slid my hands over his forearms. "Right now, you're thinking you shouldn't have been so firm in your reassurances that I had nothing to worry about from you."

"No, I'm not."

My hands continued on a slow path over his biceps to his chest. "You are. You're starting to realize that soon you'll be alone on the couch while I'm in the next room." I gripped the material of his polo shirt, bunching it between my fingers. "You're just now beginning to realize how much you don't want me to sleep alone tonight."

He was silent. Must've hit the nail on the head with that one. I licked my lips again and tilted my head to the side. "Even though I'm used to sleeping alone, it bears mention that I'm not totally opposed to sharing my bed with you." After a beat, "But you're of course welcome to that lonely couch while you're here."

"Skylar..."

"I'm way off base. Right, Price? That's why you haven't so much as twitched a muscle since I started talking. Because you don't want me?"

More silence.

I moved my lips just short of his ear. "Aren't you the one who told me it wasn't smart to try conning a con?" I flicked my tongue over his earlobe. "Especially when Price, Jr. throbbing against my thigh is a dead giveaway."

With catlike reflexes, his hands moved from the counter to my back, pulling me closer. His lips were violent, kiss urgent. I loved when he kissed me this way almost as much as I loved being right.

I pulled back long enough to tug his shirt over his head and his lips sought mine out before the shirt hit the tile floor. His hands slipped down from my back, moving inside the back of my jeans to grab my ass, pulling me closer still. I circled my arms around his neck, trying to be patient with all the foreplay.

But it was hard as hell when I had a specific goal in mind and he was hard as hell against my thigh...

Hoping to move things along, I dropped my hands to his belt and made short work of the buckle. That did it. His hands moved up to the small of my back and pulled the sweatshirt over my head. Momentarily, I wished I'd put on something sexier than a faded black sports bra, but if I got what I wanted it wouldn't be on very long anyway. Still, it seemed like such a shame to let all the sexy underwear Reyna made me buy go to waste in my dresser.

Price covered my neck with kisses. "What happened to wanting me to keep my damn hands off you?"

"Change of heart." I pushed him back and he hit the refrigerator, knocking a magnet I'd never much liked to the floor where it broke in two. "You have something I want."

A sly smile spread across his face. "And what might that be?"

In two slow steps, I closed the gap between us and sank to my knees in front of him. I heard his breath snag when I unzipped the slacks and reached inside to free the erection begging for my attention. I slanted my eyes up to meet his. "Oh, I think you know what you have that I want." Then I flicked my tongue down the length of him.

A primal growl of pleasure stirred in his throat. I'd always loved when men made that sound, especially since they all seemed to get off on playing the same game on me. I swirled my tongue around his smooth head to hear it again.

"God...say the word and I will steal anything you want right now."

"You don't have to steal a thing. Everything I want is right here." I moistened my lips one more time before taking him into my mouth.

His fingers tangled into my hair, urging me for more. As if he needed to. I'd never admit it to him, but I enjoyed the way he felt against my tongue. I gave in and worked him over longer than I meant to, regretting that I might not get to finish this. Dammit, I actually wanted to taste him.

When his breathing changed and his hands were the most insistent, I backed off. Moving him from my mouth to my hand, I said, "Price?"

His voice was hoarse with desire. "Skylar?"

"I want to know Raptor's identity."

"Anything...just keep doing that." His eyelids shot open. "Did I just hear you right?"

"If you heard me say I wanted Raptor's identity, yes."

"Don't do this. You know I can't tell you." He rested his head back against the refrigerator and closed his eyes, fighting for control of himself.

"I told you that you had something I wanted." I pumped him a few times with my hands, swirling my tongue over him again, just to make sure he wouldn't have an easy time denying me. "Give me what I want, Price, and I swear I'll give you everything you want." With my lips pressed against him so he could feel my breath, I gazed up at him. "And I'll give it to you every night while you're here with me. No strings. Just pleasure."

He pressed his hands over his face and growled in frustration. "Are you seriously trying to trade sex for a fucking name?"

"It's not just any name. In fact, it's the one name I would do anything to get."

"You...*bitch*." He pushed his fingers through his hair and glared down at me. "You don't even want me, do you? You just want to know who Raptor is so badly that you're willing to fuck me to get it."

"Yes and no." I licked my tongue over his shaft. "I think we both know how much I enjoyed having you inside me at the hotel. It's not the sacrifice you're making it out to be." I gave him a long look. "Just tell me those two little words I want to hear and we can finally have some fun."

He just glared at me, so I added, "Come on. This is a good trade. Besides, Price, I haven't even shown you yet why I give the best head you'll ever get."

His face was hard as stone. "No. I'm not playing your game. I won't give you Raptor just to get into your pants." He gave his head a tense shake. "I won't do it."

I rolled back onto the balls of my feet and stood, giving him a nod. "All right then. You have a good night with the couch." I glanced down at the lonely erection. "And with your hand, apparently." I started to walk away, but thought better of it. Splaying my hands over his chest, I moved close to his ear. "But if that couch gets so cold and lonely that not even your precious secret can keep you warm, you know where to find me. Two words, Price. Two words is all it takes to have me again." I tugged on his earlobe with my teeth and headed to my room. "Don't pretend it's not tempting."

FOURTEEN

"Do you have any idea what time it is?"

Jackson jumped at the sound of Jenna's voice from behind him. He was trying to avoid waking her up as he left this morning, but apparently he wasn't as quiet as he'd hoped. Turning around he answered, "I was trying not to wake you."

"You failed," she said as she pulled the blanket up around her shoulders to fend off the chilly morning. "Why are you getting dressed at four-thirty in the morning anyway?"

With a sigh, Jackson sat on the edge of the bed next to her. "I have to get home so I can get ready for work."

"You're telling me I can expect to be woken up two hours early every morning from now on then? I may love you Jackson, but if you keep this up much longer, I will have to kill you."

Jackson bent down to kiss her forehead. "I'll try to remember to bring some stuff over with me tonight so you won't have to commit a homicide just yet."

"You should just move in here with me. It would be so much easier," Jenna replied, yawning.

Her statement surprised Jackson. They had only been back together for a few days and had never even discussed that possibility. Granted, their alone time hadn't been filled with very much conversation since the night of the gala, but it still seemed sudden.

"You can't be serious," Jackson said.

"And why not?" she asked, a hint of irritation entering her voice.

"It just seems a little soon for a step that big, that's all."

Jenna pushed herself up on her elbows and met his stare. "And that should matter why? We'd only known each other for what, two weeks, three weeks, before I offered to move across the country with you when I thought you were going back to D.C."

She had a point, Jackson realized. Nothing about their relationship followed any sort of a conventional time table. He just didn't want to wreck things the way he had last time by jumping in too quickly.

"It isn't that I don't want to move in. I just...wait. Does this have anything to do with what I said after the gala? About requesting a transfer back after I closed my case?"

"Well..." She pursed her lips then closed her eyes. Sighing, "I'd want to live with you even if that particular threat wasn't still fresh in my mind."

"Jenna...honey...it wasn't a threat."

"So you want to move away then." A look of pain crossed her face. "That explains why you don't want to live with me."

He cupped her face in his hands. "Stop. I love you. I want to be with you." He searched her face, trying to figure out how to make her understand. "When I said I was requesting a transfer...It was before I knew how you felt about me. It was when I thought we had zero future and it was too painful to live so close to you and know you didn't care about me."

"I never..."

Jackson covered her mouth with a finger to silence her protest. "I know that now. I'm just telling you how it felt at the time."

She moved her head to rub her cheek against his hand. "Then I need to tell you how it feels to be me."

"Okay." Considering the traffic he'd have to fight on the way to the office if this went on much longer, it wasn't the ideal time for a conversation. But Jackson wasn't about to stop it.

"I don't like sleeping alone now that I have you back in my life."

"I don't either."

"And when I left your apartment Sunday night..." Jenna averted her eyes. "I cried the whole way home."

That might be the last thing Jackson ever expected her to say. "You could've stayed." He put two fingers under her chin to turn her back to face him. "You *should* have stayed."

"Jackson...I couldn't. Buddy and Chloe..."

"Have dry food and wouldn't have starved to death in one night."

She sighed. "This is the second time you've told me you were going back to D.C. while we were in a fight. I...I need to know you're really in this. I need to know you aren't going to run halfway across the country after a fight."

That she would feel that way never occurred to him. "It doesn't matter whether I live here or in my apartment, I'm really in this. All the way." He brushed away the rogue tear sliding down her cheek. "I swore to you I wouldn't leave you. I meant it."

"You realize it doesn't make sense that you don't want to live with me when you've sworn to never leave me...right?"

She had a point. "I just think we should talk about this a little more, maybe when you're more awake, before we make any decisions."

"Fine," Jenna said. "What time are you coming over tonight?"

"As soon as possible."

She frowned at him and crossed her arms across her naked chest. "Nope. No good."

"Huh?"

She looked at him slyly. "It isn't soon enough," she answered, reaching over to pull off his shirt.

"What are you doing?"

She smiled. "Well, you woke me up and I know I don't have a prayer of getting back to sleep now. I can either go to work in a bad mood because I'm tired, or I can go in with a smile on my face." She pulled him back onto the bed with her. "I choose the smile."

"But I have to go to work."

"Call in and spend the day in bed with me."

"You have to work."

"I don't have to be in court today, so it can all wait." She gazed up at him with a hopeful expression and bent her leg until her bare thigh was against his side.

God she was sexy when she was naked.

"You know you'd rather spend the day with me than Brandon. I'm better looking."

"No argument." His hand strayed to grasp the hip writhing around him.

Her hands snaked between them to fight with his belt. "Stay in bed with me. Make love to me."

"I have a bank robber and murderer to catch." Even as he said the words, his hand was making short work of belt, button and zipper.

"It's been two years." She shoved slacks and boxers over his hips. "Is one day really going to make that much difference?"

"It could." Jackson didn't know why he was still protesting when his lips were on her neck and a hand was between her legs.

Jenna moaned and arched her back against him. "You don't know who Raptor is. You don't know where Ramsey is." Her breath was coming faster now. "But I'm right here and I want you. Now."

How well he knew that. Jackson fought to still the exploring, teasing hand so he could bite out the words he didn't want to say. "But I still have to go." He squeezed his eyes closed and tried to pretend his body wasn't screaming for the release he'd only find with her. "I don't want to. I have to."

She let out a small gasp when he moved his hand away from her and clutched at his shoulders. "Leaving me in this condition is cruel and unusual punishment. Even worse than waking me up before dawn."

"Jenna..."

"Just go in late. You can't leave now. You can't." One of her hands slid down his thigh until it found his pocket. When she found what she wanted, she smacked the condom against his torso and said, "Compromise. Put this on."

"Not much of a compromise."

Her teeth nipped at his neck. "This isn't going to take long...for either of us. You'll get to work by nine-thirty instead of eight-thirty. More than enough time to satisfy me and hunt bad guys." She pulled back to meet his eyes. "Stop pretending you haven't made up your mind and make me smile already."

Well, when she put it that way...

I felt a rush of cold air hit my sleep-warmed skin and slowly began to realize I was not at my father's retirement party, but that I just had the comforter pulled off of me. I opened my eyes and blinked several times to get them to adjust to a light that felt brighter than the sun shining down on me. Price was standing next to the bed, arms folded over his chest, scowling down at me.

In confusion I asked, "What's going on?"

"What's going on is that I've been trying to wake you up for twenty minutes. You told me you were getting up ten minutes ago," he snapped.

"I don't remember that. I must not have been awake," I yawned. I shook my head in an attempt to clear it and looked over at the clock. "Why are you trying to wake me up at five in the morning anyway?"

"I need to get you prepped before your meeting with Raptor."

"That can't possibly take however many hours we have until then."

"No, it won't, but you need to change your sleep cycle."

I reached for the covers and pulled them back over my shoulders. "Why? I like my cycle just fine."

Price let out an aggravated sigh and ripped the comforter off the bed. "It may work well for you, but I need you to start thinking like the criminal you need to be in twenty hours. Songbird would be up late into the night and napping during the day. You can't seem tired when you meet Raptor. I need you to look every bit as awake at night as Chill does."

"Chill looks like a ghost at night," I muttered to myself as I sat up and swung my legs over the side of the bed. "You had better already have coffee brewed."

"I'll pour you a cup as long as you're really getting out of bed this time," Price said before leaving the room.

He was really being grouchier about this than he needed to be. What the hell was wrong with...Oh. If he'd left me primed and ready to go the way I left him last night, I'd be pissed off too.

No, I probably would've beaten him awake with his pillow.

I've never been a morning person by anyone's standards, but this morning it was extra difficult to get myself into gear to wash my face and brush my teeth. Despite being relatively early when I went to bed, sleep didn't come for me until sometime after one. I pulled on the sweatshirt I wore the previous evening over my pajamas and went to the dining room.

Even after thinking about it for hours, I still couldn't sort out my feelings for Price. I wondered if he shared my dilemma or if this was all business as usual for him. Both prospects, I finally decided around midnight, were equally bad for me and I gave up that line of thought.

Price handed me a steaming cup of coffee and sat across from me. The hint of a smile on his face irritated me. Of course, everything was potentially an irritant this early in the morning, so I tried to make my voice sound light when I asked, "Something funny?"

"Not especially," he answered between sips. "You're just cute when you're asleep and not snapping at me."

I took a sip of my coffee and ignored his statement. It was far too early to verbally joust with him. "Well, I'm awake enough now, so why don't you tell me whatever you woke me up to tell me."

"Okay," he began as he set his coffee mug on the table with purpose. "Raptor will want to know what your plan is. Basically, you'll give him the same plan I told you Saturday night, but we'll tweak it just enough so it doesn't sound like something I came up with. We'll also make sure there are a few holes in it so Raptor can feel like he's in control when he makes the suggestion to do what we've already done."

I set my cup on the table and frowned at him. "How can you be so sure he'll think of the same things you did?"

Price shrugged. "I know how he thinks. Security is so tight that there are very few ways to pull off this heist the way he likes. Besides, because he knows I'm back from the dead, he'll consult with me before he finalizes anything. The only problem could be getting him to put Cherry on the crew."

"Do we really need her?" I asked, still wondering what was really between them. "It seems like the tension between her and Chill could be a problem."

"I'm afraid so, but you don't have to worry. Chill knows how to play it cool."

"But why her? We already know we can't hack the system. She seems useless."

"There are a couple of reasons. Raptor will want to confirm for himself we can't hack in and he'll want his own person to prove it for him. Let's face facts. He doesn't trust me and he doesn't know Songbird. Chill is just a broker he uses occasionally. I've worked with him enough to know he'll want someone he feels he can trust. I just can't guarantee he'll want her on this, which will pose a problem for us."

I thought that over for a moment before asking, "What will we do if he pulls someone else into this?"

"We'll still be fine, but it's more difficult to con two people than one."

"I guess you would know."

He tossed me a look and continued, "Anyway, you'll be disguised so he doesn't know it's you, but you'll need to change your voice and mannerisms."

"I've got the southern drawl down cold, but what do I need to change about my mannerisms?"

"Everything. You have a very distinctive way of walking; standing...it all has to change. You've got to keep in mind you've just spent quite a bit of time with Raptor as Skylar. It's all over if you do anything that would make him think you and Songbird are one in the same."

I picked up my coffee and took a long, slow sip. Everything he said made perfect sense. There was no time to back out now, even though I knew I wasn't ready to pull off something like this.

"I can see I have your attention now. Let's start by getting your story down and then we'll work on the rest," Price said.

I nodded my agreement. "Okay. I'll do whatever you tell me." Too late, I realized how that must sound.

Price grinned. "That has potential, but we'll have to explore it another time."

Brandon looked at his watch for the second time to confirm he was reading it correctly. It was after ten and he hadn't heard from his partner yet. Where the hell was Caldwell? Now that he knew his partner wouldn't be out investigating him, it was a valid question.

When his phone rang he looked at it in irritation before he picked up the receiver. Thinking it was Caldwell, his greeting was gruffer than usual. "Dinsley."

"Get up on the wrong side of the wrong woman's bed this morning or what? This is Tim with the Irving PD."

Generally speaking, it was always the wrong side of the wrong woman's bed when he woke up alone in his apartment.

Brandon only got to work with Tim a few times in the past, but held a great deal of respect for the man on the other end of the line. "Rough morning. What's up, Tim?"

"I think we might have a new player in town you should know about," Tim replied.

"What makes you say that?"

"Some guy was brought in this morning for trying to knock over a gas station ATM. Literally tried to knock it over. Anyway, he cracked the second they got him to the station and started trying to hand us every perp he's ever known."

Brandon's eyes widened. Only one reason why Irving PD would call him about a botched burglary. "Raptor?"

"Naw. I think Raptor's a little out of this kid's league. He did tell us quite a story about some woman who wants to take down a bank. The M.O. sounds a little like Raptor's style."

Brandon looked up when he heard the sound of his office door opening. He shot Caldwell an irritated look as he walked in and motioned for him to sit down. To Tim, he asked, "Do you think this new player is working with Raptor?"

Tim was quiet for a moment. "Don't know 'bout that, but the perp goes by the name Songbird. If they aren't workin' together, I think they'd be a good match." He paused. "Aw, hell! I gotta go. Some drunk's raising hell in here. I'll let you know if anything turns up on this Songbird character."

"Thanks for letting me know, Tim."

After hanging up, Brandon turned his attention to his partner. There was no sense in harping on his tardiness, since the damage was already done, not that he missed much in his absence. Besides, Caldwell put more effort into doing his job than half the agents in the office combined.

"We've got a new player in town, Caldwell."

"Any connection to the case?" he asked, obviously grateful not to have to explain himself. From the dopey grin he was doing a piss poor job of suppressing, it was obvious why he was so late.

Brandon shook his head. "Not so far, but that doesn't mean this Songbird character won't end up on our desk at some point."

"Has there been any word from Ramsey?"

"No and I don't expect there will be. This guy has vanished once before and he won't turn up until he has to – or he's dead for real. Either way, he's no good to us. Have your sources been able to turn anything up?"

"Not that would help us. Raptor's been off the scene for too long and it doesn't look like he's planning to come back any time soon, at least not that anyone I've talked to knows about." His partner paused to pull a long, dark hair from the inside of his collar and grinned before continuing. "I was able to get it confirmed that Jonathan Price is a figment, though. Everything he used for that alias was tied to a social security number for someone who died more than thirty years ago, but I'm sure that doesn't come as a surprise to you."

Brandon shrugged. "It doesn't. It's the same story with Parker Ramsey; appeared from nowhere and vanished to nowhere. You don't know what I would give to know who this guy really is."

"Wouldn't it be something if Ramsey, or whoever he really is, was Raptor?"

"That isn't possible."

"No, it isn't probable, but it is definitely a possibility, Dinsley."

Brandon arched an eyebrow and frowned at his partner. "How do you figure?" If nothing else, his partner's musings would be entertaining.

"This is all just speculation," Caldwell began, "but what if Ramsey staged the whole thing? One of the people on his crew had just killed a man when he stood up and called him Raptor. The guy couldn't risk the time it would take to start fighting about which one of them was really Raptor. Ramsey would have been able to kill everyone who knew the truth and then fake his own death to throw us off."

"Let's say that you're onto something, but for the record, I don't think you are. We would be missing a body."

"True enough, and don't you think Raptor would be smart enough to know we'd think that? From what you've told me, all of the bodies were left for us to find. It would be just as easy for him to get rid of one body in a way we wouldn't find so we'd think one of them was really still on the loose. Now, Ramsey surfaces and offers to help us look for Raptor."

Brandon shook his head. "But why would he do that? It doesn't make any sense."

"Maybe, but go with me on this. It puts him in the perfect position to have us running around here chasing shadows while he gets to move around freely to plan his heist."

"It still seems like a risky move to make when we weren't any closer to finding him before Ramsey came to me," Brandon muttered.

"Maybe that's half the fun of it. Tricking the federal agent assigned to hunt him into helping him."

That remark stung. Caldwell continued before he could snap back at him.

"Okay, I was just toying with that idea anyway. Neither of us thought it was all that likely anyway."

Christ, were case theories his idea of pillow talk? "Neither of you, huh?"

It was Brandon's turn to be the recipient of an irritated glare. "She's a prosecutor who's spent some time looking into the case with me. It's bound to come up over lunch." Shaking his head, he changed the subject. "It's possible they were working together the entire time. Ramsey could have been working with you to make sure your attention was diverted from what Raptor was really doing." After a beat, "It makes about as much sense as the rest of this case."

Brandon nodded. Caldwell had a backwards way of getting at things, but at least he eventually came up with something that made sense. Now the real challenge would be figuring out how to do anything with that.

"I like that scenario better, Caldwell. Do you have any thoughts on what to do with it?"

"I have a hunch that if we can find out enough about Ramsey, he'll lead us straight to Raptor."

Brandon rose, taking his jacket off the back of his chair. "Then we'd better hit the streets and see what else we can find."

Parker turned on the television and debated whether or not to wake Skylar yet. It was past nine o'clock, but she hadn't gone back to bed until after noon. After pointing out that Raptor couldn't know she was Songbird, he felt like they accomplished something. He only wished he'd be there tonight to make sure nothing went sideways with her meet with Raptor.

Actually, he wished he hadn't pulled her into this in the first place.

At the time, it made sense to him, but now...Having her as a partner was turning into a liability for him. She was too inexperienced and Parker knew he couldn't protect her if she slipped up in front of Raptor – not tonight; maybe not at all. The other members of his crew knew what they were getting themselves into and they enjoyed the danger. Chill was a seasoned con artist who dealt with the criminal element every day. Cherry was driven by her hatred of Raptor, but at least she had the skills to back her up.

But then there was Skylar.

She shouldn't be part of all this. If all of her anger could just be set aside then she could have a good life. Intelligence was obviously one of her gifts, but she didn't use it to see what was right in front of her face. The truth about what was going on and Raptor's true identity was so obvious to Parker that he was amazed Skylar was still in the dark.

Parker could only hope his luck would continue to hold. It was a lucky break the FBI left Skylar alone after her phone call to them. Dinsley was forthcoming with him, but the last thing he needed was a dozen agents hanging around making it difficult to get things done. While the resources Dinsley had at his disposal could still be useful, it was definitely better that they were out of the picture now. Besides, they never would have gone along with what he was doing; it was illegal, after all.

Parker was so lost in his own thoughts that he didn't hear Skylar until she crossed into his line of sight. There was something different about her, but he couldn't quite figure out what it was. Of course, he thought absently, she's practicing for tonight.

"Why didn't you wake me?" she asked as she sat down on the other end of the couch.

Parker shrugged. "I wanted you to be rested."

"I'd rather be ready than rested."

"Have it your way." Parker rummaged for a moment in the bag next to his feet on the floor until he found what he was looking for and stood. "Come with me."

He was moderately surprised when Skylar followed him into the bathroom without question. She must be more nervous about tonight than she was letting on. Rather than draw attention to it, he decided to get straight to business.

"Do you wear contacts?"

Skylar seemed surprised by the question. "No. My vision is twenty-ten."

"How nice for you. What about color lenses?"

She shook her head. "I like my eyes just the way they are."

"Well, that makes two of us, but we need to hide them from Raptor. What color do you want?"

Skylar gave him a blank look, but remained silent.

"Okay then, let's try hazel. That should look natural on you with your coloring," Parker said, handing her the packet containing the lenses.

She looked at it for a second and set it on the counter. "I can't."

Parker sighed. "What do you mean you can't?"

"What can I say? I'm weird about my eyes."

"You'll just have to get past that, then. We don't have a lot of time here, Skylar."

"I know," she whined, "but I can't even put drops in them without freaking out."

Parker put his hands over his eyes and then rubbed his temples. "Look, either you wear the damn lenses or you don't meet with Raptor and you're out of this right now. Anyone who's looked at you for two minutes will recognize you by your eyes, regardless of the rest of the disguise. There are no other options."

Skylar's jaw dropped in protest, but she didn't say a word. Instead, she picked up the packet and looked at it for a second. She put it back down and cast a pitiful look in Parker's direction.

"Okay, don't be an ass about this, but I don't know how to do it. You're going to have to show me how to get these things in."

Parker suppressed a smile and shook his head. "You have got to be the only person I know who can make a guy feel like a jerk because you need help." Before she could respond he added, "Watch carefully."

Parker touched his finger to his eye and skillfully removed his lens.

"I had no idea you wore contacts."

"There's a lot you don't know about me. Anyway, that's how you get it out. To put it back in..." Parker let his voice trail off as he pulled down his lower lid slightly and put the contact back on. "See, nothing to it."

Skylar tossed him a skeptical look and opened the packet. "I'd prefer it if you didn't watch me do this."

"Suit yourself. I'll be watching the news," Parker replied, before turning and walking away.

After fighting with the lenses for almost an hour, I finally had both of them in. I looked at my blurry image in the mirror and gasped at what I saw. It pissed me off that Price was right about my appearance.

I looked like a completely different person.

Price walked into the room and leaned back against the doorframe. "How's it coming?"

I shot him an annoyed look and he let out a long, low whistle in response.

"What," I snapped.

"They look good, that's all," he replied, moving closer to inspect them.

"Really?"

He tilted my chin up so I was looking directly into his eyes. "I like your natural color better, but these definitely do something for you." Price abruptly removed his hand and cleared his throat. "Raptor will buy it."

"Is it supposed to be this blurry?"

I thought I saw Price smile, but, let's face it, I couldn't really see anything very well so I didn't comment.

"It usually is at first until your eyes adjust. The light might be a little too bright in here. Why don't you come out in the living room and try to get used to it?"

I didn't bother to fight him on that point. It *was* bright and the light *was* bothering my already sensitive eyes. Wordlessly, I let Price lead me by the hand out to the couch.

"Are you hungry?"

My stomach turned over at the mere thought of food. I knew I should eat something to keep my stomach from rumbling and growling when I met with Raptor, but...I couldn't even think about it. Food was the furthest thing from my mind right now. In just a few hours I would be face to face with the man who had murdered my father.

And I couldn't see a freakin' thing.

"Skylar?"

I wasn't aware of how much time elapsed since his original question. Probably more than I'd like him to comment on. "No, thank you. I'm fine."

"You're lying and you are eating something," he insisted.

"Whatever."

After he left the room, I picked up the remote and aimlessly flipped the channels. A kaleidoscope of images flickered in front of me, but I didn't see any of them. Despite my inner panic, I knew I was finally getting close; that this nightmare would soon be over.

I was startled when Price walked up behind me and handed me a plate. I eyed its contents, a sandwich and chips, before setting it down next to me. My stomach turned again. Stop it, I silently ordered myself. I was going to have to pull it together if I was going to get through this night. In frustration, I picked up the sandwich and took a bite.

Price sat on the couch and eyed me cautiously. "Does it always take so much concentration to eat a sandwich?"

I set the sandwich back on the plate and dusted the crumbs off of my hands. When I was reasonably confident that my voice wouldn't shake I met his gaze and said, "Don't. You know as well as I do what's wrong with me right now and I really don't want to talk about it. Please...don't make me, Price."

He shrugged. "Fair enough. How's your vision?"

"It's getting better."

After I resumed eating, he started to run through the evening's itinerary.

"Cherry dropped off some clothes for you earlier when you were asleep. Most of it will probably be too big for you, but that's not necessarily a bad thing."

Why hadn't he mentioned sooner that Cherry had come over when I was asleep? I hated the wave of jealousy that washed over me at the thought and hoped it wasn't evident on my face. There was no reason for it, anyway, because there was nothing going on between us anymore.

Not after he'd turned me down cold last night, anyway.

How was I supposed to fool Raptor when I couldn't even fool myself? With every second I spent with Price it became clearer to me that something was going on. I only wished I knew if it was indeed a mutual feeling or if this was all just business to him.

I dismissed that thought the moment it occurred to me. If nothing else, from his reaction during my bath and my failed extortion attempt, I knew he still wanted me. At the very least, he was physically attracted to me.

I could feel my cheeks growing flush as memories, first of the tension during that bath and then to the passion in his hotel room, flooded my mind. This was hardly the time to stroll down sexified memory lane. It took every ounce of my willpower to tear my thoughts away and focus on what he was saying.

"...will be here at about midnight. He wants to make sure you're ready before he takes you to meet Raptor. Apparently, he thinks he'll have to coach you for an hour before the two of you leave."

"And you disagree?"

A smile played at the corner of Price's mouth. "We made a lot of headway this morning. I think that, as long as you stay focused, you'll be just fine."

"And if I can't," I fished.

"Then it's a good thing Chill will be with you. He's a master of talking in circles when he wants to distract people." A faint smile touched his lips. "He always has been."

I swallowed the last bite of my sandwich and frowned.

"What's the matter, Skylar?"

"Something's been bothering me."

"What's that?"

I wet my lips. "If your real name is Jonathan Price, why do the two people who have known you the longest still call you Parker? Surely they don't think that they have to hide the truth from me."

I could have sworn something flashed through Price's eyes, but things were still a little bit hazy.

On so many levels.

"They know that they can trust you. Parker is…a nickname."

"I would have thought Jon would be a more natural nickname for you. How'd you end up with Parker?"

"We were always scheming at boarding school; God knows there was nothing else to do there. Anyway, I never got caught, no matter what I did. I had a knack for getting out of bad situations, I guess. There was a television show on around that time about a high school kid who always got away with doing stuff. The character's name was Parker. It started out as a joke, but the name stuck." Price studied me intently for a moment. "What about you, Skylar? Any nicknames?"

"Well," I began uncertainly, "you already know my dad used to call me his songbird. I had a boyfriend once who used to call me a little lark. Other than that, it's just been the people who think that they get to shorten my name to Sky."

"You don't like that?"

"No. If my parents had wanted people to call me Sky they would have named me Sky."

"I'll remember that. Do you feel like going over the story one more time?"

Inwardly, I sighed in disappointment. The subject always seemed to change when I felt like I was starting to learn something about him. "Why not?"

Chill parked his car in the deserted parking garage and killed the engine. Skylar hadn't said a word since getting into the car and that concerned him. Not only was his reputation riding on her performance, but possibly both of their lives.

He slid a glance in her direction and was satisfied that Raptor would not recognize her. Despite the tight-fitting black leggings she wore, her figure was hidden by a baggy black sweater. It was a damn shame too, Chill thought as they waited. Parker had made it clear she was off limits to him, but he could've at least enjoyed the view.

And enjoying the view was about all he could do these days. The Covington name attracted a certain type of woman, as did his criminal persona. He was tired of dabbling with either. What he needed was a woman who could handle swimming in both ponds with him.

Like Cherry.

Fuck.

Not that nagging thought again. Not tonight. Not now. Better to keep his thoughts on the woman next to him.

Skylar's long hair was braided and hidden by the black ski mask she wore. The length of it was tucked into her sweater. And her eyes...Oh, Ramsey had done a number on her with his little bag of tricks. The hazel contact lenses hid the natural sparkle in her eyes and replaced it with an odd greenish glimmer.

Chill realized he'd been staring when Skylar turned to face him. "Don't tell me you're about to come onto me again?"

He flashed a wolfish grin at her. "Would that be so bad, sweet?"

"It might be a tad inappropriate, given the circumstances," she replied softly.

Chill immediately picked up on her tone. "We still have time to leave if you can't do this."

Even through the cover of the contacts Chill could see defiance flashing in her eyes. "I can handle this and there will be no more discussion about it."

Chill shrugged casually. "Suit yourself, but you should know something first."

"And what's that?"

"This hardcore bitch thing you have going right now is really turning me on."

Skylar stared at him in shocked silence, clearly unsure how to react. Finally, her lips cracked into a wry smile. "You don't have any sort of an interior monologue working in your brain, do you?"

Chill was about the respond when his ears heard the faint sound of an approaching vehicle. Skylar must have heard it too because her eyes widened. He acknowledged her silent question with a nod of his head.

A nondescript Suburban appeared at the far end of the garage and the driver cut its engine. After a minute, the Suburban's high beams flashed twice. Chill flashed his once and waited. Their high beams flashed once more and then were shut off altogether.

Chill followed suit and looked over at Skylar.

"Show time. Is Songbird ready?"

Skylar swallowed hard. In a thick, southern drawl she replied, "Songbird's good to go, sugar."

FIFTEEN

Raptor cautiously eyed the approaching couple. He'd known Chill for a number of years and used him to set up numerous jobs over that time – in other towns, of course. Chill's reputation spoke for itself. The woman with him, on the other hand, would have to prove herself to him.

And quickly.

As usual, Chill skipped the pleasantries and got right down to business. "Songbird, this is Raptor. Tell him your plan."

Her brown eyes regarded Raptor coolly as she spoke. "I intend to take down a highly monitored bank without ever having to reach for a weapon."

Raptor arched an eyebrow at her statement. "You're naïve if you think that will work."

"No, hon, just confident." Songbird tossed him a haughty smile from behind her mask and continued. "Should I even go on?"

Raptor was intrigued at her arrogance. Clearly, she had no idea who she was talking to, but he decided to let it slide. He wanted to hear what made her think she had reason to be so smug.

"Go on."

"The bank I have in mind has a fairly large staff and a security guard posted behind the counter in case anyone gets any ideas. I've gotten my hands on this precious little chemical that you can treat paper bills with. It's completely safe to the touch, so we needn't worry about ourselves, but it becomes active once it's airborne."

"Then why are you treating money with it?" Raptor demanded. Alluring drawl aside, he was bored and wanted her to get to the point.

"Because I've done my homework on this bank. The tellers are required to run all of their drive-up deposits through a currency counter after a hand count. I've done my homework on that, too. It moves the money quickly to count it and will release the chemical into the air for us."

Raptor was skeptical. "Are you suggesting that we go in there with gas masks?"

Songbird cast him another haughty look. "Hon, you don't get the big picture, do ya?" Without letting him respond she said, "There will only be enough to affect the people behind the line. Besides, it dissipates quickly. Everyone will be out cold before we make a move."

Though he was annoyed by the lack of respect she showed him, her plan had merit. "And what do you propose we do about all the people who aren't behind the line?"

"They'll be too distracted by all the bodies on the floor to pay us any mind."

Chill, who remained unusually silent during the exchange, asked, "Do we have a deal, or am I wasting the best part of my day?"

"Slow down. There are still the cameras and alarms to dispense with."

Songbird's eyes narrowed. She jutted out her hip and placed her gloved hand, fingertips up, on it. Her tone was harsh, despite the silky drawl, when she spoke. "Hon, this ain't recess here. Of course we'll hack their systems."

Without reply, Raptor returned her fierce stare, and then let his eyes drop. Her figure was cloaked by the black sweater she wore, but he could imagine her creamy curves just fine. She was confident, even cocky, and he wondered if that would carry over to the bedroom, running things, taking what she wanted. Or maybe she was more timid without her mask to hide behind, taking orders as she was given. It would make no difference, Raptor finally decided with a smirk. He would make her moan when this heist was complete.

"Time is ticking," Chill reminded.

Raptor tore his eyes away from Songbird - and his thoughts - turning his attention to Chill. "The idea has merit, but let's flesh it out. Has Ramsey contacted you yet? He was supposed to."

"Yes. It was an unpleasant surprise."

"To me as well. Get the two of them in contact. Have him fill in the blanks for the kid."

Songbird made an irritated sound, but Chill spoke before she could make her displeasure at his statement known.

"Should I recruit a hacker?"

"No," Raptor said with an air of finality, waving the statement away with a gloved hand. "I already have one in mind. You just worry about keeping this one in check."

Chill smirked. "That will be entirely my pleasure."

"For now." Raptor turned his back on them, satisfied by the flash of defiance in Songbird's dark eyes. "I'll be in touch."

He started to walk away, but stopped. Without turning, he asked, "Which bank?"

The silky drawl was immediate. "First Alliance Bank and Trust, sugar."

"I've already had that bank."

After a beat, "Not much of a conquest back when the bank's security was archaic. Not half the satisfaction you'd get this time."

He turned, looking her up and down once more before responding. "Oh, I've no doubt of that." His lips curved into a hungry smile. "Especially if you're part of the conquest." Before she could protest, he added, "And you are. If you're in, you're...*in.*"

After Raptor drove for over ten minutes, and was certain no one followed him, he removed his mask. Everything was beginning to come together in his mind: the heist, the conquest, the satisfaction of it all. Songbird would never know what hit her when he was through with her. She could play it cool, for now, but she would succumb to his will in the end.

Just like everyone else.

"You did well, Skylar," Price said finally.

I didn't respond. Listening to the way Chill described the encounter with Raptor, you would think I had all of the skill and grace of the village idiot. It felt like they expected me to freeze up or give myself away, which was totally absurd in my opinion. I had eight years of theater under my belt and there was no way I was going to blow the performance of my life.

More time must have passed than I realized because I heard Chill say, "She's been like that since we left the garage. Not sure what her trauma is all of the sudden."

I cast a withering look in their general direction and rose from the couch. "I need to get these...these *things* out of my eyes. What do I do with them?"

"You can throw them out. We've got plenty more," Price answered with some hesitation.

A guilty feeling invaded me when I realized I was taking things out on him, things that had nothing to do with him, but I was not about to give Chill the satisfaction of hearing me admit it. Instead, I nodded and fled the room. Hot tears began to sting my eyes just as the bathroom door clicked shut behind me.

I had played a lot of roles, done a lot of crazy things, in my life, but this...The meeting with Raptor seemed surreal, almost dreamlike. All of the mannerisms I so carefully practiced flowed naturally and the hostility came so easily – though not because he was the better criminal and I wanted to make a name for myself. Still, I was grateful Price forced me to practice for hours this morning, yesterday morning, whatever.

I shook my head in an attempt to clear my thoughts and focus, but I was struck by the realization that I was on the floor, knees drawn up to my chest, actually shaking as silent sobs consumed me. Murderous rage had flowed through my veins when Raptor had looked me over. It had taken everything I had to control my...Like it even mattered. This man had easily murdered my father and he would make short order of me if he discovered who I really was, what I was really doing.

But who the hell was *he*? Behind the mask and faint European accent was a man who I should have recognized. Dammit! It shouldn't be this difficult. Price had confirmed one of the three men I suspected was Raptor. Why couldn't I just see it?

Drake. Eric. Trevor. Eric. Trevor. Drake. Trevor. Drake. Eric. Their names ran through my head like a mantra, but didn't bring clarity. The monster I talked to didn't remind me of any of the men I knew.

But I didn't really know any of them, did I? Not if one of them could be a cold-blooded killer who decided bedding me was a foregone conclusion.

This was all insane. I buried my head in my hands and let that thought wash over me. Raptor had killed my father with no more thought than he would give taking a breath and I thought that I could bring him down. Raptor had taken the lives of his crew as an after-thought and I had the nerve to think I could stop him. How naïve was I?

"Is everything all right, Skylar?"

I looked up and met Price's worried eyes. The door hadn't made a sound when he'd opened it, at least not that I heard. He knelt beside me and brushed a loose strand of hair from my face. I tried to turn away from him, but he brushed the back of his hand against my cheek and said, "Hold still for a second."

I felt his hands on either side of my face and then his thumbs gently rub under my eyes. At first I thought he was wiping the tears away, but I realized the contact lenses had come out of my eyes during my sobbing and were stuck to my face. There was such genuine concern in Price's eyes, in his touch...I didn't know how to respond.

"Chill is insensitive, well, most of the time, but especially when his mind is on the job," Price said quietly.

I shook my head and averted my eyes. "This isn't about..."

"I know," he interrupted. "I know it couldn't have been easy for you to face Raptor tonight. Chill told me about the way he treated you. I should have prepared you for the..." Price paused. "I should have prepared you for his Adonis complex."

I mustered a weak smile and looked back at him. "It wasn't so bad. Chill is worse when he's coming onto me."

"I'm serious, Skylar. I had hoped you wouldn't have to deal with that on top of everything else," he said, brushing a tear off of my cheek.

His touch sent a tingle of excitement through me, as though we weren't just discussing a monster. Our eyes locked and I froze. He had felt it too; it was evident by the look in his eyes. I tried to let out my breath slowly, but it came out as ragged. Something unfamiliar was stirring inside of me and I didn't know how to respond to it, just as I didn't know how to read Price's expression.

He pulled his hand away a little too quickly and rose to his feet. "You should try to get some sleep. You have another meeting with him tomorrow night." Turning to leave, he added, "We all do."

With that Price left me alone on the floor.

*****

Wednesday, March 31

Jackson crumpled the page he was reading and chunked it at the trash in frustration. He and Dinsley had spent all of yesterday pounding the streets, working over every informant the Bureau had, and there was still nothing. Now, it was almost noon and he hadn't turned up anything new, despite the stacks of reports he read.

"You missed," Dinsley commented without looking up from his computer.

"Yeah and we're missing something important."

Dinsley glanced at him. "You mean like the missing years of Trevor Brightman's life?"

Jackson was about the say something smart, but recognized the edge to his partner's tone. "What'd you find?"

He turned the monitor so that Jackson could see. "I found out exactly why our friend's past was so difficult for the DA's office to trace."

At first, Jackson didn't understand what he was reading, but then it snapped into focus. "You've got to be kidding me."

"'Fraid not, Caldwell. It's been under our nose the entire time."

"But *Witness Protection?*" Jackson shook his head in disgust. "You would think we'd have found something in our own databases about that one."

Dinsley shrugged. "You have to have special clearance to access the files on that particular server, which we don't have. Apparently, they think field agents are susceptible to bribery."

"If we don't have clearance, how are we looking at this?"

A smile crept across his partner's face. "You don't last as long as I have in this office without learning a few tricks along the way. I kept seeing the same story in all of the intel we had on him. It made me think about this one guy's file who I escorted to testify. It read pretty close to Brightman's."

"Is there any chance he could be Raptor?" Jackson asked, though he knew the answer.

Dinsley's face grew grim as he turned his attention back to the monitor. "No. It looks like we're still keeping a close eye on him for some reason. Oh, there it is. He has one more trial to testify at and it looks like this is the big one." He closed his eyes and rubbed his temples. "If he had even looked at that bank the wrong way, we would have known about it before he did."

"Well hell, Brandon. This narrows it down some, but we still don't have anything on Wyndham or Sauters." Jackson stood up. "I'd better call Jenna and let her know not to bother with Brightman anymore."

"Wait," Dinsley said quickly, his eyes wide. "You can't tell her why."

"Are you trying to tell me you don't think we can trust her?" He quirked an eyebrow. "I think we both know she's not some kind of a sleeper assassin."

Dinsley shook his head. "No, that she isn't. I'm trying to tell you there are ears everywhere around here, probably in her office, too, and I can't afford for anyone to find out how we got the information. I don't need another black mark in my file. Tell her tonight for all I care."

"All right, I'll just tell her we've discovered he has an airtight alibi."

"Thank you," Dinsley said without the usual gruff tone. Remembering himself, he added, "Just make sure that's all you tell her."

Jackson nodded and turned before his partner could see the smile forming on his face. "Consider it done."

Maybe, he thought as he headed into one of the conference rooms to make his call, Jenna was right about Agent Brandon Dinsley after all.

"Are you even listening to me, Skylar?"

"Hmm? Oh...yeah."

Parker covered his face with his hand and sighed loudly. Skylar had been acting strangely ever since she got up earlier that evening. It was as though she didn't understand how crucial tonight was to their operation.

In just a few hours, all of the players would meet with Raptor and everyone would have to play it cool. Chill phoned earlier to confirm that Cherry was approached by Raptor and everything was set. They simply could not afford for Skylar to lose her grip at this point. Too many lives were now on the line.

"What the hell is the matter with you today? I need you to focus on what I'm telling you. This is important."

Skylar looked hurt. "I know, I know. I'm sorry. I'm listening."

Her tone was just a little too agreeable. Parker realized her meeting with Raptor must have upset her even more than he originally thought. The moment he found her huddled on the floor last night he knew she was badly shaken. She'd seemed vulnerable and, in other circumstances, he might have taken advantage of that.

Hell, he almost had.

In that brief instant when their eyes had met, he'd considered pulling her into his arms, kissing her, making love to her, until she'd forgotten all about Raptor. It would be a lie to say he didn't want her every time he touched her, but the way she'd looked at him made him wonder if she might feel the same way, if there wasn't something there beyond all the games she kept playing. Despite all of the pent-up desire, he had called upon every shred of self-control he possessed to walk away from her.

No, Parker would not let himself take advantage of her in the state she was in last night. There was no denying that he wanted her, and that he would have her again, but he would not on *those* terms. The next time he took her to bed, he would not give her another excuse to run away.

"Do we need to take a break?" he asked in a softer tone.

Skylar shook her head. "No. Please go on. I know we don't have a lot of time left."

"Good. You know the story, but let me do as much of the talking as possible."

"Won't that seem odd to him? I mean, I did practically all of the talking last night."

"No. He'll assume I treated you the exact same way I treat all business associates I consider amateurs."

"And how exactly is that?"

"Like idiot children."

"I hate to be the one to tell you, but Songbird isn't exactly the type to just take it lying down."

"No, she's not," he agreed, wishing that she hadn't just conjured a memory of the two of them at the hotel.

Why was he even so distracted when there was so much else to focus on before tonight? Staying with Skylar was a clear mistake, but it served the dual purposes of giving him time to prep her and maintaining his cover story with Raptor. If he couldn't figure out a way to get his mind solidly back on business before that night's meeting, they were all sunk.

Trying to shake the image before it got out of hand, he added, "That's why you should treat me with open hostility. Of course, that won't really be anything new to you."

Parker was surprised when Skylar didn't snap at him over his remark, so he remained quiet and waited for her to say something.

"Yeah, I've been meaning to apologize to you for that. I haven't really meant to be so standoffish."

This wasn't the time for the conversation that was about to happen. Parker could feel the tension growing between them and he knew it was up to him to diffuse it before she started down a line of conversation he couldn't control. Too much was riding on tonight.

He cleared his throat. "It's not a big deal. Anyway, you should know I'll be in character tonight. Some things might get said that you won't like."

"Like that's a shock. I don't like anything about any of this. You don't need to worry about me. I'll be fine."

Parker dropped the subject, but he didn't stop worrying. Raptor was possibly the worst part of the criminal element he knew and that was saying quite a bit given Parker's past. And it had nothing to do with his skill at taking down banks. Any idiot with the balls to ask a teller to hand over their cash could take down a bank.

Didn't have anything to do with Raptor's planning prowess either. Parker knew he was clearly the better of them.

The one area in which he could never compete with his nemesis was ruthlessness. Parker was a con man; Raptor was an unadulterated sociopath. That he was only considered a bank robber and murderer by the authorities was a true testament to the ineptitude of law enforcement agencies at connecting the dots.

If Skylar knew what kind of monster she was really up against...he didn't know how to finish the thought.

What he did know for sure was that Skylar would not be pleased at what was sure to be said in a few hours. He couldn't warn her either. That would just put her on edge from the moment they got to the meet. Hopefully, she'd be able to hold it all in until they were safely away from Raptor. If she couldn't, none of their careful planning would matter.

They'd all be dead.

SIXTEEN

"What are you still doing up?" Jackson asked as he closed the door to the condo.

Jenna looked up from her computer and smiled. "I've been so busy lately that I've neglected my writing." She took off her reading glasses and set them on the desk before stretching her arms over her head. "I figured you'd be home late again tonight, so I thought I'd make good use of the alone time."

Home. He liked the way that word pinballed around in his mind.

He noticed the mischievous glimmer in her deep brown eyes. It never ceased to amaze him how beautiful she was, even when she was wearing flannel pajama pants and a tank top just as she was now. She'd pulled back her hair to keep it out of her eyes while she typed, but nearly half the strands around her face had already come loose. It didn't make sense that she could look so ridiculous and still be so beautiful at the same time.

That was the exact moment Jackson knew he was going to spend forever with her.

"That sounds like an excuse to wait up for me."

Jenna shrugged. "Let's just say I was trying to help time pass a little more quickly." She turned back to the computer for a moment before shutting it off. Rising from the chair she asked, "So how did you eliminate Trevor?"

Jackson followed her into the kitchen. "It seems that he made some powerful enemies several years ago. He's in the Witness Protection Program."

Jenna shut the refrigerator door loudly. "That explains why I couldn't find anything on him."

"Well, you're in good company. Brandon had to break into the system to find out."

"You're kidding," Jenna said; her eyes widened in surprise. "I can't believe Brandon would do that."

"Me neither, but I'm glad he did. We could have spent days trying to dig up dirt on Brightman otherwise."

"Hmm. One down, two to go, I suppose."

Jackson nodded. "I just wish I had some idea of how to narrow it down further. They're both equally unlikely suspects."

"Do we have to talk about work right now?" Jenna asked suddenly. "I haven't seen much of you this week."

More of him than she'd seen in all the weeks prior. "You brought it up."

"I know, but I only did that so I could steer the conversation the way I wanted it to go and wrap it up quickly."

Jackson cocked his head to the side. "Okay."

"Don't give me that look. You know as well as I do that asking you how your day was can sometimes merit an hour-long response. I almost think I liked it better when you had to talk about your fictional job instead of your work with the Bureau. You never offered up any details and then you'd change the subject...or just carry me off to the bedroom."

"I don't think I'll ever understand you."

Jenna smiled. "Maybe you aren't supposed to. Now come on, let's go to bed."

Without another word, Jackson followed her down the hallway. Even though he pretended to be annoyed, he was grateful for the excuse to go to bed. Sleep had been the farthest thing from his mind over the last few weeks and it was finally catching up with him.

Jenna flipped on the bedroom lights and paused. "I forgot to tell you something earlier. I've been running across the same name in Drake's file quite a bit, but I can't find anything on the guy."

"I thought you didn't want to talk about work anymore."

"I don't, but this might be important. What was the guy's name?" Jenna looked up as if the answer was written on the ceiling for her.

"You can just call me tomorrow and..."

"Simon Templer."

Jackson's eyes grew wide. "Isn't that the guy he sold his partnership interests to?"

"That's the one."

What Jackson didn't tell Jenna was that he'd seen that name come up that very day in Drake's file, but he couldn't remember where. It might not have been important; just what she'd already told him. Still, the name stuck in his mind long after Jenna fell asleep.

He would have to take a closer look first thing in the morning.

Raptor waited until he was certain his crew was already there before he got out of his car to meet them. Maybe it was a power play, but he always enjoyed making his crew wait. It went a long way to show them who was really in charge.

He especially enjoyed making Ramsey wait, knowing he wasn't used to being kept waiting for anything. Ever.

As he expected, Songbird and Ramsey did not seem to be getting along. For all of Ramsey's talents, endearing himself in the hearts of women had never been one of them – unless the woman was the mark. That probably explained why Skylar Montgomery was so taken with him. She would have a rude awakening coming once Ramsey tossed her aside like the rest of his unwanted toys.

"Where are we?" Raptor demanded as he joined the others.

Ramsey took the lead. "Some of her ideas were good; others were total crap. I think I can salvage it, but I'll need the system hacked by tomorrow to do it. I've met your hacker and I can see *why* you chose her." He cut his eyes to Cherry. "Do you even know how to hack?"

In a quiet tone, she answered, "Better than you."

"Not saying a lot." He turned back to Raptor. "Can she handle the pressure? It has to be done tomorrow. Not Friday. Not when her manicure's done. To-*mor*-row."

Raptor let his eyes sweep over Cherry's tightly clothed figure before he answered. He was so tired of her. As a conquest, she bored him. Only her continued fear kept her somewhat enjoyable. "She'll be fine, but what's your rush?"

Ramsey rolled his eyes. "I want to do this thing on Monday, that's what."

Raptor was annoyed by his tone. Though he never particularly cared for him, he did admire his guts. Besides Chill, he was the only one of them who was unmasked – even in the last crew. Then again, cons like Parker Ramsey didn't think more than a move or two ahead of the game, so they didn't realize the benefit of a hidden identity that allowed them to move freely through society.

If he had, he wouldn't have had to stay completely off the social radar for two years while pretending to be dead...

"What's so special about Monday?" Cherry demanded, more fire in her question than she offered in her own defense.

Ramsey turned on her. "The men are talking, sweetheart. Don't bother me with *blonde* questions right now." Turning back to Raptor, he said, "Daylight savings is this Sunday. After losing an hour of sleep, people will be less likely to be out and about as early as they normally would, especially to run errands. If we hit the bank as soon as they open then we'll have less chance of someone walking in on us and fewer customers to keep quiet."

"That doesn't give us much time to case the place, Ramsey," Raptor challenged. While he'd already cased that particular bank on multiple occasions, he wasn't privy to all the security procedures Traymoore put in place. Wisely, that was something the bank president kept close to the vest since the last heist.

"I've already told you I cased it before I met with you," Songbird chirped in.

Ramsey glanced at her and shook his head. "The kid's not nearly thorough enough, but you have me now, so that doesn't matter. I have a *friend* who's in good with the bank president."

Raptor nodded. "Yes, Skylar, but how are you going to get the information from her?"

Ramsey shrugged and let a smug smile tug at the corner of his equally smug mouth. "She's chatty in bed. Besides, you give her too much credit. She isn't very bright. She'll never realize what she's telling me." The smile turned into a smirk. "It'll just take a little finessing to get her on the right subject, but I know all the right buttons to push with her."

Raptor nodded his agreement. No, she was not very bright if she had been fooled by Ramsey enough to believe he cared about her in the slightest. Perhaps he had given her too much credit. To Cherry, he asked, "Can you have the system hacked by tomorrow?"

Cherry looked annoyed, but knew better than to take that type of a tone with him. He had ways of dealing with her attitude and she knew it well. "I haven't looked at it yet, but I don't foresee a problem...as long as I start as soon as we leave here."

Raptor understood what she was implying and decided he would let her take the night off. He had someone else in mind for the night, anyway; someone who was a little less professional. Someone who hadn't yet seen the reason for Cherry's constant fear. "Then let's get to it...unless anyone else feels the need to offer their two cents."

He looked from face to face, waiting. It was a pleasant surprise when Songbird remained silent. Pairing her with Ramsey was turning out to serve multiple purposes. A little bit of that fire seemed to have moved out of her dark eyes and she was more reserved, more submissive than she'd been just last night.

Just the way Raptor liked his women.

He settled his gaze on Songbird for a long moment, hoping to make her squirm, but pleased with the defiant glare he received in return. "I've worked with everyone else, so I feel I must ask only you this question. Your original plan of no guns is out. Can you handle a weapon, kid?"

"I can handle anything you put in my hand and I would appreciate if you would not forget that, hon," she drawled.

Raptor felt the smirk unconsciously take hold of his mouth. "Oh, I won't." He turned his attention to the rest of the crew. "We're done here. Ramsey, stay behind a minute."

Driving home, Parker let out a sigh of relief. It was lucky that Raptor wanted to talk to him before leaving. It gave Chill a chance to get Skylar home without risk of Raptor tailing them and discovering the secret.

They just had to keep up the ruse for just over four days and then it wouldn't matter.

Luckily, for now, he was still buying the act. In Raptor's mind, Skylar and Songbird were two different people, Cherry was still on his side and Chill was impartial as ever. But he still regarded Parker as hostile, making it clear exactly what he would do if he was betrayed. In and of itself, that was amusing when Parker already knew Raptor planned to kill him after the heist.

Parker let his thoughts turn from that unsettling thought to the remainder of the conversation. As expected, Raptor had a thing for

Songbird, never so much as considering that not every woman alive was interested in hopping into bed with him.

Then again, Parker knew a woman's willingness wasn't exactly something Raptor cared about.

Chill's car was long gone by the time he got to Skylar's. He paused briefly at the door and let himself remember the cozy picture he painted for Raptor of what it was like living with Skylar. It was entirely necessary to assure him he could get the information they needed from Skylar, and to convince him that he had no time or interest in bedding Songbird.

He lingered a few moments longer than necessary, relishing how good he and Skylar could be together once this was all over. But it was all resting on her, on what she wanted. In just under five days, he might have to walk away from her and the knowledge of what they could have if she still wasn't convinced she wanted him.

Timing where she was concerned always seemed to be working against him.

"You sonofabitch," Skylar shouted from the couch as soon as he closed the door. "Chatty in bed? Not that bright! Where the hell do you get..."

Parker held up his hands in protest. "I warned you I would be in character; that I would have to say things you wouldn't like. You said you were fine with that."

Her eyes, now void of the contacts, gleamed with anger. "I didn't realize I was going to be personally attacked in front of everyone!"

"Look," he began, crossing the room to the couch and kneeling down in front of her, "Cherry and Chill know all of that was said for Raptor's benefit. It was just the kind of thing he would expect me to say." Belatedly, he wished that hadn't come out as though that was something the *real* him would say. "You don't see Cherry over here griping about the way I treated her, do you?"

"I could be wrong, but you didn't just have sex with Cherry a few days ago," Skylar snapped.

Parker covered his face with his hands in frustration. Why were they fighting about this? The sex didn't matter. She had made it very clear that she wasn't interested anymore – unless he was willing to trade Raptor's identity for it.

He ran a hand through his hair and returned her glare. "For the record, Cherry is like a little sister to me, so you can drop the attitude on that. I do not think you're a fool, quite the opposite in fact. As for the pillow talk…" He shrugged as his words trailed off. "You bolted out of my room before I could find out, so you know as well as I do that that was a total fabrication."

Skylar looked away. "Fine. Whatever."

Parker stood up and sighed loudly. "Drop the attitude."

Her head whipped around and her eyes locked on his. "Excuse me?"

"You heard what I said. We have a lot of work to do before bed and I need you to pay attention."

Skylar rose to her feet, eyes still locked on his. "And what might that be?"

"I have to teach you how to use a weapon before our next meeting. Unless I miss my guess, you've never so much as held a gun."

Defeated, she sank back down to the couch and Parker went to find his bags. He'd have to triple-check that nothing was loaded. Now wasn't the best time to give her a loaded weapon.

I was amazed at what a fool I really was as Price demonstrated how to hold and use the gun with which I would have to appear comfortable. How did it not occur to me before now that I would have to know about this to fool Raptor? It would have been so much simpler if I had made up some excuse about how I didn't like to use guns during a holdup because of the possible jail time, or that I was against guns – which was partially true since my father had lost his life because of one. If I had thought of anything to say other than what I had then I wouldn't be in the predicament I now found myself in.

The instant I felt the weight of the cool steel in my hands, I knew that I was in trouble. Price made it all look so easy, but there was something *wrong* about the way they felt. When he held them and gestured, each gun looked like an extension of his own hand, like something he'd held his whole life. Surely it was just the lack of practice that made me feel so out of place holding them.

No…not even close. Something just like what was now in my hand had ended my father's life. I would *never* appear comfortable because I would never *be* comfortable.

Unemotionally, I mimicked the movements Price had just shown me, but I could tell from the disapproving look in those green eyes that this was not the sort of thing I was a quick study at. He stood up and crossed the short distance of the living room to me.

"Here," Price said as he motioned for me to give him back the guns.

I shook my head and frowned at him. "No. I can't learn by watching you. I have to do it for myself."

"Okay," he replied, "suit yourself, but you are going to have to look more comfortable. When you leveled the guns and brought them out to the side I thought you had a better chance of taking yourself down than a bank."

"It isn't exactly the sort of thing I do all of the time."

"Well, I can't exactly tell you how to be comfortable and you can't follow an example so I would say we have a problem."

"I know." I let them dangle from my index fingers and added, "Is it too late to pretend I have an aversion to guns?"

"I would say so. It was too late the first time you got in touch with Chill." He appeared thoughtful for a second and then gave me a guarded look. "I have an idea, but I don't want you to freak out on me."

"And why would I do that?" I asked, skeptical. It wasn't like I freaked out over every little thing he said or did. Did I?

"I think I can guide you if I get closer to you..."

"Whatever."

I hoped my tone sounded as nonchalant to his ears as I had intended it to. The reality of the situation was that I had to force myself to breathe normally when he walked up behind me. He was so close to me as he guided my arms through the motions that I could feel his breath on the back of my neck. Despite the heat of it, a chill swept throughout my body, forcing me aware of my emotions.

The decision to sleep with Price had never been one I made consciously – at least, not that night in the hotel. I had only intended to talk to him when I followed him back to his hotel, but things happened so quickly that I let myself get caught up in the moment. The champagne I was drinking that night undoubtedly was a factor as well because I was not a woman who randomly took lovers. Then again, not getting laid in two years was also sure to be a major part of it.

It took several minutes to become comfortable with the weapons in my hands. The air between us was tense – sizzling with tension, actually – which made me wonder whether my very private thoughts were obvious to Price. I got my answer when he let go of my arms and spoke to me.

"That's good. Better. I think you have it now." His voice was on edge, but he didn't move away from me.

I turned around slowly, fully aware of his nearness. The knowledge that something might be about to happen, that I actually wanted something to happen, was electrifying. My pulse was racing, but I didn't attempt to conceal it from him as I looked into his eyes.

I didn't have to.

We stood as still as stone statues, gazing into one another's eyes, for what felt like a lifetime. Neither of us spoke; neither of us moved. I might have been holding my breath, but I didn't really know. The only things that seemed to register in my mind were the butterflies in my stomach, dancing in anticipation.

Suddenly, as though moved by some elemental force, the gap between us was bridged. The passion in his kiss caught me off guard and I heard the soft thud of the guns hitting the carpeted floor. Guess they weren't loaded. Good thing, too. I had no desire for an errant bullet to cut this moment short.

Price made a rough sound when he encircled my waist with his arms to pull me nearer and I wrapped my arms around his neck in response. I wasn't sure how long we stood in the middle of my living room that way and I certainly didn't know at what point I decided I wanted him more than Raptor's identity. Perhaps I had made that decision a long time ago and was only now finally aware of it.

All I was really certain of was that I wanted to take this further. I was tired of hiding my physical responses to him. I was tired of playing these coy little games.

I wanted him and I wanted him to know it.

I let my hands slip from his neck down to his chest and began working the buttons on his shirt. His heart pounded against my hands, much the same way my heart was pounding in my chest. The number of buttons on his shirt infuriated me as I fumbled along blindly, hating that the space between our bodies to accommodate my hands was necessary.

Before I was halfway done, Price abruptly broke away from me and gathered my hands in his.

"What?" I asked breathlessly. I knew there was a dazed look in my eyes, that I appeared vulnerable, but I didn't care. For the first time, I didn't care.

"I'm sorry," he began in a slow, measured tone. "I shouldn't have done that. You should probably get to bed."

I caught my breath and chose my words with care. "Come with me," I offered from beneath lowered lashes.

"We both know that isn't a good idea," Price said. His voice was so quiet that I wouldn't be sure he'd spoken if I hadn't just watched his lips move.

"You don't want me?"

"Don't do that. You know good and goddamned well that isn't it, so don't even play the wounded dove routine with me." After a long moment, he hesitantly added, "I've never denied wanting you."

If we were on the same page about his, what were we still doing fully clothed in the living room? "Then what's the problem?"

Price shook his head. "I know what you really want from me and I'm not prepared to give you Raptor's real name. I'd rather not even get into something we aren't going to finish." His eyes narrowed. "Again."

"I'm willing to put a pin in that one for tonight." I brushed a light kiss against his lips. "I can't deny that something is going on between us. Not anymore." I nuzzled my head against his neck. "You can't either."

"I won't try to deny it because I can't, but I'm not sure that it's enough to keep you from turning on me again once you're done putting pins in things." He waited for me to meet his cautious look. "You've already leapt out of bed to hurl accusations at me once. That was enough for me."

I blinked in surprise. "I can't believe you're using that against me. *You* kept information from me that I should have known first. You're still keeping it from me."

"I'm not going to fight with you about this, Skylar. Not tonight. Not for the next four nights."

"You're a real bastard," I snapped. "You won't give me anything I need. What the hell good are you?"

I could tell that my words hurt him, but he recovered his usual cool demeanor before he spoke. "I'll be a bastard to you no matter what I do here tonight. I would rather be a bastard for not going to bed with you than for being accused of using you. Again." He dropped my hands and turned away from me. "Goodnight, Skylar."

Without another word to him, I stalked off into my bedroom, changed clothes and crawled into my lonely bed. What the hell just happened?

SEVENTEEN

"He sold it to himself," Jackson said in disbelief as he rushed into Dinsley's office.

Brandon looked up from the stack of reports he was sifting through. "Who and what?"

Jackson sank down into the chair across the desk from him. "Wyndham. He sold his partnership interest to himself."

This could be the break we're looking for, Brandon thought. Maintaining his composure, he set down the papers in his hand and said, "Why don't you back up and fill me in?"

His partner nodded anxiously. "Jenna told me that she kept running across this name, Simon Templer, but she couldn't find anything on him except for the fact that he bought Wyndham's partnership interest from him."

"And?" Brandon asked, hoping that bland information would somehow lead them to a bust. So far, none of this seemed cause for excitement.

"And Simon Templer is not a real person, he's an old television character."

Brandon shook his head. "Lots of people have names used on TV. That doesn't make him a…"

"Yes, it does."

"Have you been getting any sleep, Caldwell?" With all the long brown hairs he kept pulling from his clothes, Brandon was willing to bet he spent every night with Jenna…probably not sleeping.

Jackson's eyes flashed with anger, almost as though he'd read his mind. "Just hear me out for a second. I spent all day yesterday going over his file. In letters of recommendation, yearbooks…everything, people kept referring to him as *The Saint*."

"Okay. Where are you going with this?" Brandon asked in confusion.

Jackson stared at him in disbelief. "Have you ever watched television or gone to the movies?" He waited with an expectant look on his face and added, "Roger Moore? Val Kilmer?" After a long moment, he pounded his fists on the desk. "Simon Templer *is* the fucking saint."

This is it! Brandon wanted to jump out of his skin and race over to the bank where he could arrest that smug bastard. That would wipe the phony smile off his face. But reason wouldn't let him show his excitement over the revelation. It could still be a coincidence and he wasn't ready to stake his career on a hunch.

Even a damn good one.

"So how do you explain the infusion of cash he received from the sale? We've gone over all of his financials and we would have noticed that large of a check being written from one of his personal accounts."

"I can't explain it, Brandon. Unless…"

"Unless he robbed his own bank and needed a way to launder the money. I want this case to be airtight. Let's see what we can dig up on his association with Brightman. He's in an excellent position to help us."

Jackson was on his feet before Brandon was done talking. "I'm on it."

Once the door snapped shut, Brandon smiled and picked up the phone. There was someone he needed to talk to. Sophia wasn't around anymore to share in his excitement, but he knew there was someone else he could call who would.

If only she weren't still married…

*****

The evening had dragged on endlessly for me. An uncomfortable silence filled the house and I still couldn't quite understand what had happened. One minute it had been obvious how much Price wanted me and the next...I had never been rejected before in my life – the failed blow job extortion attempt didn't count – and I didn't know how to cope with the feelings it caused.

So I stayed quiet.

It was a good thing that Price didn't seem especially conversational because I didn't think I could be cordial. I was hurt, confused, exhausted...scared – both of what I'd been doing for the past two years and of my feelings for him. There was no way I could carry on a conversation without further alienating myself from him.

Sleep hadn't come easily for me after his brush-off so I had plenty of time to think through the situation. This was very clearly my own fault. There was no blaming Price's behavior on him after the way I had treated him over the past few weeks. God, I really was more like a spoiled, petulant child than a grown woman.

I wouldn't want me, either.

The one time we had spoken, it was all business. Chill called to let us know that everything was going according to plan. Raptor was furious when Cherry informed him the system couldn't be hacked. Price had to spend a great deal of time on the phone to convince him that the plan could work without the hack and told him that Cherry would need to procure a signal jammer. I thought that an odd statement to make since I knew Chill already had that, but I soon realized he was only trying to get Cherry out of Raptor's path of rage.

That knowledge softened my anger towards him. I had only seen him as some sort of a monster who used me and lied to me at every turn, but all of that changed. Price was protective of Cherry, almost brotherly, just as he'd told me. Knowing that she had to be so intimate with Raptor must be killing him.

Just the thought of it made me a little sick inside as well.

It annoyed me when he'd told Raptor he didn't want to meet tonight, that he'd need to work over his *source* to get the information they needed in time, but I realized there was too much tension between us to pull off the charade in front of Raptor. It would have been madness for everyone to meet with so much animosity between him and Songbird. Despite all of my acting abilities, I knew I wouldn't be able to pull that one off. Not tonight.

The last phone call came over an hour ago and it had been silent ever since. We were silent. Price had finally informed me he was going to take a shower and left me sitting on the couch alone. For a split second I entertained the thought of hopping into the shower with him as an apology for my behavior, but...having your advances rebuffed while fully clothed was one thing; getting turned down while naked and visibly vulnerable was something completely different.

I had tried to find something on TV to chase away thoughts of rejection. Nothing seemed to hold my attention for very long. Finally, I turned it off and found the book I was trying to read earlier in the week. The paperback's pages were a little wrinkled and crinkly from their dip in the tub, but none of the text had bled through.

I was about ten pages into it when I felt a warm, slightly damp hand close over my shoulder. "Skylar, there are a few things we need to straighten out."

Skylar set the book beside her and glanced up at him. "Okay, Price. What's that?"

Parker walked around the couch and sat down on the other end from her. While in the shower, he decided they would never be able to pull this off if the current tension between them persisted. But now, sitting across from Skylar, her sapphire eyes coolly narrowed at him, the words seemed to escape him.

"We can't go on like this, Skylar. I think you know that."

She nodded. "I'm aware."

Clearly, she wasn't going to make this easy for him. The hostility from last night was gone, but her tone was still very guarded. Parker cleared his throat and decided to come at this from a different angle.

In a soft voice he said, "I know your life changed two years ago. For my part in that, I'm sorry. I can't go back and change any of what happened, but I can help to set things right. That's a large part of why I sought you out in the first place. I assumed you would be as motivated to take Raptor down as Chill and I were. What I've discovered is that you are not just motivated, you're obsessed."

"So what if I'm obsessed with destroying the man who murdered my father? Is there a point to this conversation?" Her fingers drummed against the cover of her dog-eared book. "I could be doing something else instead of listening to you state the obvious to me."

"Honestly...I'm worried about you, Skylar."

Her eyes widened. "You're worried about me?"

"You've expended so much of your time and energy since that day to finding Raptor. What are you going to do in a few days when this is all over?"

"I'll get on with my life, I suppose. Maybe take a vacation. Get a good night's sleep for the first time in two years. What does it matter to you?"

Parker sighed. "It just does. I'm worried that this is consuming you; that you won't be able to let it go when the time comes."

Her expression hardened. "I'll be fine. Is this really the most pressing thing on your mind, or are you just too chickenshit to bring up the real issue?"

"Fine, Skylar, let's get down to the heart of it." He paused and chose his words carefully. "You are becoming a liability to this operation."

"Me?"

"Yes, you. You're allowing your emotions to get in the way of good judgment."

"You're talking to me about good judgment? Now?" Her lips curved into a humorless smile.

"Something about that funny?"

"If I'd been exercising good judgment then I never would have agreed to meet with you at the park that day. I wouldn't have done all the things I've done in the past two weeks at your request. I wouldn't be dressing up like a cat burglar to meet a murderer in the middle of the night. And I sure as hell wouldn't have a con man living on my couch when..." She seemed to think better of her words and shook the thought out of her head. "It's a little late to expect me to use better judgment, don't you think?"

Parker ignored her outburst and continued. "None of us can afford for Raptor to pick up on how emotionally involved you are with this heist."

She raised an eyebrow. "Or with you?"

"He especially cannot know that," Parker agreed. "He'd kill you before he'd let me have you." Absently, he shook his head and added, "Not that I get to have you regardless."

"Then why did you start something with me?" she asked, her voice oozing with innocence.

Parker slumped back against the cushions of the couch. "I didn't intend to. That just...happened."

"And your first night here? Or last night," she pressed. "Were those just accidents, too?"

Parker searched her face and then shrugged. "I'm not going to deny my attraction to you. You fascinate me, Skylar Montgomery."

"You sure could have fooled me."

"What do you expect from me? One minute you're screaming at me and the next you're kissing me. I can't figure out what you want."

Skylar averted her eyes. "I want *you*, Price. It isn't really all that complex."

If only it were as simple as she made it sound. If only he could believe they really wanted the same thing. If only...

"But it is," Parker replied softly. "What we're trying to do here requires all of our attention. We can't afford to be distracted. I meant what I said to you the first day we met. I really had no intention of starting anything with you until I could prove to you that I was on the up and up."

"Why is that so important to you?"

Parker frowned. "I want you to trust me."

"But why?"

The answer to that question should have been fairly straight-forward since he had known for quite a while. For the first time, Parker didn't just want to take a woman to bed, enjoy her for a few days, and then toss her aside. There were feelings, real and unfamiliar feelings, stirring inside of him, compelling him to change.

Compelling him towards Skylar.

But it was still too soon to let her know any of that. That was for a conversation when anger and pain weren't radiating at him from her body language. "We can't work together if you don't trust me. Not effectively, anyway."

"So this is what it's all about: work. Am I just a business associate to you?"

Parker met her gaze and realized she was hurt. "That's all you can be until this is over. Raptor can sense these things."

Abruptly, Skylar stood up and said, "I understand. I'm going to bed."

He wanted to go after her, to let her know that he cared about her as so much more than a business associate, that they only had to wait a little while longer, but he stayed where he was on the couch. The bedroom door closed loudly, with an air of finality, and he had to wonder if he was making the biggest mistake of his life.

Maybe it was just better this way.

*****

Friday, April 2

"Do you guys have any idea how much I'm risking to be talking to you in my office like this?" Trevor demanded.

"You'll be risking a whole lot more if you don't talk to us," Brandon retorted.

Jackson knew showing up at Trevor's office was sure to cause a violent reaction, but he went right along with it anyway. If this man could offer any information that would help them apprehend Raptor, well, he was just going to have to deal with them on their terms. The FBI had spent far too much time tiptoeing around the suspects because of their stature.

"Look," Jackson began calmly, "We just want to know a little about your business dealings with Drake Wyndham."

Trevor appeared defeated. "Fine. Sit down and I'll tell you whatever you want to know."

"Excellent," Brandon replied, still standing. "Why don't you start by telling us about Simon Templer?"

Trevor shook his head. "I can't. I've never met the guy."

"But you're partners," Jackson questioned.

"We were partners for a time, yes, but he was very hands-off. He seemed content to let the business run itself and collect his checks."

"Okay, then, how long have you known Drake?" Jackson asked.

"It's been a while. Ever since you boys moved me out here. I laid low for a while, but then decided to go into business again. I met Drake shortly after that when I needed some financing and he was just a peon at the bank."

Brandon looked thoughtful. "When did you start working together?"

"About four or five years ago, I guess."

The conversation wasn't moving quickly enough for Jackson. It was clear that Trevor was only giving them enough information to appease them. There was something he knew, something he wasn't telling them, that could very well be what they needed to crack the case wide open.

"So, you worked together for over three years. That must have been rough when he had to sell out," Jackson commented, deliberately baiting him.

Trevor's eyes darkened with contempt. "I was glad to be rid of him."

"And why is that?"

Something flashed through Trevor's eyes and Jackson was certain he'd said more than he'd meant to say.

"We had a falling out," he answered in a guarded tone.

Brandon raised an eyebrow. "Over?"

"I don't remember."

"You don't remember?"

"Yeah, I don't remember. It's been over two years and I have better things to do than to think about the past. If your people would hurry up and make their damn case, I could testify and put all of my past to rest."

Jackson glanced at his partner before turning his attention back to Trevor. "Well, then. You've been very generous with your time, Mr. Brightman, and I can see that you're very busy." He reached into his jacket pocket and retrieved his business card. "Please call if you remember anything you think we should know about Drake Wyndham."

Once they were in the safety of Brandon's car and heading back to Headquarters, Jackson said, "He knows something."

Brandon nodded. "Yeah. The trouble is...we don't know if that something is relevant to us or just random bullshit he's trying to hide."

Despite another near sleepless night, I was up before noon. I toyed with the idea of hitting the gym, something I hadn't done in a few weeks, but quickly dismissed it. Everyone was meeting again that night and I knew I would need all of my energy to maintain my focus.

Price was probably right about the level of my emotional involvement with what we were doing. Though I was not exactly thrilled by what he'd said, it lessened the sting of his rejection enough that I reasoned I would be able to make it through the next few days without blowing my cover in front of Raptor.

I found Price at the dining room table intently studying a mound of papers.

"Good morning," I said softly.

He turned his attention to me as I sat across from him. "Did you sleep?"

"No, not really."

"Skylar, about what I said last night..."

I cut him off with a dismissive gesture of my hand. "It didn't really have anything to do with that. I think I'm just nervous about everything that's going on in general." The lie sounded flimsy even to my own ears, so I quickly added, "What is all of this, anyway?"

Price held my gaze for a moment longer than was necessary before turning back to the table. "These are maps of the city. I'm plotting out our best escape routes and a few alternates."

I forced a weak smile. "You don't like to leave anything to chance, huh?"

"No, I don't. I've found that thorough planning is the only way to ensure things don't go wrong at the last second. Everything must go as planned if I'm going to clear myself with the FBI. One hiccup and I'm sunk."

The FBI. I hadn't given them any thought since my first meeting with Raptor. This whole thing was about revenge and justice for me, but I was forced to remember that this was something wholly different for Price. He was a fugitive and would stay that way unless everything went according to plan. In his shoes, I imagined I would be unwilling to commence any sort of a relationship either.

In his shoes, I'd be a nervous wreck shaking in the corner, a far cry from his casual demeanor.

"Do you really think the FBI will be okay with what we're doing?"

He chuckled. "No. I wouldn't be hiding myself in your living room if I thought they would approve. Nevertheless, I do think they'll be grateful enough to have Raptor in custody that they'll be willing to let me off with a slap on the wrist."

A slap on the wrist for armed bank robbery? He seemed so confident that it was hard for me to acknowledge how delusional this was. I turned my attention to one of the maps while I pondered that. I was about to ask him what he planned to do if they weren't, but something caught my eye. Instead, I asked, "What do the stars on the map mean?"

"Those are the most isolated spots that also have access to a number of major roads. I plan to place a getaway car at each of them."

I didn't try to hide my confusion. "There are only five of us. Why do we need so many vehicles?"

Price shrugged. "I like for everyone to be able to switch vehicles a few times to make sure that they aren't followed or made by what they're driving."

I nodded. "That's good. Is there anything else we need to accomplish today? I'm starting to get a little stir-crazy around here."

"I'm glad to hear you say that because there's somewhere I need to take you."

"Where's that?" I asked with some hesitation. If he was so worried about the FBI that he was hiding in my living room, I was hard pressed to think of a safe place we could visit in the middle of the day.

"Get your jacket and you'll see when we get there. It's time for you to learn how to shoot."

Jenna groaned when she looked at the clock and realized what time it was. Ever since she had agreed to help Jackson dig up dirt on his suspects, her days went by considerably faster. There were a few instances when she'd completely ignored her own inbox to look through the files she was compiling for him. She had never actively tried to neglect her responsibilities, but his case was just so much more fascinating than the ones that made their way onto her desk.

Now she found herself forced to play catch-up with her workload. Despite having read each of the briefs that she had put off, she still didn't feel any better acquainted with the facts. Her mind kept wandering away from her. She had been toying with the idea of turning the First Alliance robbery into a novel, but so far had been unable to commit all of her thoughts to paper.

Instead, Jenna let the ideas dominate her mind, clouding her attention to anything else. She'd known it would be hard to push her writing aside when she'd made the decision to work in the DA's office. What she hadn't known was how much she had taken for granted the time she'd had to stay at home and focus on her writing. If she had realized how strong her desire to continue writing had been in the first place then she probably would never have accepted the job.

But she loved her job, just as much as the writing. Almost. Maybe.

On the other hand, it had come in handy right when she'd needed a solid distraction from her life. Things with Jackson had only recently improved and Jenna had welcomed the chance to focus on something else while she had tried to sort out her feelings on the situation. Besides, the knowledge that she was keeping criminals off the street always brought a smile to her face.

It wasn't criminal defense, not by a longshot, but she knew her parents would still be proud of her.

Jenna opened the next file, but quickly closed it. It was close to five o'clock and she was ready to start her weekend. Jackson would probably be home late again which should afford her enough time to get most of her ideas down on paper before they got even more muddled than they already were.

While clearing off her desk, Jenna realized she hadn't even bothered to look at the latest information on Jackson's case. She received it earlier in the day, but was so determined to complete her own work that she'd tossed it aside. The note scrawled on the front of the manila folder informed her that the last of the information she had requested was contained within.

Part of Jenna wanted to stay and find out if there was anything useful in the file, but she resisted the urge, instead grabbing her jacket and heading out to her car. She enjoyed helping Jackson with his case and was glad to let him use her to sound his ideas on. However, she knew that bringing the file home with her would transform the weekend into just another workday.

And that was unacceptable. She was going to get some uninterrupted quality time with her boyfriend that weekend even if she had to smash his phone to pieces.

Again.

Besides, there was an excellent chance the file held no new information at all. Regardless, the investigation had been ongoing for the last two years and no one else had been able to produce any results. It was unlikely she'd found what the rest of the FBI and local law enforcement had been missing for two years.

One more weekend couldn't possibly make a difference to the case.

EIGHTEEN

Chill let out a curse under his breath as he looked at his watch...again. Coming out in public so early in the evening was a risk he didn't enjoy taking, but it couldn't be helped. He typically preferred to conduct business at Blaine's Rain where he knew he was on his own turf. Unfortunately, the man he was meeting also enjoyed having home court advantage.

His contact's bar of choice was in a bad part of town and was far seedier than any Chill would have set foot into by his own volition. Not exactly the kind of place you ever wanted to park the Jag in front of, that was for sure. He'd thought enough in advance to drive the older one with fake plates, but...still.

After waiting for ten minutes, Chill considered leaving and seeking out a new source. This guy may come highly recommended by their mutual clients, but if he wasn't punctual for the meet, could he be trusted to deliver the goods in time? He was about to make a call when a slight man in a large coat pulled out a chair at his table and sat down.

"You Chill?" he asked suspiciously.

"Yeah. You are late, Splice."

He rolled his dull eyes. "Do you want to gripe about the time or do you want to do some bi'ness?"

Chill conceded. "Fine. I need fifteen cars by Sunday."

Splice let out a low whistle. "That's pretty ambitious of you. Could get pricey."

He didn't really need that many cars, but he knew that it was easier to negotiate price in bulk. Besides, he was playing with Raptor's cash, so he'd buy a ride for the waitress if she'd been even slightly hot. "How pricey?"

"Ten large per car. Half up front."

"No deal," Chill replied, shaking his head. "I can call anyone else and get what I want for half of that." Just because it wasn't his money was no reason to get raped on the price.

"But not on this short of notice...not without risking that they've already been reported stolen."

Chill rose to his feet. "I will just have to take my chances on that."

He made it to the door before he heard the sounds of footsteps approaching quickly from behind. "Wait. We can work something out."

Chill let the grin creep across his lips and turned to the desperate car thief. "Now, we can do business."

Parker kept a watchful eye on Skylar as Raptor approached. Her emotions seemed to be much more in check than they had the previous day. When they went to a cheesy amusement park, she had questioned him, but he thought she'd ended up having a little fun at his idea of teaching her how to shoot. However unorthodox it may have seemed, she had gained a good deal of skill with the laser tag gun in a relatively short period.

Besides, it was probably therapeutic for her to chase after him with a gun.

As usual, Raptor got right to the point. "Do we have what we need, Ramsey?"

Parker regarded him carefully, gauging his words before he spoke. "I have the contact numbers that I need and all of the access codes."

"And how did you manage that?"

"I have my secrets," Parker replied with a wink, attempting to keep up his chauvinist façade without further upsetting Skylar.

Raptor seemed satisfied with his answer and moved on. "What about transportation?"

Chill smiled smugly. "I got a bargain and we'll have what we need by Sunday."

"And firepower?"

"Taken care of," Chill replied.

Parker watched the exchange with a sense of detachment. Skylar and Cherry had remained quiet and he was grateful for that. Raptor, too, seemed detached, almost as though he wasn't in the mood to be meeting.

Raptor glanced at his watch and Parker thought it was brazen of him to wear the same watch he'd worn to the gala, especially since Skylar might be able to recognize it, but he dismissed the thought when he began to speak.

"I'm afraid that I need to go before I'm missed elsewhere. Tomorrow we'll have to meet much earlier. There's an engagement I must attend."

Parker eyed him cautiously, but didn't say anything. He understood the strain that every one of these needless late-night rendezvous with the rest of them must be causing on his home life, not that he cared. The only reason he even considered everything Raptor had made, or taken, for himself was so that he could enjoy how much farther he would have to fall as a result of it.

And he would fall if that was the last thing Parker ever did.

They were calling to me. Everybody was waiting on me. Couldn't start the retirement party for my dad until I got there with the cake.

But why was it foggy? I could hear them calling to me, I just couldn't get to wherever they were. I couldn't even see where I was going and stumbled over something. I fought to regain my balance before I dropped the cake.

I wasn't holding cake anymore.

Just as well. I needed both hands in front of me to make sure I didn't slam into a tree or a house or something. Why was the fog so thick? It didn't make any sense.

My hand felt something cool and smooth. Glass. I felt my way along its surface until I felt handles. That was good. Maybe I could wait inside until the fog lifted. Then I could find everyone.

Wait. I was at the party. Why was it at the bank? Why were Reyna and Eric, Drake and Suzanne there? They shouldn't all be at my father's retirement party. I only invited Eric.

Michael walked out of his office, punch in hand, grinning from ear to ear. "Now, that's a good one, Monty. You got me." When he walked past me, he added, "Your father is hilarious with his practical jokes."

Sounded about right to me. He was always hell to be around on April Fool's Day. I walked into Michael's office and stopped just inside the doorway. "Dad, I don't get the joke."

He didn't answer me. He was slumped back in Michael's chair, phone in hand, eyes staring, unseeing. I took a few steps forward, trying to get his attention, and noticed the dark red stain on the front of his shirt. Barbeque sauce, I guess.

Well, he was a man who enjoyed his food often to the detriment of his clothes.

"Okay. I give up. What are you supposed to be?"

"Why, he's dead, of course," Suzanne said, walking into the room. She laughed and shook her head. "You're so cute to still believe in happy endings."

I looked at my father then back to her. She was already gone. In fact, everyone was gone. Turning my attention back to my father's lifeless image, I said, "Okay, ha ha. You got me. Stop playing around now."

Silence.

Growing scared, I approached the desk slowly. That was when I caught my reflection in a mirror. Did Michael's office have mirrors? Even better question...Why was I in my cap and gown at the retirement party?

Why didn't anything make sense today?

"Daddy?"

Silence.

Icy dread settled in my stomach. As I knelt next to his chair, waiting for him to shake himself out of it and scare the life out of me, I smelled pennies. At first, it was just the faint coppery smell of one or two in your hand, but it grew to a sickening aroma so thick I could taste it, bitter and terrifying on my tongue.

Where the hell were all the pennies? I looked down at my hands to see if I'd brought them in with me and nearly gagged when I saw the blood coating my hands.

Oh. God.

It wasn't barbeque sauce.

"Somebody call 9-1-1!" I pressed my hands over the gaping hole in his chest to try stopping the blood gushing out of it. "Just hold on. Please." Holding one hand over the hole, I reached up to pat him on his cheek a few times. "Come on...wake up. Please. Please. Please."

Without warning, his head slumped forward and I wasn't strong enough to hold him upright. His head hit Michael's desk and he shattered into ten trillion shards of red.

"No! Daddy!" I fell back onto the cold marble floor of our bathroom at the house.

Silence.

Through my weeping, I gradually became aware of gasping breaths behind me. I tried to pull myself around carefully on the floor, slow and steady to avoid cutting myself on all the red shards. They weren't there though.

They were pills.

"M-m-mom?"

She was motionless and cold on the ground, glaring at me as her breaths slowed. In a slurred voice she said, "You did this. If you hadn't been graduating, he wouldn't have wanted me to pick up that damn suit from the cleaners." She shot into a sitting position as the last breath left her body, her dead face inches from mine. "You killed your father, Skylar."

"No."

"You killed him."

"I didn't."

She reached out and grabbed me by the shoulders, shaking me hard. "You killed him. You, Skylar. Skylar…Skylar."

I screamed and opened my eyes. Price replaced my mother in front of me. He stopped shaking me, but he didn't release me. "You were having a nightmare, I think."

"It's my fault he's dead."

His hands released my shoulders to wipe the tears from my eyes before cupping my face. "No, sweetheart. It's Raptor's fault for pulling the trigger. It's my fault even for picking the location. But it's not your fault."

"But it is." I searched his face. Why didn't he understand? "My mom told me it was my fault when she died."

"I thought she was unconscious when you found her?"

"She was. She told me after that…after she died."

Price gathered me to his bare chest where he was kneeling beside the bed. "It was just a nightmare. No one would ever think or say you were responsible for what happened that day."

I tried to pull away and look at him. "But…"

"No." He held me tighter. "None of this is your fault. None of it."

"It is…it is…it is…it is…"

After I'd worn myself out with protests and run out of tears, Price kissed the top of my head and released me. "You should try to go back to sleep now." He rose to his feet. "You know where I'll be if you need anything."

I grabbed his wrist before he could disappear into the darkness. "Don't go." I tugged at his arm. "Stay. Please. At least until I'm asleep again."

He sighed, but let me pull him into bed next to me. Gathering me to him, he pulled the covers over us. "Just until you fall asleep."

"I know. Nothing's changed. It's okay."

I rested my head against his shoulder and realized he wasn't wearing a shirt. How could he sleep like that when it was so cold out? But his skin was so warm, so nice. It was like being curled up with him back in the hotel, only this time I didn't have any illusions about whether he was hiding things from me.

I knew he was.

After a long silence, I said, "I had that same dream every night after she killed herself for nearly a year. This is the first time it's been back since."

His arms tightened around me, but he remained silent.

"I know it wasn't my fault. Not that they died. He would've been in that bank anyway because he was always there." I cleared my throat. "And I couldn't have stopped her. I couldn't have been with her every moment of every day." I paused, remembering something. "It's funny...Reyna and Eric and Suzanne and Drake were never in the dream before."

"Maybe it's your mind's way of trying to make sense of everything from over the last few weeks." He hesitated before adding, "It's almost over. Maybe the dream will stop altogether once this is all behind you."

"And you're gone?" For the first time, I moved my head to glance up at him. "It doesn't matter. I know you're going back to your old life once you clear your name." I looked away. "It's okay."

In lieu of a response, he tilted my chin back to face him and covered my mouth with his. The kiss was sweet, tender emotion stirring within it. I didn't know where the kiss came from or how long it went on, but when his lips broke away from mine, he was leaning over me and my arms were wrapped around his neck.

I blinked a few times, becoming aware that I was on my back. I tried to make sense of what was happening when I felt his lips brushing over mine again. I wanted him, but did I want him when the pain of the dream was still so fresh in my mind?

Tapping him on the shoulders, I said, "I can't. You know I want to, but right now, Price...I just can't."

He stared down into my eyes for a long time, caressing my face with his hand. "I know that. A kiss isn't always a prelude to sex, Skylar. Sometimes a kiss is just about the kiss." He pulled his hand away. "You should get some sleep."

"Okay." I turned to face him. "You're still staying though, right?"

Price gathered me to him and I rested my head on his chest. "Just until you fall asleep."

I woke several times during the night. Each time, I was still safe in his arms.

Saturday, April 3

Trevor was still shaken after the previous day's meeting with the FBI agents. Arthur Pintauro, the man he had once been, was dead as far as he was concerned and that life was in the distant past. There was only one person in this town who was supposed to know the truth about him; only one person who he had told the whole story to.

Unfortunately, there were two people who knew his secret.

He was set to testify at his final trial in a few months and then he would be able to put the whole ugly mess behind him. The trouble was that he hadn't bargained on falling in love. Trevor had only meant to pass the time in this town and let himself be relocated again after it was over. Now, he had too much to lose if the FBI found out what he was hiding from them - and they would find out. His lucrative investment holdings, his place in society, his immunity, even the woman he loved could all be taken away from him in the blink of an eye over one mistake he made.

At first, he hadn't even realized what he did was wrong. It was only after he had taken a deeper look that he discovered its true criminal nature. Trevor had wanted out, had wanted to set things right, of course, but then *it* happened and there was no turning back.

Maybe he could still set things right. It was possible that he could talk to the agents and make them understand why he had done what he'd done. There was a chance he could make them believe he hadn't intentionally broken the law and that there were very real reasons why he hadn't come forward sooner.

Yes, he would see them first thing Monday morning, but there was something he had to sort out first. Trevor reached for the phone and dialed the number he knew by heart, even though he hadn't called it in years. When he heard the familiar voice on the other end he said, "I need to see you. There's something we need to discuss." After the briefest of pauses, "It's important."

Price was gone when I opened my eyes. In the light of day with him sitting out in the living room as he always did, it was hard to be sure whether I'd really spent several hours wrapped safely in his arms. If it weren't for the faint aroma of his cologne clinging to my pillow, I'd think it was all just a dream.

A dream. Dreams were like nightmares. I may have to let the nightmare plague me while I slept, but I wasn't about to think about it during the day. Not when I had the opportunity to be in control of my thoughts.

Of course, my thoughts were fickle bitches today.

I couldn't explain what was bothering me as I flipped through the pages of a magazine. It felt like I knew something unconsciously, but it still hadn't registered in my brain yet. Whatever it was, I thought with a sigh, had better be pretty damn important to be bothering me this much.

Even the fact that Price ran off after a phone call without explanation wasn't bothering me as much as the nagging thought that I should know something. And the way he left was just...*odd.* He didn't say anything about who was on the other line, but his whole demeanor changed and he'd slipped into the other room to have the conversation.

Once he was off the phone, he'd breezed by me to tell me he was going out for a while and not to worry because everything was fine. I didn't believe him. Running off in the middle of the day when he could get picked up by the feds didn't sound like reasonable behavior.

But I supposed he knew what he was doing.

At least, I sure hoped he knew what he was doing.

I stood and crossed the room to the window. The sun would set soon. Weird how that single, normal fact caused new feelings of apprehension to bloom inside of me. Time was quickly running out. We were set to meet one last time in a few hours. Tomorrow would be ours to relax and then...I couldn't let myself finish that thought.

It was difficult to admit to myself how shaken up over all of this I really was. I couldn't stand how low I let myself sink since my first encounter with Chill just over a year ago. All that I had ever wanted to do was avenge my father's death by finding the man who murdered him and now I was allied with him to rob the bank that my closest friend ran.

This was all so insane that I didn't understand how any of it made sense to me.

But I knew the answer. Two words: Jonathan Price.

Yes, he'd talked me into criminal things, but he'd also shown me there were more people whose lives were changed by Raptor, more people who wanted revenge than I knew. It wasn't just me operating in a bubble of sorrow. Cherry and Chill lost someone important to them and I couldn't deny them the justice they so rightly deserved.

I let out an exaggerated sigh. And there were Price's motivations. I knew Raptor tried to kill him and that he was a fugitive until he could turn him over to the FBI. But what else did I really know about him? For all of the crazy things I was doing at his request it would have made more sense if I knew something more about him than what I did.

Knowing he was good in bed wasn't exactly a decent reason to follow him on this little reckoning of his...

Not that it mattered. I was so deeply involved in this heist that I couldn't back out now, even if I wanted to. Knowing more about Price would be nice, but it was unnecessary at this point. He would be gone in a few days and that would be the end of that.

I should actually consider myself lucky I hadn't gotten any more involved with him than I had. Maybe that would make it easier to deal with it when he was no longer around. Maybe that would make it easier to say goodbye to him, assuming I was even given the chance before he slipped out of town in the fog from which he'd first appeared.

Maybe...

A persistent knocking at the door tore me away from my more maudlin thoughts. That was just as well. I didn't want to dwell on what my life would be like after Price was no longer a part of it.

I opened the door without bothering to check who it was first. If this was one of the few times Price was knocking like a normal person instead of magicianing his way in, I could stand the surprise.

Except...it wasn't Price.

My jaw went slack as I looked at the last person I'd expected to see on the other side.

"I needed to see you, Skylar." His tone was guarded when he asked, "Is it all right for me to come in?"

I held the door open a little wider to let him by. "Why wouldn't it be?"

Eric moved past me and shook his head. "Your boyfriend, what's his name."

There was no sense in telling him Price's name again. He wouldn't remember because he didn't care enough to. "He's out at the moment."

He nodded. "That's good. I didn't want to apologize in front of him."

"What are you apologizing for?"

"For how I acted last weekend, Skylar. It...wasn't fair to you."

It really wasn't. "No big deal. It's forgotten. You can make yourself at home." I shut the door and realized he was still standing near me instead of moving to the couch. "What's going on, Eric?"

He took my hands into his with a light touch. "I'm sorry for putting you in an awkward position with your boyfriend, but I'm not sorry for anything I said. I meant it then. I still mean it now."

"Eric..."

"I'm still in love with you. I tried not to be after you pushed me out of your life." He squeezed his eyes closed and shook his head as though trying to chase away a painful memory. "For a while, I didn't want to be in love with you. I got on with my life, started my business...I tried to move on. I thought I had moved on, but..." He opened his eyes and unfettered emotion swam within them. "Once I saw you...I knew."

"I don't know what you want me to say. I didn't even know you'd be there at first. It certainly wasn't some kind of an attempt to hurt you."

He released one of my hands so he could touch my face. "I never thought that. Not for a second. It's just..." His eyes searched my face. "You still love me, too. Please don't pretend you don't."

Wow. He wasn't pulling any punches tonight. "I'll always love you, Eric. That doesn't mean I'm prepared to hurt two people who care about us over it." Well, one person. Reyna was the only one who'd get hurt since my boyfriend was a fake.

"I don't love her, Skylar. She's a good person and I care about her, but...she isn't you. Deep down, you know you don't feel about this other guy the way you do about me."

"Well...no, but..."

THE SHATTERED ALLIANCE | 251

"No buts. Come away with me. Let's just get in the car and go. We can get away from this town and all the painful memories here."

"Memories will just follow us, Eric."

"So we'll make new ones. We'll make so many good memories that the bad ones can't get to us. I've made plenty of money with my work. We can go anywhere. We don't have to worry about anything."

"I have my own money."

Why was I responding to the least dramatic thing he said? Holy shit. This was my out. Leave now and forget about the robbery, about Price...about everything.

"Fine, we'll use your money too then. I don't care who pays for what. I don't care where we go or what we do. The only thing I care about is having you next to me when we get there. Stop overthinking everything and just come with me. Now. Tonight."

"I...can't." For the first time, I faltered in my protest. A part of me, a very large part of me, wanted to grab my purse and go with him.

"You can. You just...Oh, to hell with it!"

His hands moved to frame my face and he kissed me with violent abandon. I should've pushed him away or somehow protested. I didn't. Instead, I kissed him back until I could barely breathe.

It was easier with Eric than it was with Price. It always had been. There was no talk of keeping things professional. No hesitation.

No games.

Eric wanted me and he didn't care if I knew. He loved me and he didn't want to mince words about it. His feelings were what they were.

Standing there by my front door, kissing Eric, feeling my body melt against his embrace, I couldn't imagine why I'd ever tried to pretend I didn't still have feelings for him. He loved me. I loved him.

Nothing else mattered.

Since he wasn't operating under the cover of total darkness yet, Parker staked out the street in front of the townhouse before parking. He'd be damned if he got nabbed by the FBI just days before the heist. That was unacceptable this close to the end of the game.

He hadn't expected to see anything other than the usual, but he noticed an expensive car parked in front of the townhouse. Skylar had company. That simple fact wouldn't be alarming if there weren't another car parked down the street with someone slumped down in the seat, probably watching the townhouse.

To play it safe, Parker drove around the block and approached the townhouse from behind, well out of view of the surveillance. He'd have to remember to warn Chill before he headed this way. As he slid through the bedroom window, he realized Chill getting thrown into jail would bother him more than his own incarceration.

For one thing, Chill would still be bitching about it ten years from now.

Parker was about to walk into the living room when he heard a frantic voice say, "Oh...to hell with it!"

Peeking around the corner, he felt sick at what he saw. Skylar in another man's arms. As quietly as possible, he flattened himself against the bedroom wall and tried to breathe.

How the hell did this happen? Even though all they'd done was sleep – well, she'd slept – Parker thought they might've turned a corner. Maybe, just maybe, he'd thought they were finally getting to the same page about what they wanted from each other.

But no. Apparently, Skylar wanted her ex. Losing her, despite the fact she was never really his to lose, was like an icy needle being pierced through his heart. And three days to go before he'd be free of the threats from Raptor and the FBI.

He'd lost her with three fucking days left to go.

"Wait. Eric...this isn't right."

The tiniest ember of hope lit inside Parker.

"But it is. So right." More kissing sounds.

"No. Will you stop and listen to me please?" After a pause, "If you're going to end things with Reyna, you need to do it the right way. Sneaking out of town with me isn't right and you know it."

He heard the other man sigh. "I can be back over here in under an hour."

So they were leaving town together. Skylar wouldn't give up her revenge quest when he asked, but she'd do it for Eric. More icy needles pricked Parker.

"That isn't what I mean. You don't see it because you haven't been a part of it, but I do have a life, Eric. I have things I need to do. I have people in my life. I can't just pick up and disappear with you tonight."

"But...you want to."

"It doesn't matter. There's a right way to do things. You know this isn't it." Long pause. "If I'm really what you want...give me time. Give me time to put things in my life in order."

"Skylar..."

"No, Eric. If I'm going to end a relationship, I need the time to do it the right way."

"If? How come you don't sound sure you're leaving him for me?"

Parker held his breath, wanting to know the answer as much as Eric did.

But no answer came. There was only silence, a lengthy silence stretching across three eternities.

Finally, there was the rustling of a coat. "You know I was going to propose that night, don't you?" Silence. "I never got rid of the ring. I think you should have it." More silence. "I've kept that for two years, Skylar Montgomery. I can handle waiting for you to decide what you want."

This time, the silence was broken by the sounds of footsteps and a closing door.

Parker waited only long enough to ensure Eric wasn't coming back in before he went to Skylar. Tears were rolling down her cheeks, hitting the open ring box that held the ring she stared at. She barely even registered he was there when he locked the door. After a moment, her eyes went wide and she opened her mouth to speak.

"Don't lie to me, Skylar. I was here for the whole thing."

She shook her head. "He kept the ring." Her eyes searched his hard expression for a moment before she moved past him to the kitchen.

"And?"

Parker followed her into the kitchen and watched as she set the ring on the counter and got a diet soda out of the refrigerator in a daze. With a trembling hand, she lifted the can to her lips and gulped. Twice.

"And nothing, Price. Drop it."

He grabbed her by the elbow to keep her from walking away. "No fucking way do I let this go. Are you leaving with him or not?"

"Not." Her voice was calmer than he'd ever heard it. "We have a meeting in a few hours and a bank to rob in a few days."

"And after that?"

"I don't know."

"You don't know?" He realized his voice was rising, that he was starting to sound like a lunatic, but he didn't care. "You don't know if you want to be with him?"

She looked through him. "I hardly see why you care. It's not like you'll still be here."

Last night, he hadn't said anything about his plans after the heist because he didn't want to push her by moving too fast. He didn't want to scare her away, not while she was in his arms. But now...

"I wasn't actually planning to leave right away."

Her expression was unfazed. She pulled out of his grasp and asked, "Why do you even care who I'm with? It's none of your business."

Parker didn't know how to answer that. He didn't understand why she was suddenly so pissed off at him again. Was it because he was up and dressed before she woke up? God knew he wanted nothing more than to hold her. He'd forced himself to stay awake as long as he could, just so he could memorize the way she felt against him, her scent, the little sounds she made in sleep. The only reason he got up before she was awake was to avoid upsetting her if she didn't remember she'd asked him into her bed.

Snapping into action, Parker chased her out of the kitchen and spun her around by the wrist just inside her bedroom door. "It may not be my business, Skylar, but I...*care*."

Before she could respond, he pressed her back against the wall and kissed her as though the sheer force of his desire could make her understand. He released her wrist and wound his fingers into her hair, holding her prisoner against the kiss. She may not be prepared to answer whether she wanted Eric, but she was damn well going to figure out if she wanted Parker.

"Your phone's vibrating," Skylar murmured against his lips.

"I don't care about that. I care about whether I'm the one you want or if I'm just the one you're biding your time with until you can have the man you really want." His phone started buzzing again, but he didn't move a muscle. "I need an answer."

"You know I want you."

"More than him or instead of him?"

Skylar pressed against his shoulders to regain some breathing room. "Is there a difference?"

There was. She just wasn't understanding. He started to respond when the insistent ping of incoming text messages interrupted him. Absently, he pulled out his phone. "Chill's on his way."

She didn't respond. She just stared.

Shit. He had to warn him about the surveillance before it was too late. "Yes, there's a difference." He started dialing Chill's number. "I just need to tell Chill something before he gets here."

"And that's the reason it doesn't matter whether I want you or not." She shoved Parker out of the bedroom and shut the door. "I need to get ready."

Before Parker could respond, he heard the door lock and Chill answered his call.

NINETEEN

Raptor was agitated when he met the others. While he often enjoyed the company of women, he never got used to all of their needy questions. He did not have the same amount of time to devote to a relationship that women did, especially this woman. Perhaps it was time to begin cutting ties and move on.

As Ramsey ran through the order of how things would occur on Monday, Raptor found his mind wandering. Ramsey. He would get what he deserved when this was all over, he would make certain of that.

There was something about the way Songbird and Ramsey regarded one another tonight that made his blood boil. It would be a serious mistake if Ramsey had disregarded his warning and had made a play for Songbird when he had a beautiful woman stupidly waiting for him at home. Originally, he'd planned to kill him quickly. Now he might have to devise something a little more fitting.

Songbird was another issue. She still seemed oblivious to his interest in her. Either that or she was not interested in him, but that was hardly a possibility. Raptor firmly believed there were only two sorts of women in the world: those he'd slept with and those who hadn't been lucky enough to share his bed yet.

Songbird would be no different than the rest.

There was something special about Songbird, something intriguing about her. When Ramsey was finally done talking and Chill had gone over where everyone could find their first vehicle and weapons on Monday, Raptor approached her casually. She regarded him coolly from beneath her thick lashes.

"Can I help you with something, hon?"

Raptor smiled wickedly. "You bet you can."

"Oh. And how might that be?"

"I think you know how, Songbird."

Raptor wished he could have taken off her mask right then and seen the flush he was sure was creeping across her cheeks.

"Maybe you should chat with Chill. I don't mix business with pleasure, sugar. I never have and I never will," she drawled at him.

Raptor put his arms around her waist and pulled her towards him. "Our business will be complete in a few days and you won't have an excuse." He smoothed his left hand against her masked cheek, noticing a spark flash briefly in her dark eyes. Placing his lips against the material of her mask over her ear he whispered, "Even with all of these layers, you look beautiful tonight under the night sky."

Raptor felt her stiffen and allowed her to pull away.

"I need to be going. We can finish this discussion when our business transaction is complete," Songbird replied stiffly.

After she turned to leave, he replied, "Get plenty of sleep. You will need it, my sexy little bird."

Songbird stayed on Raptor's mind for a long time after he left the meet. There was a sense of familiarity about her. Did they know each other in the world where masks weren't a requirement?

Did she know who he really was?

If she did, it wouldn't be a problem. Cherry knew his daylight identity, yet she remained firmly under his thumb – at least, she would remain that way until he was ready to crush her under it.

But he'd have to put some effort into answering the question of who Songbird really was before things went down Monday. It might be nothing. It might just be the infuriating way she pretended to be disinterested in him.

Or it may be a reason to make sure this songbird would never sing again.

No matter how long I stared at the walls of my bedroom, things still didn't make sense. Why didn't I see it? Why had I been so blind, so foolish, when it was right there in front of my face the entire time? Why had it taken that bastard flashing his watch in front of my eyes for me to recognize it?

Price had been right after all: knowing Raptor's true identity was worse than not knowing who he really was.

He walked into the room and leaned against the doorframe. "Is everything all right, Skylar? You haven't said anything since the meet."

"Yeah," I said as I hugged my knees to my chest and rested my chin on them. "I just..."

"You figured it out, didn't you?"

I looked away. Price didn't say anything for a long time. He just sat next to me on the bed and put an arm around my shoulders to comfort me. It didn't work.

I was beyond comfort.

Price slid his finger under my chin and turned me to face him. "I know I've been telling you it's too late to back out, but I'll stop all of this right now if you don't think you can do it. I can go back to the FBI and fill them in, let them know who Raptor is and see if I can help them build a case against him legitimately."

His statement puzzled me. "Why would you do that? This is important to you."

"So are you, Skylar," he said softly.

I cocked my head to the side and studied his face. "You mean that?"

He nodded and a horrible thought occurred to me, causing my blood to run like ice water in my veins. There was no logical reason why he was telling me this now. My eyes grew wide and I gasped audibly.

"We're going to die, aren't we?"

"Eventually."

I shook my head slowly. "Don't do that. Please don't play games with me right now. Raptor's going to kill..." I let my words trail off because it was too awful a thought to finish and my voice was trembling. I sucked in a deep breath to steady myself and continued, "Please just be straight with me."

Price took my hands in his and said, "Raptor is a very dangerous man, but we have this covered. There is a contingency plan in place if we need it. Everything about this situation is dangerous and I will completely understand if you want out. I know I never should have pulled you into this in the first place."

"If you hadn't, I would have just done something stupid and gotten myself killed anyway. I'm...I'm glad I met you."

It was probably not the most intelligent thing for me to say, but it needed to be said. Price's words went a long way in consoling me, despite the fact that my insides were still twisted with panic. Nevertheless, if there was any chance at all that Price could be wrong, that we might only have a few days left, I wanted him to know how I really felt about him.

I needed him to know.

Price brushed a soft kiss against my forehead and stood. "You should probably get some sleep. You're starting to talk crazy."

"No, I'm not. Price, you make me feel," I whispered.

He gave me a blank look. "I make you feel what?"

"You make me feel," I repeated as I rose to my feet. "I died inside the day my mother took her life and I haven't felt anything since."

I could tell that my words shook him. There was a curious mixture of emotions in his eyes that I couldn't quite decipher. He ran his fingers through his light hair and slowly exhaled.

"What are you trying to say, Skylar?"

"I'm trying to say that, even with all of your careful planning, something could still go terribly wrong. If that happens, I don't want to know I wasted what time I had."

"Skylar..."

I shook my head. "No. I'm not done yet. There's something between us. We both know it. I don't know what it is, or if it will even amount to anything, but I'm willing to find out. If you are, that is."

Price stared at me as if he'd been struck dumb. Were our roles reversed, I knew I would be every bit as confused as he must be. I had done an about-face where he was concerned. Several times.

While he was still turning my words over in his mind, I added, "I'm even willing to overlook that you read texts and make calls when you're supposed to be more interested in me."

He sighed. "I had to warn Chill about the car watching the place. If I didn't do it that moment, I wouldn't have had time to warn him."

"Your timing still sucked."

He nodded his agreement and grew thoughtful. "There are still so many things that you don't know about me. Are you okay with that, Skylar?"

His was a valid question; a question that deserved an answer. Unfortunately, I didn't know how to respond. How could I? It was impossible to gauge what some future reaction to the unknown would be.

On the one hand, Price had proven to me, repeatedly, that I could not trust him. He'd hidden things from me, lied to my face, and revealed just enough to keep me from questioning him. Even when he was trying to show me that he wanted the same thing I did, he was the king of mixed signals.

But then there was the other hand. Price had unleashed a storm inside of me, body and mind, which I had never before felt. The desire I felt for him was long since elevated from want to need and I had the vague awareness that I would drown under the force of my feelings without him.

I wasn't sure how long I waged this battle with myself, trying to decide the best way to answer, but too much time must have passed because Price cleared his throat to capture my attention. A pensive look invaded his eyes, overshadowing the usual glint of humor they possessed. His lean body was rigid with tension; his voice stiff and measured when he spoke.

"I need an answer, Skylar. I...have to know."

For a split second, I was able to see through his eyes down into the depths of his soul and I knew everything was riding on what I said next. From just that brief glimpse I gained the knowledge that he wanted me to say it didn't matter. I realized he felt the same longing for me that I felt for him. I alone had the power to decide what happened next.

Price's eyes were full of cautious expectation as he waited for my response. What I wanted was so close now that I could reach out and snatch it up if I so chose, but I would not lie to get it. As much as I wanted him, as much as I wanted whatever was to come for us, I could not lie. Not about this.

Finally, I said, "I don't know how to answer that, Price."

"It's a straightforward question, Skylar. Either you are or you aren't." His voice was soft, but I could still detect the strained desperation.

I shook my head. "But it isn't. Nothing has ever been straightforward with us and you know that."

"Well," Price began, his face crestfallen, "I guess that gives me my answer."

"No, it doesn't. I need to know one thing before I can answer you." I swallowed hard and exhaled slowly. "Does any of this other stuff I don't know involve Raptor?"

"No. You know everything I know about him, about my past dealings with him. Everything important, I should say. There are no more bombshells left where he's concerned."

"Then I can wait to learn the rest until you're ready to tell me."

"Are you certain?"

"I'm not certain about anything in my life except for the fact that I wish I could go back in time and save my family. I know that isn't what you want to hear, but it's all I've got to offer."

Price looked at me for a long moment, silent, almost as though in shock. His eyes were unreadable and I couldn't be sure if what I'd said helped or hurt the situation. All I could do was wait.

Raptor walked through the doors and surveyed the inside of the club. Blaine Ranier had done a good job promoting his club and it was quickly becoming a hot spot in the town. He regretted, briefly, the fact he had turned down the opportunity to invest at the beginning.

"Hindsight is twenty-twenty," Raptor muttered to himself as he headed towards the bar. The guy serving drinks didn't look familiar and Raptor was reasonably certain he hadn't met him anywhere before, which was something he would definitely remember. He never forgot someone once he met them so he figured he could risk getting some information.

"Hey, bud, what can I get for ya?" asked the lanky man behind the counter.

"Scotch neat."

"You got it."

After Raptor took a sip of his drink he narrowed his eyes slightly and asked, "You know Chill?"

"Doesn't everyone?"

"Is he around?"

The man shook his head. "I haven't seen him yet, but the night's still young, man. You want me to give him a message for ya?"

"No, but I could use a little bit of information."

The bartender inhaled slowly and clicked his tongue in his mouth. "Chill's kind of a pal of mine. I think he'd wanna know about some guy asking around about him."

Raptor smiled a mirthless smile. "I get what you're saying. How much?"

"I dunno," he answered with a shrug. "How much is it worth to you to keep him from finding out you were here tonight? I've seen your picture in the papers, ya know."

Murderous rage flashed through Raptor's eyes, but he knew the kid behind the bar didn't have a clue with whom he was really dealing. Raptor wanted the information and he knew he would have to play along, at least until he could get this guy alone. No one would think twice about a dead bartender.

After retrieving his wallet he put a few hundreds on the bar and his phone, a picture he'd snapped from the gala visible.

"You must really want this kept quiet, huh?" He pocketed the money and glanced at the picture. "Pretty girl."

"Yeah. You ever see her around here with Chill?"

"Lots of pretty girls come here."

Raptor scowled and tossed more money on the bar. "Does that help your memory?"

"Hmm. She's been in here with him a few times before."

"When was the last time?"

"I'm not sure. Maybe a week or two ago. They were with another guy, but I've never seen him before. I think they called him Ramey...Randy...hell, I don't know."

"Ramsey," Raptor whispered, forgetting the bartender was still talking to him.

"Yeah, that was his name."

"Thanks," Raptor said as he turned around. "You've been a help."

"Anytime, buddy. Anytime."

Two hours later, Raptor tightened a piece of twine around the bartender's throat in the alley behind the club to cut off his air supply. So satisfying. Such a rush. He really should make this his last heist and get back to what he was really good at, what he really enjoyed...

Taking lives.

Once the struggling stopped, he retrieved his money from the man's pocket and calmly strode down the block to where he'd parked his car. He started the car and instinctively headed to a home other than his own, a home where there wouldn't be any nagging questions about where he'd been. This new bit of information brought several complications with it and he needed a woman's help to unwind tonight.

"I should have known you would betray me, Ramsey," Raptor whispered into the night. "Hindsight may be twenty-twenty, but foresight is flawless."

Price reached out and smoothed his hand over my cheek until his fingers tangled into my hair, freeing it from the loose ponytail that contained it. "Skylar, do you have any idea how beautiful you are when you aren't on the defensive with me?"

I averted my eyes. "This isn't really the right time for a clichéd pick-up line. You already have me," I responded.

"It's no line," Price said in earnest. "Why can't you just see what I see? It's been maddening to spend this last week with you, wanting you, but not able to have you."

"You're wrong. You could've had me."

"No I couldn't. Not with that secret hanging between us. Even with a pin in it, it would've still been there."

Before I could respond, Price's mouth closed over mine in a tentative kiss. Warm lips moved over mine with a barely-contained force. The tip of his tongue slid along the inside of my lower lip, pressing me for more, but waiting for my invitation. I parted my lips for him and he deepened the kiss. Every nerve ending in my body was alive with sensation as he circled his arms around my waist to pull me against him. The smell of him, raw sensuality and the spicy musk of his aftershave, filled my body with tension and desire.

Price trailed kisses across my jaw line and down my neck. Despite the intensity of the moment, I couldn't be sure if it was going anywhere. I had to know that he wouldn't turn away from me and shut me out again. I needed to know that he would stay with me tonight before I got swept away by the storm, but I couldn't find the words. Even if I had known what to say, it was unlikely I'd be able to form a coherent sentence.

His hands slipped under my sweatshirt and his fingertips began to lightly tease my breasts through the silky material of my bra. I fought to control my quickening breath and to focus, not on his sensual touch or the fact that my insides were liquefying, but on finding the words I so desperately needed to say to him. He pulled my shirt over my head and his eyes raked over me, darkening with desire.

I opened my mouth to speak, then my mind turned to mush as he bent down and flicked his tongue over one of my nipples. Thank God Reyna convinced me to buy something other than simple cotton underwear when we were at the mall. Practical cotton just couldn't hold a candle to sensual satin.

Price's mouth covered mine again. His kiss became more urgent, his desire obviously overpowering him, and I hoped the time for turning back, for stopping, was gone. I fumbled blindly with the buttons on his shirt for a moment before I felt his hands on top of mine. It was unclear at first whether he was helping me or stopping me again, but then he pushed my hands away and ripped open the remaining few.

His skin was warm to the touch, almost feverish, as I ran my fingers slowly down his muscular torso, teasing him, until I reached his waist. Hooking a finger into his belt, I pulled him nearer so that I could feel his skin, his heat, against me. It didn't surprise me that he was already hard and I rubbed my body against him provocatively.

Price broke his lips away from mine and our eyes locked.

"Skylar, I can't wait any longer. I have to have you," he said, his voice hoarse with desire. "Tell me that you want me, too."

That was what I had been waiting to hear. I sat on the bed and reclined back on my elbows, letting the straps of my bra slide invitingly off of my shoulders. "You know I want you, Price. Stop wasting time."

In an instant, he was with me on the bed. We fought to remove the last of each other's clothing like a couple of teenagers, getting in each other's way at every move. I felt his hands, his lips, all over my skin, sending electric sensations throughout my body and a realization came to me like a bolt of lightning.

The night I'd spent with Price at his hotel was possibly the most satisfying sexual experience of my life. With the exception of what came afterwards, there wasn't a single thing I would change, that I would have wanted him to do differently. I had been certain that nothing could have topped that night, but I was wrong.

A cry of pleasure escaped my lips when I felt Price inside me, but it was caught by his hungry kiss. There were no games this time, no power plays, no teasing; there was just the two of us. That night in his hotel was about heat and temptation.

This was something else.

Wanting him the way I had for the past week, imagining this, dreaming about him had only intensified my longing for him. I felt the waves of pleasure break over me almost instantly. The power of it caught me off guard and my body trembled violently.

When I managed to open my eyes, Price was gazing at me intently, his body still on top of me. It was dumb, especially given everything that had gone on between us, but I felt suddenly self-conscious. "What?" I managed.

"That was so beautiful, Skylar."

"Price..."

He silenced me with the brush of his lips on mine. "I want this to be different than before. I don't want you to have any regrets this time," he murmured.

I wrapped my arms around his neck and held him tight. "No regrets," I agreed.

Price stared into my eyes as he began to move inside me. Sure, I'd had sex before, but I don't know that I'd ever really made love. Not like this. There was a connection between us that went beyond the physical. I knew he felt it, too, by the intensity in his eyes. His mouth covered mine, an unspoken promise in his kiss.

When I thought I'd be content to stay like this for all of time, he thrust deep. My nerve endings exploded; my body shattered by the sensations that began at my toes and worked their way to the ends of my hair. Price held me tightly as he quickened his rhythm, driving me to the brink and then easing back just enough to slow the storm. I buried my head against his neck and clung to him as though he might vanish. He whispered wordless reassurances into my ear as the tension built, pleasure bordering on pain, and then the world fell away.

By the time he collapsed on top of me, both of us satisfied and utterly spent, time ceased to have any meaning and I wouldn't have been able to tell him what my own name was if he asked – not that I thought he would be able to form a complete thought at the moment. I didn't actually remember screaming, but my throat was dry and sore so I must have. When Price finally pulled himself off me and gave me a kiss so soft and sweet that my heart could have melted from it, I remembered what I'd realized before my mind shut down. A new terror filled me, replacing my euphoria.

I was in love with him.

"Where are you going?" Skylar asked sleepily from the bed.

Parker turned around at the door and smiled at her. "I want to make sure the doors and windows are locked. I'll be right back."

"Trying to protect me now?"

"Something like that."

"Hmm..." Skylar grinned. "Well then, hurry back so you can protect me some more."

It was obvious Skylar was just playing with him, but Parker knew he really would have to protect her. He chided himself silently as he walked into the living room and checked the door. Things were very different now and going back was not an option.

In a single night, everything had changed for him.

Parker sat on the couch and stared into the blank screen of the television. He was no fool; he knew sex always changed things between people. The first time with Skylar almost blew apart all of his plans, but this was different. There was a connection between them now, at least for him. It might be the same for her, too, but he couldn't be certain yet. She seemed to have let down her guard around him, seemed to have let go of some of that anger she always dished upon him...she seemed like a lot of things.

There was this new quality about her, almost a vulnerability, which somehow scared him. Parker had wanted to see exactly this side of her, but not yet. It was too soon to feel the way he did about her. What they would have to pull off in a few days was never something that could be considered easy, even before things heated up between them. Now, he knew he would have to be even more cautious around Raptor so he didn't figure out there was something going on between him and *Songbird*.

The mere thought of what Raptor might do with that knowledge gave Parker a sick feeling deep in his stomach. Skylar could talk a good game, but there was no way she would be able to stop Raptor's vengeance if he discovered her part in it. Losing Skylar was a disquieting possibility, one he hoped never to have to face.

But losing Skylar was unavoidable now.

So many things remained in his past that she didn't know; so many things were there that could potentially get in the way of whatever was happening between them now. Parker slumped back into the couch and sighed at his own stupidity. He should have handled things differently, but he had wanted her so badly, so desperately, that he couldn't have done anything other than what he had; said anything but what he had said.

Parker had lied. Knowing his answer would mean volumes to her, he had looked her directly in those gorgeous sapphire eyes of hers and lied.

Of course, she would find out the truth; there was never any question about it. Parker had actually intended to tell her himself several times despite the fact he would lose whatever shred of credibility he may have in her eyes. Now it wouldn't matter if she found out on her own or if she heard it from his mouth. All that was going to matter was that he lied to her about something as crucial as this.

There was still a bombshell where Raptor was concerned – an unforgivable secret that would drive her away from him forever.

"Hey," Skylar said from behind him. "What are you doing out here sitting in the dark?"

Parker took in the image of her as she crossed into his line of sight in the darkened room. She had his shirt around her like a robe. Only one of the buttons was fastened, leaving very few of her silky curves to his imagination.

He shook his head absently. "Just thinking."

"Is everything all right?"

Even in what little light there was in the room, a hint of concern was evident in her beautiful blue eyes. Parker reached for her and pulled her onto his lap. "Uh-huh."

Skylar made a little sound as he unbuttoned the shirt and gently brushed one of his hands across her breasts. "What were you thinking about, Price?"

"I was trying to figure out how to top what just happened," Parker replied, casually sliding his other hand up the inside of her thigh.

It was hard to believe he was a skilled con man with a cheesy lie like that, but at the moment, Skylar was a soft touch. Her body trembled in response to his touch and his need for her replaced his feelings of guilt. Carefully, he repositioned her and pulled her body down onto him. She let out a moan as he slid into her and he knew she would hate him for his lie by the time everything was said and done.

But not tonight.

TWENTY

Sunday, April 4

"No, Drake, there will be no more discussion about this. I want a divorce and that is final," Suzanne said sharply.

"Of course you know you're overreacting." Drake's tone was void of emotion when he spoke.

Suzanne looked at her husband through narrowed eyes. She hadn't known this was the direction the conversation would head when she'd started it, but she was relieved to finally have the words out. The decision to leave Drake Wyndham had been easy for her to make. She'd made that decision years ago.

Telling him was the part she'd grown to dread.

Despite the fact he had never so much as raised a hand to her, she knew there was a violent streak in him; an uncontrollable rage boiling just below the surface that seemed to dare her to cross him. Perhaps it was a side his girlfriend had seen...

She realized how completely absurd that thought was given the look on his face. Drake had the expression of someone who was just informed it was a day of the week ending in 'y'. No shock. No anger. Just silence. Suzanne had told him she was leaving him and he had no reaction at all.

"No, Drake, I think I'm *under*-reacting and I have been for years. I've been very tolerant, but last night was it for me."

He gave her a condescending look. "And why might that be?"

"Don't patronize me. You sauntered in here at four in the morning reeking of cigarettes, booze, and cheap perfume."

"I understand that," Drake replied in his even tone, "but what I don't understand is why you suddenly care, Suzanne."

She pursed her lips before letting a smile creep across her face. "I don't care, Drake. I've never cared about you or this marriage...or anything, for that matter. Oh, but now I do care about something and divorce seems to be quite fashionable these days. I've tolerated you for far longer than I've cared to and now it's time to end it."

He was silent for a moment and his eyes darkened. "I sincerely hope you don't think you're going to dredge up that mess you made two years ago."

"Hope all you like," her tone became haughty, "but to dredge it up would imply it was ever really over."

"You will not do this to me again," he warned, a hint of danger entering his tone.

"No, Drake, you will not stand in my way again. I've been the perfect little wife to hang on your arm at dinner parties for years and now it's time for me to get what's due me."

"If you do this, you walk away with nothing."

Suzanne considered his statements and chose her words carefully when she spoke. "On the contrary, you'll give me exactly what I want and you'll do it with a smile on your pompous face."

Drake's eyes filled with contempt. "And why would I do that? You're nothing. You never were. I'll let you leave, but you can head back to that one-horse town I found you in with the clothes on your back."

"Nice try. You'll give me what I want because I know about every little detail of your less than legal activities and I have all the proof I need to ruin you – professionally and legally. We both know your ass wouldn't last a day in prison."

Her words had hit a nerve and Drake averted his eyes in defeat. Suzanne brushed passed him and retrieved her coat from the hall closet. She paused at the door and looked over her shoulder at her husband. "Be a good little boy and pack your bags. I'm keeping the house and I expect you to be out when I come back."

After turning away from him and opening the door, she added, "And yes, I'm going exactly where you think I'm going tonight."

*****

We had stayed in bed – making love, napping, holding each other - for the better part of the day. Neither of us said anything about it, but we both knew our time was quickly running out. Tomorrow was the day everything would happen. Once we handed Raptor over to the FBI, Price would be back in their good graces and would no longer be a fugitive.

But what then?

Sure, Price had told me just less than twenty-four hours ago that he wasn't planning to leave town right away, but that didn't mean much. He'd said it when he thought I was on the verge of heading off with another man. Besides, saying that he had no plans to immediately leave didn't mean he wouldn't leave at some point.

I found myself sitting in the window seat, staring into the dreary dusk, as I tried to answer the question of how long he'd stay. Price didn't want to leave me, or so I thought, but we weren't exactly having deep conversations about how we'd spend the next several years; just the next few hours. The line I had to walk was a fine one. On one side, I desperately wanted to get to know him better. On the other, I knew it was too early for me to tell him I loved him. That was the quickest way to send any man running for the hills.

Was it too soon to ask him why he preferred I call him by his last name? That one had driven me nuts for the last week...

When the rain outside slowed to a trickle, Price entered the room and walked up behind me. His arms were comforting when he put them around me and I instinctively melted back against him. Why couldn't it already be tomorrow night? Why couldn't this feel like a beginning instead of an hourglass slowly counting grain after grain until the end?

"Are you okay, sweetheart? You've been quiet since we got up," Price asked.

I mustered a weak smile and turned to face him. "I'm just nervous, I guess."

"I know I've said this before," he began slowly, "but it isn't too late to turn back. We can always do this with one less person."

"And I'm sure Raptor wouldn't think that was in the slightest bit suspicious."

His face hardened. "I don't really give a damn what he thinks where you're concerned. After tomorrow, he won't be an issue for us anymore."

Us? I sighed. "I know." Turning my gaze back to the darkening scene outside I added, "I should probably take you up on that, but I can't, you know. This is something I have to be a part of."

"Your father would understand, Skylar."

Clearly, Price could read my mind. Parts of it, anyway.

"Maybe, but I owe it to...I can't explain it. I just have to see this through. Please don't try to talk me out of it. I don't want to waste any more time fighting with you, not even for another day."

"I won't," he said simply. "It's always been your call." He cleared his throat and looked out the window. "You should probably get dressed."

"Tired of me already?"

He knelt until his face was only inches from mine. "On the contrary, sweetheart," he began in a low, sultry tone, "I could stay in bed with you for the next month and still not have had enough of you. I just need you to get dressed before Chill and Cherry get here. Your bare skin is too much of a temptation for me." His hot gaze swept over me. "Even after the way we spent the day."

Though his comment soothed me slightly, I was still on edge. He must have sensed my apprehension because his expression changed. There were so many things I wanted to tell him, so many emotions I still needed to sort out on my own, but I managed a weak smile and said, "I'm just ready for all of the planning to be over with so that I can have you all to myself."

Price brushed a kiss against my lips and rose. "It's just one more night and then I'll be all yours. Maybe we could go somewhere with a better climate to celebrate when this is over. Belize is nice this time of year. There's also a small, private island off the Australian coast I enjoy. I should take you there. I think you'd like it." A slight smile touched his face, but he shook away whatever he was thinking about. "You should get dressed. They'll be here in a few minutes, but we can talk about it more tomorrow afternoon."

I stared at the spot where Price had stood for a long time after he had left the room. It was far from a declaration of love, but it was something, some glimpse of a shared future, albeit brief. No, it wasn't all I wanted from Price, not even close; however, it was something for me to cling onto.

For the first time, I honestly believed Price might stay with me once all of this intrigue was over.

*****

Dinner with Jenna's family was a welcome change from the pressures of solving a case with no new leads. Near the end of the evening, Jackson decided he was glad he'd accepted the invitation, despite his reservations about it. With the exception of the charity gala, he hadn't spent any time with her family since coming back to town. They all made it very clear before he left that he was no longer welcome, but all must have been forgiven since he hadn't received a single hostile glare.

"So, Jenna, have you heard anything new about the murder at Blaine's Rain last night?" Daniel asked.

For a split second, Jackson was taken back to the night he found his partner, murdered, in the alley behind the club. After six months, he could still feel the sting of loss every time he thought about it. It was such a shame; Collin could have been such a good agent if...Jackson stopped that line of thought. There was no sense dwelling on what could have been.

Nothing he could do now would bring back Collin.

Jenna shook her head and sipped her water. "No. Trista and Blaine are out of town, so I only know what I've heard on the news."

"Such an awful thing to happen to someone so young," Elaine mused. "Did you know him well?"

"No. Why would I?"

Her sister frowned. "I thought he might be one of the men you dated there."

"I didn't date the guys who worked there, 'Laine. I met dates there."

Why hadn't Jackson known about any of that?

Elaine rose to her feet and began to clear the dishes from the table. "Well, thank goodness for small favors."

Instinctively, Jackson also rose. "Let me help you with that, Elaine."

She nodded and carried the plates she had into the kitchen. Jackson collected what was left over and followed her, trying to focus on the task at hand. Jenna dating while they were apart shouldn't bother him, but it did.

It bothered the shit out of him.

"What are you doing, Jackson?"

"Helping you with the dishes."

Elaine let out an aggravated sigh. "That isn't what I mean and I think you know it. I want to know what you're doing here with Jenna."

"I was under the impression you invited me."

"Not exactly. Jenna asked if I'd mind if she brought you to dinner and I told her I'd never be rude to a guest in my home."

Clearly, all was not forgiven.

Jackson folded his arms in front of him and scowled. "It won't happen again. I'll make sure I'm not around when Jenna spends time with your daughter."

"Don't be that way. There's no reason for it." She sighed. "I just don't want my sister hurt by you again."

"I have no intention of hurting her again."

"Well, you didn't have any intention of hurting her the first time around, did you?"

"I don't know what you want me to say, Elaine."

"The truth would be nice." After a beat, her expression softened and she added, "I realize I'm being a bitch right now, by the way. It's just...you aren't the one who had to see the pain she was in after you left. When she wasn't manically studying for the Bar, she was crying. If she wasn't serial dating, she'd stay in bed for days at a time." Tears sprang to her eyes. "Lana kept making get well cards and asking to take them over because she couldn't understand why her aunt didn't come see her anymore."

"I didn't know."

Her eyes met his. "And you'll never let her know you know now. She'd never forgive me."

Jackson tried to clear the emotion from his throat. "It stays between us."

"Thank you, but you still haven't answered my question. Not in any real way."

It didn't surprise him that she was stuck on getting an answer. Still, the answer was not as cut and dry as he would have liked. There were so many unanswered questions in his mind that he didn't feel certain he would be able to allay her concerns. But he would have to try.

He knew he owed her that much. She was the one who was there for Jenna when he wasn't.

Her and Lana were apparently the ones to clean up the destruction left in his wake.

"I'm here because Jenna wants me to be and I will stay for as long as she'll let me. Despite what you might think, I love your sister more than anything in this world, more than I even thought was possible, and the last thing I would ever want to do is hurt her again."

Elaine's eyes were impassive as she looked at Jackson. In a cool voice she replied, "You had better mean that. I would never threaten a federal agent, but you'll regret it if you break her heart again." She paused long enough to let the gravity of her simple words sink in. "How's your case going anyway?"

Jackson was taken aback, but he was grateful for the change of subject. "I don't know if we're really getting anywhere, but it seems like we should have everything we need to put it together. It's like a small detail is staring us in the face that doesn't make sense yet."

"I would never presume to tell you how to do your job, Jackson, but I do hope you know what you're doing. I know the men you consider suspects, all of them, and I can honestly say I don't believe any of them could have killed a man in cold blood. If the press gets the names..."

"You don't have to worry about that, Elaine. The FBI knows how to be discreet with its investigations."

"Yes. I remember a little too well."

Jackson opened his mouth to respond, but Jenna poked her head into the kitchen. "Hey, are you two almost done? I'm not trying to be rude, but I have an early morning."

Jackson exchanged glances with Elaine, who nodded. "I can take care of this. You two should get going."

It didn't occur to Jackson until they were almost home that Elaine shouldn't have known who the FBI suspected to be Raptor. Jenna never shared the details of a case with her sister for fear she wouldn't be able to keep the information confidential. How could her sister have known if neither of them told her?

"I can't even explain what a special breed of asshole he is," Cherry fumed as she accepted the drink Price offered her.

"What did Raptor do now?" he asked.

Cherry shook her head. "It's Trevor. Apparently, he and Suzanne are back together."

I blinked back my surprise. "Suzanne? Suzanne Wyndham? But she's married to..."

We were interrupted by a soft rap at the door. Price jumped to his feet and let Chill into the townhouse. Chill said something in a hushed tone to Price. He nodded in our direction in greeting before the two men disappeared into the bedroom.

"That was odd."

Cherry smiled. "So are they." After taking a sip of her wine, she added, "Get used to it. Those two have been like that since I've known them. They aren't about to change and I can tell he'll probably be around for a while."

"Why do you say that?"

The blonde shrugged. "Call it whatever you like...hunch, intuition...You're different from the others. Parker's hooked."

Cherry's words should have soothed me since she'd known Price far longer than I had. Instead, the conversation unsettled my already frazzled nerves. My stomach knotted and I scanned my brain for a way out of the conversation.

I wasn't ready to get my hopes up. Not yet.

"So...Suzanne and Trevor?"

Cherry rolled her eyes in disgust. "Yeah. I'm told they're in love, have been for years. I was just the distraction until she could get out of her marriage. I hate that condescending bitch. It enrages me to think I ended up serving drinks in that filthy club because I didn't want to hurt her."

"What are you talking about?"

She took another sip of her drink. "I had to get a job after Marcus was killed. I lucked into a cushy job at the bank working directly for Drake. I was nowhere near qualified to be an assistant, but I figured it was just my lucky day. Didn't take long for me to learn I only got the job because of the length of my skirt. I knew Drake was married and I fully respected that. Whatever people might think or say about me...I'm not a slut and I would never move in on someone else's man. I turned him down and I was fired shortly thereafter."

"That's illegal, Cherry. Why didn't you do something?"

"You can turn down the righteous indignation." She slouched back into the couch. "I don't know. For starters, I had falsified half my resume to sound legitimate. Then there was the fact that the only real skills I had were hacking into computer systems. Can't you just image how unsympathetic I would have looked in court if I sued?"

I realized how completely I had misjudged her. Cherry wasn't the opportunistic tramp everyone made her out to be. It struck me funny: under other circumstances, we might have never become friends. The old Skylar would have written her off as just another bleached blonde gold digger and never given her a second thought.

It's what I was prepared to do the night of the gala.

"Then why does Suzanne hate you so much if you didn't sleep with her husband?"

"I didn't find out until today, but she and Trevor were having an affair a few years back. The night I put an end to Drake's advances, he went straight home and caught the two of them together. I suppose that pretty well ended his friendship with Trevor and the affair."

"That doesn't explain why she hates you."

Cherry grimaced. "Think like a cold-hearted bitch, Skylar. If I had been fucking her husband like a good little tramp, he wouldn't have come home early."

"Seems like she could have just divorced him."

"Um, well...Drake Wyndham isn't exactly the kind of man you get to walk out on."

"Oh," I said, not really knowing what else to say to that. "I guess that makes sense."

"Yeah, well, I don't really care anymore. Those two deserve each other. They're a real match made in hell, if you ask me."

I nodded. "You're lucky to be rid of him. Trevor was a bore. I don't know how you stood him."

"I liked that he was boring. It made me feel...safe, I suppose." She leaned forward conspiratorially. "I thought he was someone who was on the right side of the law. I thought he was different from the other men I'd dated."

"Like Chill," I asked.

Her face grew solemn. "Yes, but I always felt safe with him."

I studied her face intently. It was obvious she didn't have many friends, at least many friends she could talk to about this sort of thing. It was also obvious that she needed to talk.

"Do you want to tell me about it?"

She eyed me cautiously and sank back into the cushions of the couch again. "I'm going to need another drink before I get into that mess."

I refilled her wineglass and waited for her to take a sip from it before asking, "So?"

"We were friends practically from the first day we met. Parker was like a brother – a very protective brother who didn't let me go out with the wrong sort of guy. It was annoying, but I know he meant well, especially since I seem to be a sleaze-magnet."

"And Chill?"

A faint smile touched her lips. "He wasn't Chill then...Everyone just called him Rand. I think I was the only person who ever got away with calling him Crandall to his face."

"Did you start dating right away?" I asked, trying to imagine anyone calling Chill by anything other than Chill.

Cherry shook her head and took another thoughtful sip of her wine. "Actually, we were both friends with Parker, but were thoroughly annoyed with one another for the first few years we knew each other. Things changed about a month before graduation...he was my first. I think I might have been his, too, but I've never known for sure."

"Why didn't things work out with the two of you?"

"That," she began in a dark tone, "is something I definitely do not want to talk about until the bottle of wine is gone."

"It was Raptor, I know it was," Chill said as soon as they were out of earshot of the women.

Parker regarded him carefully. He had only found out about Aaron's murder a few hours earlier when he flipped to a local news station. It was definitely not good news to find out one of the few bartenders Chill trusted had just been killed outside of the club where much of their business had transpired, but it didn't necessarily point to Raptor.

Strangling sounded about right though. Familiar.

"We don't know that for certain, Chill. It's too late in the game for us to come unglued and jump to unfounded conclusions."

Chill's usual cool demeanor returned before he responded. "I am well aware. I have contacted my sources and Raptor most certainly was in the club last night just a few hours before Aaron was strangled. Does it not concern you that one of the only people who can confirm our affiliation is in the morgue?" He eyed him for a moment before adding, "Might I just add that he was there the night you, me and Skylar had drinks. He's also seen me talking to Cherry...*before* Raptor made the call on her hacking."

"I wasn't aware you'd been seeing Cherry socially."

"It wasn't like that. Not for more than a dozen years now." He sighed. "That's not the point anyway. Me being seen talking to *any* of you before Raptor started the ball rolling is bad. Me being seen talking to Skylar *ever* is worse. Aren't you even in the least bit concerned?"

Actually, that was the only thing that had been on Parker's mind since he heard the news. Aaron was a good guy, but everyone had their price and Raptor had plenty of cash to throw around. If he knew...

Parker pushed the thought out of his mind. He couldn't afford to play the what if game right now. Cherry was pissed, Skylar was emotional and Chill was on edge. One of them had to remain calm and focused; one of them had to keep their game face on.

"It concerns me as much as it does you, but there is nothing we can do about it at this stage. This is going down tomorrow morning at nine sharp, just as we've been planning," Parker said with cool authority.

"This is your score, your call. What do we do about them?" Chill nodded in the direction of the living room.

He frowned. "We can't let them know anything is wrong. The two of them will come unhinged. We could pull this off if it was just Skylar we had to worry about, but we need Cherry on top of things."

Chill cocked his head to the side and twisted his mouth into a taunting grin. "Shall I assume it has not been all bubble gum and sunshine over here this past week?"

"Assume whatever the hell you like."

"All kidding aside," Chill began, his tone cautious, "there's something going on with the two of you, isn't there?"

Parker hadn't wanted to discuss this, but when he met his old friend's gaze, the words tumbled out as though by their own volition. "She's in love with me."

Chill's eyes softened. "She told you that?"

"She didn't have to...I can just tell."

"Well, Parker, I don't see what the problem is then. You clearly want her. Seems like a good predicament to be in. I wouldn't mind it if a beautiful woman was in love with me."

Parker sat on the window seat and buried his face in his hands. He wasn't sure how to make Chill understand and he wasn't sure if he should try. He didn't even want to try understanding it himself.

With a sigh, Parker looked up and said, "This isn't good timing. I don't need something frivolous like love clouding my judgment tomorrow."

Chill sat next to him. "That's a grim outlook, even for you."

"What if something goes wrong, Chill? What if I have to choose between destroying Raptor and being with Skylar? How do I even make that kind of a choice?"

"You won't have to; it isn't going to come down to that. Besides, if it did, there's only one choice you can make and we both know that."

Parker was about to ask what Chill thought that choice was when Cherry burst into the room and closed the door. "We have a visitor," she whispered once she'd shut off the lights.

Reyna's clear blue eyes were bloodshot and cold when Skylar opened the door.

"Can I come in?"

Skylar looked confused, but opened the door a little wider. Reyna pushed passed her and flopped down onto the couch. It was difficult to set her anger and hurt aside long enough to find words, but it all tumbled out as soon as Skylar sat next to her.

"I thought we were friends, Skylar. How could you do this to me?" Reyna demanded.

"What are you talking about?"

"I sat right here in this room and you lied to me! How stupid do you really think I am?"

Skylar held up her hands in protest. "I swear I don't know what you're talking about. At least fill me in before you continue yelling at me."

She narrowed her eyes. "I'm talking about you and Eric," she hissed.

"There is nothing between the two of us anymore, Reyna. I've already told you that."

"Oh, that's the story you keep trying to sell, but I'm not buying it." She felt hot tears welling in her eyes and wiped at them impatiently. "You say it's over between you two, but I saw the way you were looking at him at the gala when he was dancing with you. I noticed how the two of you snuck off before dinner last Sunday night. I've noticed the way he's started to pull away from me ever since the day you walked back into his life."

"Reyna..."

She shook her head and cut her off. "Don't *Reyna* me. And don't lie to me anymore, either. I followed him yesterday. I know he came here, you...bitch." She could barely speak over the betrayal she felt. "Everything was going so great and now...and now he keeps coming in at all hours. He doesn't return my calls the way he used to."

"I'm not encouraging..."

"I don't care." Reyna glanced over at the coffee table and was infuriated by what she saw. "You know, he wasn't home when I called him earlier. Have you seen him, Skylar?"

She shook her head emphatically. "No, Reyna, I have not. Not since yesterday."

"So do you always need two glasses of wine for a quiet evening at home alone then?"

"When I said that I haven't seen Eric, I was telling you the truth, but," Skylar began heatedly, "I never said I was here alone." She turned towards her bedroom and called, "Can you come out here for a second, hon?"

Reyna folded her arms over her chest and waited. When Jonathan Price entered the room, an expectant look on his face, she felt her cheeks grow warm. She looked from him to Skylar and back again before dropping her head into her hands. The tears that rolled down her cheeks made her feel like such a fool.

In a soft voice Skylar asked, "Would you mind getting Reyna something to drink? Thanks."

Reyna looked up and cautiously met the brunette's look. "I don't know what's wrong with me. I'm sorry. I'm so sorry."

Skylar shook her head. "Don't worry about it. I understand. I know what it's like to feel like you're losing someone you care about. But if he's pulling away from you, it's not because I'm trying to steal him from you."

She brushed a damp strand of her dark hair off her face. "I just thought..."

"I'm not going to lie to you, Reyna. Eric did make a play for me last Sunday and again yesterday, but I didn't encourage it. You can ask Price if you don't believe me. He walked in on the scene. Whatever is up with Eric has been going on since before he saw me again."

Jonathan walked back into the room and handed Reyna a glass of water. She thanked him and took a few gulps. Apparently, it was worse than she thought.

Reyna let out her breath slowly to calm herself. "It would have been so much easier if it had been you. I can deal with another woman, but I don't know how to deal with whatever this is. I hope we can still be friends."

Skylar nodded and Reyna decided it was time for her to go. Clearly, she'd come at a bad time. With most of the lights out and wine on the table, it was obvious she had interrupted something private, intimate.

She walked with Skylar to the door. "I've got to go." In a lower tone, she whispered, "I didn't mean to ruin your evening."

"You didn't. Please don't worry about it." Skylar glanced back into the living room and then stepped out onto the porch. "I want you to know that, if you and Eric are able to patch this up, you don't have anything to worry about from me. That ship has sailed. Even if it hadn't..." She shook her head. "I care about the man in there too much to hurt him like that."

Reyna plastered a weak smile on her lips. "I know how you feel. Thanks for understanding." Something occurred to her and she added, "I think it's so cute the way you call your boyfriend by his last name."

With that, Reyna hurried down the sidewalk to her car and sped away.

"Where do you think you're going, Cherry?"

She groaned. "Don't start with me tonight, Chill. Trevor kicked me out so I don't have many options except for going over to Raptor's and..."

"Dammit, Cherry! Staying with Raptor for one more second is not an option. Why don't you understand that?"

I watched the exchange in silence. Once, I glanced over at Price to see if I should say anything, but he shook his head. It was clear I didn't understand their relationship well enough to get in the middle of the argument. There was no way I could let her stay with me; Raptor could find out about that, so I stayed quiet until it was over.

"What would you have me do, Chill?" she screamed. "We both know the police will be checking out hotel and motel registries after shit hits the fan tomorrow. My name can't turn up there." She gestured to me and Price. "And even if it wasn't obvious these two want to be alone tonight, I couldn't stay here either. It's too risky."

No one said anything for a long moment and Chill's expression softened. "Stay with me."

"Oh, and I'm sure Raptor won't find that odd in the slightest," Cherry retorted before laughing. "You know how it is...Chill didn't want to treat all the seed money with the chemical by himself so we had a little pre-heist slumber party." She shook her head. "Sorry, but I didn't bring my Care Bears sleeping bag."

"I know you're trying to be funny, but I have a guest room. Several, actually."

"Yeah, well...It's just one more night. He's not going to hurt me the night before a heist. It's too late to get a replacement."

Anger flashed in Chill's eyes as he advanced on her. "You aren't spending another second with that monster. If I'd known then I would have gotten you out of there sooner."

"I'm not your problem to deal with anymore, Chill. Just let it go."

He grabbed her by the shoulders. "I don't care if Raptor likes it or not. You aren't a problem, Cherry. Don't you see...Even if you were, you never should have stopped being my problem!" He kissed her roughly. "You never should have left school the way you did. Things would have been so different...for both of us."

Cherry's jaw dropped for a second before she shook herself back and regained her sarcastic expression. "Yeah, okay. If it's that big a deal to you, I'll help you treat the bills and crash in your guest room. There's no reason to stand here trying to con me."

His grip on her shoulders visibly tightened. "What the fuck is wrong with you? I've never conned you. Never lied to you either, not even when I wanted to. Not once." He spared a glance in our direction before continuing, almost as though he'd forgotten we were here. "You realize you're the only person in this room who seems to think I actually want you to crash in my guest room...unless that's the bed you'd prefer."

Again, I glanced at Price. He shrugged. From the look on his face, it appeared he'd considered this exchange between them an inevitability.

When Cherry didn't respond, Chill released her and muttered, "I've only spent half my life in love with you. Is it so much to ask for you to notice?"

The blonde's jaw dropped again. When she regained her composure this time, there was no sarcasm in her voice. "I'll follow you over in my car." She turned to us. "I'll see you guys in the morning. And Skylar," she crossed the room over to me and gave me a quick hug. "Don't worry so much. I'm right, you know."

After they left Price turned to me and asked, "What did she mean by that?"

I shrugged it off. "You know; the heist tomorrow. No big deal."

I hurried into the kitchen and dumped the excess wine from our glassed into the sink before turning on the water to rinse them. It was a lie and I hoped Price wouldn't pick up on it. For whatever reason, I wasn't willing to admit the conversation I'd had with Cherry before Reyna had shown up.

Unfortunately, Price wasn't buying it. He followed me into the kitchen and leaned against the doorframe. His slight smile melted my resolve and I shut off the water.

"Do you want to tell me what she really meant by that?"

I dried my hands on one of the kitchen towels. "I would prefer not to."

He approached me slowly and I found myself pressed between him and the counter. "Does it have anything to do with what you were whispering to Reyna before she left?"

"In my defense, you weren't supposed to hear that," I replied, nervously biting my lower lip.

Pressing his forehead against mine, he asked, "Why do you insist on hiding your thoughts from me?"

I wet my lips before I spoke. "Because I have too much to lose now that..."

"Now that what?"

I averted my eyes, but then felt braver and looked back to meet his gaze. "Now that I'm in love with you, Price."

At first I wasn't sure if telling him was a mistake. Price didn't say anything and instead stared at me with darkening eyes. I was about to say something else, anything else, when he caught me in a kiss.

Price's hands slid up my back, pulling me closer, and my body trembled in response. It sounded like he might have whispered against my lips that he loved me too, but I couldn't be sure. My ears weren't trustworthy right now. He could've muttered something about needing to file his taxes, for all I knew.

Did con men file taxes?

Price pulled away slightly and asked, "Are you ready for bed?"

"I thought you'd never ask."

TWENTY-ONE

Monday, April 5

Parker was awake hours before the alarm was set to go off. The moon had long since set and the gray pre-dawn light had begun to seep into the room. He brushed a strand of hair off her face and watched her as she slept.

A tropical getaway would be just what they needed when today was over. Parker toyed with the idea of getting online and purchasing their tickets, but decided it might be a little premature. The point of what he was doing was to clear his name with the FBI and he knew it could take some time to convince them of what he was trying to do. He also knew he didn't want to spend the rest of his life looking over his shoulder for the cops when he could be looking at Skylar.

She stirred beside him. "Is it already time to get up, Price?"

Parker repositioned himself and pulled her into his arms. "No, you can go back to sleep." He gave her a light kiss on the forehead. "I'm sorry I woke you."

She smiled and buried her head into his chest. "Okay."

Parker kissed her forehead again and her breathing became deep and even as she slipped back into slumber. Skylar seemed so peaceful now that he couldn't imagine her robbing a bank in just a few hours. It would be so easy to slip away while she was still asleep, shutting off the alarm before he left. The whole ugly mess could be over before she got out of bed and she wouldn't have to deal with any of it. Raptor would think it was odd, but it would be over for him soon enough.

But that wasn't an option.

As much as Parker wanted to protect her from what they would have to do to bring down Raptor, he knew Skylar would be furious at him for keeping her out of it. She was stubborn to a fault. She would never forgive him for that.

Parker turned his thoughts away from protecting Skylar to what they could do after the day was over. He absolutely dreaded the inevitable meeting that would take place between Skylar and his mother. When his mother had called to inform him on Saturday that her plane had just landed and she wanted to see him while she waited on her connection, he had dropped everything and left.

She was the only person that could always see straight through him and it was difficult to make her believe he was really in Dallas on business. Once he'd admitted it started out as business and grew into something else, she insisted that she meet Skylar as soon as he could take a break from work.

Parker realized that once Raptor's identity was revealed and it was on the front page of the paper that his mother would take note of it. The connection he had to Raptor was too strong and there was no way he would be able to keep her from saying something about it in front of Skylar. No matter how he tried to excuse his lie, there would be no way to make Skylar understand.

Parker slipped into a fitful sleep knowing he was about to lose the only woman who'd ever made him want to be a better man, the only woman he'd ever truly loved.

I realized I was alone in bed before I opened my eyes. A quick glance at the clock revealed it was still a few hours before the alarm was set to go off. My first thought was that Price left without me, but that was silly since I could smell the coffee brewing in the kitchen. Besides, we had agreed the night before that there would be no more discussion about it.

I was going and that was that.

The chilled air hit me as soon as I stepped out of bed. I scanned the room and found the sweatshirt from last night on the floor by the bed. I pulled it over my head and slipped into the bathroom as quietly as I could. Price had clearly gone out of his way not to wake me up yet so I didn't want him to know I was up.

I needed more time before I saw him anyway. My hands were still trembling so badly from the thought of what I was about to do that I could barely splash water on my face. If Price saw me in this condition then he would certainly try to talk me out of going again.

"Coffee?"

I nearly jumped out of my skin when I heard Price behind me. "You scared me."

Price set the coffee mug on the counter and placed his hands on my shoulders. "You're tense, Skylar."

"A little, I guess."

"Let me help you with that," he offered, skillfully massaging my shoulders and neck.

I let my head drop forward and counted my lucky stars he hadn't realized how unnerved I really was. My resolve was too fragile at this point to handle another conversation about my staying home today. It had to be done.

He pressed his lips to the back of my neck. "You're still very tense, sweetheart."

"Hmm…" I leaned back against him. "Maybe I just have a lot of excess nervous energy right now…"

"Really?" He slipped his hands under my sweatshirt and circled my waist. "I might be able to help you out with that."

I turned around and met his gaze. "You think so?"

I'd intended for my tone to be more playful than it came out, but when I looked at him for the first time that morning, I felt my heart melt. Even though he'd obviously been awake for longer than I had, his hair was still tousled, not in the usual carefully practiced way, but the way it really looked when he first woke up. It was possible that I was the only person who had ever seen the real him.

If this was the real him.

"What is it, sweetheart?"

Well, I could hardly tell him I couldn't stop thinking about how much I was in love with him. After confessing my feelings last night, we'd made love once and gone to sleep. There had been no more discussion on the matter. I wasn't sure how I really felt about that fact.

I cleared my mind and forced a slight smile. "I was just wondering something."

Price leaned against the doorframe and folded his arms across his bare chest. His lean physique never ceased to amaze me. Though I had never seen him work out, not even once, his whole demeanor exuded his masculine strength. Even now, wearing only a faded pair of grey sweats, I could still remember the strength of his touch, the firmness of his body against mine...

"What were you wondering?" he asked, dragging my mind away from my thoughts.

I mustered another weak smile. "I was just wondering if you really could help me get rid of *all* this excess energy. Do you really think you're up for that?"

I saw the mischief flash through his eyes for a split second before he reached for me. He pulled my shirt over my head, but I didn't have time for the chill to set in. The heat from his body seeped through my skin the instant his body touched mine.

Pressing me up against the counter, he said, "Oh, yeah. I'm definitely up for it." He gave me a rough kiss. "Are you?"

In lieu of a response, I tugged at his pants until he removed them. Price lifted me up onto the counter, knocking over the cup of coffee he'd brought me in the process. It shattered on the tile floor as my legs were nudged apart.

"I was looking forward to drinking that."

Price grinned. "I can get you another one."

"There's glass on floor."

"I'll clean it up later. Sweetheart, I'm more interested in you right now." He pulled away from me. "This isn't just about nervous energy, is it?"

"Don't do this, Price."

"I have to. Please stay out of this today."

Were we seriously going to have this discussion now? Naked? "We've already discussed this and agreed I was going through with it."

"Things are different now."

"I don't understand. What's changed?"

He took my face in his hands and gently caressed my cheek. "Sweetheart, everything's changed. Raptor's an unpredictable factor that I can't control. I don't want to risk you."

"Risk me? What about you, Price?" I placed a hand on his chest. "I'll stay out of it if you will."

He shook his head. "I can't do that. Raptor is taking down First Alliance with or without me. If I'm there, I can make sure things don't get out of hand. I'm not letting anyone get hurt like..." His voice trailed off.

"Like before," I finished for him. "You don't have to do this to atone for the past."

Price looked me squarely in the eyes. "Neither do you." He brushed his lips against mine. "Stay here where it's safe."

I wished I could do just that, but I couldn't. Even though I would be safe, I would be a nervous wreck wondering if he was all right. At least if I was with him, I would know he was safe.

"I can't do that," I answered, hugging him tightly. "I'll only stay here if you do."

"Skylar..."

"No. If you can risk your life...so can I."

"No you can't. Your life is worth more than mine." He pulled away from me. "You know how I feel about you, don't you, Skylar?"

There was no way to answer that question. I wanted desperately to believe I knew, but he'd been pulling cons for years. Though every fiber in my being told me he loved me, how could I really know anything for certain?

"You really don't know." Price gathered my hands in his and gave me a soft kiss. "Skylar, I..."

I pulled one of my hands away and pressed a finger to his lips to silence him. He was about to tell me he loved me and I was falling apart inside. In theory, it would put my mind at ease, but it probably wouldn't be that simple. Price was skilled at lying to people without them ever knowing. I just didn't want to hear the words from him if I couldn't be completely sure he meant them. "Don't say it."

"Why? I don't understand."

I shook my head. "It doesn't mean anything when you say it in bed."

"But we aren't in bed," he said, puzzled.

"Well, we're naked. We could be." I grinned. "But you'll have to stop talking to get me in there."

Price scooped me up into his arms. "This subject is far from closed, but we're under a deadline so I'll drop it. For now."

Jackson looked at Brandon in disbelief as he told him the news. He knew Trevor was hiding something from them, but he hadn't thought he would cave over the weekend and be ready to talk to them so soon. He certainly never thought he'd be waiting for them up at Headquarters before most agents were in for the day.

He just hoped that what he had to tell them was going to help them make their case against Drake Wyndham.

Trevor was reclined in his chair staring at the ceiling when they joined him in the conference room. "It took you guys long enough," he complained without looking at them. "Feel better now that you've both had your morning coffee?"

"Cut the crap, Brightman," Brandon demanded. "You asked for this meeting now get to the point."

Trevor cleared his throat. "I didn't tell you everything I knew about Drake the other day. Are you still interested about the details or should I go?"

Jackson leaned forward in his chair. "Go on."

"I've been a party to many illegal activities with Drake. At first, I didn't know we were doing anything against the law, but it was too late once I knew."

Jackson shook his head. "Why didn't you go to your handler with the information?"

"You don't get it. By the time I found out, I was already in too deep."

"You're usefulness to the Bureau would have outweighed any of your crimes, with the exception of murder, of course," Brandon said. "What exactly were you involved in?"

"A drug smuggling operation. I think Drake may have been laundering the money through his bank, but I stayed out of that side of it. Actually, I tried to stay out of most of it."

Jackson was puzzled. "What did you mean when you said that you were too involved to get out?"

"I met his wife. What can I say? I fell in love with her and I didn't want to hurt her with a scandal."

"Is that really all there is to it, Brightman?" Jackson asked. He was grateful Trevor had come forward, but he was skeptical that they were getting the whole story yet.

Trevor let out an exaggerated sigh. "Drake found out about my past. I tried to get out and he told me that he would make certain the people who are looking for me got a tip about where I was hiding out. Things went on for a while after that, but then he caught me with Suzanne. She wanted to leave him to be with me, but we both knew what he would do, so...that was the end of that."

Brandon drummed his fingers restlessly on the conference table. "So why now? What's changed?"

"Suzanne's finally had enough," he replied, shrugging. "It's always been her call. I know she has her place in society here and I couldn't have asked her to give all of that up to go into hiding with me."

"And that's not an issue anymore?" Jackson questioned.

Trevor nodded. "I called her this weekend. I had to let her know I couldn't hold all of this in anymore, that I was going to tell everything, with or without her. She told me she knew how to get her hands on all of his records and she was coming with me if I had to go somewhere."

Brandon's eyes widened. "What kind of records are we talking about here?"

Again, Trevor shrugged. "I haven't seen everything she has yet, but I'm pretty sure it will be everything you guys need to put him away for drug trafficking, bribery, money laundering, embezzlement, you name it."

This definitely had all the makings of a big bust, but Jackson couldn't be sure whether any of this was useful to the bust they needed to make. There was no choice except for him to lay their cards on the table, especially since it sounded like he was about to be relocated yet again by the Bureau. The time for discretion with this man had come to an end.

"As you may know, we're trying to apprehend a man who goes by Raptor."

"The guy who robbed Drake's bank a few years back, right?"

Jackson nodded. "That's right. Do you think Drake could be that man?"

Trevor frowned and thoughtfully rested his chin on his hand. "I honestly don't know. The man steals small sums from that office every day, so I don't know that I would put it past him to put on a mask and march in there with a gun."

"This is important," Jackson urged. "Can you think of any specifics?"

Trevor shook his head. "That happened right about the time he found out I was in witness protection. I spent as little time with him as possible." His eyes suddenly brightened. "I do remember Suzanne saying that she couldn't see me because of something to do with Drake. She might know something that could help you guys out."

Jackson nodded and stood up. "Okay, well thanks for your time."

Trevor shot up to stop him from leaving. "Wait a minute. You'll protect Suzanne from Drake and his associates, right? You have to," he pleaded.

Brandon crossed the room to the door and, in an authoritative tone said, "If she can prove any of what you just said, then we'll help her. Call her and get her over here. Until then, we have work to do."

Parker pulled the covers up around them and held Skylar close. It never ceased to amaze him how good making love to her felt or how spectacularly blue her eyes were when she'd gaze at him afterwards. It also surprised him that he could just hold her forever without getting sick of her being around.

Love was a funny thing.

Of course, love was another issue. He didn't fully understand why Skylar tensed up when he tried to tell her how he felt, but he knew enough not to press the issue right now. Even though he'd done everything in his power to change it, she was still tense. It was probably best not to get into any heavy conversations until the day was over and they could both relax.

"What happens now?"

Parker locked fingers with her and pulled them to his lips. After kissing them lightly, he asked, "What do you mean? I thought you said you understood how things were going down at the bank."

"No, I do, but..." Skylar's voice trailed off as she rested her head on his shoulder. "What about after?"

Though he'd known she would eventually wonder about that, Parker wasn't prepared for the question. The FBI could still be a problem; they could still toss him in jail for his part in things. Or they could let him off with a slap on the wrist as he'd hoped and he could get away with Skylar.

But then what? They couldn't just stay in a tropical paradise forever. Parker loved her and wanted to have a future with her. In order to do that, he would eventually have to tell her who he really was. Skylar might not be able to accept his deception about his identity. If she couldn't accept who he was then Parker knew she would never be able to accept the truth about him and Raptor.

So much was at risk right now.

Now wasn't the time to spring everything on her. Parker cleared his throat and said, "Well, you know I'll have to spend some time with Agent Dinsley. I imagine that it will take at least through the

THE SHATTERED ALLIANCE | 293

afternoon, so I probably won't be home until tonight." He hadn't realized until he said it that he thought of being here as home.

Skylar nodded against his shoulder and remained quiet.

"I'd like to spend a quiet night before we head out of town so we can talk."

"I'd like that, too," she agreed softly.

Somehow Parker doubted she would say that once she heard what he had to say. "After that, we can go anywhere you want."

Skylar raised herself up onto her elbows and met his gaze. "What if I want to stay right here, just like this?"

Parker kissed her tenderly on the lips. "Then that's what we'll do."

It was hard to leave Price's warm embrace once the alarm went off. I wasn't sure why, but I had this nagging feeling something was going to go wrong at the bank. It took every ounce of willpower I could summon to pull myself together before he realized what a basket case I was.

He must have sensed how tense I still was because he remained fairly quiet as we got ready to go. A part of me wanted to run away from all of this, to ask Price to run away with me, and be done with all this madness. Now that I knew the name of the man who killed my father, it almost didn't matter to me who took him down as long as Price was safe with me.

But I never asked. After our earlier conversation about him staying out of it...I didn't want to know whether he'd pick revenge against Raptor or staying with me.

I might not win that one.

We all agreed last night that Cherry would meet Raptor before the heist and they would ride together. It was a good thing she was okay with that because it meant someone would be able to keep an eye on him and make sure he didn't switch weapons. I could only imagine how much she wanted this day to be over.

Chill was the one who needed to make the deposit so he would be in his own car. Once he called to confirm that the package had been delivered, we were supposed to make our move. He'd monitor the police scanners and meet up with us at the rendezvous site.

Price and I would ride together. Even though it would have been safer for all of us to be in separate cars on the way from the bank to the first switch site, I didn't think I'd be capable of making my usual offensive maneuvers behind the wheel. If nothing else, it would give us an extra choice of vehicles for the switch.

Just before eight-thirty, I made the call to the monitoring center. Despite knowing my impersonation of Michael's assistant was dead on, my heart was pounding so badly that I could barely make it through the call. Somehow I managed to complete the task and we had one hour to take care of things. The cameras and alarms would remain in maintenance mode until it was too late for them to be useful.

First Alliance was blind and deaf, a sitting duck.

Price made one final sweep of the townhouse to make sure we had everything we'd need and asked, "Are you ready to get going?"

No. "Yeah." Inwardly, I shuddered because I was anything but. "Let's do this thing."

TWENTY-TWO

Jenna decided to go into the office early when she realized she wouldn't be able to get back to sleep after Jackson left that morning. He said he wanted to go in early so he had a shot of getting off in enough time to take her out to dinner. His statement had amused Jenna slightly because she knew it would be well past dinner time before he made his way home from work.

"The weekends just aren't long enough anymore," she mused before taking a few sips of her coffee.

Turning her attention back to her work, Jenna familiarized herself with the facts of two of her more pressing cases before she remembered the file she still needed to go through for Jackson. Sighing, she set aside her case and pulled the file in front of her.

It was much thicker than she remembered and took considerably longer than she'd anticipated to read through. Twice, Trista had poked her head in to see if she needed any help. Jenna found that she had to read several passages over just to make sure the interruptions hadn't caused her to miss anything important.

After thirty minutes of reading, she found it. It hadn't seemed like a very important detail at first, but Jenna had written it down anyway. She realized she was misspelling it when it nearly jumped off the page at her.

Jenna reread the document twice, just to be certain she hadn't been mistaken about what she thought she'd seen. It was only when she was certain she hadn't made it up that she reached for the phone. Jackson wouldn't believe his ears when he heard what she had to tell him.

Jenna couldn't believe that he had fooled everyone for so long. He'd almost gotten away with armed robbery and murder.

My heart was pounding in my chest as we entered the building and I plugged the signal jammer into the fire jack. As I had known it would be when we'd selected this date and time, the bank lobby was void of customers. I fought to keep the trembling I felt in my knees from reaching my hands. Songbird was supposed to be a criminal and I couldn't afford for Raptor to find me out, even at this late stage in the game.

Not if I wanted to avoid a fun-filled afternoon of questioning by the FBI, that is.

The teller staff was already passed out on the floor and Chill had already pulled out of the drive-thru where he made the fake deposit. Michael was running from teller to teller trying to revive them. He froze the moment he saw the four of us. The look of sheer terror in his eyes broke my heart. He was a good man who did not deserve to have this happen to him twice in a lifetime.

This would all be worth it once Raptor is brought to justice, I reminded myself.

Just as Price taught me earlier in the week, I crossed to the far side of the lobby and quickly turned in a circle, guns drawn in either hand, to take stock of the situation. The weight of loaded guns was heavier than I'd expected, even though I'd known there would be a difference. I would never be a fan of holding them, even in gloved hands.

A group of employees were at the desks, but Cherry walked over to them and motioned with her gun that they should be down on the ground. Obediently, they did as they were told and she nodded at us. Price took his position by the front door and started his stopwatch.

"Three minutes," he said to Raptor.

"Open this," Raptor ordered Michael, nodding to the door which would let us behind the teller line.

Michael wordlessly did as he was instructed. Raptor and I walked past him and stood at the door to the vault. Being so close to the man who had shot my father in this very building with a loaded gun in my hand brought several images to my mind, but I knew I couldn't act on any of them. Once we had the money this could all be over.

"You know the drill," Raptor said to Michael.

Michael nodded and knelt down next to one of the women on his staff. He took a set of keys from her limp hand and led us into the vault. Raptor tossed the two black bags at Michael and told him to fill them both while I went back to get the chemically-treated cash out of the currency counter.

As we waited, I could feel Raptor's eyes on me. I had gone to every precaution during our previous encounters to disguise my voice and keep my hair tucked into my ski mask. Though I'd done the same for the heist, my clothes weren't as baggy as they were last week. After drying the borrowed clothes from Cherry on the wrong setting yesterday, they hugged my body snugly. I could only hope that, as one of the men who possessed an intimate knowledge of the curves of my body, he would be too distracted by the money we were about to take to notice.

I'd also forgotten about my contact lenses until we'd already left, but Price assured me it wouldn't make any difference at this point.

Within one minute, Michael had filled the bags. Raptor took one of the bags and handed me the other. We made Michael lead us out of the vault and into the lobby. I began to cross the lobby to the door, but Raptor stayed behind.

"I know what you're thinking, manager. You're wondering if this is going to be the last moment of your life. I could make that happen, you know," Raptor taunted.

I watched as Price and Cherry exchanged a look, but because of the masks, I could only read the eyes. There had been a contingency plan for this, but none of us wanted to have to use it. A dead bank robber wasn't the same collateral that a live one could be.

Cherry crossed the lobby to Raptor quickly. She placed a hand on his shoulder to calm him. From what I could see, Michael was holding his breath, waiting for the shot which I prayed would never be fired.

"Let's go, Raptor. We have what we came for," Cherry said firmly.

"I know you do, slut," he replied without taking his eyes off Michael.

In one fluid motion, Raptor dropped his weapon and placed his hand over Cherry's hand on her gun. He spun her around to face where

Price and I were standing. Almost as though in slow motion, he pulled the trigger.

Jenna's tip about Raptor couldn't have come at a better time. Brandon was skeptical at first, but Jackson had neatly laid out all of the evidence for him and he conceded. It was so simple that Jackson didn't understand how he could have missed it when he was researching the case himself.

He created a shell company to *hire* himself and the funds were deposited into the business account in plain sight. No one had ever bothered to check out the company further once he provided all of the necessary business documentation. Jackson was amazed that it took two years for anyone to realize that Protra Enterprises was an anagram for Raptor.

The smug sonofabitch had been daring them to catch him.

It was still part of the morning rush hour when they drove over to his house. Jackson could practically taste the anticipation he felt at every red light as they came closer to arresting him. Raptor would never see them coming.

Brandon parked the car in the driveway and took his gun from its holster. Jackson followed suit as they approached the front door. To their surprise, it was not only unlocked, it was slightly ajar.

The major items were still present, but all of the personal contents of the house had been cleared out. They split up to make a quick sweep of the house. How had Raptor known they were coming for him?

Jackson was about to put away his weapon when he heard a sound at his back. He spun around, gun still drawn to find out who was there. Reyna Vinson was sitting on the floor with her head buried in her hands. He quickly holstered his gun and rushed to her side.

"Are you all right, Miss Vinson?"

She looked up at him from behind a curtain of black curls. "The bastard didn't even have the guts to break up with me in person. He wrote me a letter and left it in my refrigerator for me to find this morning when I was getting the milk for my cereal. What kind of monster does that?" she sobbed.

Jackson regarded her carefully. "What are you doing here?"

Reyna sniffed. "I thought I could come over here to get a few answers, but it looks like I'm too late for that."

"Do you have any idea where he might be?" Jackson asked.

She shook her head. "No. I've already tried him at the office, but his secretary said she hasn't heard from him yet today."

Brandon burst into the room. "We've got to move, Caldwell. Tip called in that our pal Raptor is robbing First Alliance again."

Jackson rushed out to the car behind Brandon without giving another thought to the young woman in the house who was so upset. Reyna would get over it. She was better off cutting ties to Eric Sauters anyway.

He was about to go to prison for a very long time.

"Songbird, get down," Price shouted the instant Raptor pulled the trigger.

People always talk about how the most traumatic moments of their life happen in slow motion. I always thought they were full of crap or just trying to make things seem more dramatic than they actually were. Now I know that isn't true.

Time slows down and speeds up at the same time.

I felt myself hit the ground before I fully understood what was happening. Shards of glass were cutting into me before I realized a bullet shattered the glass door behind me. Price's body was heavy on top of mine. His weight felt...*wrong.*

Just like in the dream, I smelled pennies.

Raptor had now succeeded in wrestling the gun away from Cherry and was pulling her out of the bank. Her eyes were pure desperation when they met mine. She didn't expect to live to plot another day. But, more than that, I could see the question in her eyes.

Why wasn't Price moving?

Raptor paused to smirk at the two of us, me trapped under Price's dead weight and Price...No finishing that thought. I looked him squarely in the eye as he passed me. I didn't care if he recognized my eyes anymore.

Fuck him. He'd already ruined my life. Twice. He could pull the trigger and end what little was left.

But after I made sure of one thing.

"I know it was you, Eric Sauters," I screamed loud enough for everyone conscious in the bank to hear.

Rather than anger, his eyes turned amused. "You didn't know it Saturday," he murmured, dropping the fake European accent. "You wouldn't have kissed me like that if you had."

He pointed the gun at me, but I didn't so much as blink. I would not give him the satisfaction of my fear. Eric had already taken enough from me.

Eric nudged Price's leg with his foot, seeming satisfied by what he saw. "And I've known what my little lark was up to this whole time."

Something sticky was wet against my arm, but I didn't feel anything else anymore. God. My blood or Price's blood?

The shot I dreaded was never fired.

After Raptor and Cherry left, I felt movement on top of me and Price pulled me to my feet. He wasn't dead, but the blood was real, an obvious darker stain against his black sleeve. If it weren't for the stain, I could believe he'd stayed motionless as a ploy to keep Raptor in the dark, to keep him from finishing him off for good.

I could almost see Price's split second planning in my mind. He'd rightly guessed that Eric wouldn't be able to kill me, not when he believed his nemesis was dead on the floor. In saving me, he sacrificed Cherry though.

Her eyes hadn't been desperation after all, just acceptance. She'd known the next bullet would be for her.

"We have to go, Songbird. Now!" Price's voice was a hoarse whisper in the utterly silent bank lobby, bouncing off the tile at us.

Things were never so silent as they were after firing a gun.

I looked back at Michael once more as we fled the building. A look of recognition flashed across his face when our eyes met. I had just been made. I paused briefly at the doors, but he mouthed for me to go.

Michael would take his knowledge of my involvement to his grave. Of that I was certain. I followed Price to the car and we sped away, the sounds of police sirens whining faintly in the distance.

Jackson and Brandon arrived on the scene just after local law enforcement. He instantly recognized the bank president from the gala where they had met. As soon as one of the officers was done taking his statement, Jackson made his way across the lobby to him.

"Mr. Traymoore? I'm Special Agent Caldwell with the FBI."

Recognition flashed through the man's eyes. "Of course. We met at the charity gala." He accepted the hand Jackson extended to him. "It's a shame that we have to meet again under these circumstances."

"I'm afraid I need to ask you a few more questions."

Michael nodded. "I've already given my statement, but I'll co-operate in any way I can." He gestured towards his office. "Please come with me. There will be fewer distractions in there."

Once they were seated, Jackson got straight to the point. "Was it Raptor?"

"Yes," Michael answered uncertainly, "but I know who it is."

"Eric Sauters?"

"Yes. How did you...Of course you already knew. That must be how you got here so quickly."

The bank president was going into shock. This was certainly a nightmare for anyone in the banking industry, especially given that it was the second time around. Jackson decided he would need to get right to the point before he shut down completely.

"Mr. Traymoore, how..."

"Please, call me Michael."

"All right, Michael. How long have you known Eric Sauters was Raptor?"

He absently shook his head. "I never even suspected him. He was taunting me with his gun and then something snapped in him I suppose. He turned on two of the members of his crew; shot at them. One of them called him by name and then it all snapped into focus for me."

"Did you recognize the person who outed him?" Jackson asked.

"No, I did not," he answered, automatic.

Drake burst into the office, oblivious that he could be inter-rupting something. "How much did they get this time, Michael?" he snapped.

Michael's eyes shone with contempt. "We don't have an official count yet, but I'm sure it will be a total loss beyond what they left in the cash drawers. They were quite thorough, Drake."

"I'm not taking the fall for this one with the board of directors."

Michael rose to his feet. "Oh, yes you are. If you hadn't cut back my armored car service, then most of that money would have been safely out of here by now. And, don't worry; I intend to let the board know about that. They need to know what kind of man is making the decisions for this bank."

"That won't be necessary, Michael," Jenna said, leaning against the doorframe at the threshold to the office. "I don't think Mr. Wynd-ham will be around long enough to warrant that."

"Who the hell are you?" Drake spat out the words as though the question was somehow distasteful to him.

Instead of answering, Jenna simply smiled and made a motion with her hand. One of the detectives entered the office and handcuffed Drake. He began to read him his rights as he escorted him out.

"Thanks for the tip. This was an important bust for my office," Jenna said to Jackson. Turning her attention to Michael she said, "It appears your boss has been involved with numerous criminal activities, Michael, including embezzlement. I'm sorry to have to take away your leadership, such as it is, at a time like this. It couldn't be helped."

Michael grinned, but it didn't quite reach his eyes. "Drake was more of a problem around here than a leader. You did me a favor, Jenna. Please say hello to Elaine for me." Turning back to Jackson he said, "If you'll excuse me, Agent Caldwell, I can hear a few of my staff talking. I'd like to check on them."

Jackson nodded and Michael hurried from his office.

"How did you get here so quickly?"

Jenna shrugged. "I thought it might be a good time to bring Wyndham in, what with all of the commotion from the robbery. Fewer people will notice him being taken into custody this way. He'll appreciate saving a little face in the long run."

"Probably good thinking. No one likes taking the perp walk," Jackson agreed. "Even still, you got here fast."

"I rode in with one of the detectives. Lights and sirens tend to expedite a commute."

"Good thinking to catch a ride." After a beat, he added, "How well do you know Michael?"

"Not well. Just through Elaine. Why?"

Jackson shook his head. "I just get a strange vibe from him, that's all."

"Cut the man a little slack. He was just robbed at gunpoint."

"I know. I just can't shake the feeling that he's not telling us the whole story."

Again, Jenna shrugged. "Whatever it is, it'll come out in the end." She looked around and pulled Jackson farther into the office, out of view of law enforcement and security cameras. Circling her arms around his neck, she said, "I've been thinking about something."

He grazed her lips in a brief kiss. "If it's the same thing I'm thinking about, there are too many cameras around to risk it."

She smacked at his shoulder in play, but the smile didn't leave her face. "I've been thinking about moving in together. If you don't want to live in the condo, it's okay. But your apartment doesn't have enough space for us and the cats. And Lana would have to sleep on the couch when she stays over."

"Jenna..."

She cut him off. "So I guess we could look for a new place. It will take me some time to sell the condo or find a tenant, but it's fully paid for and the monthly dues are fairly low so that wouldn't be a hold up." Her expression was thoughtful. "But we'll have to look for a three-bedroom because I'd want a room for Lana to use and an office so we can still have a place to eat."

"Honey..."

"And you've still got a few months left on your lease so we'd have plenty of time to look before..."

Jackson cut off her flow of words with a kiss. "Or I could just break my lease and move into the condo with you."

"Really?" Her eyes lit up. "If you're not sure, I don't mind selling and moving."

"I am sure. I'll look into breaking the lease as soon as things calm down a little at the office."

She frowned and nodded towards the pandemonium going on in the rest of the bank. "I don't know, Caldwell. That sounds like a stall tactic to me."

"Now that we know Raptor's identity, how long can it really take us to find him?"

"Took two years to get the name."

"And now that we have it, he can't hide in plain sight anymore. That's when criminals start to make mistakes."

"You were brave in there, Skylar. I know that was hard for you," Price said softly.

We had planned everything out to the last detail, even thinking to replace the bullets in Raptor's gun with blanks. In all of our planning, I never dreamed he would anticipate what we had done and grab Cherry's gun. I just had to hope Raptor would show up at the meet soon. I knew how ridiculous a hope that was, but it was possible he might come back to finish me off and get the other half of the money.

If he did, we could still take him.

I wasn't really sure why I kept thinking of him as Raptor in my mind. It was Eric, but it wasn't the Eric I had been in love with once upon a time. It wasn't even the same Eric who'd been trying so desperately to get me back. The man he had become was cruel and calculating. No, I decided finally, this man was Raptor, not Eric.

"Why do you think he grabbed her gun?" I asked Price.

"I don't know unless he figured out he had blanks."

I didn't like thinking about the guns. The moment we got to the rendezvous point, I'd frantically pulled off Price's shirt to check his wound, despite his protests that it was little more than a scratch. I'd cleaned and dressed it using the first aid kit he carried in the car, but I didn't stop worrying. I couldn't.

There had been a lot of blood for a scratch.

"What are we going to do, Price? He has the other half of the money."

I knew he could hear the panic in my voice and I didn't care. His entire plan revolved around us being able to go to the FBI with all of the stolen money and Raptor. The way things stood right now, we were nothing more than a pair of bank robbers.

The worst part was that I had enabled him to get away, despite the tracing beacon in the money. By plugging the signal jammer into the fire jack at the bank they would be unable to trace the cash until we had enough time to separate the cash from the beacon. Part of me wanted to call Michael and tell him about it so they had a chance to catch Raptor, but I knew I couldn't do that.

"Let me worry about that, Skylar," he responded after a lengthy silence.

I stared out the window of my car. We had already changed our shirts and had been waiting for over an hour for Raptor or Cherry to show up, even though we knew both would probably never happen. Chill had come and gone after a brief conversation. Neither were vocalizing it, but Chill's grief over Cherry was palatable.

My thoughts turned to the gym bag crammed with cash in the trunk of Price's car, not more than ten feet away. Things happened quickly in the vault with Raptor, but I knew there must be at least a few million dollars in there. Combined with the first heist, it was enough money that the FBI would never stop hunting for us.

When a car approached on the dirt road, I instinctively put my hand on the key in the ignition. I was unfamiliar with the approaching car and I worried that we may have to make a quick escape. Price put his hand on mine to stop me and I removed the keys from the ignition.

"It's Cherry," he said, relief evident in his tone.

She parked her car about twenty feet from where we were. We got out and met her halfway, Price pulling her into his arms and hugging her for a long time. The look on her face when he released her didn't lend me much hope.

"Does Chill know?"

She nodded. "I called Rand from a pay phone when I finally got to the last car."

"What happened, Cherry?" Price asked.

"I don't know how, but he knew. He pulled over in an alley about three blocks from my car and put the barrel of the gun up against my temple. He told me I had until ten to be out of his sight and started counting. I bolted," Cherry answered, shuddering.

Price swore imaginatively under his breath before replying. "Did you see which way he went?"

Cherry shook her head. "I'm sorry, Parker. I just wanted to get out of there before he put a bullet in me."

"You know you have to go into hiding now."

"Now that Trevor is out of the picture, I'm going back to my old job. I don't think Raptor will be back. Not now that he's been made."

"That's not good enough." Concern was etched across his face. "Eric will kill you, Cherry. I've told you exactly what he's capable of doing."

She laughed a mirthless laugh. "You didn't have to tell me anything. I already have the scars." His face grew serious. "Look, I'm getting out of town for a while anyway. It's going to be too hot here for me for a long time. Rand's booking the trip now, I think. He was talking so fast on the phone that it was hard to catch everything."

Price nodded. "Okay, but..."

"No, Rand can protect me. Stop worrying." She paused, looking from him to me and back. "I'm so sorry, Parker. I know how badly you wanted to end this thing with him." Her gaze came back to rest on me. "I can't imagine what you'll do now."

I watched as Cherry walked back to her car and pulled away. Part of me couldn't help feeling sorry for her. She had been trying to start over when she got pulled into all of this. It wasn't her fault that she was attracted to the wrong kind of men.

That was something I knew a little bit about.

Price paced back and forth in front of me, swearing under his breath. I knew there was nothing I could do or say to comfort him, so I remained silent. After a moment, he stopped pacing and walked over to me with a wild look in his eyes.

"Did Eric ever hurt you?"

"Other than murdering my father?"

He grabbed my shoulders, frantic. "Physically. Did he ever do anything to you when you were together?"

"Price, what's wrong with you?"

"Dammit, Skylar, just answer me!"

"No, he never even raised his voice to me that I can remember. What's all this about?"

He ignored my question. "You'll be safe then. I have to go after him. I know I can find him."

Price turned away from me and headed in the direction of his car. I followed him. I didn't know how to stop him, but I knew I had to think of something. Raptor would kill him if Price succeeded in finding him. Every ounce of my being told me I was right about that.

"You have to let this go, Price. It's too dangerous."

"Look, Skylar, no one knows you were involved. Go back to your life and let me handle this."

"I don't want to go back to my life without you in it. Look, I have plenty of money. We can tip off the cops where they can find this and we can get far away from here, maybe one of the places you were talking about yesterday."

"You'll be a fugitive if we do that, Skylar."

"None of that matters to me. Raptor will *kill* you."

"I don't care," he snapped while he opened his car door.

"I care. I've lost everything and everyone in my life that means anything to me. I'm not ready to lose you too," I said quietly.

Price turned to look at me. I could see the hardness that had taken over the features of his face a moment ago was gone. It was probably just my imagination playing tricks on me, but I could have sworn his eyes were moist.

Price took me in his arms and kissed me fiercely. When he pulled away, he snatched my keys out of my hand and tossed them into the brush several feet away. He sat in his car and looked up at my stunned face.

"You won't lose me, Skylar. I have to finish this right now, but I promise I'll come back to you once it's over."

I made one final plea. "Price, please don't do this. If you ever cared about me even a little, then you won't leave me like this."

Price started the engine and looked back at me. "You don't understand how much I care about you, you never did, but I can't stay here, Skylar. Raptor will go after my family. As much as I want to stay with you, I can't let that happen." A pained look etched itself into his face and he looked away. "He's my...my responsibility. I have to stop him."

"Don't do this, Price. I don't understand what's going on, but he's not your responsibility."

His eyes met mine. "I could have stopped him fourteen years ago. Eric was maybe eleven or twelve when we were at the lake together and he met a girl. It was my responsibility to keep him out of trouble that week, but I wasn't much older and thought the puppy love thing between them was cute. When I found him on the last day of the trip, the girl was dead and he was freaking out. He swore choking her was an accident, but..." Pain swam in his eyes. "I never should've helped him cover it up. Even at sixteen, I knew what he was, what he had the potential to be."

"You knew Eric as kids?" I couldn't comprehend what he was telling me.

"Yeah. Skylar...your father's dead because I didn't stop Eric when I had the chance."

His words knocked me off balance, so he didn't have to push me very hard to make me fall away from the door. "I'm sorry, sweetheart. I'm so sorry," he said before closing the door and leaving me alone on the cold dirt.

EPILOGUE

Love wasn't a fickle bitch.

She was a cruel, calculating sadist, bent on showing people a few meager moments of happiness so their pain would be more intense when it was ripped away. What Nightmare Suzanne said to me about still believing in happy endings made more sense now. I had believed in them, right up until mine was ripped out of my hands.

Love must be having a good laugh over this now.

I didn't try to find my keys until I had watched his car vanish down the country road. Unemotionally, I retrieved my keys from the brush, not even flinching as a thorn pierced the skin of my wrist. The drive home was automatic for me.

The garbage men were only just now making the rounds down my street, so I tossed our bloody shirts into the can and wheeled it out to the street. I wanted to be furious with Price for lying to me as I changed out of the last of the clothes I'd worn to the bank. He'd said there was nothing else I should know about him and Raptor. I'd say the fact they knew each other as kids was something.

But I couldn't feel anger. Not yet, at least.

My home felt cold, empty, without him and I felt more alone than I'd ever known possible. I wandered from room to room with a sense of detachment, remembering the last few weeks. Every conversation, every caress, every unspoken promise played through my head in an endless loop. There wasn't a single room that didn't remind me of my loss – and his betrayal.

The kitchen was particularly painful. Eric's ring was still in the box on the counter, taunting me. If he hadn't killed my father, I would've married him in a heartbeat. I would've been his devoted wife, never knowing what he really was inside.

I half expected for Price to walk out of the bedroom at any moment, almost as though everything that had gone on at the bank and after was just another bad dream. But he didn't. At some point, I would have to come to terms with the fact I had been used, but I couldn't.

It wasn't until I went into the bathroom to splash some water on my face that I realized it was probably over. Maybe this was how all of his cons ended. Maybe all I would be left with were some of his belongings and my memories – shattered like the coffee mug still on the tile floor.

My heart skipped when someone pounded on my door. Had the FBI come for me? No. No one but Michael knew and he wouldn't tell.

"Price?" My lips formed the word before I gave my heart permission to hope. I threw open the door and my face fell. How many times must that happen to delivery guys?

"Miss Montgomery?"

I nodded and a guy in ripped blue jeans and a faded brown leather jacket dumped a manila envelope into my hands. "Have a nice day."

Hastily scrawled address with no return information. This wasn't through any courier company. My hands were shaking so badly as I sat at the table, I could barely open it. When I finally ripped into it, a car alarm remote and a sheet of paper fell onto the table.

I picked up the remote and discovered it wasn't exactly like one you'd use for a car. It had two blue buttons and a red one. Had I seen this with Price's keys?

With hands still shaking, I picked up the letter.

S-

Enclosed is the spare of the device I've been using to disable your alarm. I want you to have it so you can feel safe. Pressing and holding the red button for fifteen seconds will destroy the hack and render the one I still have useless.

I've been trying to tell you for weeks, but I lose my nerve every time I look at you. Even today, I couldn't. I have to go after him because he's my brother. I'm sorry I kept that from you for so long. I'm sorry for the way I left things with you this morning. I miss you already.

I'm sorry.

-P

Through blurred vision, I watched a tear hit the page long after I'd finished reading Price's words. I picked up the clicker again, rubbing my thumb over the red button. I pressed it and held it just shy of ten seconds before releasing it and setting it aside.

I wasn't ready to give up on Price yet.

There were so many things I didn't know about him. Hell, I couldn't even be certain if his real name was Parker Ramsey or Jonathan Price or something else altogether given that Eric's last name was Sauters. The only thing I was certain of as the tears started to stream down my cheeks and I began to feel the first waves of loss was that he had meant what he said.

If Raptor didn't kill him, he would come back to me.

The End

WHAT'S NEXT FOR SKYLAR?

Turn the page for an extended preview of

Foresight is Flawless
Undercover Series Book Three

Available September 2013

PROLOGUE

He looked up from the papers on his desk when he heard a faint knock on the door. A glance at the clock revealed it was well past the agreed-upon time. There would be a good explanation or there would be hell to pay.

"Enter."

The door opened and a slender woman in her late twenties walked into the room. Her every movement exuded defiant confidence, but her violet eyes betrayed her. She was terrified of him, as she should be, and he was very much aware of it.

"You're late," he stated.

Her voice trembled when she spoke. "I know and I'm sorry, but it couldn't be helped."

"Of course," he replied. "And why exactly is that?"

She wet her lips. "His flight was delayed and I couldn't just leave him there." She tucked a silky strand of her golden hair behind her ear and continued, "And I certainly couldn't call you while I was with him."

"Very good then. Does he have my money?"

"Not yet, but he is aware..." She let her voice trail off as his eyes cut through her.

He was pleased by her reaction to him and rose to his feet. "As I am sure you know, my dear, I am a businessman. Now, this man entered into a business transaction with me and I expect his part to be executed as expediently as was mine."

Her eyes were on him as he crossed the room and poured a drink for himself into a crystal glass. He offered her one, but she shook her head in response. It satisfied him a great deal that she remained silent rather than offering any more naïve statements.

"So, as you can see, I only want what I am due, what I am entitled. You have spent a great deal of time with this man at my request and I would be intrigued to know what you think would impress upon him the urgency with which this transaction must be concluded."

"I..." She paused to clear her throat. "I wouldn't know. He doesn't seem to hold anything as sacred. Perhaps..."

He walked over to her and placed his index finger over her lips to silence her rambling. "Listen carefully because I will not repeat myself. Every man, regardless of his morals, would be destroyed to lose one thing in his life. This man is no different. I suggest you think carefully before you answer my question this time or I may begin to think I can no longer trust you. Certainly, we do not want that, do we?"

She took in a shuddering breath. "He has a daughter, sir. He doesn't talk a lot about her, but she can't be much more than five years old."

"Excellent," he said as he returned to his chair. "I suggest you explore that option and swiftly. I would like to conclude my business with Mr. Whitman before the end of next weekend's festivities."

She nodded. "Yes, sir, I'll take care of it," she said, exiting the room.

"Yes, my dear, you most certainly will or there will be very real consequences for you."

ONE

"As I've told you before, Agent Caldwell, I did not immediately recognize any of the thieves who took over my bank. It wasn't until Raptor was taunting me that I recognized him to be Eric Sauters."

"And what gave him away, Mr. Traymoore?" I asked.

"His eyes," he replied. "And please, call me Michael."

I nodded. "Did you recognize any of the others who were with him?"

Michael sighed. "I can only assume that the other man with them was Parker Ramsey."

I lifted an eyebrow. "You mean Jonathan Price?"

"Whatever he calls himself now, yes."

I nodded and looked at the pad of paper in my hand. "What about the woman who called Sauters by name, this Songbird, did you recognize her?"

"I did not."

"The voice was not familiar to you?"

"No."

"You're sure?"

"Yes. As you know, Agent Caldwell, I have been performing the duties of both President and CEO of this bank since the day of the robbery and I'm afraid I must cut our meeting short. I have pressing bank business with which to attend."

I nodded and stood. "Of course, and if you think of anything else…"

Michael opened his office door to show me out. "I'll contact you if I learn of anything you should know."

Despite having no solid evidence to support it, I knew he was lying to me. The only slip he made was calling the abrupt end to our meeting as soon as I mentioned Songbird. Of course, I already knew Skylar Montgomery was Songbird, and now I knew Michael Traymoore knew it as well. My most difficult task would be proving it.

I thought about all of the dead ends I encountered in the three months since the second robbery of First Alliance Bank and Trust as I started the tedious drive to FBI headquarters in downtown Dallas. Eric Sauters, the infamous Raptor, had most certainly left town after his last heist. Parker Ramsey had vanished into the same thin wisp of fog he had come out of and ten million dollars was still nowhere to be found.

To say the least, my transfer to the Dallas Financial Crimes Unit was not going well.

The only good thing that had come from moving to Dallas was Jenna. Things had gotten off to a bumpy start, but they improved right before the robbery and, despite the fact that my career with the Bureau was not going as planned, I'd never been happier in my life. We'd been living together since right after the robbery and I knew that my life was better with her in it.

The only problem was that I wasn't sure if she felt the same way about me. There was no disputing the fact that she loved me. I just couldn't be sure if she was in the same place that I was in. What I wanted became clear to me one night shortly after we got back together, but I'd only let myself acknowledge it a few weeks ago.

I'd been carrying the ring around with me ever since.

Sure, most men probably would have tried to find out if their girlfriend even wanted to get married before they made a trip to the jewelry store. Not me. I'd always been the sort to play fast and loose with my heart when I finally managed to let someone get close. Besides, nothing about my relationship with Jenna had been conventional by anybody's standards so it didn't make sense to change gears now.

It was moments like this that I was forced to realize how drastically my life had changed in a relatively short period of time. In my younger days, I wouldn't have been desperately trying to figure out how to pop the question; I would have been trading on my black hair, crystal blue eyes, olive skin, and rigorously maintained physique to ensure that I was never alone in bed unless I wanted to be. That part of my life had surely come to an end when I'd met and married the woman of my dreams, only to later have her toss away our marriage for my partner and mentor at the Bureau.

Being divorced by the age of thirty-three sure hadn't done much for my romantic resume or my ego. When I'd met Jenna while working undercover, I'd never even imagined that she'd be the one to jump-start my broken heart. It was amazing to me all of the things we'd been through together in the months since we'd first met. It was even more amazing to me that she'd been able to get past my deception about my career.

Really, it was like I was living in a dream and I could wake up at any second and find myself back in my old apartment in D.C., alone and miserable.

After almost an hour on the road, I was finally able to fight my way through the morning traffic to Headquarters. I looked at the ring again for a minute before putting it in the glove compartment. If I had any chance of capturing Raptor then I would have to stop trying to find the perfect way to propose and start trying to find my partner. Maybe Brandon had some ideas about how to get the truth about Skylar out of Michael.

God knows, we needed something to give right now.

After finishing her second cup of coffee of the morning, Jenna Monroe felt ready to dig into her caseload. She normally preferred to get an early start on Fridays so she could put in a full day's work and still get off relatively early, but that had simply not been an option that particular morning – not that Jenna really minded. The unconscious grin still plastered on her face was evidence enough that a woman simply did not get much sleep with Jackson Caldwell in her life.

Or her shower, as was the case that morning.

Jenna looked up from her desk the moment she heard Trista greeting someone in the outer office. She assumed her message would summon a speedy response, but she hadn't imagined Skylar Montgomery would show up at her door within an hour of the call. Based on the angry voice on the other side of the door, she made her point loud and clear.

Skylar's face was flushed with anger when she burst into the office. Jenna studied the younger woman intently, trying to figure out what the best approach would be with this woman. Athletic, but petite build in an aggressive posture, disheveled auburn hair, and facial features twisted with contempt all let Jenna know she would not have an easy time with this particular interrogation. Luckily, she didn't have the opportunity to dwell on it for too long.

"How dare you call my house and leave me a message telling me not to leave town. Who the hell do you think you are?" Skylar snapped, defiance burning in her sapphire eyes.

"A prosecutor in the DA's office." Jenna was unaffected by the display of emotion. "Please have a seat, Miss Montgomery."

"I'll stand."

Jenna shrugged. "Have it your way." She turned her attention to the file on her desk before closing it. "I'm sure you're aware that you're a suspect in the First Alliance robbery."

"You have got to be kidding me with this."

"No, I'm quite serious," Jenna replied. After brushing a strand of her deep brown hair out of her eye and deliberately tucking it behind her ear, she continued. "I do suggest you take a seat."

"Fine," Skylar huffed as she sank into the chair. "I don't know why you're wasting my time with this. There was no evidence against me when it first happened and there is no evidence against me now."

It was obvious to Jenna that she was being lied to by this woman, just as she had been lied to by Michael when she'd questioned him about it. There was no way that her boyfriend turning out to be one of the bank robbers was merely a coincidence. Besides, if Jackson was certain this woman was up to no good, that was enough for Jenna.

"Miss Montgomery, you need to understand something. Just because my office hasn't charged you yet does not mean there is no evidence against you."

Skylar narrowed her eyes. "I'm well aware of that, but perhaps *you* should be aware of something. I know there is no evidence against me because I didn't *do* anything."

"Of course," Jenna replied. After walking to the other side of the desk and leaning against it she added, "Then I suppose you wouldn't mind helping to clear up a few minor details, since you have nothing to hide?"

"What now?"

"There are a few factors that don't add up if you did nothing."

Skylar sighed loudly. "Such as?"

"Well, for starters, we know Jonathan Price is Parker Ramsey and we know you know that as well. We believe he was involved." Jenna caught the panic that flickered through Skylar's eyes at the mere mention of Ramsey. "How do you explain that?"

"I've made no secret of my disappointment when the FBI was unable to capture my father's murderer. The opportunity to expose him presented itself to me and I took it."

"You took it?" Jenna asked. "It didn't bother you that he was involved with your father's death?"

"He didn't pull the trigger so, once I was convinced that he wanted to find Raptor as much as I did, no. He informed me that he'd found Raptor at the gala and I considered my part in it over. I didn't see him after that."

Jenna smiled and cocked her head to the side. "It didn't occur to you that he was just toying with you?"

"As I've said, he was very convincing. Besides, I assumed I could trust him if the FBI was willing to do the same."

"Okay," Jenna replied, reaching back for the file on Skylar. She flipped through a few pages until she found what she was looking for and asked, "But you said in your statement that you didn't know that he was working with the FBI until the night of the gala when you found him talking with Agent Dinsley. Which is it, Miss Montgomery?"

Skylar's tone was icy when she replied. "That's correct. I didn't know for certain until the night of the gala, but I had overheard him on the phone before that and I had my suspicions. Look, am I honestly supposed to believe that you consider me a suspect because I got mixed up with a man who I thought would be able to capture Raptor?"

Jenna shook her head. "No, I don't. You and the bank president, Michael Traymoore, are close, are you not?"

"He was a friend of my father's before he died. He tried to look out for me once I lost my parents."

That statement hit too close to home for Jenna. She had also lost her parents too soon and she could vividly remember the siege of emotions that she'd dealt with. At least she'd had her sister to help her through it. Skylar didn't have any close family left. Jenna would not have questioned her in such a harsh way if she hadn't been positive that this woman knew far more than she was saying.

"So, he's tried to protect you?"

"You could say that, yes."

Jenna knew that Jackson would have already completed his questioning of Michael that was supposed to take place that morning, so she felt secure in laying her cards on the table. It would be interesting to see if either of their stories changed once they began to feel the heat. She would have to remember to call Jackson to compare notes after Skylar left.

"We know that Mr. Traymoore has been lying to us and, Miss Montgomery, we believe that you are the reason why. It is just a bit too convenient that the security tape from the precise time of the robbery is missing. Everyone in the bank at the time was too traumatized to accurately identify Songbird's voice and your good friend claims that he did not recognize the voice."

"Well, Michael would have recognized my voice, so what does any of this have to do with me?"

"If he's taken on the role of your protector, then it makes perfect sense that he would try to protect you from this as well. Give it up, Skylar. I know that you're Songbird, Michael knows that you're Songbird and the FBI knows that you're Songbird. Are you really going to make him an accessory after the fact in this?"

Skylar sprang to her feet and stared directly into Jenna's eyes. "You should know that I was very much in love with Eric Sauters before my parents died and I was devastated when I was told that he was Raptor; that he shot my father in cold blood, murdered him. Do you honestly believe that I would have been able to control myself enough to work with him if I'd known the truth? Do you even realize how asinine that sounds?"

In her experience, emotional outbursts typically meant that the suspect was on the verge of cracking. "Yes, Miss Montgomery. That's exactly what I believe you did."

"Then you're the queen of Fantasy Land and your boyfriend is the king. I didn't do what you people are trying to pin on me!"

"Of course. Any thoughts on why the FBI considers you a prime suspect then?"

More composed now, Skylar sank back into the chair. "Because I got under your boyfriend's skin when I made a move on him that first day we met. He's looking for any excuse to be around me."

"I doubt that."

"If that's what you need to tell yourself. But it's the reason you're coming after me so hard right now, because you know I could have had him if I wanted him." Fire burned in her eyes. "I still could."

Jenna was about to respond when the door to her office was thrown open. Trista's eyes were wide and all of the color had disappeared from her face. Whatever had caused this reaction in her had to be bad. Trista was one of the toughest people Jenna had ever known.

"Jen, sorry to interrupt, but I just got a call from your sister..."

She walked around Skylar as though she wasn't even there. "What's wrong? What did Elaine say?"

"She said...It's, uh...You just need to get to her house as quickly as you can," Trista stammered.

Jenna hurried to the other side of her desk and grabbed her keys and purse. She caught Skylar out of the corner of her eye and realized that she was still there. Taking a deep breath to calm herself she said, "We're done, for now. As I've said, don't leave town."

Jenna rushed out of the office before she could respond. Elaine was not the type to call with a false alarm and Trista was certainly not the kind to become alarmed over nothing. She tried to figure out what was wrong on the drive over, but all she could think was that something had happened to her brother-in-law's flight that was supposed to be arriving this morning. Elaine would be devastated if something happened to Daniel, so Jenna tried to prepare herself to be the strong for her.

Nothing could have prepared Jenna for what she was told once she arrived at her sister's house.

Skylar left the Collin County DA's office in a state of panic. All she wanted to do was bring the monster that killed her father to justice, but she had only succeeded in ruining everything. Now, the most awful part of the whole fiasco, Michael might lose his job or go to jail because of what she'd done.

She should've turned and run the other way the first day she met Price in the park.

The same hot tears she'd been plagued by since the day Price left stung her eyes as she drove. How had she been so stupid as to believe him? She'd been asking herself since that day if any of it had been real between them, but she honestly didn't know. Everything had felt so right, even when she knew he was still holding things back from her.

Of course, there was nothing right about the way he told her Eric Sauters was his brother in a typed letter after taking the half of the money his brother didn't already have and abandoning her in the middle of nowhere. As that annoying prosecutor had said, it was just too convenient to be a coincidence. It had been three months since Price had vanished and he hadn't called, hadn't written, and hadn't sent word through Chill or Cherry since that day. If he really cared about her then she should have heard something from him by now.

Something more than his pathetic brush-off note...

The truth was so glaringly obvious that Skylar mentally kicked herself every day for not seeing it in time. They both had the same disarming smiles; the same intense, piercing eyes; the same lean athletic build...She had always known her attraction to blondes would be her downfall one day.

At least she could take some solace in the knowledge that it made perfect sense for her to fall in love with two brothers. The first brother had stolen her father's life and the second had stolen everything she had left to give.

Every moment they spent together kept flashing through her mind and each time the memories became increasingly painful. By this time she was quite certain that neither Jonathan Price nor Parker Ramsey was his real name, despite his claim that the former was the truth. It wouldn't make sense to a rational person, but the sudden realization that he'd lied about his name brought a measure of comfort with it.

Skylar had tried to track him down by hiring a private investigator to look into Eric's parents. Since she didn't know Price's real identity, she figured she could track him down through Eric's paper trail. Unfortunately, Eric's mother didn't name the father on his birth certificate and gave him her maiden name. Irene Sauters had no other children and her search ended up being fruitless.

Why did that dead end even surprise her? Any man who knew how to fake his own death to hide from the FBI would definitely not be easy to find by anyone's standards.

She'd given up on that rather quickly and turned instead to Chill and Cherry, but they were on an extended vacation to Mexico – that someplace tropical she was supposed to visit with Price. There was no telling when they'd return, or even if they would return, so she'd had to abandon that idea as well.

Skylar had been through the full spectrum of emotions since he left. She remembered thinking he would come back for her once Raptor was no longer a threat just as vividly as she remembered the sadness his absence caused. Once she understood she was nothing more than a pawn to him, the anger had set in. Now, as she drove home, all she felt was contempt and a murderous rage. He had better pray they never crossed paths again.

She hadn't intentionally planned on taking this particular route home, but all of the memories of Price – whoever he really was – must have subconsciously led her down it. The park where they'd first met was coming up on her left. Just beyond that Skylar knew she'd find the cheesy amusement park where he'd taught her how to shoot a gun.

It had felt so right at the time. All of it.

Skylar angrily swatted at the fresh batch of tears welling in her eyes. "Damn you, Jonathan Price. Damn you to hell for this!"

A wave of nausea, something else that had become a common occurrence, hit her with a sudden intensity that almost doubled her over. Every time she thought about him it would come, almost as though to remind her that it was a waste of her time to reminisce about him. Skylar was able to pull the car over to the side of the road just in time.

Hindsight may be 20/20, but...

Foresight is Flawless

Coming Soon

Sydney Katt has been writing books for as long as she could string words into sentences. Today, her books are more complex and feature romance, murder and mayhem, all subjects her grade school teachers frowned upon.

Happily married since before the beginning of time, Sydney and her husband live in the Dallas area, where three demanding cats rule their lives. When they aren't slaying video game dragons, the five of them keep a watchful eye for the first signs of the Zombie Apocalypse.

For more information about Sydney's adventures in Dallas, new book projects and upcoming releases, visit www.authorsydneykatt.com if you dare.

You can also join the Katt Lovers Community at www.facebook.com/authorsydneykatt